D1064135

Books by Donald Harington

The Cherry Pit (1965)

Lightning Bug (1970)

Some Other Place. The Right Place. (1972)

The Architecture of the Arkansas Ozarks (1975)

Let Us Build Us a City (1986)

The Cockroaches of Stay More (1989)

The Choiring of the Trees (1991)

Ekaterina (1993)

Butterfly Weed (1996)

When Angels Rest (1998)

Thirteen Albatrosses (or, Falling off the Mountain) (2002)

Thirteen Albatrosses
(or, Falling off the Mountain)

Thirteen *Albatrosses*

Henry Holt and Company, New York

(or, Falling off the Mountain)

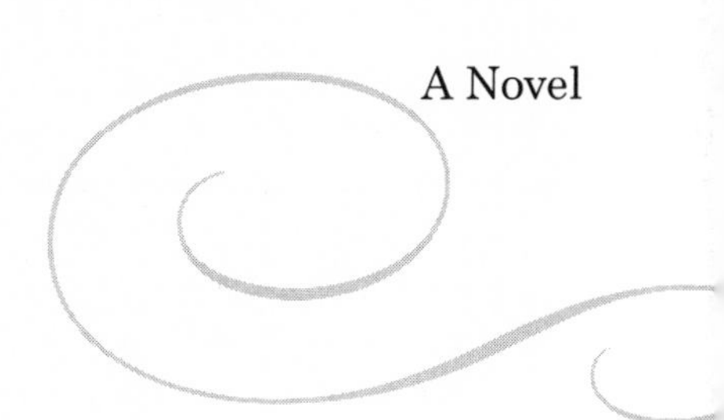

A Novel

DONALD HARINGTON

Henry Holt and Company, LLC
Publishers since 1866
115 West 18th Street
New York, New York 10011

Henry Holt® is a registered trademark of Henry Holt and Company, LLC.

Distributed in Canada by H. B. Fenn and Company Ltd.

Library of Congress Cataloging-in-Publication Data
Harington, Donald
Thirteen albatrosses (or, falling off the mountain) : a novel / Donald Harington.—1st ed.
p. cm.
ISBN 0-8050-6855-4 (hb)
1. Governors—Election—Fiction. 2. Political campaigns—Fiction. 3. Ozark Mountains—Fiction. 4. Mountain life—Fiction. 5. Politicians—Fiction. 6. Arkansas—Fiction. I. Title.
PS3558.A6242 F35 2002
813'.54—dc21 2001024501

Henry Holt books are available for special promotions and premiums.
For details contact: Director, Special Markets.

First Edition 2002

Designed by Fritz Metsch

Printed in the United States of America
10 9 8 7 6 5 4 3 2 1

For Jacque and Micky Gunn

Perfect folks-in-law

Some of the backwoods farms in the Ozarks are pretty steep, and steep also are the stories that the natives tell about them. Many of the wildest of these tales are true, at that. The old gag about the farmer falling out of his cornfield sounds like a tall tale, but people who live in the Ozarks know that such accidents are not uncommon.

—Vance Randolph, *We Always Lie to Strangers*

ex•tir•pate *tr. v.* 1. To pull up by the roots. 2. To destroy totally; exterminate.

—*American Heritage Dictionary*

First Part

Primary

Chapter One

You've never heard of Vernon Ingledew unless you've read a book by the name of *The Architecture of the Arkansas Ozarks*, but that's not essential. That book, under the cover of being a scholarly examination of the vernacular buildings of a lost but pastoral backwater, was a chronicle of generations of Ingledews in a village called Stay More, founded by the first of them, Jacob, and still inhabited by the last of them, Vernon, who was last for several reasons, most particularly because the woman he loved could not conceive a child if she'd wanted to, and she didn't want to for several reasons, most particularly because Vernon was her first cousin.

Now, *that* book ends when Vernon becomes so wealthy from raising razorback hogs and processing them into the Ingledew Ham that is sold in gourmet shops everywhere that he and Jelena, his cousin, whose last name is also Ingledew, build themselves a fabulous house on a mountaintop above Stay More and set out to live happily ever after.

That book appeared twenty-seven years ago, when Vernon was just turning twenty-one and Jelena was eight years older than he, and sure enough they have been living as happily as June bugs, happier than Heaven, ever since, with never a word about any afflictions or problems or even stresses that bothered them.

Jelena had a lovely garden that I'd heard a lot about but never seen. I'd hoped, at the end of the architecture novel, "that on my next visit to Stay More I will be invited to sit with them in that garden." But I never had. I didn't visit Stay More very often. Neither Vernon nor Jelena had anything happening to them that would have merited even a good short story, let alone a novel. Happiness doesn't inspire books, although books can cause a lot of happiness.

Speaking of books, that's supposedly how they spent most of their time, reading them. And supposedly it was one or more books he read that gave Vernon the peculiar notion to run for governor.

He had no political experience whatsoever when he made his romantic decision. He had few friends; not one of them was an elective official on the local, state, or national level. His only qualification for office was that he was the great-great-great-grandson of Jacob Ingledew, who had been governor of Arkansas during Reconstruction and was remembered as a courageous Unionist in a hotbed of the Confederacy. While Vernon Ingledew had inherited his ancestor's courage and independence and sense of ethics, as well as his mountaineer's fierce pride and native wit, he ran for governor in spite of an avowed disparagement of politics. In addition, he had no experience at all in law (a fact that would earn him a lot of votes), and indeed he was not even a college graduate.

As for Jelena, she was not only eight years older than Vernon but was also a mother of two sons by her divorced husband, and even if she were not Vernon's first cousin he could not have married her, not because of his pathological woman-shyness (somehow he was never shy with Jelena) but because it was his destiny never to marry. Yet he chose to live with her (or *cohabit*, if he'd ever learned a legal word), and he was still living with her almost thirty years later when he decided to run for governor, and one of his first all-night sessions with his campaign manager (or political consultant, as they're called nowadays) concerned the best spin to put on the relationship he had with Jelena. Never mind the jokes about Ozark hillbillies loving their cousins. Never mind the fact that Jelena had been valedictorian of her high school class and, if she'd ever had her IQ measured, was possibly as much a genius as Vernon himself. Never mind that she had not borne children to Vernon (she'd requested a tubal ligation following the birth of her second son). Never mind, even, the fact that handsome Vernon and beautiful Jelena had created the most gorgeous love story that a specialist in the field could have ever imagined. There was simply going to be no getting around the fact that, as incumbent Governor Bradfield put it (somewhat desperately), "Those two have been living in incestuous sin long enough that God ought to blast 'em both with plague upon plague."

When Vernon Ingledew made his decision to seek the governor's office, the first person he told, apart from Jelena, was his best friend of many years, a forester living in Stay More named Day Whittacker. Although Day, who was the same age as Vernon, the same age as my wife, Kim, had lived in Stay More for most of his life, he was a native of New Jersey and possessed an outsider's perspective on the ways of the Ozarks. He and his wife, Diana, had been back-to-the-landers years before the influx of hippies had hit the Ozarks, and they had not permitted themselves to be caught up either in the turned-on and tuned-out lifestyle or in the drug culture that briefly tainted the lovely mountains and left a lingering odor into the eighties. They were an eminently sensible couple, and their son Danny had gone away to college and was now living and working in Rome.

On the average of once every two years, Day and Diana drove the two hours from isolated Stay More to Fayetteville, the shopping and cultural Mecca of the Ozarks and my home for the past couple of decades. Naturally, on these trips they stopped by to say hello and bring me up to date on what little news the languishing village of Stay More managed to generate. Kim was always delighted to see them, because in fact it was their story in my early novel called *Some Other Place. The Right Place.* that had first made her aware of the obscure novelist who wrote it and had led, indirectly, to our meeting and eventual marriage. We exchanged Christmas cards with Day and Diana and, on those very rare occasions when we could find time and incentive and nerve to take ourselves to Stay More, we always stayed at their house, a 1930s cottage painted a fading yellow, up Banty Creek a mile or so from the remains of the once-thriving but now defunct village. The house had been built by Diana's grandsire—or sire, too—a strange hermit by the name of Daniel Lyam Montross, who has appeared in several other of my novels and even narrated one of them, and who might even turn up in this one too.

Unlike Vernon and Jelena, who may have borne me some resentment for laying bare their history for all the world to see, Day and Diana knew that all the world was too busy to pay much attention to them, and thus they'd never complained about my invasion of their privacy, not even my shocking revelation of who Diana's real father had been, not even my mention of Day's youthful habits of prodigious masturbation, nor any of the other details of their private lives. I once asked them if they'd ever had any strangers knocking at their door who had been inspired to seek them out by having read *Some Other Place. The Right Place.* Their answer, which on one hand was an unpleasant reminder that this novel had never really enjoyed a large audience but on the other hand reassured me that I had not caused Day and Diana any real embarrassment or inconvenience by revealing their story, was that once in a blue moon somebody would turn around in their driveway after having satisfied themselves that that yellow house did in fact exist. But nobody stopped to inquire if it was really true that they'd been to all the ghost towns the novel said they had and done all the strange things it said they'd done.

I served a supper of my barbecued butterflied leg of lamb (with parsleyed new potatoes and asparagus) to Day and Diana on that particular visit when, after I'd broken out the second bottle of Merlot, Day said, "Did you know that Vernon plans to enter the gubernatorial primary?"

Since I'm very hard of hearing, he may as well have been telling me that Vernon was entering a monastery or a psychiatric hospital.

Kim helped by giving me the sign-language gesture for *governor*, a circling of the temple with the index finger, just a few inches removed from the common gesture for *crazy*. She said, "It's about time. When I first moved in with Don, he was writing a novel about Vernon Ingledew as governor of Arkansas. That was seventeen years ago. He couldn't finish it." She turned to me. "What was the title of that novel?"

All the King's Horses, I said. It was loosely based on Robert Penn Warren's *All the King's Men*. But Vernon was just thirty then, too young to be governor, and naturally I wasn't going to get any cooperation from him in the project.

"You tried to talk Vernon out of it, of course," I remarked to Day.

"Of course," Day said. "I still can't imagine what's possessed him."

"Jelena hates the whole idea," Diana said. "She told me that if Vernon runs into problems because they're first cousins and not married, she will be only too happy to 'leave the country.' She doesn't want to be a politician's consort. Not if she has to live at the governor's mansion in Little Rock."

"What does George think?" I asked. Jim George Dinsmore was Vernon's plant manager, his farm manager, his majordomo, his right-hand man, and a very strong and level-headed Ozark hill-billy. I had known him since my childhood.

"We don't know yet," Day said. "Vernon hasn't told him. That's his next step. He showed me his schedule; he's taking this whole thing step by step. He plans to tell George this week, and then the two of them are flying around the country to interview some prospective campaign managers."

I fished my index cards out of my shirt pocket and took my ballpoint and began jotting notes. I really didn't want to start a novel about Vernon running for governor; my problems with the previous attempt, although only a vague memory now, still came too readily to mind. I was immersed in a critical study of Arkansas painter Carroll Cloar, actually in the form of his "autobiography," and I expected *Cloar* to keep me busy through the next several breaks and vacations from my teaching duties. "When Vernon told you of his decision," I asked Day, "did he indicate any event or person or circumstance that prompted him to it? Was it just a spur-of-the-moment thing?"

Day smiled. "Last year he got to the *P*'s in his program, and the second *P* was politics. So you can imagine what he's been doing for the past six months."

I could imagine. I knew about Vernon's program, which was exactly that: a programmatic system of self-enrichment, almost rigid in its demands—although Vernon would have preferred calling it *orderly* rather than rigid—and going all the way back to Vernon's teenage years (which I summarized in the conclusion of my architecture novel), when he had discovered that, on a trip to a used-book store in Harrison, all the areas of knowledge and inquiry were tantalizingly available in softcover. Since then, Vernon's whole life had been devoted to reading and study, a kind of continuous, obsessive adult education, a pursuit I could only envy. What I envied most, perhaps, being a slow reader of the sort who "hears" every printed word as I read it, is that Vernon was a speed reader, phenomenally rapid, reading pages as fast as he could turn them. Not only that but he was apparently able, when he chose, to ignore sleep; he could stay up all night if he had thirty books to read before breakfast. And after breakfast, supervising the swine rearing and the ham making consumed only a small part of his daily hours (George and his crew handled most of it), and, since Jelena was an inveterate bookworm herself, they deliberately did not possess a television (in all the Ozarks, there were fewer than half a dozen similar households, but the reason most of the other few did not possess a television was that they couldn't afford one).

The walls of both chambers of the strange "double-bubble" house Vernon had constructed in the early seventies, before the first hippie had erected the first yurt or geodesic dome anywhere in the Ozarks, were lined, floor to ceiling, with bookshelves fitted to their circular surfaces. In fact, a decade ago Vernon had been required to build a barn-sized annex for the purpose of housing the overflow of books. I had never seen Vernon's weird house; I had included a vague illustration of it in my architecture novel, based on a smudged Polaroid that Day had taken and sent to me. When I took Kim on her first trip to Stay More, I spent all of one afternoon trying to find Vernon's dwelling to show it to her, but I could not, and I had to respect Day's determination never to reveal its location to anyone, not even God. But I knew the place was overrun with books.

I knew also that Vernon had decided many years ago to take a certain array of subjects in alphabetical order and, devoting a steady six months to each one, attempt to master it completely, or at least as much as one could master a subject. He made it through one letter of the alphabet and two subjects each year. He had started, sixteen years before, with art history and astronomy, and within a year, aided by a fabulous collection of art slides, portfolios, and monographs and a quite expensive Celestron Ultima telescope, he had acquired the equivalent of a PhD in both subjects. No, that's wrong, because a PhD implies a kind of limited academic expertise, a certain narrow, specialized knowledge. Vernon literally knew *everything.* I recalled from my previous aborted novel that like Willie Stark of *All the King's Men* he possessed an elephantine memory: if you quizzed him at breakfast on those thirty books he'd read overnight, he wouldn't give you many wrong answers. And since art history was my own professional field, I greatly envied Vernon his knowledge of that subject and often wished he would be willing to discuss it with me, if nothing else (especially nothing else). After he had published in *Art Bulletin* an astounding study of van Gogh drawings proving that van Gogh was not an expressionist after all, I wrote him a nice letter proposing an exchange, either by mail or in person. Jelena answered with a note to the effect that Vernon was totally absorbed with wrapping up his study of botany and running behind schedule, with biochemistry waiting impatiently for him.

Another year, and they were followed by chess and Christianity; Jelena proved such an able partner for the former that it did not surprise me to learn that both Vernon and Jelena had acquired Grand Master status as chess players. As for Christianity, the Ingledews, since time immemorial, by tradition and genetic disposition, had been atheists, and Vernon's profound investigation of the birth and development of a way of belief based upon a Jew of Nazareth named Yeshua was not at all pious or godfearing but totally objective and scholarly, and he came away from it no less a nonbeliever than ever. The next two subjects, under *D*, were drama and dance, requiring Vernon and Jelena to spend most of the year in New York City, in order to attend performances. The year he did entomology and English he stayed home in Stay More, and a paper he published in *Journal of Insect Behavior* on the mating habits of *Periplaneta* inspired me to write my novel *The Cockroaches of Stay More.* (Day told me that Vernon was not at all amused that I called him "Gregor Samsa Ingledew," or Sam, in the novel and had him romantically involved with a female cockroach, Tish, who was not at all Jelena.) Vernon's study of *Titus Andronicus* has been acknowledged by Harold Bloom in his *Shakespeare: The Invention of the Human.*

Year by year this program of Vernon's greatly increased his knowledge of the world and even contributed to the world's knowledge of itself. His ultimate motive, perhaps, was a theme I had stated toward the end of my architecture novel and which is originally set forth in that Ozark funeral hymn "Farther Along": the idea that, farther along, we'll know all about it; farther along, we'll understand why. Vernon really did intend to understand everything eventually, even if he could do only two subjects a year and might have to start all over again when he reached the end of the alphabet. Getting into the *F*'s, Vernon's factotum George Dinsmore helped him with some practical applications of his intensive study of finance, and he received much willing help from all the old-timers of Newton County in his study of folklore, which was not limited to Ozark folklore but encompassed that of the whole world. Indeed, Vernon made and published important studies of the parallels between Russian and German folktales. Two years were devoted to geology and gods and history and horses, respectively. (Day reported that Vernon had found horses a more extensive and difficult subject than gods.) When the letters of the alphabet brought Vernon to *I*, he was hard-pressed for a pair of subjects but settled on Irish and Indo-European linguistics, the former requiring Vernon and Jelena to rent a cottage in County Meath for six months, where, according to Day, they made friends with the reclusive and eccentric novelist J. P. Donleavy, once again to my everlasting envy.

Vernon discovered a clever way to combine his next two subjects, Japanese and journalism. For the five months that he and Jelena spent in Tokyo he was the Japan reporter for the *San Francisco Chronicle* and was invited to become Tokyo bureau chief for the Associated Press at just the time he was getting into knight errantry and the Koran; he could find no connection between those two other than, of course, that many of the knights had been bent upon destroying Islam. Undoubtedly his study of the former subject required a lively reading of *Don Quixote* without his realizing that he himself would become quixotic in his eventual quest for the governorship.

One of the *L*'s was easy to choose: Latin. He already knew how to read it; even before he'd started his program, his first intensive act of autodidacticism as a young man was to teach himself Latin for the purpose of translating a certain old book, *De Architectura Antiqua Arcadiae*, he'd found in a bookstore in Rome on the first *wanderjahr* that he and Jelena had taken. Latin was a subject I'd flunked in the ninth grade (although I've pretended to knowledge of it in some of my books); Vernon was so fluent in it that throughout his program he had not hesitated to acquire books in Latin on art, Christianity, gods, horses, et cetera.

Choosing the other *L* was a bit more difficult, and he was strongly tempted to pick law. Given his amazing assimilation of all the topics he chose, he could doubtless have been admitted to the Arkansas bar if he had, but he would unknowingly have defeated one of the strongest selling points for his eventual gubernatorial campaign: the very fact that, unlike most of the other candidates, he had no background in law at all. He also considered the possibility of locution and its many subcategories, and perhaps he should have picked that, because when he ran for governor he would discover to his dismay that he had no talent at all for public speaking. But I must stress that all these topics were undertaken without any inkling on his part that any of them would have any connection with his entry into politics.

The topic he chose was love. He was to discover that of all the subjects he had devoted himself to, it was the most boundless. A month into his investigation he began to realize he could never hope to cover it, not even in a lifetime, certainly not in six months.

Knowing Latin, he read and reread Ovid on the subject, as well as Seneca and Tibullus. He read Dryden and Stendhal and Goethe and Dickens and Oscar Wilde. He even read Henry Miller. When his eyesight was strained from reading and he needed to close his eyes, he listened to a plethora of love music, from ancient ballads and lays to modern pop and rock and funk. His eyes rested, he stared long at certain paintings: Giorgione's *Tempest*, Rembrandt's *The Jewish Bride*, Kokoschka's *Tempest*, or *Bride of the Wind*. He even read a few Harlequin romances, just to discover the source of their appeal to the masses.

As in so many of his courses of study, he enjoyed always the willing assistance of his consort, Jelena, who could not only match him game by game in chess but could match him, pang by pang and throe by throe, in love. He discovered, very quickly, that love can be written about, it can be painted, it can be composed into music, it can certainly be felt, but it cannot be discussed, not between lovers. Lovers can endlessly tell each other how much, how deeply, how endlessly, they love each other, but they cannot discuss love itself and its meaning. One knows love by not knowing it.

Learning that, Vernon was free. He went on down the alphabet. In recent years, Vernon's plunge into mathematics and music resulted in actual contributions to the knowledge: Vernon's paper on "New Approaches to Game Theory Suggested by John von Neumann's Study of the Rings of Operators in Hilbert Space" appeared in *American Journal of Mathematics*, and his study of " 'Ranz des Vaches' and Other Mountain Airs in Relation to Appalachian/Ozark Folk Music" was acknowledged as the inspiration for Benjamin Fisher's haunting *Symphony No. 2 in C Minor*, which premiered at the New York Philharmonic not so long ago.

N was for nature and for nuclear physics. Oh, he had some fun with *O*: occult and Osage, the latter the name of the tribe that had inhabited Stay More before being displaced by white settlers, principally Vernon's ancestor, Jacob Ingledew. For years I'd known that Vernon owned and jealously guarded the original holograph of *The Memoirs of Former Arkansas Governor Jacob Ingledew*, in which, it may be assumed, that founder of Stay More detailed his earliest encounters not only with the last remaining Osage Indian but especially a brief liaison with that Indian's squaw, which supposedly had resulted in a pregnancy. These things, however, were not part of Vernon's motive when he undertook to read all the dozens of volumes about the history and culture of the Osages in Missouri, Arkansas, and ultimately their reservation in Oklahoma, especially V. Kelian's recent *Dawn of the Osage*, which inspired Vernon to master a speaking ability in the Osage language with the help of Francis La Flesche's *A Dictionary of the Osage Language*, published by the U.S. Government Printing Office in 1932, and also by hiring and importing to Stay More from Pawhuska, Oklahoma, for two months one of the few remaining mixed-blood Osages still fluent in the language. Day wondered if the man, whose name was James Big Eagle, realized he was temporarily a resident of a hunting ground that had once belonged to his ancestors.

In alphabetical order, politics comes after philosophy, so Vernon had spent the first half of the previous year trying to read as much as possible of the enormous literature on philosophy, aided by and starting with a "popular" classic, Will Durant's *The Story of Philosophy*. The subject of philosophy was almost as deep as the subject of love; it was almost as unknowable. Jelena told Diana that Vernon had doubled his consumption of coffee during this course of study. He gleaned some personal mottoes that would come in handy when he got into his next subject: for example, Socrates' "Let him that would move the world first move himself" and Francis Bacon's "It is a miserable state of mind to have few things to desire and many things to fear: and yet that is commonly the case of Kings."

Quite possibly, in his determination to cover all the subjects in his program, he was consciously or unconsciously jumping ahead to the next one. He made frequent note of how the great philosophers had viewed politics, such as Plato's "The punishment suffered by the wise who refuse to take part in government is to live under the government of bad men." (Arkansas itself was currently under the thrall of Governor Shoat Bradfield, one of the baddest.)

The first thing he learned about politics is that, like all art, it is a lie meant to refresh truth. The deceptions of politics, like those of art, are not necessarily meant deceitfully but for the magic regeneration of life. The promises of good politicians are not meant to cheat but to inspire. In every society, there are two kinds of people: those who, like most of us, assume that there is somebody around who is going to take care of everything, and those who believe that the only caretakers are themselves. All politics are based upon the indifference or the apathy of the majority.

Slowly, as he rapidly devoured writings by Plato, Bacon, Edmund Burke, Thomas Jefferson, Carlyle, Benjamin Disraeli, Henry Adams, and Woodrow Wilson, he came to realize that he could no longer be part of the indifferent majority. By the time he began reading such things as Harry Lee Williams's *Forty Years Behind the Scenes in Arkansas Politics* and Diane D. Blair's *Arkansas Politics and Government: Do the People Rule?* he had pretty much made up his mind that he should seek election as Newton County representative to the state legislature, and he was so taken with the notion that he could think of nothing else. George Dinsmore went to Jelena to report that Vernon was just standing out in the middle of one of the pig pastures, not tending his swine but staring off into space. Jelena went and got him and told him he had been reading too much or too heavily. She recommended that, if he had to read, he ought to read something light, like novels. She reminded him of how much he'd learned about love just by reading Harlequins.

So he began reading some novels. He ordered from his Internet bookseller a whole slew of political fiction. He started with William Brammer's *The Gay Place*, about politics in Texas, and found it so readable he began to devour a political novel at the rate of several a day, reading Allen Drury's *Advise and Consent* and *Capable of Honor* before lunch, and novels by Salinger—not J. D. but Pierre, who had been Kennedy's press secretary—in the afternoon, along with Fletcher Knebel, William Safire, and Ward Just at night. He enjoyed Joe Klein's *Primary Colors*, based upon that Arkansas governor who had ascended to the presidency. According to his reading schedule, during the days he consumed Robert Penn Warren's *All the King's Men* and lesser novels by Jeffrey Archer, Anton Myrer, and Stephen Longstreet. He even found time, late one night in December, to read my *When Angels Rest*, which was not, strictly speaking, a political novel, or rather was concerned with the make-believe politics of children, a bunch of kids whose names were all familiar to Vernon because they had attempted to set up a government for the village of Stay More during World War II, before Vernon was born. He found the novel honest and accurate in its depiction of the village of Stay More and of the way of life then, and he even felt an intense pang of nostalgia for a world he had never known except in his imagination of the way it might have been if he had lived at that time.

That modest little novel should have convinced him that politics (like the warfare that is its handmaiden) is best left to innocents and idiots and idealists. There is no room in that country for the truly wise.

But instead he decided that, as he told Jelena at breakfast, the only way he could learn politics was to spend some time as a politician. What she answered is not known but can be imagined.

Chapter Two

George Dinsmore took another sip of his bourbon, which didn't help him figure out an eight-letter word ending in *y* with the second and third letters as *de*, meaning a system of beliefs. He didn't have him a pencil; a-working these goddamn things with a ballpoint pen was like a rattlesnake with piles trying to get home. He could flip over to page 113 of this here *Sky* magazine and find the answers, but that wouldn't be honest. Hell's banjer, he wouldn't've tried the dumb puzzle in the first place except that nobody else before him had already started messing with it, the way you can usually count on some dumb-ass previous passenger to've already screwed up the puzzle before calling it quits when the plane landed. But this here one had been clean until George got aholt of it. Now look at it. And he wouldn't've even started the dadburn puzzle if Boss had been awake for him to talk to. It was the first time in his life he'd ever seen Boss a-sleeping. No kidding, he'd known Boss ever since he was just a little squirt and ever year of his life except the four years George was doing his duty in Vietnam, and he'd even asked his niece Jelena, who lived with Boss, "Don't he never sleep, even way off of a night in the early hours?" And Jelena had laughed and explained that Vernon sometimes went for days without a wink but usually got on the average four or five hours each night.

Now Boss was sawing logs so vigorously he didn't even notice the air pockets this 747 kept hitting, one of them so bad George's bourbon sloshed onto the lap tray and would've wet his pants if he hadn't mopped it up with the napkin. George realized that Boss probably had a good reason for being dead to the world: he was plumb wore out from this project, not so much the hard work of it and the flying around from place to place, but the total shuck doodly poo *going nowhere* of it. It sure was a good thing that Cincinnati was the last stop, the bitter end maybe but down into the short rows, don't you know? Boss hadn't made no promises, but George had the feeling that if Cincinnati was a bust they could get their butts on back to Stay More and live happy ever after without anymore of this here politics foolishness. George sure did hate to admit it, even to himself, but he had under his hat swore to his niece Jelena, 'cause she asked him to, that he would do everything in his power to crumb the deal, to louse up the whole project, short of wasting any poor sucker who was dope enough to swallow the bait. George didn't like being put on the spot like this, being a two-faced four-flusher, pretending to Boss, who he liked more than any man on this here earth, that he was helping him out at every turn, not to mention costing him a chunk of money for airfares and hotels and eats etsettery, when in fact he was a double agent, working for Jelena, who didn't want her man wasting his fortune running for governor.

Not that they couldn't afford it. Last time George had looked—or, that is, the last time that Rowena Coe the bookkeeper had told him—there was so much in the sock or under the mattress, so to speak, that Vernon could shut down the pig works and spend the rest of his life taking Jelena around the world once a week, not to mention buying out the Library of Congress, which he'd likely care to do. Way back in the seventies, when the money first started rolling in, Boss had got his broker over to Fayetteville to buy up no end of Wal-Mart stock when it was selling for diddly, and now look at it: what with stock splits and the bull market etsettery, Boss had come mighty nigh to owning as much of the company as old Sam Walton hisself, rest his bones. So it wasn't that Jelena was worried the campaign would put them in the poor farm; she just didn't cotton to the idea of spending so much money on something she didn't believe in and she wasn't convinced that Vernon himself believed in.

For that matter, who could possibly believe in it? On this trip, George had asked himself, more than once, "Would *I* vote for Vernon Ingledew if he wasn't my boss and my buddy and my sort of nephew-in-law?" And the well-considered answer was a loud and clear *Nope, noway.* Of course, George wasn't much of a voter anyhow. He'd voted only once for Clinton himself for governor, and once for him for president, and that left eight other chances he'd had to vote for Clinton but stayed home. Not that he'd ever had anything against Clinton, unlike some of these here loud-mouth clodhopper naysayers who had thought they'd looked smart running down the boy just on account of he was practically family, like killing your brother or your dad or leastways your cousin. George had been pure-dee proud of Clinton being family, and he hadn't never held it against him. The odd thing was, he had a little bit of trouble trying to think of Vernon as family, even though Vernon really and truly was kinfolks. Not because he was Boss and not even because he was so all-fired brainy, but because he just didn't somehow seem like he was *one of the folks*.

For one thing, he didn't sound like one of the folks, what with those big words that fell out of his mouth like crumbs of caviar. And he didn't exactly *look* like common folks but some godburn Hollywood movie star or somebody. Sure, he looked like an Ingledew. Anybody who'd ever known any of the Stay More Ingledews for generations back would say that Vernon was pure Ingledew, but come to think of it, the Ingledews had always stood out from everbody else.

George remembered when he was just a kid, growing up in that shack his momma tried to keep up yonder on Dinsmore Mountain, the least'un in a family of thirteen brats, he'd been learnt from the word go that the Ingledews was quality folks, the upper crust, never mind that Stay More couldn't've been divided into classes any way you'd slice it. After old John Ingledew, Boss's great-grandpa, had lost his money in the Crash, none of the Ingledews had had any money to speak of, but they still kept their pride and their feeling that they were a cut above everbody else. Boss didn't wear his pride like some goddamn epaulets on his shoulders, but you could feel it surrounding him like a invisible raiment. How had that Avenel feller in Salt Lake City put it? "Mr. Ingledew, I don't want to hurt your obviously well-earned self-regard, but my experience is that most people who aspire to politics without ever having endured any of the tests and trials of the campaign are doomed to discover that they have inflated images of themselves." George wondered if Boss was really capable of seeing himself as others saw him.

But George also wondered how others really and truly did see him. How did Jelena see him? How did Day and Diana? How did his own sister Sharon and that college professor husband of hers, Larry? How did his grandma, Latha Dill? How did all the other seventeen employees at Ingledew Ham? Well, George could probably speak for the last group: they worshiped him. Come to think of it, George himself worshiped him. Why else would he be on this goddamn bouncing 747 working this goddamn crossword?

He took another sip of his bourbon and wondered if he himself could say anything to discourage this Pharis feller they were a-fixing to meet in Cincinnati. More than likely, it wouldn't be necessary. The way it looked, Pharis was a lost cause irregardless of how the offer was made to him, but there remained, nevertheless, one possible selling point that separated Pharis from all the other guys they'd interviewed: he was a ole Arkansas boy hisself.

The others—Fred Avenel in Salt Lake City, Matt Spears in Washington, D.C., Gene Kubby in Atlanta—didn't even seem to have a clear idea of where Arkansas was, though they damned well knew a former president of the United States had come from the state—which was not, as another former president name of George No-W. Bush had misplaced it, somewhere between Oklahoma and Texas. Two of them, Kubby and Spears, had both wondered if Vernon had been inspired to run for office because the former president had once held that office. Boss had replied that Clinton's tenure as governor of his state had been "proceleusmatic," whatever that meant, but he didn't have any presidential aspirations himself; he just wanted one term in the statehouse to see what it was like.

Matt Spears, who was an old man who had helped elect seventeen United States senators and eight governors, had understood what proceleusmatic meant but had concluded, "You certainly have Clinton's *duende*, and his eupatrid mien, but you don't have enough of his track record to dissuade me from carrying out my long-anticipated and well-earned retirement." On the plane to Atlanta, George had asked Boss if he wouldn't mind enriching George's impoverished vocabulary. *Proceleusmatic* was just one of them fancy Greek words meaning "inciting, animating, or inspiring." *Duende* was Spanish dialect, meaning the ability to attract others through personal magnetism and charm. And *eupatrid mien* ("He was just poking fun at me when he threw that in," Vernon explained) simply meant aristocratic bearing or manner. I live long enough, I might learn a thing or two, George said to himself.

Gene Kubby had come pretty damn close to accepting. Of the three, he had given Boss the most of his precious time, nearly three hours, including lunch at Atlanta's best rib joint (although George had slapped down his AmEx card to cover it), and George knew that Boss had got the feller just to the point where he was fixing to say, "Let me think this over," but they never made it that far. Kubby's credentials wasn't nothing to write home about, not compared with the others; he'd elected the governor of Georgia twice and of Alabama once, as well as a whole slew of jackleg and peanut hopefuls, and the man wasn't timid about talking price. When Vernon asked him flat out to name his figure, he had come up with some bad news so steep it made George choke on his spare rib but didn't even make Boss blink. All Boss had said was, "When can you start?"

The man had carefully wiped all around his mouth with the cloth napkin and then had put to good use the bowl of water with the lemon wedge in it, and when he finished wiping off all his fingers he said, "Gentlemen, as you can plainly see, I'm not in this line for my health. I require not just a handsome fee but I require practically a guarantee of winning. Frankly, I don't see any clue of that in your case. Why don't you hire a local manager? I can recommend a good man or two in Little Rock."

But Vernon had told him he was determined to find the very best, and he was sorry the very best was turning him down. He wasn't interested in the "amateurs" in Little Rock. "So where do you go from here?" Kubby had asked. Cincinnati, Boss had said. Bolin Pharis. The man had laughed his fool head off. "Jesus God, you *are* ambitious, aren't you? The good news is, if there's a man on this earth who could overcome your insurmountable odds, it's Bo. The bad news is, you don't have a prayer of talking him into it. When he quit the game after Al Gore lost, he made it clear to everyone he's never coming back."

George winked at the stewardess, who was just sitting there like she didn't have nothing else to keep her in business except waiting on him and Boss, who didn't need anything because he was asleep and wouldn't bother her none if he was wide awake because he was not only shy with womenfolks in general but pretty airplane stewardesses left him speechless and petrified; in fact, when Boss first dozed off, George figured he was just trying to escape the pretty gal, who was bent on serving them. Now she brought George another Jack Daniel's. He reached down and opened his briefcase and got out the file on Bolin Pharis. George earned his stiff salary, and not just at the pig works. He had spent a good bit of time rounding up everything there was to know on all these fellers, and he had half a dozen pages on Bolin Pharis, who was practically folks, born in Harrison up in Boone County just forty miles from Stay More. George had never known any Pharises, but for that matter he hadn't known hardly anybody up Harrison way. His niece Jelena had gone to school there, when Jackson Ingledew was a-raising her after her dad got killed in the War. Of course George had done a lot of business and trading in Harrison; everbody did. If Mr. Bolin Pharis wanted to chew the fat about his hometown, George reckoned he could manage.

Pharis had gone to the university at Fayetteville in the late sixties on an academic scholarship *and* a football scholarship, had played for the Razorbacks, and was Southwest Conference academic All-American. He had got hisself a bachelor's and a master's degree in business administration and had worked for a while in management back home at Hammerschmidt's lumberyard before Hammerschmidt's campaign manager offered him a job as assistant in one of Hammerschmidt's early runs for United States Congress. Pharis had accepted, even though Hammerschmidt was a Republican and Pharis was a Democrat. Pharis celebrated Hammerschmidt's victory by marrying a Harrison girl he'd dated throughout his university days. They'd had two kids, the boy now in college in Texas and the girl working in Chicago; the wife had divorced Pharis some years ago but he hadn't remarried. Pharis's work for Congressman Hammerschmidt had led to a campaign managership when a Republican had tried to beat Dale Bumpers for senator; the guy had lost, but that was the last time Bolin Pharis's man ever lost a campaign, until Al Gore and the Florida fiasco.

It was also the last time he ever worked for a Republican. After helping elect several people in Arkansas, Pharis had been lured to neighboring states, Oklahoma and Missouri and Tennessee and even Texas, and had elected a bodacious list of senators and congressmen and governors. With some other fellers, he had set up a whole factory of campaigning, calling it Pharis Carville & Begala. They went nationwide and elected governors, senators, and congressmen in Pennsylvania, Florida, Georgia, Ohio, etsettery; all they could handle. James Carville left the firm to manage Clinton's successful first campaign for president, and while there had been rumors that Bolin Pharis had been mortified because Clinton had passed up a fellow Arkansawyer in favor of Carville, a Louisianian, he and James Carville remained good friends, and in his memoirs of the Clinton years Carville had praised Pharis as practically his mentor. "Hey, the dude taught me all I know about strategy, which aint much, but hey," Carville had said.

When his man Al Gore won the popular presidential vote but narrowly lost the electoral vote to that dumb Texas governor, Pharis had no problem finding a top job out of politics. He was offered and accepted a position as public relations director for this great big company whose headquarters were in a tower in Cincinnati, although the factories were all over the earth. They made everything. They turned out soaps and drinks and beauty products and coffee and medicines and God knows what all. Hell, George himself was an occasional user of some of their stuff, like Pepto-Bismol and NyQuil and Crest toothpaste, not to mention Head & Shoulders and Old Spice. But he wasn't fixing to think their name out loud right here, where any fool could see it. He was only going to notice that if you took out that ampersand and replaced it with an *I*, it would spell *PIG*. He was also going to notice that he wasn't too partial to the company's name because the first part of it reminded him of some sessions he'd had to have with a St. Louis medical specialist called a proctologist, who caused him some pain and embarrassment.

He didn't hold any of this against Bolin Pharis. From everything George could find out, Pharis had been doing a really bang-up job handling the public relations for the company, and the company truly appreciated it and paid him accordingly, with bonuses and stock sharing and enough perks to keep any man happy and working his ass off. George knew there was no way on God's earth they could hire him as campaign manager. They couldn't afford him. Aw, hell, of course they could afford him even if he asked for a million dollars, yet surely Boss had set some kind of limits.

Bolin Pharis was even in line to become Chief Executive Officer of the company. He was such a big man that the very thought of him reassured George that they would get a quick, easy, and indisputable turndown, maybe even strong enough to make Boss give up his fool idea, and Jelena would feel good. But George had to play along with Boss, who was now stirring and waking up, mumbling something that sounded like "Ugithew," probably one of those Indian words he'd learned last year when he was studying the Osages. "Where are we?" Boss asks.

"We're a-fixin to light down," says George.

"Where?"

"Cincinnati," George tells him.

"Why?"

"You're running for governor, and we need some help."

"Right," Vernon Ingledew says.

It was late before they got away from the baggage carousel, and by the time they'd checked into the Hyatt Regency it was nigh onto suppertime, so they got them a bite at the Champs Italia Chop House and took a stroll afterwards. There was snow on the ground but they still had their boots on. George had never been to Cincinnati before. It was a right nice old town. There was hills all around it. They walked past the General Offices Tower Building of their destination for the morning, so they already knew how to get there. The very size and shape of the building ought to have warned Boss he didn't have a dog's chance.

They both wore business suits next day for breakfast and for the goings-on ahead, and they both carried briefcases, although Boss didn't have anything in his except some books because George carried everything they needed. They rode up the elevator to the man's suite of offices, way up yonder; he sure did surround himself with a fancier environment than any of those other fellers they'd visited; he had a real swell view of the Ohio River and all. The man's secretary didn't keep them waiting very long, hardly long enough for Boss to get out one of his books and read a bit.

The man didn't have his secretary usher them in. He came out himself, with his hand extended and a smile on his face. Bolin Pharis was about fifty, and George was surprised to see he had a beard, still dark, not much gray in it, neatly trimmed on all sides. George had grown a beard when he came home from 'Nam, that time he discovered his wife had left him and taken the kids with her and he got so mad and so drunk he went around beating up any man in Newton County who crossed his path and some who didn't, including Boss, who wasn't his boss yet and who didn't get beat up, as far as that goes, but in fact gave George the beating of his life, or rather the two of them walloped the crap out of each other, off in the woods, for half a day until they couldn't move, and then they got drunk together and healed their wounds and their bruises together, and Vernon offered George a job. George sobered up and shaved off his beard.

Bolin Pharis had a right powerful handshake, but George matched him in the strength of it and said, "Please to meetcha,

Mr. Pharis." He noticed out of the corner of his eye that Boss grimaced just a tiny bit when his hand was squoze in Pharis's mighty grip. Probably wants us to not forget he was a Razorback linebacker, George thought.

It was the fanciest office George had ever seen, big enough for six or seven fellers, but Pharis had it all to hisself. There was Razorback souvenirs and stuff all over: flags and a hog hat and a couple of footballs and team pictures and etsettery. George's chair was so big and so comfy he near about fell asleep right away. The secretary brought coffee.

The man kept looking back and forth between Boss and George and finally he says, "It sure is a pleasure to see some Arkansas people. Sometimes I think I'm the only one in Cincinnati." He took a sip of his coffee, and then he says, "I'm not sure I've been to Stay More, though. Is it down in there somewheres around Parthenon?"

George offers, "Just six mile or so kindly southwest of Partheeny."

"I may have fished the Little Buffalo in your backyard without knowing I was there," says Pharis.

"The town's so untenanted and necrotic you'd not notice it," says Boss.

Pharis stared a little bit at Boss, and then he asks, "Are you any kin to Jelena Ingledew?"

"We're own cousins," says Boss.

"I'm her uncle," George puts in.

"Well, well," says Pharis, and shakes his head and says, "I never knew her myself, but she was a legend at Harrison High. She was a few years ahead of me. Highest grades in the history of the school and valedictorian and all, you know." Pharis chuckles a little chuckle. "My teachers were always telling me, 'If you'd just work a little harder, you might be as good as Jelena Ingledew.' " Pharis appreciated that George and Boss both chuckled along with him a bit. "Whatever became of her?" Pharis asks. "Is she married?"

"Naw," George offers. "Not no more, leastways. Her and Mark Duckworth was married for a while and had a couple kids, but they split up, oh, I reckon it must've been going on thirty year ago."

"Really?" says Bolin Pharis. "She didn't remarry?"

"Nope," says George.

"She's not still in Arkansas, is she?"

"Matter a fack, she is. Her and him"—George inclined his head toward Boss—"they kindly live together."

Bolin Pharis gave Boss a good looking-over for a second or two, and then all he says is, "Well." Then he sort of coughed, and after a while he says, "I sure do eat Ingledew Ham, I can tell you. Every chance I get, I buy it."

"George gets most of the credit for the quality of that meat these days," Boss says. George shook his head to deny it.

Pharis smiled and says, "You boys aren't here to suggest that we buy you out, are you? Despite the diversity of our products, we don't do anything fancy in the food department. I'm sure lots of people eat our Pringles with their Ingledew Ham, but we aren't planning to diversify into meat."

Boss shook his head. "No, Bolin—may I call you Bolin?"

"Just call me Bo, please," says Bo.

"Bo, we're here to get you on board my campaign for governor."

"On board?" says Bo. "If you plan to run against that bastard Shoat Bradfield, I'd be glad to make a contribution—"

"The contribution we want is your expertise as our campaign manager," says Boss.

George tried to figure whether Pharis's smile was kindly wistful-like or just politely negative. He didn't say sorry or nothing, though. He asks, "Who recommended me to you?"

"Everyone," says Boss.

"Didn't Everyone tell you I've sworn off politics?" says Bo.

"Yes, but they didn't tell me why," says Boss.

Bo looked at his costly wristwatch. "Listen, fellows, we're having this talk on company time, you know. If I had known the purpose of your visit, I would have declined outright and spared you the trip, but if you had insisted on pursuing it I would have courteously offered to discuss it with you at any hour when I was free from my daily routines working for this company."

George admired the man's honesty. He himself made a point of never letting salesmen into his office if they were trying to sell him something for his own use, not the company's. Since he had been responsible for setting up the appointment with Pharis, he felt obliged to apologize. "Sorry," says George, and waited for Boss to lead the way out the door.

But Bolin Pharis asks, "How long are you boys in town?"

"Our plane home is late this afternoon," George declares.

Pharis stood up. "Wish you could stay more," he says, slipping in that little mention of their hometown in such a way it told them he knew they knew he was slipping it in. They stood too, and he walked them to the door and offered his hand for another one of those iron-man handshakes.

Boss wouldn't let go of Bo's hand. "Don't you want to hear *why* you should be my manager?" Boss asks him.

"If you told me it would ensure my passage to Heaven, I still couldn't do it," says Bo, without blinking an eye. "But if you could tell me on my time, not the company's time, I could meet you for drinks downstairs after five. Better yet, I'd love to have a couple of Arkansas boys go to dinner with me tonight."

George blinked. Had Pharis forgotten that out home in the Ozarks *dinner* always meant the noon meal? Boss says, "We'd be delighted." And that was that. It was George's job to call the airline and cancel their afternoon flight and make a new flight for the following day and then to tell the hotel they were staying another night. Then they had a whole day to kill so they split up; Boss took off to the Cincinnati Art Museum to see a van Gogh painting called *Undergrowth with Two Figures*, and George went out to the Cincinnati Zoo to look at the undergrowth with big cats.

The way it turned out, they didn't just have drinks and dinner with Bolin Pharis, they come mighty nigh to spending the whole night with him. It was pretty close to midnight before George finally got to bed, and he was not used to that. When he got close to sixty, he learned he needed to go to bed each and every night at the same time, ten-thirty on the dot, and it really bothered him to miss out on that. But there they were, shooting pool in the feller's game room way past George's bedtime.

The supper had been at this real swank place called Maisonette, where they was waited on not by gals but by men dressed like for a wedding, and for that reason Boss was able to speak to 'em and George didn't have to order for him as he would've if they'd been waitresses. Chances are, I'll never find myself in a place like this again, George told himself. So he passed up the idea of just a good old steak, which wasn't on the menu anyhow, and he tried the Scottish wild pheasant, because Bo recommended it. Boss had the Scottish hare saddle, not to be contrary, but maybe on account of he'd rather eat rabbit than fowl. Pharis had the venison medallion. And they had a couple of bottles of the bygoddest wine George had ever swilled. When it was all done, Bo Pharis, being an old Razorback linebacker, had much quicker reflexes than George and managed to grab the check about .037 of a second before George could reach it.

Things started out with Pharis saying an odd thing. "I apologize for my hypocrisy in refusing to use my company's time to discuss this matter with you," says Bo, "when I've spent a good part of my company's time today looking into it. I've made calls to quite a number of my acquaintances in Arkansas, people in the know, you know, some pols who go way back with me, as well as a few people in the press." The man stopped to make sure that George and Boss both understood just how much he'd been checking around, and then he says, real serious, "Not one of them has ever heard of you." He let that sink in, and then he says, "Even Orval Faubus, who came out of nowhere in the Ozarks to run for governor back in 1954, had at least been elected to minor county office beforehand. *You*, Vern—may I call you Vern?—have never been elected to *anything*."

George gripped the man's biceps in a mighty hold. "Don't never call him Vern," he says, low and mean as if he didn't want Boss to hear him, although of course Boss could. He repeats it. "Don't *never* call him Vern."

Bo Pharis gave George a look as if they were about to square off right there and have it out. But he turns to Boss and says, "I was beginning to suspect that you are some kind of impostor, maybe running a scam on me."

Boss just smiled. He showed teeth when he smiled, George reflected, just like old Bill Clinton had always done. "The very fact," says Boss, "that you went to all that trouble to check me out would seem to imply that you are not dismissing, out of hand, my request for your services."

"Whoa," says Bo. "Let's get this straight before we go another step. I will not, under *any* circumstances, serve as your campaign manager. Or anybody else's. Would you like to know how much Al Gore paid me to handle his run for president? No, you don't want to know. But it wasn't enough to erase the pain of the defeat. Let's please understand clearly from the outset, good buddies, that we are not going to negotiate my services. But we owe it to each other, as Arkansas men, as good old hillbillies—even if the part of Harrison I grew up in is actually flatland—we owe it to each other to understand each other: I want you to understand just why I will not under any circumstances operate your campaign, and in return I'd like to hear why you think you should be governor of Arkansas and how you think you could scare up enough votes to be elected. And I might even offer you, free gratis, some advice."

But the funny thing was, they never did get around to talking about that, not during the supper, leastways. They didn't talk about politics at all. The closest they got to talking politics was this here great joke that Bo told. It was about that bastard governor, Shoat Bradfield, who got hisself reelected even though everbody hated him. 'Course *Shoat* was just his nickname, and a shoat is a young pig after he's been weaned, and the joke was about a pig, but there wasn't no direct connection with his name. Seems this here state trooper who was Shoat's chauffeur was driving him down the road on the way to a speech he had to give in some little Ozark town, and maybe the trooper was a-drivin too fast, but anyhow he don't see this pig a-crossin the road and he hits it. The state trooper knows he hit the poor pig hard enough to kill it, and he wants to stop and see, but Shoat's in a hurry to get to where he's givin that speech and makes him drive on. But that trooper is a good man despite his employer, and he keeps tellin the governor how awful it was to hit that pig. And finally he says, "Sir, while you're givin your speech, would it be okay if I just drove on back down there to find out who owned that pig and tell 'em I was sure sorry?" And Governor Bradfield says, Well, if you have to, and gives him permission. So the governor gives his speech and the party's all over but that trooper didn't come back. The governor waits and waits for hours, until finally his car comes back into view, weaving back and forth across the road, and there's the trooper, drunk as a coot, and the backseat loaded up with enough meat and produce and jams and stuff to feed the entire state police. The governor gets in a rage and demands what the hell happened to him, and the trooper says, "I done what I thought was right. I went back to the farm where I hit that pig. When I knocked on the door and give them the news, they loaded me down with all these victuals and they fed me a big dinner and gave me a demijohn of fine whiskey and afterwards their real pretty daughter insisted on giving me a blow job in the car before I could finally get away." The governor demands to know exactly what the trooper told those folks. And the trooper says he don't understand it hisself; all he said to them was, "I'm Governor Bradfield's chauffeur, and I killed the pig."

Boss was about two or three full seconds ahead of George in getting the joke, but they both laughed so hard that people stared at 'em. George wasn't the laughing type; he hardly ever heard or saw anything that struck him as funny enough to waste a guffaw over, and he couldn't remember the last time he'd had one of those laughs that was completely involuntary and natural, without him having any control over it. He blushed a good deal, realizing he'd let the laugh get away with him. But Bo Pharis sure appreciated his audience.

From then on, George was sort of left out of the talk, which wasn't about any sort of governors or governorship or campaigning or nothing. Bo Pharis happened to ask what they'd done that day, and George mentioned he'd seen the zoo with all those big cats and that was about the last time he got a chance to open his mouth. When Boss said he'd been to the art museum, the two men got to talking about van Gogh, and Bo Pharis even could quote the exact words that the artist Vincent had wrote to his brother Theo about that particular painting, *Undergrowth with Two Figures*, and then Bo and Boss got into this long talk about whether or not van Gogh was really as wrought up as he'd been cut out to be, and Boss seemed to really blow Bo away with his theory that the *Undergrowth* painting wasn't spontaneous but calculated and orderly. After they'd talked about art for a good bit, Bo just says, "*Ars est celare artem*" and Boss says "*Sutor ne supra crepidam*," and before you know it the two fellers was doing their chitchat in Latin, and poor George had nothing to do but look over the various ladies in their finery who were eating their supper at other tables. It wasn't too bad, studying all them pretty gals and wondering what-all *they* was a-talking about, you could bet not in Latin.

Bo and Boss discovered they shared a passion for astronomy, and they talked about black holes through dessert, when they also discovered their interest in geology and talked about rocks until Bo beat George to grabbing that check. Then Bo put them into his sleek black Jaguar and took them out to a place called Indian Hill, where Bo had this huge mansion, the finest house George had ever been inside of. The bar alone was bigger than George's house. They had drinks and Bo and Boss talked about all kinds of stuff, horses and Ireland and nuclear physics and the Osage Indians.

Maybe George had a little too much to drink, feeling left out, because when they were shooting some eight ball on this ten-thousand-dollar pool table in the game room (there was also a Ping-Pong table and a shuffleboard and a chess table, but Boss declined Bo's offer to play a game of chess because he didn't want to clobber him) and at one point Boss had to go to the bathroom and take a leak, so George and Bo were alone together for the first time, and George laid his cue stick down and put his face up pretty close to Bo's and says, "Lookee here, I reckon I ought to tell ye. I know ye aint a-fixin to jine the campaign anyhow, but afore ye git too chummy with Vernon I think ye ort to know something. Jelena don't want him runnin for governor. Hell, *I* don't want him a-runnin for governor. Aint *nobody* wants him runnin for governor."

Bo Pharis he just smiled and looked at George kind of tolerant, like George had crapped on the rug but he forgave him for it. Then he arched his eyebrows and says, "But what if *I* would like to see him running?"

Chapter Three

Bolin Keith Pharis III drank an extra cup of breakfast coffee and thought out loud, which had been his habit in this house ever since he'd moved into it. Kristin, his maid, no longer lived in but came to work each day after he'd left, so he was alone. "If George is Sancho Panza," he said to the empty house, and not just rhetorically, "then who or what am I? One of the windmills? The rascally publican who dubbed the knight? The Biscayan squire? Or perhaps"—he permitted himself a laugh—"I'm just the bony old nag Rosinante!" If there weren't something so godawful ludicrous about the whole situation, Bo wouldn't have wasted another minute of his considerable powers of cogitation on it.

Surely his contempt for the present governor of Arkansas, the misbegotten Bradfield, would not have been enough excuse for him to get involved. If he truly cared about getting rid of Bradfield, there were any number of ways he could swing it and any number of candidates he could back who had a good chance to defeat the man. Not that it mattered all that much who was the present—or future—governor of Arkansas. Although Bo still felt some concern for his native state, he had long ago severed most of his ties with it and had been indifferent to the string of politicians such as Jim Guy Tucker and Mike Huckabee who had followed Clinton into the governor's office, although when news of the election of Shoat Bradfield reached him he began to pay attention, because his experience with Bradfield was that the man was utterly without scruple or altruism. And the good Democrat whom Bradfield had defeated, Caleb Burdell, had used as his campaign manager one of Bo's dearest old friends, a bright, bouncy woman named Lydia Caple, who, Bo had learned, had been truly wounded by Bradfield's campaign tactics.

Bo still wrote to his mother in Harrison three or four times a year, and he still called her at Christmas and on Mother's Day. He followed, at least in the back pages of the *Enquirer*'s sports section, the fortunes of the Razorback football team. He paid his annual dues to the University of Arkansas Alumni Association. He kept in touch with several old friends, such as those he'd called yesterday, including Lydia Caple, to see if any of them knew anything about this Ingledew. Lydia hadn't been soured on politics to the extent of giving up the trade of political consultancy, but she'd told Bo that whoever this Ingledew fellow was, however much money he had, she didn't want to mess around with any more "amateurs."

Bo still had a few calls to make. He had told Ingledew, when he'd dropped him and George Dinsmore off at the Hyatt Regency late last night, that the least he could do was find a good man (or woman) in Arkansas willing to run the campaign for him. Ingledew had said, "I'm not interested in any amateurs in Arkansas." Bo had resisted the urge to tell him Lydia Caple had bestowed the same epithet on *him*. Instead, Bo had kidded him about not having enough faith in the talent to be found in his own state. There were a few men and women in Arkansas who were anything but amateurs, and Vernon Ingledew could expect to hear from one of them in another day or so. Still, even in that last moment together, Vernon had not been willing to concede Bo's refusal. "I'm offering you," he had said, "something far greater than an obese salary with all conceivable expenses. I'm offering you a chance to do something that will save your soul."

"Coming from anybody else," Bolin Pharis said to his empty house over an unprecedented third cup of coffee, "such a statement would have been inexcusably presumptuous, or at best hopelessly quixotic. But coming from Vernon Ingledew, it is disquietingly thinkable." It was thinkable, Bo realized, because Vernon had thought it, and Bo had come to believe that Vernon was capable of better thought than any other man he'd ever met. They had got to know each other remarkably well in the few hours they'd had together. Bo had understood Vernon well enough to know that when he said *soul* he wasn't talking in any religious sense. Indeed, whatever notion Bo had been developing that Vernon just might be electable, because of his intelligence, his kindness, and his good looks, not to mention his money, was given a severe jolt when Bo learned that Vernon was not religious. Of all the things that Vernon had going against him—and these were formidable, such as his lack of experience and his relationship with his "own cousin" Jelena—his lack of any church affiliation would practically kill him with the Arkansas electorate.

Bo knew that just as he had come to understand Vernon in ways that transcended the various weighty topics they had discussed, Vernon had probably come to understand him too, and thus, he realized, he might even have sensed that there was something lacking in Bo's soul. "What did I say to him?" Bo asked the house. "What clue did I possibly give him that there is anything about my soul that needs saving?" Perhaps Ingledew had just been guessing. Or perhaps Ingledew had looked into his eyes and found there a hint of what one of his most recent girlfriends—had it been Lisa or Jan?—had called "a certain indescribable void."

Bo enjoyed and appreciated being by himself and was never given to brooding about his soul or feeling that anything was missing in his character or his personality. Ask Patricia, his once-upon-a-wife, and she would tell you otherwise; she would call him selfish and stubborn and, her favorite insult, "a little boy." But the fact remained that he was happy with himself, he was not bothered by any frustrations or resentments or yearnings, and he was not aware of anything he ought to do to change himself or his life. He had a great job and he was damned good at it. He had not cast a backward glance at his career in politics for quite some time. He never gave it a thought . . . unless somebody like Al Gore or Vernon Ingledew made him an offer that was excruciatingly difficult to refuse.

He loved Cincinnati. He was a die-hard Bengals fan and remained convinced that if only the Bengals could learn to tackle, learn to pass, learn to establish the run, and quit missing assignments and dropping passes, they had a good chance to make it to the Super Bowl someday, and Bolin Pharis intended to be here when it happened. His company had a skybox in the spanking-new Paul Brown Stadium, and he never missed a home game. His company also had a booth at Cinergy Field, and Bo occasionally went to a Reds game. He would be even more of a sports fan if he didn't dislike crowds so much. The older he got, the more uncomfortable he felt—a form of agoraphobia, he supposed—around large numbers of people. What he really liked to do with his spare time was a couple of private things, all by himself: fly-fish and garden. He was really good at fly-fishing, had practiced for years, owned the very best Orvis equipment, and liked nothing better than jumping into his second car, a Nissan Patrol 4-by-4, and heading for Twelve Mile Creek or Mad River or one of the creeks up in the Kentucky hills to spend a day reading the stream. There was only a bit of conflict, in that the best season for fly-fishing coincided with the times when he needed to get out into his vegetable garden. Bo's eleven-acre spread included a half acre of good loam that he had devoted much time to enriching and planting and harvesting. He had the only vegetable garden in Indian Hill, and he'd had to plan it and screen it so it couldn't be seen from the road or the neighbors'. He never reflected that his green thumb had anything to do with his Arkansas heritage, because after all his folks back home in Harrison had never had a vegetable garden. Gardening didn't make him a rustic. There was just something in it that was a handy metaphor for life and work: starting with a seed that contains the incredible amount of information needed to make cells expand and multiply into a living plant, watching it grow, tending it, giving it everything it needed, knowing what it didn't need, and being rewarded, finally, by the abundant, succulent harvest. It was too bad there wasn't anybody here to share the harvest with him. On occasion, he could serve his own fresh vegetables to his guests and his girlfriends, but usually he just put a couple of ears of still-in-the-husk corn into the microwave and ate them himself, and if there were too many ears he had to throw them on his compost pile. Maybe it wasn't fair of him to do so, but he judged his girlfriends on their taste for radishes. He hardly ever had a date who could eat a radish, not just the Champion and Cherry Belle but even the French Breakfast and White Icicle. He was crazy about radishes himself, their earthy taste, and, thinking of them, he realized that the planting season was just a few weeks away. His orders to Burpee and Shumway and Park had all been filled. He had a dozen heirloom tomato plants already thriving in the south windows.

Thinking of the nuisance of having to hide his garden from view, he realized he wasn't entirely happy with his residence or its location. One reason he'd taken it was a nearly unconscious wish to reconcile with Patricia, and he had persuaded her to come and visit at least once, but she had pronounced the manor too damn big and ostentatious. Bo had tried to sell her on the zoning: only single-family houses were allowed, and about 60 percent of those were on five-acre-minimum lots. There were no traffic lights, no supermarkets, no gas stations, no convenience stores, no barbershops, no four-lane roads, no apartment buildings, and almost no crime. Bo belonged to the Camargo Club, a private country club whose restaurant was the only "business" in Indian Hill. Although nobody but Bo had a vegetable garden, within the city limits of Indian Hill were at least three working farms raising cows and sheep, and there were horses all over the place. Sometimes when Bo was rounding a hilly curve in the road, he could almost pretend he was back in the Ozarks. But there was nothing anywhere around to remind him of the courthouse square in Harrison, which had been his favorite hangout as a kid. What he had liked to do most, even more than playing football, was sit on the south side of the courthouse, where the old men whittled and swapped yarns. Bo had had a darn good Barlow pocketknife himself, and he could whittle too while he listened to the old men talk, spinning their fabulous myths. There was nothing at all like that in Hamilton County, Ohio.

The people who lived in Indian Hill and appreciated all that quiet and serenity and seclusion were mostly family people, sometimes with both parents working in order to support such a lifestyle but with lots of kids taking advantage of the best school district in the nation. Bo was one of the few single people living in Indian Hill. After Patricia had failed to respond to his not fully articulated invitation to forget their differences and move in with him, he had tried to persuade his widowed mother to move to Cincinnati, but she wouldn't leave Arkansas. His daughter, Sarah, worked in Chicago as a promotion underling for a department store; he had tried for years to convince her that a much better job was waiting for her in Cincinnati. His best hope was that his son, Bolin IV, due to graduate this spring from Rice University, might want to take a job with Bo's company.

And of course more than one of Bo's girlfriends had wanted too earnestly to move in with him, but he hadn't yet dated one he'd truly care to live with, never mind their dislike for radishes. So he was given to wondering if he was destined to spend the rest of his working career as an aging man living alone in a house much, much too big for him.

"But what has that got to do with lacking a *soul*?" he asked, rhetorically this time, of that empty house, and then he got into his Jag and drove to work.

One of his deputies, Castor Sherrill, had already left him a memo to the effect that he was on top of the latest problem involving the recurrent false rumor that the company had Satanic ties, a calumny that had derived from an old misinterpretation of the company's logo of moon and stars (abandoned fifteen years ago). During his time with the company, Bo and his large staff had been required to respond to thousands of calls and letters regarding the false rumor. Now bright young Cast Sherrill was devising a plan to squelch it, once and for all.

Bo really didn't have much to do. Cast and the other deputy, Jim Tompkins, worked zealously running the show. Despite Bo's pretense, to Vernon and George, of not wanting to use the company's time for personal matters, Bo had no compunction about using the company's time for whatever he wished. At least two or three mornings a week he sneaked away to his athletic club for a good workout and a good swim. But this morning, instead, he began making some more calls to old friends in Arkansas, trying to scare up a good campaign manager for a worthy but callow gentleman named Vernon Ingledew. His first call went to Jerry Russell, but he learned the man was already committed to another candidate in the Democratic primary. "Ingledew?" Jerry said, and after a long pause, "No, Bo, I can't say I've ever heard of him. Is he in the state senate, maybe?"

Two other prospective managers he called were also already committed to candidates. Bo learned that there was going to be a pretty broad slate. So eager were the Democrats to find someone to run against and defeat Shoat Bradfield, there had already been eight filings for the primary, including a former governor, the present secretary of state and attorney general, a powerful county sheriff, a state senator, a rich and powerful automobile dealer, a popular minister, and a former congressman. "Good heavens," Bo remarked to his informant, "my man Ingledew is going to be caught in a horse race."

"With a name like Ingledew," the man remarked in return, "who would bet on the nag, let alone jockey him?"

"Hey, names don't mean anything," Bo said. "What about Eisenhower?"

"Ike was a famous general," the man replied. "Does your Ingledew have any war record?"

Bo realized that there was one more albatross (he was keeping count, and this was number thirteen) for poor Vernon's neck: he had no military service at all. Not even ROTC, because he'd never gone to college. Bo felt obliged to mention this to the fourth person he called, the same woman he'd called the day before, Lydia Caple, who had not yet signed up with any candidate and was in fact trying to decide whether to keep shopping for a candidate or accept an offer to be one of the other manager's assistants or perhaps a press secretary (she had first entered politics from her career as a political reporter for the state's top newspaper). Bo told Lydia that yes, she was right, Vernon was a crass amateur, but he was "the most personable, clever, handsome, engaging, outright lovable aspirant" that Lydia could ever hope to meet. He could palpably sense that Lydia might actually be refraining from giving him a second flat refusal. But because she was such a dear old friend (they had in fact enjoyed each other in bed on one wild, memorable occasion) he felt obliged to inform her candidly of the thirteen albatrosses he had identified as obstacles in Vernon's path and to mention one in particular: Lydia could expect to find Vernon extremely uncomfortable in her presence, not because of her but because Ingledew men going back to ancient Anglo-Saxon times had always been hopelessly bashful around women.

There was a long silence on the other end. "Bo, honey," Lydia said at length, "are you teasing me? Is this some kind of joke? Or have you just lost touch entirely with the Arkansas electorate?"

"Lyd, sweetheart, think of it as a huge *challenge!*"

"The challenge is so huge that not even a seasoned pro like Bolin Pharis would want to handle it," she said, and changed the subject, and that was that.

Bo was thinking he ought to spend the rest of the morning at his athletic club. But he made one more call. "I am saving my soul," he told the four spacious walls of his office. He put in a call to Archie Schaffer, an old college classmate at the University of Arkansas who had been the closest thing to a best friend Bo had had during his junior and senior years. Arch had successfully managed the campaigns for Dale Bumpers as governor and later long-term U.S. senator from Arkansas. In fact, in a place where everybody was kin to everybody else, just as Vernon was Jelena's own cousin and George was her uncle, Bo was not unmindful that Arch Schaffer was Dale Bumpers's nephew. When Arch had run his Schaffer & Associates political firm in the eighties, he had provided some stiff competition for Bo Pharis on occasion. It was Arch's withdrawal from the political scene into a public relations career that had inspired Bo to do likewise: Arch was vice president of Media, Public & Governmental Affairs for the huge chicken company Tyson Foods, which was headquartered in the Ozark town of Springdale. Bo realized, while the call was going through, that he couldn't hope to persuade Arch to go back into politics any more than Vernon had persuaded Bo, but there was no harm in trying.

"Arch, you old bastard," Bo said.

"Bo, you old rascal," Arch said. "Hey, congratulations! Now I'll have to call you Doc Pharis."

"What's this?" Bo wondered.

"You haven't heard? Hell, maybe I shouldn't be the first to tell you. The university's giving you an honorary degree at May graduation."

"No shit?" Bo said. "No, I hadn't heard yet. That's swell. I guess I'll have to accept it in person."

"You sure as hell will. And Beverly and I are expecting you to stay with us instead of the Hilton."

"Of course. And maybe we can go the next day to the tailwaters of Beaver Lake Dam and catch us a few rainbows."

"You bet." There was a lull in the conversation, then Arch asked, "What's up, Bo? What can I do for you, or vice versa?"

"I don't suppose you've ever heard of Vernon Ingledew," Bo said.

After a reflective pause, Arch said, "Which Vernon Ingledew did you have in mind? The fellow who runs Ingledew Ham? Or do you mean the fictional character in *The Architecture of the Arkansas Ozarks*?"

"I don't know about the latter," Bo said. "I never read that."

"Well, could be they're one and the same. He's the owner and CEO of Ingledew Ham. I've met him. We tried to buy them out a few years ago, but they weren't for sale. Are you thinking of buying them out? I can save you the trouble."

"No, it's something else. Have you heard any news about Ingledew entering the Democratic primary for governor?"

"Give me a minute," Arch requested, and Bo visualized him running a check on his computer's high-powered search engines. Less than a minute before Arch came back. "Nope. He hasn't filed as of this morning, and there's really nothing at all on him except a bunch of books he got on interlibrary loan from the university."

Bo told Arch about the visit from Vernon and George in Cincinnati. He gave him the rough outline of Vernon's position. He told him about Vernon's thirteen albatrosses. "You laughed him out of your office?" Arch asked.

"Not exactly," Bo admitted. "I took them to dinner. After that, I took them up to my house for a few hours. We got to know each other real well. I made it clear to Ingledew that I'm no longer available as a political consultant. But—" Bo paused, took a deep breath, and gave a long moment's meditation. How to say it? If anybody he knew could understand, probably Arch Schaffer could. "Arch, listen, I'm telling you—or I'm trying to tell you—that Vernon Ingledew is a *natural*. If I lived in Arkansas, I couldn't think of anybody I'd rather have as governor. He just sends off this feeling that he could solve any problem on earth. He knows everything. He can *do* anything."

"Wow," said Arch. "Coming from *you*, that's high praise. But I think I know what you mean. When Johnny Tyson and Buddy Wray and I and some of the other guys here met with Ingledew, he sort of projected that same feeling, that he not only knew exactly why we should not and could not buy them out but he knew we shouldn't diversify from chicken into pork. Turns out he was right, too. We made a big mistake when we expanded into fish and beef and pork."

"He could make Shoat Bradfield wish he'd never been born," Bo declared.

"So what you're telling me is that you're having second thoughts about turning down his overture, and you want me to tell you you're doing the right thing."

"Aw, shoot, no!" Bo quickly exclaimed. "I'm *out*. What I'm telling you is that if you ever had any desire to get back into campaigning, here's your best chance."

"I'm like you, Bo. I have no desire to get back into

campaigning. You know how cops and firemen can retire real early because of all the stress they've had to put up with? I think political consultants ought to have the same consideration."

"Could you at least *think* about it?" Bo pled.

"Could *you*?" Arch returned.

"I have been," Bo told him. "I haven't been able to think about anything else."

"I don't know about you, Bo, but I'm a real slow thinker. I'll have to get back to you on this, but don't get your hopes up. Beverly wouldn't let me do it, for one thing. But I'll think. And I'll think. And I'll also do some checking around and see what I can scrape up on Ingledew. Meanwhile, let me strongly recommend that you read *The Architecture of the Arkansas Ozarks*."

Bo Pharis asked his secretary to call some bookstores and find him a copy of the book. Later that day she reported back that Barnes and Noble had told her the paperback was out of print. Bo asked her to try some used-book stores. She finally found a hardback original marked down to just $4.95 at a place called The Dust Jacket and asked them to hold it, and Bo left work early to pick it up. He took it home with him. In his home mail was a letter from the president of the University of Arkansas notifying him that he would be awarded the honorary doctorate of laws degree, and the pleasure of his robing at the May graduation was anticipated. He would not be required to give the commencement address; a senator was doing that. Bo realized that commencement was being held the weekend that he usually set out his tomato plants, but he supposed they could wait another week. (The plants, not the university.)

He read the book. Not all at once, for he lacked Vernon's reading speed, but he managed to get through it in two nights and one day at the office. It was a riot in places. He laughed till his ribs hurt, beginning with the first chapter and the story of Jacob Ingledew, Vernon's ancestor, and how Jacob "evicted" an Osage

Indian from the future site of Stay More but impregnated the Indian's squaw in the process. Bo wondered where the author had got all this stuff. The book reminded him a bit of *One Hundred Years of Solitude*, but there was nothing outright fantastic in it—that is, nothing that couldn't actually have happened.

When Jelena Ingledew was born on page 314, and Vernon Ingledew was born on page 342, and nearly everything that happened to them was related in bold detail, Bo wondered how the author could have got away with that, writing a supposed "novel" about real people whose privacy he was invading. When Bo was in high school, he'd had a crush on the *idea* of Jelena, whom he had never met, and now he was reading about her actual lonely childhood and it made him practically fall in love with her. Her obsession with the boy cousin who was eight years her junior was made perfectly plausible but no less painful, and Bo found himself identifying with Vernon, and even believing it when Vernon wears a magic wristwatch that enables him to become aware of the reader of the novel! Bo thought it was real tricky: to find himself inside of Vernon at the same time that he found himself being the reader that Vernon is watching and communicating with. There were some spooky things in the ending of that book.

Bo felt hideously homesick. More than satisfying his curiosity about Vernon and Jelena, the book gave him a sense of the destiny of the whole long lineage of Ingledews who had inhabited this place in the Ozarks called Stay More. The narratives evoked for Bo those old tales he used to listen to the old-time whittlers spin on the courthouse square at Harrison. In fact, Harrison itself appeared in the book in several different places. Bo realized that the people of the Ozarks had had a fabulous history, filled with hardship but also with a rich sense of excitement and a texture that was entirely gone from current life.

"By God," Bo declared to his empty house, "when I go back in May to get that doctorate they're giving me I'd better plan on doing my fly-fishing on the Little Buffalo, or even Swains Creek, and maybe even see if those old whittlers are still there on the square in Harrison."

And behold, his empty house answered him, for once. **"Bo, son,"** it said, **"that's not until May. Can you wait that long? Why don't you go back *now* and help a good man start running for governor?"**

The house didn't say anything more for the rest of the night, but Bo had trouble sleeping. Early the next morning he went to see his boss, the CEO of the company, and told him he needed some time off, a few months perhaps, for "spiritual enrichment." No problem. Couldn't Castor Sherrill and Jim Tompkins hold down the fort as long as need be? Sure thing.

He called Cast into his office and laid it on the line. He told Cast he had decided to take a leave and "reenter the lists" as campaign manager for an offbeat visionary in Arkansas named Vernon Ingledew. Cast would be put in charge, even allowed to boss his rival Jim Tompkins, for at least three months and possibly longer, if Vernon Ingledew managed to survive the primary and make it to the general election. Cast was a bright, able kid; although he was a native Hoosier, he'd taken his MBA at Harvard. Tompkins's MBA was from Stanford, but Jim lacked Cast's lively personality. All Cast needed for advancement was a little managerial experience, and here was his chance to get it.

But Cast said, "Please take me as your disciple, sir."

Where have I heard that line before? Bo wondered. Was it something in *Don Quixote*? No, maybe Bo hadn't heard it but had read it in the subtitles of a movie. "Listen," he replied, "I don't have anything to teach you. I had a lot of experience fighting political campaigns, but for your own good you don't want to get into that."

"No," Cast said. "I've made up my mind. I'll follow you to Arkansas even if you won't accept me."

"I forbid you to do that," Bo said, and showed him to the door. He was flattered, but he owed it to the company not to leave Jim Tompkins solely in charge.

Late that afternoon, while Bo was clearing off his desk, a call came in from his pal Archie Schaffer. Arch was dramatic. "Bo, because of you, I accept. I'll do it. Tyson's will let me off until the general election."

"But Arch," Bo said, "I've talked myself into doing it!"

Was Arch's silence bitter disappointment? But it didn't last long. "Great," he said. "Really. I'm happy for you."

As consolation, Bo offered, "Would you consider being my second-in-command?"

"Being second fiddle to *you*, Bo, would beat hell out of being first fiddle all by myself."

Bo Pharis laughed. "I hope you mean that. We could make some real music together. But who else would we need for our orchestra?"

"We would have to get four or five more. We'd need a press secretary, a headquarters manager, a head of opposition research, and we'd need a good media advisor."

Bo made a scoffing noise. "Hell, I know all *that*," he said. "I mean, who do we want for those *jobs*?"

Arch sought clarification. "Money's no object?"

"Ingledew is more than loaded."

"Okay, so how about Carleton Drew for media advisor?" Arch suggested, naming a prominent DC consultant who had elected numerous senators and governors by the crafty use of television ads.

"Fine, if we can get him," Bo said. "But he might not appreciate Vernon's opposition to television."

"God." Arch sighed. "How opposed is he?"

"Won't allow it in his own house," Bo said. "Although I suppose he wouldn't object to other people having it."

"But he would object to using it for advertising his candidacy?"

"I'm afraid he might," Bo allowed.

"All right, you give Carleton a buzz and ask him, hypothetically, if he would consider himself capable of electing a candidate *without* any use of television. Now, who's the best oppo man you ever knew?"

Of course Bo understood the euphemism; the head of opposition research was in charge of digging up all the dirt on the other candidates. "Would you buy Harry Wolfe?" Bo ventured.

"Harry Wolfe's our man," Arch said. "But I haven't talked to him yet. I think maybe you'd better talk to him."

"Right. And we'll need an office manager and some conspicuous headquarters in Little Rock."

"Better check with our man Vernon on that," Arch suggested. "He might prefer having headquarters up here in the Ozarks."

"Will do. We'll also need a top-notch press secretary."

"Shall I call Lydia Caple? Or do you want to?"

"I've already talked to her twice," Bo informed him.

"Was that before or after you made up your mind to do it?" Arch wanted to know.

"Before," Bo admitted, and began to feel good all over with the prospect of getting Lydia for the job. For years Lydia Caple had been the ace political reporter for the *Arkansas Democrat-Gazette*, and when her job and her political savvy had been challenged by the popular columnist Hank Endicott she had decided to leave the paper and get into politics herself. She'd had legendary good luck with all the candidates she'd worked for, including briefly Governor Clinton himself, but his well-known propensity for requesting a certain sexual allegiance from his female underlings had cost him her services. Bo had not been able to resist feeling proud that he had succeeded in doing something the then-governor and future president had not succeeded in doing.

"Okay, I'll call her again," Bo said. The only thing he'd left on his desk was his appointment book, and he was jotting things down in it. Reminders: *Call Lydia tonight.*

When he'd finished his long talk with Arch, he needed a drink to help him catch his breath. He was pouring it at the little bar in the corner of his office when Cast Sherrill came back into the office. "Excuse me, sir," said Cast, "but have you reconsidered?"

Bo had so much on his mind he couldn't figure out what Cast meant. Something about the old logo? "What's that?" he said.

"I want to go to Arkansas with you and be your disciple," Cast said.

"Hell, Cast, you've been my disciple ever since I hired you. Now it's time for you to run the show in my absence."

"Don't hold it against me, sir, but I don't want to work here after you've gone. This place wouldn't be the same without you, and I'd be lost."

It was a long drive to Arkansas, Bo realized, and it might not be too bad to have a traveling companion. Maybe Cast could help drive. Thinking of this, Bo realized something more important. Which of his two vehicles would he be taking? The Jaguar was the object of his greatest affections, and he couldn't conceive of being without it. But it wouldn't be any good in the back roads of the Ozarks. If he had to go to Stay More, six miles beyond where the pavement ends at Parthenon, he would need the Nissan 4-by-4. How about taking the Jag himself and getting Cast to drive the 4-by-4, and then he'd have the use of both?

But no, he didn't want the kid tagging along after him throughout the campaign. He was going to be so busy selling

Vernon Ingledew to the people of Arkansas he wouldn't have time to teach anything to a goddamn apprentice. Or certainly not Castor Sherrill, who, despite his brilliance in college, had a peculiar background, the details of which Bo had picked up over several drinks when he'd first hired Cast out of Harvard Business: Cast's mother, whom he hardly ever saw, was an Indiana farmgirl who had a brief career in Los Angeles doing what budding starlets often have to do, making porn movies. Cast's father was one of her costars, though Cast had never met him. The man had, however, named Cast, not after castor oil as his childhood friends assumed, but after the brother of Pollux, hatched from Leda's eggs in Greek mythology.

"I'm flattered you feel that way," Bo told him. "But the company needs you to run things while I'm gone. You don't want Jim fucking it all up, do you?"

Cast opened a manila folder he was carrying and spread it out on Bo's now-empty desk. There was a diagram that looked like an organizational chart. "Sir, if you'd take a look at this . . . ?"

Bo expected to see how Cast intended to reorganize the staff while he was gone, but instead he found, to his great surprise, the names of the eight candidates who had already filed for the Democratic primary in Arkansas and, beneath the name of each, a list of five or six "liabilities." The candidate who was a former governor, for example, had been tried and convicted in court of fraud. The attorney general had been blamed for the suicide of a legislator. The popular evangelist was suspected of child abuse. And so forth.

"Where did you find all this stuff?" Bo wanted to know.

"Sir, in the time since you left politics, the Internet has grown exponentially in a fantastic manner."

Bo stared at him for quite a while, awed by this display of swordsmanship. Then he said, "Can I make you a drink?" He had never offered a drink to one of his employees before, but this was an exceptional situation. When Cast was halfway through his scotch and soda, Bo inquired, "Can you handle a four-wheel-drive Nissan?"

"I can drive anything," Cast declared.

At home that night, checking to see what he needed to do to the house to shut it up for several months, Bo said to the house, "Well, it would appear, in answer to the question I asked you the other morning, that *I* am the Knight of La Mancha, and Castor Sherrill is my Sancho Panza." The house did not answer this time. But then, thinking of Cast's swordsmanship, Bo realized he had the wrong allusion. It wasn't *Don Quixote*. No, it was *The Seven Samurai*. He realized he had two more phone calls to make. But then, thinking of the wonders of the Internet that Cast had demonstrated, Bo decided to e-mail Harry Wolfe instead of phoning him. If his guess was correct, Harry was probably sitting right beside his notebook computer in his spacious but squalid Georgetown apartment, waiting for e-mail or keeping an eye on the inbox while he did something else, like Net surfing for porn or serious drinking. One of the good things about e-mail was that you didn't need a salutation or a closing, and Bo omitted both.

> Long time no E. Anything good up at the Phillips Collection this season? It's been awhile but I'll have to forgo a trip anytime soon. You won't believe this, Harry, but I'm coming back. Not to D.C. But to The Fences. The Game. There's a fellow running for governor of Arkansas who would be your dream, if you wanted to find a huge pile of shit on a candidate. The problem is, we're on his side. We have to find the shit on his opponents. We have to find enough shit on his opponents to coerce them into ignoring the shit on our man. Are you interested?

Just in case Harry wasn't at home, he added Arch's e-mail address to his own. And he pushed the SEND button with his left hand while using his right hand to push the phone buttons for Lydia Caple.

She was home, somewhere in Little Rock. "Do you still love me, Lydia?" he asked in greeting.

"Bo," she said, "if anybody could possibly love somebody like you, I'm qualified." There was in her tone just the gentlest, faintest of reminders that she had enjoyed that one wild night they'd had together.

"Have you given anymore thought to that personable, clever, handsome, engaging, outright lovable aspirant I was telling you about?"

"Hinkleberry or whoever?" she said. "No, I put him forever out of my mind when you told me about the thirteen albatrosses. I might handle six or seven of those birds, but not all thirteen."

"But he's a good man, Lyd. All you'd have to do is show the people of Arkansas how good he is."

"Where does he stand on the issues?"

"Honey, believe me, he is *for* everything you're for, and he's *against* everything you're against."

"Sounds wonderful," she said. "But Bo, now it's your turn to believe me: I don't have any fight in me anymore. That bastard Bradfield took it all out of me."

"That's what I thought about myself, after fighting Bush," he said. "But Ingledew is so good I'm going to be his campaign manager, and I want you to be his press secretary."

"No!" she yelled into the phone, and during the long silence that followed Bo was convinced that she had simply turned him down for a third time, but then it began to occur to him that she was simply expressing astonishment or incredulity.

"Yes," he negated her. "I mean it. And do you want to know

who proposed you for the job? Your old pal Arch Schaffer, who's also coming aboard the team."

"Arch is in it?" she said. "Really? Why didn't you say so? If he's in it, you can count me in too!"

"You're a sweetheart, Lyd," he said. "You and I will be having a leisurely lunch with Arch just as soon as I can get out there," he said. "And then we'll have to get ourselves out to a place called Stay More."

Mention of Stay More made Bo realize that there was one more very important phone call he would have to make. First, before shutting off his computer, he checked for e-mail and there was a speedy reply from Harry Wolfe. More and more people, alas, were beginning to believe that the ease and informality of e-mail precluded proper punctuation and capitalization, and Harry was apparently one of these, but there were also mistakes to suggest that he was well into his cups.

> hey, i am gladc to hear fromj you again man. real white of you tto think of me. i havent had a gigg in 2 yeares ever since i guess you mayv heardd about itt i tracked down sso much shameful stuff on senator passmore that the bastard wonb by sympathetic backlash. not my fault reallly, but anyhow haven't had a job since. what can i tell you man i'm real rusty. i mean I nee dsome practice real bad. but if you want to take a rat's chanc eon me an make me your dung beetle, jus tsay when an where an i'll be there. never been to arkansaw former home of the alltime scandalousest poiltician

Bo made a quick e-mail reply, simply giving Harry the address and phone number of Arch Schaffer and suggesting that Harry catch the next plane to Arkansas, and then he closed his laptop and put it beside his Vuitton suitcases. Finally, he got around to making that most important call. “Why have I put it off so long?” he asked the house, and, since the house wouldn’t answer, he answered it himself: “I suppose I wanted to have everything in place before making it.” Nearly everything was in place. Six of the Seven Samurai were polishing their swords. And he had given Lydia permission to select the seventh one herself.

Jelena Ingledew answered the phone, and Bo was thrilled to be speaking directly to her. He felt like a schoolboy calling his first date. He felt himself wanting to ask her if she’d like to do some homework with him. He felt giddy, almost silly, to be speaking to her. Losing his edge, he quickly asked to speak to Vernon.

“Vernon’s not here right now,” Jelena said. “He’s over at some friends’.”

“Did he tell you about me?” Bo asked. “Did he tell you that I turned him down?”

“Yes, and we’re all very glad that you did.”

“But I’ve changed my mind!” Bo declared. “I’ve thought it over and decided I’ll do it. Not only that but I’ve assembled the best team in the country!”

“Sorry for all your trouble,” Jelena said, “but Vernon changed his mind too. It’s the first time, but he’s done it. He’s going to devote himself to the study of quantum theory and put politics behind him.”

Chapter Four

Something has gone out of life, she decided. And she wasn't, for a change, thinking of herself. Or at any rate she was thinking of herself only in relation to the rest of humankind, and not just here in the Ozarks but everywhere she'd gone, which included a considerable part of the globe. Particularly in Ireland, particularly in Japan, she'd developed the same impression that people were almost suffocated with an unconscious nostalgia for a golden age they hadn't ever known and perhaps hadn't even been told about but simply knew had once existed and now did not, not anymore. Here in her familiar homeland it was inescapable: people everywhere seemed to be missing yesterday, as if it had possessed some magic no longer at work, as if tomorrow with all its fabulous wonders seemed to be a threat more than a promise of new delights.

She had long ago taught herself not only to give up the past but also to maintain the same skepticism about the future that she had maintained about everything, and if there was one word to describe her (as reporters interviewing people were in the habit of asking "What one word would you choose to describe yourself?"), it was *skeptical*. In fact, the only word that she knew that Vernon didn't know was Pyrrhonism. When she had first come across the word, years ago, she had asked him, as was her habit, what it meant. "Gee, I never heard of that. How do you spell it?" he had said. And she had spelled it, and he still didn't know. She couldn't believe it; she had stumped him, for the first time in his life. She couldn't find the word in her dictionary and had to look it up in the encyclopedia. Pyrrho of Elis founded the Greek school of Skepticism in the fourth century B.C. and taught that, since knowledge is unattainable, the only way to achieve happiness is to practice suspension of judgment.

Skeptics are imperturbable. People like Vernon who think they can acquire knowledge are constantly disturbed and frustrated. People like Jelena, learning to suspend judgment, neither affirm nor deny the possibility of knowledge but remain peaceful, still waiting to see what might develop. The Pyrrhonist did not become inactive in this state of suspense but lived undogmatically according to appearances, customs, and natural inclinations.

Once she had looked up Pyrrhonism, she didn't tell it to Vernon. She kept it as her own private word, a precious little knowledge that he did not have, one more among several secrets (her occasional cigarette, her vibrator) she kept from him. It amused her to think of the paradox: that Pyrrhonism says knowledge is not attainable but she had at least attained the knowledge of Pyrrhonism, and she took the trouble to read several books on epistemology, particularly Hume, until she had a full knowledge not only of Pyrrhonism but of the nature of knowledge itself. She didn't come to know anything about herself that she hadn't already known; she didn't become more skeptical than she had already been.

She and Vernon rarely kept anything from each other (except a few vices and virtues she's already thought of, above, and a few more she'll think of soon), not even their innermost thoughts and fantasies (well, of course she'd never told him about sexual daydreams she'd had about his best friend Day Whittacker), and there was only one other thing besides Pyrrhonism that she considered her own private province of knowledge: the fact that she had taught herself enough of the ancient Egyptian language to be able to talk to her cat. Not to converse with it, because the cat had never replied, but to capture and hold its attention in a way she'd never been able to do with English. Or with Japanese or Gaelic, which she'd also tried. Her very large and handsome marmalade tom (altered), which she had named Vernon (why not?), was like all cats totally indifferent to the speech sounds of human beings, or pretended to be. Therein was the fundamental difference between dogs and cats.

She had acquired Vernon (the feline, not the human) from Aunt Latha, who had such an awkward surplus of cats living in and around that old dogtrot log cabin she insisted on keeping despite Vernon's efforts to provide a much more modern home for his grandmother or lately, as Latha had passed her centennial, to persuade her to move to Jasper into a "residence for assisted living." Jelena had asked Latha if there was any way to talk to cats, but Latha, who'd been keeping them for a hundred years, said, "If there is, they sure do a good job of keeping the secret to themselves."

As Vernon (the cat) grew up and became fully developed, and as Jelena's studies and travels gave her new vocabularies, Jelena tried out French, Gaelic, and Japanese on the cat, to no avail. To accommodate her, Vernon (the man) even tried Osage on the cat. Osage was the only one of Vernon's several languages that Jelena had never bothered to master, but she trusted that Vernon in speaking it to Vernon was not telling the cat to get lost and never come back. Vernon the cat, however, was as indifferent to Osage as to any other language.

Eventually, secretly, keeping the book hidden in the same cabinet she hid her Bible, Jelena had learned how to speak ancient Egyptian, and to her surprise when she said "*Miw*," the Egyptian word for *cat*, Vernon perked up his ears and turned and stared at her with a dumbfounded look. She had seen cats with quizzical looks and curious looks and questioning looks but never a dumbfounded look. So she went on talking to Vernon in Egyptian, and while he didn't answer, he sure paid a lot of attention.

Once not so long ago Vernon (the man) had overheard her talking to Vernon (the cat) in Egyptian and had asked her what she was saying or what tongue she was using, but she said it was just some gibberish she'd invented to attempt to reach Vernon. "Successfully, it would appear," he remarked.

This morning she was hanging clothes on the line with wooden clothespins, not plastic, and she was wondering if they would be dry before those people showed up, and she realized she didn't care if those people saw the laundry still flapping in the March breeze like a row of singular ensigns. On a whim that was not really a whim, she occasionally eschewed her soundless, hideously expensive nine-cycle moisture-sensor clothes dryer and, instead, hung the clothes on this line, not to imitate her Stay More ancestors but simply because that state-of-the-art dryer couldn't impart to the laundry the scent of fresh air and sunshine. She said in Egyptian to Vernon the cat, who was watching her, "Does sunshine possess a scent?" And he nodded. Those Egyptians knew a lot about the sun.

This morning she was a bit more careful to use her artistry in hanging the clothes according to color and shape, just in case those people saw them. Thinking of art, she thought of Picasso dangling a cigarette from his mouth while he painted, and she fished the pack of cigarettes out of her apron pocket and smoked one while she worked. The clothesline was too far from the house for Vernon to see her, even if he happened to be looking out his window.

She was not nervous about those people. Skeptics are imperturbable, and she was skeptical that those people would have any luck at all in getting Vernon to change his mind. "What about me?" she said in Egyptian to the cat. "What about *my* mind?" Vernon (not the cat) had explained to her just who each of these seven people were, how "famous" they were in their respective areas of expertise in the game of campaign politics, which was a vocation requiring incredible powers of persuasion, and she knew these people were coming here with the full intention of selling them on the idea of occupying that mansion on Center Street in Little Rock where little Chelsea Clinton had grown up. Jelena had used as a handy excuse, to those who had sought her opinion—her best friend Diana, Diana's husband Day, Uncle George, Vernon's sister Sharon and her husband Larry, and Aunt Latha—that she simply couldn't stand the thought of living in the governor's mansion, not after over thirty years of living in this fantastic twin-orb palace on a mountaintop in the Ozarks.

When she first saw this house, when Vernon was building it in the seventies, it scared the daylights out of her. She didn't see how she could possibly learn to live in such a weird pair of giant balls, and in fact she had bad dreams the first several nights she slept here. But now, after so many years of taking for granted its fabulous comforts and amenities, she didn't see how she could possibly live anywhere else. Several times, back in the eighties, when she and Vernon had been visiting Day and Diana and they'd had too much pot or booze to drive home afterwards, they had stayed in that house, a thoroughly cozy traditional house that had been built long ago by that weird old hermit Dan Montross, who had been either Diana's grandfather or father or both. Jelena hadn't slept well, not because the place was haunted by Montross but because its walls did not make great curved spheres surrounding and hugging her like her own walls.

No, she had no intention of living within the boxy walls of the governor's mansion, where she probably couldn't find space to set up her darkroom and would have to abandon photography for four years, but that was just her most convenient excuse, sparing her the trouble of elaborating upon her more intense reasons for not wanting to be First Lady of Arkansas. Jelena's favorite reading matter was biographies, particularly women's biographies, and she had consumed a ton of books about Sappho and Marie Curie and Sacajawea and Susan B. Anthony and Simone de Beauvoir and George Eliot and Harriet Tubman and Mother Teresa, et alia. But when Vernon moved from philosophy to politics in his program, she began reading biographies of Eleanor Roosevelt, Jacqueline Bouvier Kennedy Onassis, Betty Ford, Rosalind Carter, and, more recently, Hillary Rodham Clinton. She understood how much a politician's wife had to deny her own identity and submerge her own feelings, and she was not ready to do that. Before Vernon abandoned his harebrained notion to run for governor, she'd tried to tell him this, but he had assured her, "That's not the way I'd see it. We wouldn't deviate significantly from the way we've always been living, together as equals." But she had doubted that the campaign signs would read VERNON AND JELENA FOR CO-GOVERNORS.

What she disliked most about the whole idea was that the "job" would require of her almost constant contact with the public. She'd have to give speeches to ladies' garden clubs and church socials. She'd have to shake a lot of hands. She'd have to learn to make polite but meaningless chitchat with anybody who chose to greet her, and she'd have to learn to smile when she didn't feel like smiling.

But worst of all, she and her whole life and history would become the property of the people of Arkansas. Their ownership of her would allow them to pry into her relationship with Vernon and into everything she'd ever done in her life. They would know that she'd married at eighteen a loutish Stay Moron named Mark Duckworth who built and maintained eight enormous sheds for the raising of chickens. They would be unmoved by the fact that on her way down the aisle at the church, before Uncle Jackson Ingledew had given her away, she had paused at the spot where ten-year-old Vernon was standing in his first coat and tie, she had stopped beside him and bent down and whispered urgently into his ear, "I was going to wait until you grew up. Will you marry me when you grow up? If you say yes, I'll call off this wedding." The people of Arkansas would not understand what it had done to her when Vernon had looked at her as if she were only teasing him, but then, understanding that she meant it as seriously as she'd ever meant anything in her life, shook his head and declared, "I will never marry." The people of Arkansas would not understand just why he'd said that, and they certainly wouldn't understand how right he was: he had never married, certainly not her.

There would be people who would want to know what she herself did not know and could not find out: Was she possibly a grandmother? Surely, if her two sons had grown to manhood and perhaps even finished college in California or wherever their father had taken them, they had quite possibly married, and somewhere on this earth there might be a beautiful child—or two or three—whose photographs ought to be in Jelena's wallet for her to show to people. She had nothing whatever against the idea of being a grandmother. If only she knew! She couldn't stand the suspense. And page after page of her journal was filled with letters she had written to her grandchildren, year by year as they advanced from childhood into adolescence.

She stepped back to study the clothesline and admire her arrangement. She decided that even if the clothes were dry before those people got here she might leave them hanging anyway, not to let the world know that she still did things by hand but just to add a touch of color and pageantry to these drab March woods. The house itself, two giant spheres, was a pale white surrounded by the bare trees and bushes in the woods on the eastern bench of the mountain, not even visible from the drive as it crossed the crest of the rise; her clothesline was out in the clearing, in the sunshine, the first thing those people would see when the road brought them off the plateau. Thus, she reflected, if she left the laundry hanging it could serve as a kind of beacon, to let them know they had arrived.

She stomped out her cigarette and buried the stub, then grabbed up the empty laundry basket (not plastic but wicker) and hiked back to the house to check on the ovens. In both ovens of her built-in Whirlpool double oven she had things baking: breads and pies. She was very good at pie. She would be serving a black walnut pie, just like pecan but tastier, made from nuts she'd gathered from their woods, and a cushaw pie, like pumpkin but made from cushaw she'd raised in her garden and canned. One part of that clearing on the mountaintop, which the visitors wouldn't notice because there was nothing in it this time of the year and Uncle George was coming up to Rototill it next week, was her vegetable garden, her patently substitute child, to whom she devoted all the love and attention that she had left over when she got through loving and attending Vernon and Vernon. Her orders to Burpee and Shumway and Park had all been filled. When Vernon had built the annex, as they called it, to house the sprawling overflow of books as well as her darkroom (and the building was not spherical like the house but conventionally boxy), he had added on the south end of it a greenhouse for her, and she had her plants thriving there already, waiting to be transplanted to the garden later this month and next: heirloom tomatoes, four varieties of pepper, three kinds of eggplant, and six kinds of cantaloupe, as well as flowers already blooming. She could not conceive of the state of Arkansas permitting her to convert part of the lawn of the governor's mansion into a vegetable garden.

She gave the living room another going-over. She was disturbed by the unusual number of chairs: in order to accommodate the guests, not just their side but our side too (seven of each, which was a fair balance), she had had to borrow some chairs from Diana and from Sharon, and there was an irregular assortment of old ladder-back rush-seated chairs, country rockers, captain's chairs, and Victorian cabriolets, as well as her own Eameses and Barcelonas. She could not tolerate clutter; all the books climbing the rounded walls to the domed ceiling were very neatly arranged, their spines lined up, and they were carefully dusted. There were bouquets of glads and mums and dahlias she'd forced in her greenhouse. The omnium-gatherum of furniture seemed chaotic, but on reflection she decided that it might mirror the distinctly individual personalities of all the participants. Jelena had tried to arrange the hodgepodge with two equal focal-point chairs: for Vernon a tall stately ladder-back that had been made in Stay More in the mid-nineteenth century; for Mr. Bolin Pharis an equally stately Hitchcock chair. She had considered but discarded the idea of providing pads of yellow legal paper and pencils; those who wanted to take notes would have to furnish their own.

Before taking Vernon his lunch, she hiked to the mailbox, back up on the mountaintop where the dirt road met the gravel driveway. It was a big mailbox that said simply INGLEDEW on it, which could have represented either one of them. Today it contained her orders to Coldwater Creek and J. Jill, and she couldn't wait to try on the garments but realized she'd have to postpone it until after the guests had left. It also contained three packages from Amazon.com, and she had her arms full carrying all this back to the house, along with the daily *Arkansas Democrat-Gazette*, a stack of bills and catalogs from Sundance and The Linen Source, and a letter for Vernon from someone in Louisiana named Monica Breedlove. Jelena stared at the envelope. They knew several people named Breedlove here in Newton County; it was a common name. Was this one of their displaced cousins?

Jelena made a BLT on toasted whole wheat and took it with a bottle of Dos Equis up to the "nest," in the upper reaches of the other sphere, which contained their bedroom and the extravagant bathroom (whose shower could accommodate six or seven people although it had never known more than two). The nest was Vernon's study, where he spent most of his time, usually half reclined in his Barcalounger with a book in his lap or his computer blazing away. She didn't worry that he was too sedentary; every day without fail he practiced his tai chi and then went for a long hike, sometimes all the way, three miles, down to Stay More, where his vast pork processing factory was sprawled out along the banks of Swains Creek. He also had an elaborate gym of exercise machines out in the annex, and he didn't allow them to collect dust.

Now she noticed that although he had a stack of books on quantum mechanics on his worktable, what he was actually reading was a volume called *Antipolitics* by Max Konrad. She handed him his lunch and his beer and his love letter, if that's what it was. "Who's Monica Breedlove?" she asked him.

He studied it and turned it over. "Got me," he said. "My first thought was it's Clyde Breedlove's daughter, but she's not in Louisiana, and her name isn't Monica but Mona, I believe."

"Open it," she requested.

He tore off the end and pulled out the letter. He took a bite of his sandwich and a sip of his beer and began reading it to her.

> *Your Excellency. Please don't laugh. Don't laugh at my salutation, which is practicing, not facetiousness. And don't laugh at my name. You may be aware that there are many other people in your part of the country named Breedlove, and my former husband is probably descended from Arkansas Breedloves. I have had lots of experience working in Arkansas for successful gubernatorial candidates, such as Clinton, and unsuccessful ones, such as Bristow. Also I worked for Bill Clinton for years when he was governor, and then after he became president and that Lewinsky child*

got involved with him, anytime I told people my name or tried to get a job and mentioned that I had once worked for Clinton they would break out laughing, and some of them made crude jokes. You wouldn't believe the nightmare my life became simply because I was given this name, a perfectly good and pretty name which, by the way, means "advisor," and that brings me to my reason for writing to you. I am going to become one of your advisors. I am not going to get into your pants or let you into mine. I have many talents that will prove to be very useful to you but none of them involve that sort of thing. I know you are very busy, probably over your head in quantum mechanics already, but please listen to what I have to say.

Quite possibly you will have already met me before you read this, but if my timing is as good as it has always been, you will get this letter on the same day, maybe just minutes before, you first lay eyes on me. My good friend Lydia Caple, who as you know also worked for a time in the office of Governor Clinton and was thus my colleague and dear friend, for whom I would do anything she asked me to, has asked me to join the select group of paladins who will constitute your campaign staff when you storm the statehouse.

I fully realize that you have elected not to seek election. I understand that we will be meeting with you this afternoon, maybe in just another hour or so, for the purpose of trying to convince you that you really owe it to yourself, as well as to the people of the great state of Arkansas, to change your mind and resume your previous ambition of learning politics by participating in it.

You won't hear me say much if anything this afternoon. I am a shy person, especially when there are a whole bunch of other people present who are much brighter than I. And I understand that it is difficult for you to converse with persons of the opposite sex. So I have to say here and now what I'd want to say to you: namely, that I have this feeling—and I have always trusted my hunches, which have always turned out to be true—that you could become a governor such as this state, this whole nation, has never had before. And that is why I am willing to buckle down and bust my ass for you.

Yours sincerely,
Monica C. Breedlove

P.S. The others don't know I'm writing this to you, so please don't tell them. See you in a jiffy.

"Well, how about that?" Jelena said. Vernon did not comment. He was smiling but seemed lost in reflection, as if he were actually touched by her flattery. *A governor such as this state has never had before.*

But what he was musing he eventually spoke: "It has a Farmerville, Louisiana, postmark. How could she have known exactly how long it would take to reach me so it would arrive on the same day she does? And how could she know so much about me?"

They were rhetorical questions but Jelena answered them. "Maybe just her infallible hunches." And she added, "It's touching, but I hope it doesn't sway you." When he didn't comment on that, she persisted. "You aren't going to let it—or anything—make you change your mind?"

"I'm not running for governor," he said. "Was it Coolidge who said, 'If nominated I will not run; if elected I will not serve'?"

"That was Sherman," she corrected him. "But why are we going to such trouble to have this meeting? Do you realize we've never had so many people coming to our house before?"

"Has it really been all that much trouble? And aren't you eager to serve your pies to those folks?"

"But you didn't have to buy all that beer and booze as if you expect everybody to get drunk."

He laughed. "Maybe if everybody gets drunk they'll have a good time and forget about politics."

"Maybe if you get drunk you'll change your mind and decide to run for governor."

"When was the last time you saw me drunk?"

"It's been a good long while," she admitted. She tried to recall. Maybe back in the early eighties. And she hadn't been able to tell if he was really drunk or just stoned on marijuana. She herself had been too high to discern.

"What are you serving for supper?" he asked. "Just in case we don't get rid of them before suppertime. Are you prepared to feed fourteen people?"

"Sure," she said. She had given it some thought and preparation, and she was all ready. "During the meeting, they'll smell the aroma of baking ham coming from the kitchen."

"*Ham?* That's rather self-serving, if you'll pardon the expression. Or unimaginative, as if Ingledew Ham were all we had."

"I'm not serving Ingledew Ham," she said. "I bought a nice big smoked spiral-cut Mount Nebo Ham."

"You're kidding me!" he exclaimed. But she wasn't. Mount Nebo was Ingledew's primary competition in the state and region, but comparing the former with the latter was like comparing a bicycle with a limousine. She had devised this plan not as a flaunting of Vernon's product but as a kind of test: if the guests *thought* they were eating Ingledew Ham and made extravagant compliments about it, she would know they were insincere or, like political people, too politic. But if they evaluated the ham honestly and said something like "This isn't your own ham, is it?" she would confess that it was the product of their competitor and she simply wanted them to know how inferior it was.

"I haven't had my own lunch yet," she said, and gave him a kiss and took leave of him. Then she was confronted with the decision of what to eat. She hated having too many choices, and she spent a long time staring at the interior of the huge fridge, trying to decide. Finally she closed the door and went into the roomy pantry and got her jar of Skippy peanut butter and opened it and spooned it directly into her mouth. Seven or eight spoonsful made a perfectly adequate lunch. For dessert she was also faced with too many choices but opted to get the big box of Godiva chocolates from their hiding place. She selected five but then had to take two more. She didn't have many weaknesses, but chocolate was definitely one of them.

Aware of this indulgence, she stepped into the bathroom to yield to another preoccupation: her appearance. Company was coming, after all. She knew she did not look anything at all like a politician's wife. Not even Hillary had possessed her comeliness, but she seemed to be losing it faster than she had expected, and not just because chocolate had taken the pinch out of her figure. Would these political consultants think she looked more like some aging Hollywood star or worn-out fashion model than like a homespun Arkansas girl worthy of being First Lady? Well, let them! She had to keep reminding herself that it was a series of subtle negative impressions that she wished to make. Her black hair was still too black; she ought to have allowed the gray to show more. As if in compensation, she selected a pair of earrings that were just a little too unlike her. Her third hobby, in addition to gardening and photography, was making earrings. She had made all of Diana's and Sharon's wardrobe of earrings, dozens for each. Even Aunt Latha had permitted Jelena to make some earrings for her. And for herself she had made hundreds. Now she deliberately picked a pair that she had once almost thrown away because they were too gaudy.

By two o'clock nobody had arrived. She stepped outside a couple of times to see if she could hear any vehicles coming up the mountain. The second time she distinctly heard a vehicle, but it was a familiar one, Day and Diana's Jeep Cherokee. As passengers they were bringing Vernon's sister Sharon and her husband, Larry, the former college professor. Jelena liked Larry, especially since he had gone off the hard stuff under Sharon's influence. As was customary, Jelena hugged Diana and Day. She'd done so hundreds of times, but she never embraced Day without feeling a little sexual arousal. In contrast to Vernon, who was the same age but far more intellectual, Day was strictly an outdoor type, roaming the forests of southern Newton County, and although Jelena had done nothing more with him than use him in her daydreams (and a few spectacular night dreams), whenever he hugged her in greeting her body seemed to levitate a few inches. She also hugged Sharon but did not hug Larry, who somehow didn't seem the type for such an intimate greeting.

Jelena made them comfortable, and Vernon came down from his nest and offered them drinks, and they sat around and made conversation. And wondered when the guests would come.

"How were they supposed to find you?" Day asked. "Did you draw them a map?"

"I'd never do that," Vernon said. "George is waiting for them down below, and he'll lead them up here. Assuming they can find Stay More." Vernon had forwarded by fax to Arch Schaffer a detailed map giving the complicated directions for reaching Stay More from Jasper and Parthenon, a map Vernon sent to people who wished to do business with his company.

It was Diana, finally, around three o'clock, seemingly possessed of better hearing than anyone else, who picked up the sound of Uncle George's Ford Explorer and said, "They're coming," and the rest of them perked up their ears and opened the front door and listened to the sound of strange 4-by-4s negotiating the hairpins of the trail. They all went outside and stood in the yard staring up at the clearing on the mountaintop.

In time, three vehicles appeared: George's Explorer leading a forest-green Chevy Silverado extended-cab pickup and a silver Nissan. They parked where the road came to an end, where the others had left their vehicles, alongside Jelena's Isuzu and Vernon's Land-Rover. Seven people got out, each of their silhouettes distinct in the blue air. Lined up like that in silhouette, all seven of them, five men of various sizes and two women, one large, one small, they seemed like a tableau from a Hollywood Western, the heroes coming to rescue the downtrodden. Some of them were carrying briefcases. One of the women was carrying a houseplant. And one of the men was carrying two bottles of wine. They began walking toward the house, still arranged in a broad line. They seemed like vigilantes. Or . . . what was the word Monica Breedlove had used? *Paladins.*

But there was still another word struggling into Jelena's consciousness. Although she and Vernon did not allow television in their house, they had an enormous TV screen in the den connected to their VCR and they watched a lot of films. It was this great Japanese movie she'd seen one time and could never forget. Yes, these people coming down to her house to spend the remains of the day were samurai, seven samurai. The problem was, the samurai were supposed to be the benevolent defenders of the good people against the evil warlords. These people, Jelena couldn't help feeling, were the evil warlords. She hoped that the seven on her side could defend against them, and she glanced over her own samurai to appraise their strength. Surprisingly, her glance lingered not on Vernon but on Day, as if he were the one who could do or say the right thing to repulse these invaders. Day was indeed sizing up the invaders as if he were David taking the first measure of Goliath.

One of the men was getting his single-lens reflex camera ready to take a shot of the house. Uncle George moved quickly to stop him. "No pitchers, okay?" George informed the man.

The man recased his camera and offered George his hand. "Mr. Ingledew, I'm Carleton Drew, your media man."

"I'm not him," Uncle George said. "That'un's him." He pointed, and Vernon stepped forward to shake the man's hand.

Introductions were made all around, but as usual Vernon could not bring himself to look at, let alone speak to, the women. The larger of the two women Jelena recognized, having frequently seen her picture in the paper beside her political column, which Jelena had read regularly with much admiration for her intelligence and keen grasp of the state of the world: Lydia Caple, here in person. The smaller of the two women was a pretty curly-haired natural blonde, Monica Breedlove, and Jelena was pleased with the good manners of the home team: none of them snickered or giggled or ogled at the mention of her name when she was introduced.

"Well, well, well," remarked Mr. Bolin Pharis, who was dressed casually in a woolen plaid shirt, as if he were going hunting. "This is quite a layout you have up here!" He said this to Vernon, but then he said to Jelena, "You've got a real nice garden patch up there just waiting for the plow." Jelena was pleased that he had recognized her garden patch, even if nothing was growing in it except overwintered radishes and spinach.

"Let's all go inside," Vernon suggested, and led them in.

When they got into the living room, the guests were even more openmouthed in wonder at the interior. Jelena took pride in the interior's accessories. She was very good at selecting and arranging, without excess, all of the objects that adorned the walls and tables and floor: the houseplants, the pictures in their frames, the knickknacks, the small sculptures, the candlesticks, all the odds and ends that make a house a home. Bolin Pharis moved at once to inspect some of Jelena's barnscape photographs in their frames on the walls. "Who's the artist?" he asked.

"Jelena did those," Vernon said, and she detected a note of pride in his voice.

"Fabulous landscapes," Bolin Pharis said, and beckoned to the man named Archie Schaffer. "Look at these."

"Hey, great landscapes," said Archie Schaffer. He and Pharis could have passed for brothers: they had identical beards, neatly trimmed, Schaffer's just a bit grayer.

"I call them barnscapes," Jelena said modestly. For years she had tried to document the falling, crumbling barns of Newton County, and these were her best ones, in color.

Rather than try to serve people individually, Vernon just led them to the buffet, which served as a well-stocked bar, and urged them to help themselves. Bolin Pharis and Archie Schaffer had scotch with water. Carleton Drew had a Heineken. The man named Harry Wolfe, who was supposed to be an expert in uncovering scandalous information about opponents, poured himself more than a double from the bottle of Jack Daniel's. Lydia Caple poured herself a jigger of Stolichnaya on ice. Monica chose a Coke.

Then they all sat down in the assorted chairs. Harry Wolfe plopped his corpulence down into the Hitchcock that Jelena had intended for Bolin Pharis. "Excuse me, sir," Jelena whispered to him. "That's Mr. Pharis's chair."

Harry Wolfe gave her an annoyed look and lifted himself up and into a lesser seat. Jelena realized, rather late, that the arrangement of the chairs was such that Vernon and Bolin Pharis would be a good twelve feet apart. Or was that one of her subtle negatives?

Fourteen people were more or less comfortably settled in a motley of seats. But there was a very long and uncomfortable silence before anybody said anything. Jelena wondered if her position as hostess required her to be the first one to speak. But she wasn't thinking about possible opening remarks. She was silently praying. Vernon did not know that she prayed sometimes. She wasn't religious in the sense of any system of belief or worship; she hadn't been in a church since her wedding. But occasionally she tried to communicate with her idea of God. And she was doing that now, asking God please to not let these people talk Vernon into running for governor.

Chapter Five

Who would speak first? And, assuming it was not a remark about the weather, would it carry any consequence? I will wait fifteen more seconds, and then *I* will speak, Day promised himself. He didn't really want to speak despite having given considerable thought to what he might say in defense of Vernon's well-considered decision to stay out of politics, although Day had spent hours with him recently, playing devil's advocate at his request, a sparring partner in preparation for the fight Vernon was now facing. Day had thrown at him every possible good reason why he should seek the governor's chair and really laid on thick all the good things he could do for the state of Arkansas and in honor and memory of his ancestor Governor Jacob Ingledew, and Vernon had successfully countered every argument Day hit him with.

The irony of the role reversal hadn't escaped Day: back in December and January, when Vernon was making up his mind to run for governor, Day had played the devil's advocate *against* the idea and had made a powerful case, not only for the reasons Vernon should shun politics but also for all the encumbrances he would face if he left himself vulnerable as a candidate. Day had even pretended to be his opponent in debate; they had made believe that Vernon had survived the grueling primary and was now going head-to-head with Governor Bradfield, and Day had done a fairly accurate job of impersonating that bastard, even to the point of imitating his swagger. Day let Vernon have it. He threw at him all the damaging charges about Vernon's lack of experience in elective office, his lack of a law degree—or any kind of degree beyond a high school diploma—his scandalous living arrangement with his own first cousin, his refusal to accept the existence of a God or even to subscribe to the basic tenets of the Democratic Party. But Vernon had demolished Day. In time Day had told me what he believed now: If Vernon wanted to run for governor, fine. If he didn't want to run for governor, equally fine.

It had always been thus, for as long as Day had known him. Almost thirty years ago, when they were very young men and Vernon had given Day and Diana a couple of piglets to start their "farm," Day and Vernon had discovered they were the same age, the only two males in Stay More born the same year or anywhere near it, and thus, if they were going to have coeval friends at all, they had no choice but to accept each other. The thing about their relationship is that either one of them could have done without it; neither Vernon nor Day was the type who *needed* friends. But as long as they were here, they might as well make the most of it. And they had. Day can't conceive of what his life would have been like without Vernon.

Vernon was speaking now. "I'm happy you good people could come and visit Stay More. There's not much left of the town, and you probably didn't even notice it when you passed through. It's an easy place to miss. But I mean that in more ways than one. I'd miss the place too easily if I had to leave it. When we were in Cincinnati, Bo, even before you turned me down, I'd begun to get so homesick I couldn't wait to get back. And now I'm here, I plan to stay here." These last words he uttered with the kind of conviction characteristic of him: Vernon never said anything without meaning it; he always meant what he said.

When Day had been arguing *against* Vernon's decision to

run for governor, one of Day's strongest arguments, prompted partly by his awareness of Jelena's feelings (and it must be revealed to you that Day knows everything she thought and felt in the previous chapter, even her mention of sexual daydreams she'd had about him), was that Vernon would never be able to live in Little Rock for the duration of his tenure as governor. Day reminded Vernon of the problems that his ancestor Jacob had had trying to live there. Day even reminded him of the "other" woman who had come into Jacob's life in Little Rock, the mysterious lady referred to as Whom We Cannot Name in *The Architecture of the Arkansas Ozarks*, and Day told Vernon that even if he didn't get into such an involvement himself, he would spend too much of his time pining for his homeland in pastoral Stay More. The few times that Diana and Day had ever left Stay More—to visit their son Danny in Rome, to attend Day's father's funeral in New Jersey, to visit Diana's mother in a nursing home in Little Rock—the pain began when they crossed the Newton County line and did not let up until they'd recrossed it going homeward in the opposite direction.

Bolin Pharis was speaking now. He was an impressive man, both in his appearance and his speech, the latter with just enough of his Harrison, Arkansas, background to keep him from seeming a "furriner" the way Harry Wolfe and Carleton Drew did. You should know that Day is just as familiar with Bo's chapter, number 3, as you are. Why should you have the privilege of knowing all those interior tidbits about Bo if Day can't? But even if Day didn't know such things as his habit of talking to his empty house, and the business about his soul needing saving, and all those allusions to *Don Quixote*, Day possessed the talent (if that's what it was) to read his character in his face and his movements. For example, when Bo and his lieutenant, Arch Schaffer, were pouring their scotch, Arch selected the Haig & Haig blended because he was a thoroughly up-front man who thought unblended scotch was pretentious, but Bo picked the Glenfiddich because he was one of those nifty trendy unblended drinkers.

"We understand that," Bo was saying, "and I might with equal justice point out that one of the chief reasons I decided to abandon my scruples and take on your campaign was that I too discovered how homesick for Arkansas I was in Cincinnati. There is something very special about the idea of home, whether it means Stay More in particular or Arkansas in general."

Day cast a glance at Monica Breedlove, who for the sake of the present assignment had given up her home in Farmerville, Louisiana, to return to Arkansas, which was her second home but one dear to her heart. Day, who alone of these people had the privilege of knowing the events of *Thirteen Albatrosses* as they unfolded, knew of course the contents of the letter Monica had sent to Vernon, which Vernon had received and read this very day, and Day understood of course the sly and shy looks that Monica occasionally cast at Vernon, which of course Vernon was not able to reciprocate because of his impossible shyness toward women. Monica was not going to speak, but Lydia did.

"Speaking for myself," Lydia Caple said, "I like Stay More in particular. I understand Vernon's ties to this town and I can understand his disdain for Little Rock. As a native of Little Rock, I wouldn't wish it on anybody."

Jelena smiled broadly at that remark. Diana usually reported back to Day all the many conversations she had with her best friend, Jelena (her only friend besides Day), and even if Day didn't know Jelena's chapter as well as you do he would have known how much Jelena loathed the idea of having to live in Little Rock if she became First Lady. Day also knew that even if she did take up residence in Little Rock, against her will, the media would not let her be referred to as First Lady because she and Vernon weren't married. So what would they call her, First Lover? Day personally felt she ought to be called simply First Person.

The only thing distressing about Day and Diana's long relationship with Vernon and Jelena was Day's belief that regardless of how much Diana and he loved each other, it could never match the love between Vernon and Jelena. Day didn't feel inferior to Vernon because of his vast learning and his keen intelligence and his movie-star looks, and Day certainly didn't feel inferior to him because of his money (because Diana was inconspicuously one of the wealthiest women in Arkansas, having inherited from her father a major insurance company). Day felt inferior to Vernon only because he enjoyed such a woman's love as Day could not even imagine.

You are wondering, Day is sure, if during the almost thirty years that they'd been the most intimate of friends they hadn't swapped. Back during the seventies and on into the early eighties when the Ozarks were filling up with back-to-the-land young people seeking alternate amoral lifestyles including lots of homegrown pot, they couldn't escape having for neighbors (if not friends) certain interesting but ultimately shallow characters who temporarily affected their way of life. For one thing they created noise pollution in the form of the helicopters from law enforcement that periodically flew over, scouting out the marijuana patches. For another thing their prolific cultivation of that weed led to Day and Diana's and Vernon and Jelena's brief experimentation with the use of it. And for a third thing their new friends' flagrant constant practice of "free love" provided a topic of conversation among the four of them that led, inevitably, to a desire to try it. Just out of curiosity, of course.

Day can remember the date: April 12, 1979. Young Danny, their son, then nine, was staying over at a friend's house. Vernon and Jelena were staying over at Day and Diana's, not by design or invitation but because they'd all experimentally lighted and smoked several joints made from the prime crop of a hippie friend who lived on the road to Parthenon and had been trying for years to have them sample his harvest. In the euphoria and lightness that goes with such an activity, they ceased gossiping about the constant mate swapping of various acquaintances and began to wonder, aloud, if they ought not give it a fling themselves. Day remembered the summer he'd first met Diana, ten years before, when they were camping out in the abandoned remains of Dudleytown, Connecticut, he just out of high school, she just out of college, both of them with the belief that he was the reincarnation of her grandfather, Daniel Lyam Montross. A band of pot-smoking Jesus freaks, who had wound up sharing not only their dope but also their bedrolls, had interrupted their tranquil idyll in Dudleytown.

So Diana and Day had previously been "unfaithful" to each other, when they were young and adventurous and naïve. But had Vernon and Jelena ever been unfaithful to each other? "I'll try anything once," Vernon said. "I'm game if you are," Diana said. "Suits me, I reckon," Jelena said. "Well, hell," Day said, "so long as we'd still all be friends afterwards."

They smoked another joint (enough perhaps to help Vernon overcome the appalling woman-shyness that he felt toward his good friend Diana simply because she was female), and then they repaired upstairs to separate bedrooms, Diana leaving the light off in her bedroom so that shy Vernon would not have to look at her, and Day taking Jelena into the guest room. Day may never know what transpired in the other bedroom; he never asked Diana about it, and she never told him. But he can say what happened in the guest room: nothing. Day and Jelena just stood there, facing each other, fully clothed, staring at each other with expressions on their faces that must have said *How did this happen?* Day did have an overwhelming desire for her. And after learning what she'd often felt about him, in the previous chapter, he can only assume that she had an overwhelming desire for him. Why didn't they rush into each other's arms, have a long mad kiss, strip the clothes from each other, and jump into bed? After a long moment he managed to ask, "Aren't we going to do anything?" And she answered, "If we were sneaking around by ourselves, I guess we could. But with them too? In the same house? At the same time? I think I'd be thinking of them throughout." So they went back downstairs and made themselves a pair of drinks with Chism's Dew and went outside to admire the stars and moon.

Day never smoked pot again after that night. He doesn't think the others did either. They never talked about reaching a decision not to smoke pot anymore, but they never did.

Arch Schaffer was saying, "You know, it's a little ironic, when you get right down to it. I'd like to say this on behalf of Bo, because he's too polite to bring it up himself. But he made it perfectly clear that he wasn't going to get back into politics for *anybody* after Al Gore, certainly not an unsung greenhorn in Arkansas. Then after he was persuaded to change his mind, no doubt because of the many attractive qualities of that unsung greenhorn, and after he went to considerable trouble to persuade the rest of us to join him in the crusade, he discovers that the unsung greenhorn has backed out! Can you blame us for feeling betrayed?" Schaffer cleared his throat, took a sip of his Haig & Haig, and added, "Of course I mean no criticism of the unsung greenhorn."

"Damn right!" remarked Carleton Drew, the media man. He was a short man who had long but neat black hair and the look of being uncomfortable away from the blistering operations of politics in the nation's capital. He wore an ascot, for heaven's sake. "I'm speaking only for myself, not for Harry, but we both left DC and came out here to risk our necks working for an unknown entity. I gave up a chance to handle Bergen Reed's campaign for California governor. And I did so with grave misgivings because, if I understand correctly, Mr. Ingledew would not permit television ads, which is neither here nor there in view of the fact that he doesn't intend to run anyway! Jesus." Day wondered if Carleton Drew, who had brought two bottles of good wine with him as a well-meant gesture of cordiality, was a bit miffed because his wine remained unopened.

Around the circle of various chairs, various people offered variations on this theme: Here they all were, with nothing to do, feeling led astray and frustrated. If only Vernon could give the word, they'd amaze him, they'd amaze themselves even, by organizing a campaign such as had never been seen before in Arkansas politics. They were proud professionals. Bo Pharis politely interrupted whenever any of them even hinted at the matter of what they were losing financially. Without coming out and saying so, he gave the impression that he intended to reimburse all their expenses out of his own pocket, but Vernon at one point flatly declared that he would give each of them a generous honorarium for damages. The baby of the group, young Castor Sherrill, who couldn't have been yet out of his twenties (and was drinking beer, not hard liquor), spoke up and said he was probably the one who needed damages most but didn't want any because he had "volunteered" for this "mission" in order to gain experience in politics. He said he could certainly understand and appreciate Vernon's original motive of wanting to run for governor in order to gain experience in politics, and then he said to Vernon, "Sir, if you don't want to run, could I have your place?"

Everyone stared at Cast, and it took them awhile to realize what he was suggesting, that he become the candidate. Arch Schaffer informed him that the law said you had to be a resident of the state for seven years before you could run for governor.

"I was just kidding." Cast grinned and got up to get himself another bottle of beer.

But was he? Knowing Vernon as Day did, and watching him

now as his eyes revealed his thought processes, Day could make a strong guess that Cast Sherrill's naïve, even absurd suggestion might have been the spark that made Vernon come round. If you don't want that piece of pie on your plate (and by now Jelena was serving her delicious black walnut and cushaw pies and everybody was ready for seconds), could I have it? No? So you decided to eat it yourself, after all? Just because I wanted it? Day didn't yet know Cast Sherrill well enough (Bo in his chapter hadn't yet revealed enough about him), but he wondered if Cast had deliberately made that suggestion just to prod Vernon into changing his mind.

Whatever, to switch to another metaphor, the subtitle metaphor, Vernon was beginning his slow fall off the mountain. The mighty eagle sitting on the tree limb had been hit by just one pellet from a kid's BB gun. But it was enough to make him start to fall.

The fat fellow named Harry Wolfe said, looking directly at Day and even winking at him, "If the mountain won't come to Mohammed, Mohammed had better get his ass to the mountain." Day stared at him. He was obviously well along into inebriation, his words slurred, but why had he directed that statement to Day, as if he'd been reading Day's mind at the moment when Day came up with the mountain metaphor? Suddenly—and Day wasn't stone sober himself—he had a weird suspicion that he might not be the only one of them who had the privilege of knowing what this novel is about: not merely a participant in it but a spectator of it.

Day waited until the next time Harry Wolfe got up to replenish his drink—he didn't have to wait long—and then joined him at the buffet bar and quietly inquired what he had meant by that remark. Harry eyed Day a bit superciliously and said, "You haven't heard that expression? You're Ingledew's best friend and he hasn't revealed to you the wisdom of Islam?" Sorry, Day said, wondering how Harry had unearthed his friendship with Vernon. "It's a long story," Harry said, "about Mohammed trying to throw a miracle like Moses or Jesus had done to prove his supernatural powers. He commanded Mount Safa to come to him, but of course it wouldn't, so he came up with a good excuse: Well, God was merciful because if the mountain had come to him it might have fallen on them and killed them all. 'I will therefore go to the mountain,' said Mohammed, 'and thank God that He has had mercy on a stiff-necked generation.' So you might say it means this: If we cannot do as we wish, we must do as we can. Or like this: If someone won't do this thing for you, you'd better do it for yourself. Or even like this: We may find a way to make a difficult situation better if we just think about it in different terms."

"That's very interesting," Day said. "But why did you happen to direct the remark to me, almost as if you could tell what I was thinking at the moment? You're supposed to be the top opposition-research man in the country, but your talents don't include mind reading, do they?"

Harry Wolfe chuckled. He toasted Day with his refilled tumbler of bourbon and said, "It's not just Vernon falling off the mountain. It's all of us. You too, buddy." He returned to his seat.

Lydia Caple said, "As far as the people of Arkansas are concerned, right now Castor Sherrill is just as good a candidate as Vernon Ingledew. Our big question is: What has Vernon got that Cast hasn't?"

"Good looks," said Harry Wolfe, who was in bad need of good looks himself.

"Brains," said Bo Pharis, and there was laughter at the implication that Pharis's protégé lacked brains.

"*Presence*," intoned Carleton Drew. "If they photographed Cast, the image would be blank." More laughter.

"Sex appeal," offered Monica Breedlove, the only words she'd spoken. But she got some laughs too, and a pout from Cast.

"*Duende* and eupatrid mien," said George Dinsmore, and the others did not know, as Day did, where George had picked up those uncharacteristic words. Perhaps the guests thought George was using some old Ozark dialect. Vernon laughed. Vernon laughed very hard.

"A hearty and sincere laugh," said Arch Schaffer. "That's a rare quality in politicians . . . although I haven't heard Cast laugh so I don't know if he's got it or not."

"Laugh for us, Cast," Bo Pharis requested.

"After my next beer," Cast said, and so many laughed at that remark that Cast himself laughed. It was a good laugh, but it didn't have the heartiness and sincerity of Vernon's.

The afternoon waned and they went on drinking. Eating all of Jelena's pies kept them from getting empty-stomach drunk, but they were all getting pretty light-headed and convivial. Harry Wolfe, who was a jump ahead of the rest of them in the intoxication upgrade, declared that because he'd been out of training for so long in his chosen field of uncovering dark secrets about the opposition, he had decided to get back in practice by digging up the dirt on each of his fellow members of the team, if anybody would care to hear it.

"Tell us!" several exclaimed, and Harry started with the head man himself, Bo Pharis. Despite being the valedictorian of Harrison High, Bo had been caught cheating on the final exam in physics his senior year. Arch Schaffer during the early seventies had a real drinking problem that got him into several scrapes, jails, and situations. Carleton Drew was a gun nut and not only had done much work for the National Rifle Association but personally possessed an arsenal of handguns and long guns. Lydia Caple at the age of seventeen had been caught shoplifting a handful of Bit o' Honey bars at a Little Rock supermarket. Monica Breedlove had five tickets for speeding in her Camaro. And Castor Sherrill spent his spare time sex-surfing the Internet.

"You forgot somebody," Bo Pharis said to Harry Wolfe.

"Who?"

"Yourself."

"Hell, I wouldn't need to do oppo research to find that out," Harry said. "All I'd need would be a good memory. But damn me if I can remember a single bad thing I ever did in my life." Several others joined Harry in his drunken laughter.

Vernon looked levelly at Harry and asked, "When are you going to practice on me?" Day felt it was almost a concession. It was almost as if Vernon had changed his mind and wanted to get the ball rolling.

"That's the very first thing I did," Harry Wolfe announced. They all looked at him and waited expectantly. But he said nothing else.

The aroma of baking ham filled the house and gave Day an appetite, even if he knew they would be served a meat inferior to Ingledew Ham.

Day spoke up, a bit self-consciously. "Well?" he said to Harry Wolfe. "Let's hear it. What did you find? He couldn't make the mountain come to him?"

"Mohammed's problems with Mount Safa were like nothing compared with Vernon's problems with Mount Ingledew," said Harry. He looked inquiringly at Jelena. "This *is* Mount Ingledew, I take it?"

"Actually, Ingledew Mountain is the big one you see to the southeast," Jelena informed him. "This one is called Daniels Mountain."

"After Daniel Lyam Montross?" asked Harry, and once again Day was stunned by his wealth of information. But Harry could easily have read any one of the four Stay More novels in which Montross appears.

"How did you know about *him*?" Jelena asked. "But no, this mountain was named back in the nineteenth century for an early settler whose last name was Daniels."

"Excuse my interruption of this geographical discourse,"

Day put in, "but we're still waiting to hear what Mr. Wolfe has uncovered about Vernon."

Harry Wolfe gave Day another of his supercilious looks. "What the fuck difference does it make? There's not going to be any campaign. There's no need to get personal on Vernon. Let sleeping dogs lie, for fuck's sake."

"Now, Harry," Bo Pharis said, "I haven't seen anybody else throw in the towel. If the towel is going to be thrown, I don't think you're the one to do it."

"Supper's ready," Jelena announced.

There was no dining table to accommodate fourteen of them, so they had supper with the plates in their laps in their customary places, although they were sitting as if it had been planned for a table: Vernon at one end with Lydia Caple beside him, Jelena at the other end with Bo Pharis beside her, the rest of them arranged in such a way that spontaneous conversations developed between one and another, and no attempt was made to keep the supper talk focused on the group as a whole or on the subject of the meeting. There was lots of chatter. Day was sitting on Jelena's left, and he overheard her conversation with Bo Pharis on her right. She served, among the variety of side dishes, radishes that had overwintered under straw in her garden, and Bo and Jelena devoted several minutes to talking radishes.

The Mount Nebo ham wasn't bad at all. In fact, it was tasty. But there is simply no comparison to Ingledew Ham. When Carleton Drew made the mistake of flamboyantly adoring the ham, even to the point of saying, "I can see why you made a fortune on this!" Day was not going to be the one to correct him. It was Bo Pharis.

"Carleton," said Bo, "hold on. I've had plenty of Ingledew Ham, and I can tell you: This is an impostor. Or else the hog from which it was made wandered too far and ate something abominable." Day was impressed with Bo, not just at his sensitive palate but his knowledge of the fact that Ingledew hogs are indeed free-ranging, not penned up and fed the usual commercial crap but allowed to forage for themselves in their natural element, the woods. Bo turned to Jelena and said, "So why did you do it?"

"Just to test you," Jelena said. "And you passed. Congratulations. I apologize, but this isn't Ingledew Ham. It's Mount Nebo, a perfectly fine Arkansas brand but nothing at all like ours."

"I flunked," Carleton said morosely, and there was laughter.

"Maybe they'll serve Ingledew Ham with your eggs Benedict at breakfast," Day said, "so you can see the difference."

Day got some polite laughs but also some quizzical looks: Were they all going to be continuing this session through the night?

In fact, any supper party (although Day hadn't been to many in his life) has a magic moment when everybody has a sense of the affair having run its course and people begin to leave. That magic moment didn't happen here. Day reflected that everyone knew nothing really had been accomplished, and there was a reluctance to leave the matter unsettled. Jelena, having already served her great pies at teatime, served for late dessert a light but scrumptious lemon curd. Although she offered carafes of both regular and decaf coffee, many of them preferred to make further inroads on the bar. The atmosphere was genial; people had even forgiven Harry Wolfe his snooping, and nobody was making allusions about Vernon's resolute refusal, which was, Day could detect in his eyes and manner, losing its resolution. People got up and wandered around the house and into the kitchen and, in the case of the few smokers, like Cast and Harry (but not Jelena), outside into the yard. People paired off; it was more like a party than a meeting. Day overheard Bo and Jelena, both once long-ago valedictorians at Harrison High, reminiscing about certain teachers they'd had in common and the Key Club to which they'd both belonged.

It dawned on Day for the first time that the median age of all these people was almost fifty. They weren't young. Castor

Sherrill was in his late twenties, Monica Breedlove in her late thirties, the rest of them either pushing fifty or pulling it. One of many things Vernon and Day had in common was that they lived with women older than themselves: Diana was three years older than Day, Jelena eight years older than Vernon. George Dinsmore was the "old man" at sixty-four. Vernon's sister Sharon was a year older than Vernon and her husband, Larry, the former college professor, was about the same age. Neither Sharon nor Larry had spoken up during the meeting, but they were doing a lot of socializing now that the meeting had changed to a party. Most everyone, Day reflected, had a sense of being what Jelena spoke of (or thought of) in her chapter as "almost suffocated with an unconscious nostalgia for a golden age they hadn't ever known and perhaps hadn't even been told about but simply knew had once existed and now did not, not anymore."

Speaking only for himself (and possibly for Diana), Day knew the incidents and adventures he'd known as a young man—particularly those of *Some Other Place. The Right Place.*—were experiences he could never hope to have again. As he had expressed it in his own contribution to that book, Diana's and his exploration of ghost towns had led him to realize that, as he said, "Oh, this is a story of—you know it, don't you?—a story not of ghost towns but of lost places in the heart, of vanished life in the hidden places of the soul, oh, this not a story of actual places where actual people lived and dreamed and died but a story of lost lives and abandoned dreams and the dying of childhood, oh, a story of the great ghost villages of the mind." Day knew that everyone at Vernon and Jelena's house that night, even young Cast, had an aching sense of those lost places, and a fear of never finding them, and a notion, even a conviction, that perhaps Vernon Ingledew could lead the recapturing of them.

But the time came when they could no longer cling to each other and wait for Vernon to take the first step. It was almost eleven, and the Samurai realized they couldn't hope to drive back to Fayetteville that night. Diana, bless her, was the first to offer an alternative when she suggested that they had two spare bedrooms. Sharon spoke up for the first time and said they had a guest room and a convertible sofa in Larry's study. Jelena pointed to her own sofa and said somebody could sleep on that and there's a guest room in the other bubble. The Samurai drew lots, and everybody had a place to sleep.

In this spirit of good feeling, as they were preparing to leave the Ingledew house and were putting on their coats, Lydia Caple got in a few last words on the purpose of the get-together. "Some of you may remember when Bill Clinton lost to that Republican jerk Frank White in 1980 and had to give up the governor's mansion for a couple of years. For a while he thought his political career was over. He was really down. He was the youngest 'former governor' in American history. His staff was as frustrated and depressed as he was, and some of them were pissed off at him for letting them down. He could have quit. He could have devoted himself to the study of quantum mechanics and forgotten about politics. But he got his staff together, including Monica and me, and told us that we were going to mobilize the grassroots workers who had been lazy and apathetic in the election Clinton lost. We got thousands of volunteers, mostly energetic young people, and those workers, to use one of Monica's favorite expressions, busted their ass. In all my years of campaigning, I'd never seen such spirit, such a sense of having a mission. And as you know, Clinton demolished White the next time around."

When she'd finished this story, she looked around to gauge the effect of her words on each of them, and then she took a deep breath and said, "I felt some of that same spirit in this house tonight. It's the first time I felt it since then: that willingness and that readiness to take it to the mountain, to *move* mountains."

"Even to fall off 'em," Harry Wolfe said drunkenly.

"If we fall," Bo Pharis said, "we might discover there's a thrill in free-falling."

"If we fall," Arch Schaffer said, "we might discover that we can fly."

Diana and Day were going to accommodate Lydia and Arch for the night. Monica and Harry would stay with Sharon and Larry. Bo, Carleton, and Cast were going to stay with Vernon and, as Day would later learn, sit up all night talking. As in Cincinnati, the talk would not have anything to do with politics but with their mutual interests in several areas of scientific and artistic inquiry. There was nothing Bo could say about politics to sway Vernon. But perhaps he wouldn't need to.

Vernon walked them to their cars with a high-powered flashlight. Along the way, they discovered that Jelena's laundry was still hanging on the clothesline, and Day offered to help her take it down. Everyone pitched in, unfastening from their clothes-pins all the garments and towels and linen. Fourteen people make quick work of such a thing. As Day was taking down a towel, Vernon gripped Day's upper arm in a friendly gesture that he would eventually use on hundreds of voters, a gesture that could, from one point of view, resemble that of a man clutching at a tree branch to keep from falling off the mountain. "Well, Day," he said quietly to his best friend, "I've never asked you this before. What would it do to your opinion of me if I changed my mind?"

Day clapped him on the back. "It would just confirm what I've known all along."

Chapter Six

What a weird but fabulous room. The bed was the loveliest thing Lydia had ever seen or slept in, and there was an antique chifforobe for hanging up her clothes, as well as an antique wash-stand with basin and pitcher. There was a small desk, actually just a library table with a few books on it that looked as if they hadn't been opened for years. Hadn't anybody slept here in a long time? But there was fresh water in the pitcher! And the walls . . . my God, at first she thought it was strange wallpaper, but looking closer she saw that there was writing all over the walls: a kind of longhand such as was taught to school kids in the nineteenth century, covering all the white plaster everywhere.

They'd told her, as if to make her appreciate it, that this had been the study of Daniel Lyam Montross. She wasn't sure who he'd been. Diana Stoving's grandfather? She remembered seeing this house in *The Architecture of the Arkansas Ozarks*, which she'd read when she was in high school a long time ago, and she just vaguely remembered what it had said about the man who'd built this house, some outsider who'd come to Stay More and mystified the locals because he was strange and kept to himself.

Speaking of strangeness, she thought her host, Day Whittacker, was a rare bird. Well, he looked normal. In fact, he was good-looking in a rugged sort of way, but there was something in his eyes that made him seem . . . was *possessed* the word she wanted? Maybe *weird* was the word, weird like this room, and as she'd looked around her before putting out the light she wondered if maybe Day was the one who had done this room, even writing on the walls, thinking up all those lists, nine items in each, under "Montross, His Becomings; Montross, His Leavings; Montross, His Namings; Montross, His Hummings; Montross, His Blessings; Montross, His Damnings." She fell asleep, quickly and easily, and if her dreams were haunted at all she didn't remember any of them in the morning. She would have only a slight hangover; she'd had too much of the Stolichnaya, but it was a fine vodka and everyone else had freely imbibed, except Monica, who'd stuck to drinking Coke. Lydia knew why Monica could have had something heavy but preferred Coke. Lydia wondered if she'd done the right thing in persuading Monica to come up here from Louisiana, leaving the house out in the country she'd worked so hard with her own hands to build, putting it on the same ancestral spot where her family house had burned, taking her mother's life with it. Monica had sworn off politics to go home and do that, build that house. Now Lydia felt she'd grievously misled the woman. We've all been grievously misled, she reflected. We've been had.

The smell of coffee and frying bacon was coming upstairs. Lydia dressed in dark green slacks and top, different from what she'd worn yesterday, an outfit that looked a little more countrified, as this house was such a modest place compared with that extravagant pair of globes the Ingledews lived in. Before going downstairs she paused to examine the three books on the little library table: an old, ponderous unabridged dictionary, an anthology of Elizabethan poetry, and a Bible that must have been used by some early settler.

At breakfast she asked Arch if he knew what time they'd be heading back to Fayetteville. She really liked Arch; all her many dealings with him, dating back to when she was just a cub reporter at the old *Gazette* and he was a patient teacher of the ways of the political world, and then in the eighties when he had the best PR firm in Little Rock and could be counted on to furnish her with material for a column—all these dealings were up front, white and mellow, and he'd used his years of experience as chief of staff for Governor-then-Senator Bumpers to help her learn the ropes when she went to work for Clinton.

"What's the hurry, Lydia?" he said, smiling. "Now that we've finally found Stay More, we ought to stay more." He smiled at Day and Diana. "But we don't want to wear out our welcome."

Diana said, "Stay as long as you like. Please." Lydia liked Diana. Unlike her husband, she was real and all there.

"Vernon called," Day said. "He wants to offer you a tour of what's left of the town."

She was glad she stayed more. After breakfast they drove into what once had been the center of the thriving village of Stay More but now contained only one old building, which she recognized from the *Architecture* book as the two-story verandahed house that Jacob Ingledew had built in 1868 after he returned home from his stint as governor of Arkansas. It was a handsome old building and someone—probably Vernon—had put a good bit of money into fixing it up, so it looked newer than it had when Governor Ingledew built it.

"Who lives there now?" Lydia wanted to know.

Day and Diana exchanged looks. Diana said, "The woman who restored the house. Vernon sold it to her. I don't think we'll see her, and I don't think we'll be invited inside. She is a woman who . . . well, let's simply call her Whom We Cannot Name."

Lydia laughed. She knew *that* woman from the architecture novel, Jacob Ingledew's mysterious mistress who was a young Little Rock widow and had thrown a bouquet of flowers at his feet from the gallery of the Old State House when he had stood bravely alone to vote against secession at the outbreak of war. She had later become social secretary for his wife, Sarah, and had accompanied them back home to Stay More, where she'd lived in this house the rest of her life, long after Jacob and Sarah had died. The reason this house had three doors—what that novelist had called "trigeminal" (but that reminded Lydia of her neuralgia)—was because the three of them had lived together in a kind of ménage à trois for many years.

Lydia said, "I assume that the Whom We Cannot Name who lives here now is *not* Vernon's mistress?"

Day and Diana laughed. Diana said, "Heavens, no! Nor is it likely she would ever become his mistress."

"She's old and ugly?" Lydia asked.

"She's quite attractive," Diana said, "and she's just a bit younger than Vernon and Day. But trust me: She won't be getting involved with Vernon, although they're great friends and chess partners."

"My, my," Lydia remarked. "What mystery lurks behind the doors of Stay More."

Across the road from the Jacob Ingledew house, which had once served, after the death of the Woman Whom We Cannot Name the First, as the village's only hotel, was what remained of Stay More's principal general store, which had once been an imposing edifice of three floors beneath a huge gable roof. All that was left now was the cement porch floor and the cement steps leading up to it.

It was at this porch to the missing store that all the participants of yesterday's meeting and supper party parked their cars and rejoined one another. Lydia was glad to see her friends again. The morning was sunny and growing warmer, although a March breeze kept it uncomfortably cool.

Vernon and Jelena, with help from George Dinsmore (who was quickly becoming Lydia's favorite), led them on a tour of the remains of the village, pointing out the locations of the two doctors' offices, the old bank, the blacksmith shop, and the cavernous cellar hole of what had been the great gristmill. Throughout their tour they encountered immense wandering hogs, and Vernon or George introduced several of them by name, George explaining that each of the many Ingledew hogs, male and female, had been named after a celebrated Razorback athletic star.

"Pat one if ye'd care to," George suggested. "They don't bite." Lydia gave the mammoth hog named Burlsworth a tentative pat on his head, and he grunted and rolled his eyes at her.

"If you let them run loose all over the place," Lydia wondered, "don't they ever get hit by cars?"

"What cars?" George said. "Aint much traffic hereabouts. But if one of these here hogs ever met up with a car, the car would kindly go into the shop, not the hog."

Farther up the main road they came to the ruins of what had been the Swains Creek Bank and Trust Company, and across from it the smaller general store that had been the town's last post office and the home of Latha Bourne Dill. It was now tastefully restored as the home of Sharon and Larry Brace. Sharon served coffee and homemade beignets, and the fourteen people sat or stood on the porch the same way people had congregated there in the old days when it had still been the town's post office. Those who wanted were given a tour of the interior, to see how Sharon had restored the store part, with its post office boxes, and Larry had converted a side room into his book-lined study, where an IBM Selectric typewriter was looking like an antique alongside the latest computer, scanner, and printer. Lydia felt a pang of envy and told herself she'd retreat from the world too if she could live like this.

Back on the porch, Vernon declared, "I'd like to say a word." There was something about his tone that made everyone spontaneously sit down, either on the edge of the porch floor or on the assorted porch furniture, including a couple of nail kegs. Lydia sat in a captain's chair. "This is an appropriate place for it," Vernon said, and Lydia detected that she wasn't the only one who had suspended breathing. "This was my grandmother's store, as well as her house, and it's the coziest spot Stay More ever had. It's steeped in human history. So I may as well give it a little more: I've decided to run for governor."

The first response came from George, who said, "Dad blast it all to ding-dang hell!"

"Pussy's in the well," rhymed Harry Wolfe. He hadn't started drinking yet today; it was his usual manner.

"Wow!" said Bo Pharis, and stood up to shake Vernon's hand and clap him on the back. "Let the good times roll!"

"Way to go!" said Arch.

Day said to Jelena, "Sorry."

"He woke me with the news," Jelena told Day. "About five o'clock. I was the first to know, at least. Unless he'd already told Bo."

Lydia said to Carleton Drew, "Let's take a little hike," and she led him out of earshot of the others. She and Carleton hadn't had time to get acquainted or compare notes, and she wanted him to know the chain of command. "Got your phone handy?" His cell phone was in Bo's Nissan. He fetched it. She had her own in her purse. They agreed she would do the television stations and major newspapers; he would do the radio stations and the lesser newspapers. Not that she outranked him in the media department, but she had many more media contacts than he did, as she discovered when she put in her first call, to station KFSM in Fort Smith, a CBS affiliate, and was immediately connected to the station manager, with whom she'd once had lunch. They would send a crew right out, he said, and she gave directions, as best she could remember, on how to find Stay More.

“We’d better get Ingledew’s permission,” Carleton suggested. “You know he has this thing about TV.”

“Hold on,” she said to the phone, and yelled at Vernon, “Hey! You got any objection to being on television?”

“My personal antipathy toward television,” Vernon said, “doesn’t extend to others’ use of it in any form.”

Lydia needed only a moment to figure that out, and then she told KFSM the formal announcement would be at four o’clock. To be fair to the other networks, she also called KHOG in Fayetteville and KFAA in Rogers, ABC and NBC affiliates respectively. She was pleased that the mention of her name got her a quick connection with the station manager wherever she called and with editors at the newspapers she called. Carleton Drew’s name couldn’t have accomplished that in Arkansas.

She took the trouble to write out for Carleton’s benefit the “official” release she was dictating to the media:

> “Deep in the remotest Ozarks a man has decided to learn Arkansas politics by starting at the top. Vernon Ingledew, 49, owner and operator of Ingledew Ham, declared today for governor in the Democratic primary to be held in May.
>
> He will face eight other candidates, including former governor Jim Ray Birdwell and former congressman Bob Tunney, for the awesome right to challenge Republican Governor P. T. “Shoat” Bradfield in the November election.
>
> Unlike the other eight candidates, Ingledew has had no experience at all in elective office. But his vision for the state of Arkansas in the twenty-first century and his exceptional intelligence have already drawn to his corner a team of seasoned political professionals, including such well-known consultants as Bolin Pharis III, a native of Harrison, on leave as vice president for public relations at a major national corporation in Cincinnati; Archie Schaffer III, on

leave as Director of Media, Public and Governmental Affairs for Tyson Foods, Incorporated, in Springdale; and Lydia Caple III, former political reporter and columnist at the *Gazette* and the merged *Democrat-Gazette* and a well-known political consultant in her own right."

"Are you really Lydia Caple the Third?" Carleton asked her.

"Of course not," Lydia said. She handed Carleton the handwritten copy of the release and told him to get busy.

Then she put in a call, a long one, to Hank Endicott at the *Arkansas Democrat-Gazette* in Little Rock, the state's largest and most influential newspaper. When the old *Democrat*, Hank's paper, had merged with the *Gazette*, Lydia's paper, following a typically internecine newspaper war, Hank had taken over the thrice-weekly op-ed political column Lydia had been writing, a circumstance that could have resulted in great enmity between them had it not been for Lydia's gracious and philosophical attitude. Hank and Lydia weren't exactly friends. They'd never lunched together and he'd never tried to flirt with her, and sometimes his political opinions had caused Lydia to cuss him to his face, but they had remained on good speaking terms if only because she found it easy to talk to him. Now she found it easy to give him a lot of off-the-record information about Vernon—the things investigative reporters would find out soon enough—in order to give Endicott the full picture with all the local color it needed.

When she'd finished, Endicott asked, "What's your part in all of this, Lydia?"

"My part?" she said. "I'm working for him. The minute he made his announcement, half an hour ago here in Stay More, I became his employee."

"I can't believe it," Endicott said. "*You?*"

"There are going to be a lot of things about Vernon

Ingledew you won't believe. It's going to be your job to make him believable to the readers of your paper."

"No, my job is just to say what I think about the world."

"The world of Vernon Ingledew is going to give you plenty to think about."

Bo Pharis called a strategy session that afternoon, following lunch. By lunchtime the weather was warm enough that they could eat al fresco. Good George Dinsmore disappeared and returned with baskets of food: sandwich fixings, chips, condiments, beer, and wine. Real Ingledew Ham was included this time. Sharon furnished a pot of baked beans she'd been cooking all morning. Diana fetched a plate of assorted homemade cookies.

It was a grand lunch, but as soon as it was over they had to get down to business. First, Bo wanted the Seven Samurai to meet without Vernon. Not that there was anything they were going to keep secret from him, but they didn't want to be inhibited by the candidate's presence while they bounced ideas off each other. Sharon offered them the use of the interior of the store, where they could sit around the potbellied stove and cracker barrel. Then, later in the afternoon, they'd bring Vernon into the meeting in time to get him ready for his formal announcement, scheduled for four o'clock, when the media would arrive.

During the session without Vernon, while he was presumably secluding himself to work on the draft of his formal announcement, they discussed their individual responsibilities and their ideas for making the most effective use of their ingenuity and talents, but they agreed that they'd have to wait until Monday to really get started, when Bo and Arch would begin phoning and e-mailing old friends and Arch would use his contacts in the Democratic Party organization to get the machinery rolling.

Young Cast Sherrill brought up the idea that the state's colleges and universities would soon be having their spring break, and it was important that sufficient students be "energized" beforehand to start "infecting" a considerable contingent of campaign workers. Monica volunteered to accompany Cast on a tour of the campuses the following week. Bo complimented Cast on his idea and complimented Monica for helping with it, but reminded Monica that her principal responsibility was office manager of campaign headquarters, which she would be setting up in Fayetteville, a city Vernon had decided would be a more appropriate place than Little Rock.

Lydia wanted to be complimented too, so she brought up the idea of getting early endorsements from other prominent politicians. "Arch," she asked, "could you get your Uncle Dale to plunk for us?" Arch said he could damn well try, but Dale Bumpers, who had been one of the most popular governors of Arkansas in modern times during the seventies, and who had followed that up with a distinguished career in the U.S. Senate, had consistently refused to endorse any candidates for the primaries, preferring to wait for the general election.

"And I'll talk to David Pryor," Lydia said. Like Bumpers, Pryor was a popular former governor who had also served in the U.S. Senate before his retirement.

"Good for you, Lydia," Bo said. "*Good* for you."

Harry Wolfe promised to begin digging up the dirt on the eight other candidates. Bo said he was driving in to Harrison to visit his mother on Sunday, and he'd give a Harry a lift to the Harrison airport so he could fly to Little Rock, the best place for researching the opposition.

The strategy session lasted over an hour, and then they sent Cast to find Vernon and invite him for the second or "open" part of the meeting. When Vernon arrived, Bo said to him, without beating around the bush, "Governor, do you have your speech ready?"

"Do I have to make a speech?" Vernon asked.

"Well, you can't simply say, 'Look, I'm running.' And you ought to be ready to answer the reporters' questions."

Lydia would discover, to her and their chagrin, that they needed more than a couple of hours to prep Vernon for his first public announcement and his fielding of questions. They had taken it for granted that a man with—what was that charming expression of George Dinsmore? *Duende and eupatrid mien*, for God's sake!—would be able to compose himself in front of a microphone and say something forceful and noteworthy to convince the people of Arkansas that he was a worthy candidate for governor.

"First," Lydia said to him, "I think you ought to wear a jacket and tie, not just *that* shirt."

The fact that he hung his head when she spoke to him made her think that he was ashamed of his shirt, but then she realized he was known to be shy of women. "What's wrong with this shirt?" he asked his shoes innocently, and she wondered how to tell him. The shirt wasn't bad; it was a plaid wool in an attractive color that went well with his complexion and looked like something a business executive would wear on weekends in the country.

Bo Pharis said, "When you came to my office that first time we met, I could have mistaken you for a CEO or a U.S. senator. Couldn't you wear that same suit?"

"That was Cincinnati," Vernon pointed out. "This is Stay More. The last time I wore a necktie in Stay More was when I was ten years old and they made me attend Jelena's wedding."

"Speaking of Jelena," Carleton Drew said, "what are you going to tell the media about your—uh, living arrangements with your cousin?"

"What are the media going to ask me?"

"She's going to be by your side, isn't she?" Bo said. "How are you going to introduce her?"

Vernon smiled. "I'm going to say, 'This is Jelena Ingledew, who would much prefer that I stay home and make love to her instead of running for governor.' "

"You're not going to say that!" Bo said.

"Then what should I say?" Vernon asked.

The Seven Samurai looked at one another; a couple of them actually scratched their heads in thought. Timid Monica Breedlove was the first to speak up. "Couldn't he simply say, 'This is my better half'?"

"*Bitter* half is more like it," Vernon commented, not to Monica but to the sky. "She's not going to be smiling, and I'm not going to force her to smile."

"But sir," Cast Sherrill put in, "how's that gonna look? She's so much older anyhow, she'll really look like a senior citizen if you can't get her to smile!"

"Mr. Sherrill," Vernon said. That's all he said, but his tone was such that Cast knew he'd be unemployed shortly if he didn't watch his tongue.

"Jelena is a beautiful lady, smiling or not," Bo commented. "Let's not concern ourselves with her appearance."

Carleton Drew said, "Personally, I'm for full disclosure from the beginning. Since they're going to find out everything about Vernon before the first vote is cast, we might as well put all our cards on the table from the git-go."

Arch said, "That's an admirable policy, but I think we'd better lay the cards down one at a time, in order to give people a chance to absorb them."

When Jelena returned eventually in her Isuzu 4-by-4, Lydia was troubled to see that she was still wearing the same blue jeans and sweater she'd had on that morning. While Lydia was envious because she herself couldn't fit as neatly into blue jeans and couldn't look as presentable in them, she didn't think Jelena looked like a governor's wife. Of course, she reminded herself, she *isn't* his wife.

They had to decide upon a place to serve as the setting for the announcement. Vernon wanted to use the porch of Latha's store, now Sharon's house, the same place where he'd declared his intentions earlier that day, but the Samurai were pretty much in agreement that it wasn't very photogenic: it just looked like some old country store, or an old country store converted into a house. Vernon's second choice was the porch of the Governor Ingledew house, but he was reluctant to assemble a crowd there because it might disturb Whom We Cannot Name the Second. Lydia and the other Samurai much preferred that edifice, however, so Vernon offered to go talk to the Woman about it.

Other things continued to go wrong on this most momentous of days. The announcement was scheduled for four o'clock, and therefore the television crews ought to have arrived and been set up by three-thirty at the latest, but four o'clock itself came and there was nobody there except the Samurai and the local people, including all the employees of Ingledew Ham, who had been given the afternoon off. Others of the few citizens of Stay More also showed up, including Vernon's grandmother, the regal dowager Latha Bourne Dill, who didn't look, as Lydia had been told, a full century old. Lydia couldn't take her eyes off the woman, but soon she had to return her eyes to the road and wonder what the hell was keeping those media people.

Her cell phone rang. It was one of the television people, calling from somewhere in the vicinity south of Parthenon, where all the television vans and reporters' cars had apparently taken a sequence of wrong turns and become hopelessly lost.

Lydia reported this to Bo Pharis, and he suggested that Cast take George in the Nissan Patrol and go out searching for the media crews and bring them in.

It was almost five o'clock before Cast and George returned, leading a convoy of cars, vans, and trucks. And then Lydia's attention became focused, intensely and fearfully, upon what was to become the disaster of Vernon Ingledew's formal announcement for governor.

When the microphones were in place at the top of the steps leading up to the porch of the Governor Ingledew house, Vernon sort of ambled over to them. He didn't walk with a brisk confident stride like all seasoned politicians. He *ambled.* And he just stood there with his hands in his pockets and a blank look on his face before realizing he'd forgotten Jelena, so he had to amble back down the steps and find her in the crowd and take her by the hand and pull her back up onto the porch as if he were a mother trying to get her scared kid to go to the first day of school.

Bolin Pharis, his campaign manager, introduced him. "People of Stay More, people of Arkansas," Bo said, "it is my great privilege to present to you a man some of you already know and all of you will come to know as well as you know yourselves!"

He paused and draped one of his muscular arms across Vernon's shoulders. Lydia noticed that Vernon was several inches taller than Bo, but he wasn't standing up straight to his full height. He had a kind of slouch, for God's sake.

Bo went on. "We're standing here in front of the charming old house that Jacob Ingledew built for himself and his family after he left the Governor's Mansion in Little Rock in 1868. Just why we're standing here I'm going to let Vernon Ingledew tell you. He is a direct descendant of that brave, wise, courageous governor who dared to stand on the floor of the Old Statehouse in 1863 and vote 'No!' against the motion to secede Arkansas from the Union, and who fought valiantly to keep the Union together during the Civil War, and who served as an able and foresightful governor to steer the state of Arkansas through the perilous years of Reconstruction after the war!"

Lydia admired the way Bo Pharis could say these words as if he were describing Vernon rather than Jacob.

"Look around, friends, at these lovely Arkansas mountains." Here Bo paused long enough to let the television cameras pan the surrounding landscape. "Vernon Ingledew was born here, raised here, and learned how to make a scrumptious ham that has watered the mouths of every one of you! And now his beloved hills are going to let him go. But I'll let him tell you why. Ladies and gentlemen, the most remarkable citizen of the state of Arkansas, our next governor, *Vernon Ingledew!*"

Lydia would have liked it if Vernon had said something folksy like "Howdy, I sure am proud to be here," but he just stood there for a too-long moment, staring into the cameras, his hands still stuck in his pockets, and then he turned his head and stared at the house behind him, as if he were seeing it for the first time. Lydia detected, behind one of the curtained windows, the vague but striking face of Whom We Cannot Name the Second. Lydia hoped that none of the cameramen were zooming in, trying to pick out the figure behind the curtain.

Vernon faced the crowd again and tried to speak. "G-g-good evening," he stammered. Although it was getting dark pretty fast, it wasn't evening yet, but Lydia remembered that in the Ozarks *evening* means all the rest of the day following noon. Vernon gulped and faltered onward. "J-J-Jacob Ingledew wasn't a great governor, and I'm sure he would much rather have—"

Vernon seemed suddenly to realize that what he was saying was being heard not just by this small gathering but by thousands of people all over the state, and for a moment he appeared on the verge of panic. Lydia's heart quit beating.

"—much rather have, have stayed right here in Stay More instead of going to Little Rock. He had no use for Little Rock. Neither have I." Vernon appeared to be getting in control of himself, but at the cost of beginning to make outrageous statements.

He'd already lost the big Little Rock vote. Vernon wasn't letting his eyes roam from face to face the way a good speaker should, but was just staring straight ahead at an imaginary person, and Lydia realized she had better become that person herself real fast, so she tried to position herself in Vernon's line of sight and convey instructions by sign language, to get him to stand up straight, to get him to take his hands out of his pockets, to get him to move his eyes from face to face, until she realized that Vernon wasn't looking at her because she was a woman. Her gesticulations failed to escape the notice of several media people, who snickered or laughed, and Vernon just stopped speaking, thinking he was being laughed at. He waited until it was completely silent, and then, as if Lydia's sign language had gotten through to him, he took his hands out of his pockets, straightened his backbone, and began to look intently at each person . . . at least each male person.

"I am a reluctant candidate for governor," he went on. "Jacob Ingledew was reluctant, but he accepted the job because this state was in a mess and only he with his eccentric ideas could straighten things out after the war. As you know, the state was bankrupt when he took over, and when he left office it had a surplus. He had to put a tax on everything—I think it's only a myth that he put a tax on breathing." Vernon grinned and waited to see if anybody laughed. George Dinsmore could be heard chuckling, and there was a smattering of laughter from a few others. "But he managed to hold the state together. I'm not going to ask you to vote for me because I'm Jacob Ingledew's great-great-great grandson." At first Lydia thought he was stuttering again, but then she realized he was tracing his descent. "But I'm going to tell you that my ideas may be just as eccentric as his, and they're going to save this state." Vernon swept his arm and permitted his voice to rise slightly toward the end of this sentence, but otherwise his delivery was mild, without inflection, without any semblance of oratory. Lydia, using a sign language resembling the motions of an orchestra conductor trying to get a full crescendo, attempted to get Vernon to impart more eloquence to his speech, but without much luck. He still could not look at her.

Vernon rambled on about the anfractuous direction Arkansas had taken since Republicans Mike Huckabee and then Shoat Bradfield had taken office. Arkansas might be enjoying a period of record economic prosperity, but it wasn't because of Huckabee and Bradfield. Vernon wanted a chance to show how tenebrific the state leadership had really been during the Republican years. His own programs were still inchoate and perhaps ineffable, but he wanted a chance to enunciate them. Lydia made a mental note to pass out pocket dictionaries at Vernon's next speech.

Dark had settled in, the place was as tenebrific as hell, but the TV crews had turned on their bright lights. Vernon didn't even say thank you. A good speech ought to end by expressing gratitude for the listener's attention, but Vernon seemed to think he was doing everyone a favor. Lydia was beginning to feel depressed. She knew that even if Vernon survived the primaries, if Shoat Bradfield challenged him to a debate, there would be no way that Vernon could stand up against Bradfield's powerful oratorical skills.

But the worst part of it didn't start until the question period, and the first reporter, a woman from the *Northwest Arkansas Times*, asked, "Mr. Ingledew, can't you give us any idea of just what exactly you plan to do to improve the state of Arkansas?"

Because the reporter was a woman, Vernon wouldn't look at her, and Lydia wasn't even sure he had heard her. But then he replied—to one of the TV cameras. "Certainly. For starters, I would like, eventually, to extirpate our institutions, particularly our prisons, our schools, even our hospitals."

Lydia wondered what *extirpate* meant and why he had to use such fancy words. If it meant improve, why couldn't he just say *improve*? If it meant paint and fix up, why couldn't he just say *paint and fix up*? She noticed that Bo Pharis had covered his face in his hands, so maybe Bo at least knew what the word meant. One of the reporters asked Vernon how to spell the word, and he spelled it out, but he didn't bother to offer synonyms, and none of the reporters had the guts to admit that none of them knew what it meant.

Another reporter, a man from the *Springdale Morning News*, asked, "What about churches? Do you plan to extirpate the churches too?"

"No," Vernon said. "As Plutarch wrote, 'If we traverse the world, it is possible to find cities without walls, without letters, without kings, without wealth, without coin, without schools and theaters; but a city without a temple, or that practiseth not worship, prayer, and the like, no one ever saw.' "

"Where do you practiseth worship?" the same reporter asked. "What church do you go to?"

"None," Vernon said, but then he touched his heart. "Here's my temple."

"You have no religion?" the reporter asked, rather challengingly.

"Well, you might say I follow the Tao," Vernon admitted, "so I suppose you could call me a Taoist if you had to."

Like the reporters, Lydia heard this the way Vernon pronounced it, as "Dow," and she, like they, took it to mean that the only thing Vernon worshiped was the Dow-Jones average. Which, of course, the vast majority of other Arkansas people also worshiped, even if they were Christians.

"Did you go to the university? Or where?" asked a teenage (male) reporter from the *Arkansas Traveler*, student newspaper at the university. Lydia realized she ought to have prepared in advance some bio sheets to give these people. If she had, they wouldn't have to ask such questions. But she also realized why she hadn't: a Vernon Ingledew bio would look awful to a reporter, let alone a voter.

"I'm strictly an autodidact," Vernon said. "And I'd like to see your children and your children's children become autodidacts."

This time a reporter was brave enough to ask, "What's an autodidact? How many wheels has it got?"

After the laughter, Vernon said, "A self-taught person."

"So now you plan to teach yourself politics?" asked one of the reporters. And without waiting for Vernon's answer, he commented, "I hope you're a fast learner."

Lydia *knew* Vernon was a very fast learner, but she had her doubts that he would be fast enough at learning such things as elocution, ebullience, posture, glad-handing, backslapping, and, above all, tact and restraint: in a word, politics.

After it was over and the crews were on their way home, she asked Bo, "What does extirpate mean?"

Bo rolled his eyes heavenward. "*Abolish*, dear Lydia. Literally, it means to pull up by the roots. I suppose our friend, our candidate, our employer intends the subtle implication that we find the root need for schools and prisons and hospitals and then yank out those roots. God knows. When's the next plane back to Cincinnati? Wait. I've got a car. And a chauffeur. Where's Cast? *Cast?*"

Lydia took it upon herself to attempt to give Vernon Ingledew a good chewing out. Somebody had to do it. But while she had often been unsparing in her critiques of the various candidates she had worked for, a carryover from her years of lambasting all politicians in her columns, she hadn't needed to criticize their delivery, their demeanor, and their absolutely crackpot ideas. Lydia could cuss better than a sailor when she had to.

She dragged him off into a field where the old gristmill had been, far enough to be out of earshot, even when she began to holler. She was a little rusty with some of those cusswords, but as she warmed up they all began coming back to her, in all their glory and power. Vernon could only stand there and take it, not once looking her in the eye. She was so busy cussing him that she forgot to remember the reason he was hanging his head was not because he was abashed at her chewing him out but because she was a female and he was congenitally shy toward all women, as had been all males in the Ingledew lineage going back a thousand years or more! How could she do a proper job of cussing him out if she couldn't even get his attention? But she kept on cussing him. She cussed his poor performance, she cussed his posture, she cussed his lousy *duende* and eupatrid mien, and above all she cussed his harebrained ideas. He stood there and took it like a ten-year-old boy getting a scolding from his mother, and she realized that Vernon had been only ten when his mother died.

It was not until this moment—or this sequence of profanity-laced moments—that Lydia Caple realized the real reason she was being so hard on him: She had fallen madly in love with him and believed with all her heart that he was going to be the best goddamn governor who ever governed any place on earth.

Chapter Seven

Little Rock from the air at night is a jeweled Shangri-la, a fucking fairyland. He'd never seen it before, day or night. The closest he'd come was when the Bob Dole campaign had added him to the throng of oppo men reconnoitering Clinton's whole life, but they had decided to keep him in DC and let others do the Little Rock search for secrets. To this day he remained convinced he could have found the tidbit or two that would have tipped the balance in favor of their client, but he was glad he didn't, because when you got right down to it he hated Republicans. All his life he had always preferred working for Democrats. He'll work for anybody who pays him, regardless of party, but when the great political balance sheets are drawn up, it turns out the debit side of the Republican sheet is besmirched with uglier scandals and misdeeds and sins and crimes. Look at Nixon. Harry would rather work *against* a Republican any day than *for* him. Of course the present job, at least until they got Ingledew past the primary, was going to mean lifting Democratic rocks to see what crawled out.

"Don't leave a stone unturned," Bo Pharis had said to him at the Boone County airport in Harrison. Harry had promised to give him full dossiers on each of Ingledew's eight opponents within a week, and Bo had told him not to give a thought to expenses. Really, the only commercial way to fly from Harrison to

Little Rock involved taking a Big Sky flight to St. Louis and a TWA from there, 800 miles of travel just to cover 140 miles. Ridiculous. So Bo had put him on a charter flight, hang the expense. But Bo wasn't a happy man. They'd gone to visit his mother, who lived in this cute little cottage just east of the courthouse square, and this sweet little old lady had known right away that something serious was troubling her son, but all Bo would tell her was, "I've let myself get deeply involved in a chimera, and my hopes have already been dashed." He told her he was home to stay for a while, however, at least until May, when he was due to get an honorary degree at the university and planned to have his mother attend.

The previous night, the Samurai—Bo and Harry and the others—had a Saturday night emergency session in Stay More to discuss whether or not Ingledew's campaign wasn't "dead in the water," as Bo put it; whether it could still be salvaged after such a shitty beginning. It was Saturday night, which by time-honored tradition Harry devoted to serious recreation, primarily bonded in 86 proof, but he went easy on the sauce long enough to hear out Bo and Lydia and Carleton and even the kids, Cast and Monica. Monica made a cute little speech reminding them that the first time each of them ever tried anything they blew it: the first time they walked, the first time they wrote, the first time they rode a bike or drove a car, the first time they had sex. Harry couldn't help guffawing at that last part, and he said, "The first time I had sex was the last time I had sex!" That got some laughs, and he added solemnly, "And maybe Ingledew's first speech was his last speech." Arch said they ought to blame themselves for not having coached Vernon sufficiently in advance. Carleton said all the coaching in the world wouldn't have corrected his ding-a-ling ideas about eradicating prisons, schools, et cetera.

Bo said the only way this campaign could go forward would be to "straighten out" Vernon. They might not be able to persuade him that he was crazy even to think of abolishing the school system, but they could certainly warn him that such ideas had to be kept to himself until after the election. They had to make sure that such gaffes would not occur again. They had to find out just what he was for and what he was against.

So they called Ingledew in and told him to lay it all on the line. Had he given any thought to legalizing marijuana? No, he said, he'd like to extirpate drugs. There was that word again. But Bo had explained it to any of the illiterati among them: *stirps* was Latin for roots, and *ex* meant out, so the word meant to pull up by the roots, but the way Ingledew intended it he sort of meant to find the root cause of anything, the root of drugs, the root of prisons, and eliminate that need. Which wasn't such a bad idea, if you thought about it. But then Ingledew looked at them as if he dared any of them to challenge him on that, and he added, "*All* drugs. Tobacco is a drug too. Guns are a drug."

A lot of them sighed. Was he in favor of strict gun control, then? Was he going to extirpate smoking? Well, he'd better save it for after he was in the governor's mansion, because the state had thousands upon thousands of proud gun owners who didn't think their possession of guns was a drug, and thousands upon thousands of smokers who didn't consider cigarettes a drug, and Ingledew didn't have a chance to get elected by alienating all those people. Harry wasn't sure they convinced him. But they got him to agree to tone it down, to put a lid on it, to generalize and extemporize and euphemize. In short, they got him to agree to become a politician. And from that point, they could move forward.

The charter plane, a Cessna, touched down on the same runway where a few years previously an American Airlines jet had overshot the runway and torn apart, killing eleven people. Knowing this didn't make Harry nervous. Even if he weren't such a goddamn fatalist anyway, he also knew why the airplane had crashed, he knew the pilot's error that had caused it, he knew what the pilot was thinking when he shouldn't have been thinking such thoughts at the moment he was supposed to have been thinking about deploying the wing spoilers but failed to do so. Listen: If you ever say anything, if you ever write anything, if you ever *think* anything, he can find out about it, believe him.

When Day Whittacker suspected Harry of reading his mind, that business about Mohammed and the mountain, he wasn't very far from the truth. We're decades past Big Brother in Orwell's *1984* (a date that seemed impossibly far in the future when he first thought of it over half a century ago but now seems hopelessly lost in the ho-hum Reagan years), but we've seen the near-complete erosion of personal privacy. Harry could tell you, if he had to (if he was paid well enough to), what you're wearing, or not wearing, as you read this. He has got his Compaq notebook in his lap, and this charter airline thoughtfully provides a modem hookup, and he has been plugged in the whole hour since Harrison.

He told the cabdriver to take him to a good hotel. The route went past the site of the Clinton presidential library, and the cabby pointed it out to him, what they could see of it in the dark, and although Harry can see in the dark when he has to, this wasn't one of those times. The cabby deposited him in front of a sleek glass cliff called the Excelsior, but he noticed across the street from it a Victorian Italianate oldie called the Capital, which he thought looked more cozy, even more political, than the Excelsior. So that's where he checked in. The rooms were expensive, but it wasn't coming out of his pocket. The decor was soft and old-timey and his King room had a modem line, no problem. He ordered a bottle of black Jack from room service and plugged in. It was Sunday night, but hit men never sleep. Well, actually, if they drink enough their demons will pass out, and he expected to join them in the land of oblivion, but meanwhile he'd just as soon work on Sunday night as punch a nine-to-five on a workday.

His Compaq notebook already had the chart of the Eight,

as he'd begun to think of them, mapped out. Thanks to eager-beaver Cast Sherrill, who'd make a great oppo man himself someday if he hadn't set his sights higher on a campaign managership or media expertship, Harry already had in his notebook's many gigabytes a clunky file on all the basic known scandals involving the Eight: the ex-governor's felony conviction, the evangelist's suspected child abuse, the attorney general's involvement in the suicide of the legislator. But, all due credit to the kid Cast, these things were common knowledge: Cast had found them in newspaper accounts, probably lifted off Lexis-Nexis. Harry knew places to look beyond Lexis-Nexis that the kid had never dreamed of.

When Harry had found himself unemployed after Senator Passmore's defeat (which was, he would always believe, the fault of the other campaign consultants, who violated a fundamental principle of Harry's: If you find some real poison about a candidate, use it early in the campaign; don't wait until toward the end, when it can look like desperation tactics and can backfire), when Harry found himself unemployable for a time, with nothing to do but haunt the corridors of the National Gallery, the Corcoran, and the Phillips, he decided to keep in practice by doing a complete dossier on himself: every possible existence of any sequence of bytes spelling out HARRY WOLFE on the Internet was retrieved and examined (there are 1,250 Harry Wolfes in the United States, and he didn't even bother with those in Canada, Australia, and England). Posing as a credit rating service, he obtained a complete record of Harry Wolfe's credit, which led to investigation of bad debts, a few minor thefts, countless overdrafts at the bank, and the use of a MasterCard to subscribe to "love clubs." Using the FOIA, or Freedom of Information Act, he obtained all the FBI files on Harry Wolfe, which contained some interesting revelations of how he and his activities were viewed by others. Pretending to be a consulting physician, he obtained all of Harry Wolfe's hospital and medical records, shocking in their revelations of his failure to take care of himself. And then by posing as a potential employer doing a security-clearance check, he obtained all the records of Harry Wolfe at South Hagerstown High School, as well as at Georgetown University, from which he was expelled as a junior. He hacked Harry Wolfe's computer and uncovered a cesspool of salacious material and a private diary that would sear your eyeballs.

So dedicated to this work did he become that he supposed for a while he was clinically a split personality: one Harry Wolfe was the fat, filthy, drunken loner who couldn't get a date if his life depended on it and overcompensated by doing just about anything, short of rape and murder, to give himself a good time; the other Harry Wolfe, hot on his trail, was America's premier investigative oppo man. The first Harry had a habit, at least once weekly, of drinking himself into oblivion, of not even remembering what he'd done while loaded, so the second Harry took advantage of this to hide miniature videocams in his bedroom, bathroom, and kitchenette. Further, in disguise he interviewed various persons who had contact with Harry Wolfe during his blackouts, such as fellow patrons of the nude bars he frequented. Every loathsome deed of the man was recorded in lurid detail in a log on the computer. This surveillance reached its nadir when the sleuth paid a city sanitation department truckdriver a bribe to set aside the twice-weekly collection of Harry Wolfe's garbage, an act (sometimes called "dumpster diving" in the trade) that depleted his financial resources. If you shake your head and say *Why the fuck didn't he just save his own fucking garbage?* he could point out two things: one, that would have violated his sense of being split into dual personalities; and, two, he needed to find out how hard or easy it was to bribe a garbage collector. The experience created some unpleasant moments when he had to sift meticulously through all that dreck and analyze its possible meaning.

And the conclusion? Don't, for *any* office, vote for this man!

Don't trust him. Don't buy anything from him; don't even sell him anything. Don't rent to him or borrow from him. Don't, if possible, speak to the bastard. Don't touch anything he has touched. Don't breathe the same air.

His very calling, once upon a time, was totally disreputable. Back in the seventies he'd been a newspaperman stringing for a chain of small newspapers in Delaware when a man running for state senator had come to him and "wondered" if Harry knew anything about the man's opponent. Nothing he hadn't already published, he said. The man offered to pay him, and that's how he got started. They weren't called "opposition research" in those days; they were called a lot of unflattering names, the best of which was "lepers." They were kept in small rooms behind closed doors all by themselves. It was lonely. Most of the men (and a few women) Harry worked for denied that they even knew him . . . sometimes to his face. Such researchers certainly weren't allowed into the rooms where the key campaign decisions were discussed and reached. But then the Nixon White House hired a gumshoe to research Chappaquiddick, Donald Segretti became Nixon's "dirty trickster," the Democrats answered with their own, Dick Tuck, and the muckraking escalated to the point where no politician in his right mind could live without oppo people, and they were afforded a place at the table in the highest campaign echelons.

The first thing Harry did that night was something he could've done at any time before but had postponed: He searched the Internet to see if any of the Eight had their own Web pages. A personal Web page is a flagrant display of egotism, which is another way of saying that every politician has to have one. Sure enough, six of the Eight had Web pages, some of them dignified and patriotic and stressing family values, decency, no taxes, all that crap, but also some unintentional gaffes, clumsy bad taste, and even clues for Harry to pursue in search of the candidate's extremist support or faulty public record. Having downloaded all those Web pages to his computer, he then ran a Bigfoot search on each of the Eight: for a reasonable fee per hit (charged to his MasterCard), he could get what Bigfoot.com calls a Supersearch: all the known information about the person, including names and phones of the person's neighbors (*very* handy, because your friendly neighbor probably resents the hell out of you and is more than willing to gossip and dish the dirt on you from his ringside seat), the previous addresses of the person going back ten years (politicians who move around a lot, like any fly-by-night miscreant, are fugitives from justice), as well as a summary of assets and a complete record of any bankruptcies, civil judgments, or UCC lien filings. Bigfoot is a big bargain. Harry was ready to hit the street.

Monday, after a late breakfast from room service, he put on his suit and walked over to the county courthouse to start searching for overdue property taxes, government liens, mortgage records, and lawsuits—routine basic information. He found a few lawsuits involving some of the Eight that offered juicy reading and also provided him, as a bonus, with the names of the litigants, who were all now sworn enemies of one of the Eight and would each have further secrets to share with Harry. He made a few phone calls and set up a few appointments, lunches, and cocktail meetings.

Walking from that courthouse back to his hotel, he passed the Old Statehouse, Gideon Shryock's antebellum neoclassical masterpiece. In his computer he had the entire text of *The Architecture of the Arkansas Ozarks*, and he knew the full story of how Jacob Ingledew had stood in the chamber of this building, not once but twice (and the second time all alone), to cast his vote against Arkansas's secession from the Union. As far as Harry could determine from what he considered a rather frivolous novel,

Jacob Ingledew had been just an old Ozark hillbilly, not very literate or grammatical, but possessed of enough good sense and dignity to make him vote his conscience. The thought of his bravery, which had occurred in this very building Harry gazed upon, made Harry gulp. He is a cynical man, as you've determined, but he is touched by human decency wherever he finds it.

Then he phoned Hank Endicott at the *Arkansas Democrat-Gazette*, to call in some favors. He knew Lydia had already talked to him, but she hadn't told Harry about the call. If she had, he could have told her that Hank and he went way back and were the best of buddies, at least to the extent that a pariah like Harry could have a friend. When Endicott had gone to Washington back in 1993 for a whole year to cover Clinton's early performance in the White House, out of which he'd written a great book called *Rascal: A President's First Year*, Harry had run into him in the bar of the National Press Club and introduced himself (Endicott claimed that "everybody knows who Harry Wolfe is"), and once Harry learned Endicott's motive for being in town he offered to introduce him to some newspaper pals of his at the *Post* and *Star* who could show him the ropes of the DC scene. During Endicott's year in town, Harry had met him for drinks on several other occasions, and once—just once, but that was unprecedented—he'd had him up to his Georgetown apartment to view his extensive collection of political memorabilia. So Endicott owed him.

"My God," Endicott said. "Lydia Caple told me all about this Ingledew, but she didn't say *you* were on the team too." Harry assured him he was and conjectured that Lydia had neglected to mention him because there was still an odor of ill repute about oppo men. He asked Hank if he'd care to meet him after work for a drink and learned that the bar of his hotel, the Capital, was the chosen watering hole anyhow. But Hank said, "Listen, Harry, I've got a column in tomorrow's paper about Ingledew. Maybe you'd better read it before we meet." So they set their bar date for the following afternoon.

Harry spent the rest of the day at the Little Rock Public Library. Despite whatever thrilling image oppo researching may have, most of the hard work is actually done in the library. But most oppo men just walk in, blind, and start looking around. Harry took the trouble to ingratiate himself with one of the head librarians, a splendid fellow named Bob Razer, who, it turned out, was delighted to learn of Vernon Ingledew's candidacy because he was a major fan of Harington's fictions. Razer showed Harry a case in which all eleven of Harington's books were kept in first editions. Razer was thrilled at the prospect of being able to read more about Vernon. "Maybe Harington will write a novel about this campaign," he conjectured.

"He's already started it," Harry pointed out.

When Razer learned Harry's objective, he was only too happy to direct Harry to a few sources he might otherwise have overlooked, and even to permit him to tap into some databases that were not customarily available to the public. Razer is, it can't be said enough, a splendid fellow.

The next morning a copy of the *Arkansas Democrat-Gazette* was delivered to Harry's door at the Capital, and he climbed back into bed with it and his breakfast. He turned at once to Hank Endicott's column. Harry blushes easily, and he could feel his face flushing over the headline on it:

A Clown's Hat Is Tossed into a Three-Ring Circus

Remember Monroe Schwarzlose? Remember "Uncle Mac" McKrell? How about Crazy Joe Weston or Crazy Kenneth Coffelt? And then there was always Tommy Robinson and Sheffield Nelson.

Without the ill-fated, bumbling campaigns of such colorful characters, Arkansas politics would have been even duller than it already was, given the decline of stump speaking. Schwarzlose dared to run against Bill Clinton four times, and the first time he tried he somehow got 30% of the vote (only 5% the other times).

Now comes Vernon Ingledew, whose name isn't quite as picturesque as "Monroe Schwarzlose" but who is even more of a political novice and makes old Monroe look like a sage statesman. We've all (except Paul Greenberg) eaten Ingledew Ham, "the Smithfield of the Ozarks," but that's about all we know about him.

He's abandoning his pig works in tiny Stay More, up in the remotest wilds of Newton County, in order to make a run (or at least a winded walk) against the eight other candidates already filed for the Democratic primary.

Schwarzlose had some good ideas, possibly ahead of their time: he wanted a statewide lottery, he proposed solving the problems of deteriorating roads and hazardous waste disposal by using the waste to fill the potholes, and he envisioned putting hydroelectric plants on the dams of the Arkansas River. Ingledew's ideas, what little is known about them at this early stage, appear even more ahead of their time.

His near-invisible credentials—he has never held any office and isn't a college graduate—include being possessed of extremely good looks and the fact that he's a direct descendant of Jacob Ingledew, Arkansas governor during Reconstruction, whose best-known achievement, apart from casting the lone vote against secession, was taxing the bankrupt state back into solvency.

Well, "Too-Tall" Tom McRae was the great-grandson of an Arkansas governor, but it didn't get him past Clinton in the Democratic primary of 1990. Unlike Ingledew, McRae was thoroughly familiar with politics, having served as staff coordinator for Governor Dale Bumpers.

Speaking of Bumpers, Ingledew's few supporters have probably encouraged him with the fabulous story of how young Dale Bumpers came out of nowhere in 1970 to run against and defeat Orval Faubus and his powerful machine in the Democratic primary and then to beat Winthrop Rockefeller in the general election.

Bumpers's fantastic rise from absolute obscurity in less than three months might have prompted Ingledew to seek out the man who was one of its architects: Archie Schaffer III, then just a 22-year-old college graduate who also happened to be Bumpers's nephew, who is now—or was, until Ingledew hired him—head of PR at giant Tyson Foods.

But Schaffer, best known for the "Free Archie" campaign leading to his pardon by the lame duck President for a trumped-up charge of currying favor for Tyson, took a leave at Tyson not to be Ingledew's campaign manager but only the deputy or associate campaign manager.

The top man on Ingledew's expensive staff of topflight professionals is none other than Bolin Pharis, veteran of many a local and national campaign, accused of losing the presidency for Al Gore. Pharis supposedly quit politics after that fiasco and, like Schaffer, went to work as PR chief for a Fortune 500 company, but *something* about Ingledew not only got him to change his mind about politics but, again like Schaffer, to take a leave of absence from his company. With a pair like Pharis and Schaffer, who needs anybody else? But you still want the best possible press secretary, right? So who do you hire? Somebody with *vast* experience in journalism as well as a stint in the Arkansas governor's office, somebody like . . . well, would you buy *Lydia Caple*? They bought her, and she says she hasn't been happier for years.

Enough already? No, there's more: Lydia Caple brought onto the team one of the best administrative assistants from the governor's office during the Clinton years, the unfortunately named Monica Breedlove, who bears no resemblance whatever to her infamous namesake. Also, the seasoned media expert Carleton

Drew was hired away from Washington, perhaps to find ways to circumvent Ingledew's declared intention to shun television.

Can you believe a campaign without constant spots? Ingledew, if nothing else, is going to be spotless.

The sixth member of the ferocious team is young: Castor Sherrill, Harvard MBA and Bolin Pharis's protégé in PR. And last but not least, someone who ought to strike fear into the hearts of all the other candidates: the man who will handle opposition research and is in Little Rock right now hard at work laying bare every aspect of their lives, America's paramount political spy, Harry Wolfe.

Never before has a candidate for public office in Arkansas (or any other state, for that matter) assembled a staff such as these Seven Samurai, as they call themselves, not necessarily smiling. How did Ingledew do it? Well, money of course. He apparently has unlimited resources. But also there's that *something* about him, which, if the Samurai can package it and present it to the voters effectively, might well get him past the primary.

Even Monroe Schwarzlose could have won if he'd had these people in his corner.

Harry was of course flattered to be identified as "paramount," but the first thing he said to Hank Endicott that afternoon, meeting him at the Capital Bar, was, "What gives you the authority to call Ingledew a clown?"

"They're *all* clowns, Harry," Hank said. They shook hands and clapped each other on the back and looked each other over. Harry liked to think that if he could just lose about a hundred pounds, he might look like Hank Endicott. Not that Endicott was skinny, by a long shot, but that Harry was obese.

"Do you think our clown stands a chance against the other clowns?" Harry asked him.

"In a field of nine, nobody's going to get a majority," Hank observed.

"But if the primary were held tomorrow, who would come out ahead?"

"Tomorrow?" Hank deliberated. "If the primary were held tomorrow, your boy wouldn't get one percent of the vote, which was Dale Bumpers's percentage in the first poll after he announced."

"So if the pie is sliced nine ways, and my man gets just a sliver, who gets the biggest piece?"

"Probably Barnas, the state senator. He's got the best organization, and he's leading the polls."

"That was my reading too," Harry agreed, because he was thoroughly familiar with the polls and the organizational strengths of the opposition. Then he said, "Tell me, Hank, have you heard of something called the Ouachita Militia?"

"That's pronounced Wash-it-taw," Hank corrected Harry's pronunciation. "Sure. A bunch of neo-Nazis." The Ouachita Militia was a big, rich, not-so-secret right-wing paramilitary group, operating primarily out of Mena, in the Ouachita Mountains west of Little Rock.

"Well," Harry said, leaning toward him, "they're bankrolling James Barnas."

"You're kidding me!" Hank exclaimed. "Says who?"

Harry smiled. "I can't reveal my sources, just as you can't reveal yours."

"But can it be *proved*?" Hank wanted to know. "Can it be documented? If it's true, Barnas's ass is grass."

"So there's one down, seven to go," Harry declared.

Hank's cell phone rang and he answered it, talked awhile, scoffed, talked some more, snorted, talked some more, grunted, finally hung up, and said, "No, there are three down, five to go. That was Ned Green, up at the office: 'This just in.' Three of the nine candidates in the Democratic primary for governor of

Arkansas have withdrawn from the race." And he named the three, mostly minor: the automobile dealer, the state representative, and the briefly former governor. Vernon Ingledew wasn't one of them.

Harry clapped Hank on the shoulder. "Your column did it, Hank! They're scared shitless of me!"

Hank laughed. "Don't flatter yourself. They've pissed their pants over the whole Seven Samurai, not just you." He fished out his cell phone. "Excuse me, I'd like for you to meet someone." And he made a quick call. Harry was hoping against hope that Hank might be setting him up with a desirable female of his acquaintance.

But they went on talking politics, agreeing to help each other during the campaign. Out of Hank's sense of journalistic ethics, he would not steer Harry to reports or rumors he hadn't been able to pin down or hadn't already written about, and out of Harry's sense of tightfisted management of his intelligence (referring of course not to his fabulous IQ but his collection of secret information), Harry would not reveal to him *all* the dirt he'd found.

Who joined them wasn't a lady at all but a creepy-looking little guy in tweeds and thick spectacles. Harry might not have got his name right; it sounded like "Garth Rucker." When Hank made the introductions, Harry thought the guy was going to prostrate himself at Harry's feet.

"Oh, Mr. Wolfe!" he said, holding Harry's hand in both of his and shaking it up and down. "I couldn't believe it when I read Hank's column and learned you were in town, sir! What a pleasure this is! How thrilled I am to meet you, sir!" and he went on lionizing Harry until Hank interrupted him.

"You guys haven't met before?" Hank asked. "At the national convention of Negative Researchers, perhaps?" He laughed at his own wit, and then he told Harry, "Garth is Barnas's oppo man."

"Oh?" Harry said. If there ever was such a thing as a national conference of opposition researchers, they would be the most repulsive assembly of human specimens ever congregated, either fat, slimy, and evil like Harry or tiny, fiendish, and rat-faced like Garth Rucker. Harry didn't number many oppo men among his acquaintances; they simply didn't associate, if they could avoid it.

But Hank had other ideas. He suggested that they adjourn to this nice place called The Afterthought, up in the Hillcrest section of Little Rock, a sweet old neighborhood untouched by the creeping modernization of so much of America's cities. It reminded Harry of Georgetown, and he was homesick.

When they were settled in, and munching their supper from the bar menu of meatballs *boulés*, spicy wings, and cheese focaccia, Garth said to Harry, "Sir, would you like to play Swap? You tell me all the good stuff about Ingledew and I'll tell you all the good stuff about Barnas!"

He meant bad stuff, of course. Harry had no intention of telling him Ingledew's secrets. Harry knew things about Ingledew that haven't yet been mentioned in this book, and they were going to remain his closely guarded preserve of skeletons in the closet. But he could throw this guy a sop or two. So just to humor him and keep Hank entertained, they began swapping. "Ingledew was never elected to anything," Harry pointed out.

"Already got that, sir!" Garth said. "That's a good one, but I already got it. Okay, Barnas is too conservative by Democratic Party standards."

"Got that," Harry declared. "Ingledew has no children, just him and Jelena Ingledew."

"Got that," Garth said. "He's not married to her, either, is he? Oh, we already know that one, sir! Okay, Barnas has the full support of the National Rifle Association. But maybe that's in his favor."

"Got that," Harry said. "Ingledew is opposed to guns, period."

"Really? Thanks. I didn't have that one. Barnas voted in the state senate against the highway improvement bill."

"Got that. He also voted against day care."

"Check. Did you get that he was only 187th in a class of 453 at Malvern High School?"

"Sure. And only 498th in a class of 1,248 at Arkansas State University. Ingledew never even went to college."

"Got that, sir. Man, that looks bad. Everybody goes to college."

"Barnas plagiarized his term papers in Sociology, Economics, and American History," Harry pointed out.

"Hey, touché, Mr. Wolfe, sir. I didn't know that myself. But what about your man worships the Dow?"

"That's Tao, buddy," Harry pointed out, and spelled it for him. "And he doesn't worship it, he just likes it. It's an oriental religion which teaches, among other things, that we should be kind to one another."

"But it doesn't teach that Jesus Christ is our Lord and Savior?"

"Not that I know of."

"So what's Ingledew's religion?"

"He has no religion."

Garth Rucker stared through his thick lenses at Harry for a time long enough to assure himself that Harry wasn't jerking him around. "Whoa!" he said. "You don't mean he's an *infidel*?"

"I suppose you could call him that," Harry granted.

"Wow! Boy, sir, can we use this!"

"I wish you wouldn't call me 'sir.' Maybe I can outsmart you, but I don't outrank you." And then Harry told him flatly, "But you aren't going to *use* any of what I'm telling you about Ingledew."

"I'm not? But that's the whole point of Swap, sir. We need all this good stuff to attack each other with."

"You're not going to attack Ingledew," Harry informed him.

"Hey, what is this?" He looked to Hank Endicott for help. "We're talking politics, right, sir? Politics is about attacking each other's faults and weaknesses and sins, isn't it? What do you mean, we can't attack Ingledew?"

"Because if you do," Harry warned him, "if you utter, or publish, or televise, or even leak one unkind word about him, we will reveal that your man Barnas gets his endowment from the Ouachita Militia."

Garth Rucker's mouth dropped open. He struggled to put a blank, innocent look on his face. "Huh? What's the Ouachita Militia?"

"A neo-Nazi gang of thugs whom the good people of Arkansas rightly despise," Harry informed him.

"Never heard of 'em," Garth said.

"Then you'd better go ask your client to tell you all about them. And while you're at it, get him to give you full disclosure on certain other aspects of his activities. Ask him about the weekends that he flew to Jamaica at the expense of the tobacco lobby. Ask him, since we're so concerned about religion, to tell you why he was expelled in 1989 from the Malvern First Baptist Church. Ask him to let you audit his income tax records for 1986 to 1992 and get him to account for all the falsifications therein."

There was a long silence, an absolute silence that scarcely permitted the sounds of other customers in the cozy confines of The Afterthought. Even the jazz piano seemed to be muted. Harry reflected on the seemliness of the establishment's name, because he was going to keep on rethinking and reconsidering everything he knew about James Barnas. The silence was finally broken by the sound of Hank Endicott's laughter.

"Hoo boy," Hank chortled. "You're out of your league, Garth. It's too bad I can't print any of this good stuff."

"Unless you have to," Harry reminded him.

"Unless I have to," Hank said ominously.

"So what's the deal?" Garth demanded. "Do you mean nobody can say anything bad about Ingledew?"

"You're a fast learner, boy," Harry complimented him.

"But that's not *politics*!" he whined.

"It's going to be politics," Harry assured him. "By the way, did anyone ever point out to you the origin of the word *politics*? It comes from the Latin, *poly* meaning many and *tics* meaning bloodsucking creatures."

"Hold on just a minute." Having missed the humor, Garth was trying reason. "You and me both would be out of business if we couldn't use the dirt we dig up and dish out. How'm I gonna tell my boss, 'Here's all this good stuff on Ingledew but you can't use any of it'? Do you think he'll *pay* me? I'll be out of work!"

Harry smiled. "Maybe we can hire you to help sniff around Shoat Bradfield in the main campaign." Harry was making no promises, but he was having afterthoughts about Garth Rucker's possible usefulness. "Tell you what. Make you a deal. You show me all your files on the other seven candidates—oops, there's only five left, right?—you show me all the good stuff you've got on those guys, and I'll recommend that Bo Pharis hire you for the Ingledew campaign."

So, thanks to Hank Endicott, Harry greatly simplified his workload in Little Rock. He even had a badly needed ally when, because he'd lost his license over a DWI years before, he depended on Garth Rucker to chauffeur him around, help plant a few videocams and wiretaps, and hunt for a few garbage collectors to be bribed. Thus Harry was able to escape from Little Rock sooner than he had expected, coming away from the place with all the intelligence that could have been desired about any opponent who would dare oppose Vernon Ingledew.

Chapter Eight

She was the cheapest of the Samurai, but it didn't bother her. She'd just as soon not have known how much less she was making than Cast, but among the five thousand other responsibilities in her job description was writing the checks for the weekly payroll. Of course Cast had a master's degree from Harvard, which was one reason he was making more than she was, although what he was making was still a scrimption compared with what Bo and Arch and Lydia were pulling in. She didn't really care. She would have taken the job for nothing, to have a chance to be doing something like this. They had even let her pick out the campaign headquarters. They'd told her it had to be in Fayetteville, and it had to be high profile, but beyond that they left it up to her, the way they left so many things up to her: the selection of the computer equipment, the hiring of office staff, the scheduling of Vernon's appearances. Bo had draped his big arm across her broad shoulders and said, "Monica, hon, here's the rule: Whenever you think of something that needs to be done, you do it. You don't need my say-so."

That week after Vernon announced was the busiest week of her life so far, and the first thing she'd done was find out which realtors managed the few vacant buildings in Fayetteville. Even before she found an apartment for herself, she visited several buildings around town that were available; and after thorough investigation and careful consideration (but no advice or consent from the others), she signed the lease on a building right close beside the picturesque Fayetteville Square, got in there herself and swept the floor and cleaned the windows, obtained all the necessary supplies during a one-hour shopping spree at Office Depot, visited some furniture-renting stores and got enough desks and chairs and all, and even helped the men unload them and put them in place. There wasn't anything a man could do that she couldn't do.

The second day on the job she'd had a sign company make the signs and a printing company print some banners, and she had already hired and put to work three of the office staff when Vernon Ingledew came to Fayetteville for his first visit to get himself photographed for the official campaign photo and begin his lessons in speech and deportment. He was amazed to find his headquarters already in business, not only in business but really busy, with four people on the phone and typing their computers simultaneously. Although he was not able to speak directly to her, or even look at her, he wrote a memo heaping her with praise and she was ready to die for him. In fact, she was tongue-tied as far as her own tongue was concerned, and when she tried to tell him some of her ideas for the upcoming tour that she and Cast were going to make to the state's college campuses, she found that her voice sounded exactly like Lydia's.

Vernon, whose woman-shyness didn't prevent him from *hearing* her, laughed and said, "Who needs Lydia? You've even got her voice," and even though he spoke these words to his shoes she felt that they were in touch at last. She'd always had a talent for imitating the people she admired, and way back when she'd worked in the governor's office alongside Lydia, other people had called her "Lydia Junior." When Lydia grabbed Vernon and dragged him out into a field in Stay More to jump his ass for his poor performance, Lydia had thought they were out of earshot, but Monica had followed (it was dark) and eavesdropped, and she wondered if the occasion would ever arise when she'd have to cuss Vernon herself. If it did, she knew she could cuss nearly as good as Lydia. If Cast's ambition was to make himself into another Bo Pharis, Monica's was to make herself into another Lydia Caple. And this job would let her do it.

And like Lydia, without even knowing Lydia's heart, she too was madly in love with the man and ready to die for him.

It was her assignment to take Vernon to meet Andrew Kilgore, the photographer, who shot Vernon all over the campus, particularly in the library, in what was supposed to be a staged picture in the reference room with stacks of books piled all around while he pretended to read and study. But he wasn't pretending, and Monica had a heck of a time trying to get him to leave. You'd have thought he'd never been in a real library before. Maybe he hadn't. The pictures turned out great, an official campaign photo that made Vernon look really movie-star handsome and an "activity photo" that showed him looking like the answers to all the problems of humankind were in those books about to fall on his head.

Monica and Cast had been thrown together for a whole week, the second week after the announcement, early in April. Since it had been his bright idea to visit the college campuses, he had spent a lot of time at headquarters helping her plan and order what they needed to take with them: four hundred campaign T-shirts, thousands of banners, buttons, and bumper stickers. These things were made right here in Fayetteville, but they had to wait several days for the bumper stickers. Cast and Monica had their first fight over what the T-shirt should look like and say. All they could agree on was that it should have the official photo of Vernon that was so striking. But Cast wanted a conventional campaign T-shirt, with red-white-and-blue lettering and something like VER-

NON INGLEDEW FOR GOVERNOR, whereas Monica wanted to put in big purple letters across a yellow chest INGLE WHO? and then, in smaller letters below the photo, ASK ME! This was too unconventional for Cast, so they had to take it to Lydia and get her opinion, and then all the way up to Bo, who agreed with Lydia that Monica's idea would attract more attention even if it sort of poked fun at the candidate's name.

She selected the campaign colors with of course the approval of the candidate, who complimented her again (by memo) for her ideas. When she had been studying art at UALR she'd had an obsession with color and had learned everything she could about it. One reason she wore black herself so much, apart from the way it went with her blond hair and pale complexion, was because the psychology of black connotes mystery, loyalty, authority, seriousness, and strength, not to mention death, and there had been so many deaths in her life that it was unmentionable. She chose as Ingledew's colors purple and yellow because, for one thing, he himself didn't want "trite" red-white-and-blue, never mind Cast's opinion. Purple and yellow are complementaries, meaning that one of them makes the other more intense and noticeable. Purple is associated with dignity and royalty, with frugality and melancholy, and Monica was one of the first to detect Vernon's streak of melancholy. Yellows give playfulness, gaiety, and sunlight but also confidence, esteem, and knowledge. All these things were part of Vernon's makeup. So with his full approval and appreciation, it was decided that all the banners, T-shirts, bumper stickers, and buttons would be purple and yellow. The yard signs would have been too but, as we're going to see, Vernon wouldn't allow the "visual clutter" of yard signs.

It was also Monica's idea to put together a little paper sack full of goodies to be distributed on the campuses, each sack containing stuff that college kids can always use: the campaign pencil (which, Cast agreed with her, could simply be imprinted

GOVERNOR: VERNON INGLEDEW) and the campaign ballpoint (ditto) as well as note pads, a package of chewing gum, and an imprinted lollipop. Monica's tomato-red Camaro couldn't carry all this stuff, so Cast took Bo's silver Nissan 4-by-4. They had a trial run right here in town at the University of Arkansas, getting permission from the Office of Student Affairs, setting up a booth on the quad in front of the Student Union, and contacting the Student Democrats Club to come and help out. They gave the club officers each a T-shirt and a little booklet that would tell them what to answer if somebody did take that ASK ME! literally and wanted to know not only INGLE WHO? but what he stood for.

That's where the other Samurai were needed, putting that booklet or manual together. In what little free time they had, for each and every one of them had a full plate of jobs to do, the Seven Samurai got together, sometimes with the candidate, and talked about *position papers*. Bo had wanted to form what was called a steering committee, which wouldn't have included Monica (did they think she wasn't bright enough to have ideas about issues?), but when Vernon found out about it he delivered a little stern lecture against committees. No committee in the history of the world, he asserted, had ever accomplished anything, and he defied any one of them to give him an example of a single achievement by a committee. He certainly intended to extirpate committees, right here and now. Monica was proud of the way he spoke out against committees, beginning to sound already like a forceful no-nonsense governor.

Without any committees meeting, it was commonly agreed among them that there was to be no further mention of Vernon's more radical ideas, especially those involving extirpation. It was agreed to stress Vernon's aim to bring Arkansas into the twenty-first century, to take advantage of technology and new inventions to lift the state out of the stagnation that two Republican governors had left it in. Those parts of the state Democratic platform that were not too unacceptable (Vernon could not accept "We hold that the public school system is essential to Arkansas's economic success and support") were rephrased into his own platform: It could be said that he supported law enforcement agencies without giving his support to prisons, that he expected government to refrain from undue intrusion into the private lives and personal decisions of Arkansans—no, wait; Vernon like a lot of people was adamant that the word *Arkansans*, which smacked of some kind of false connection with the state of Kansas, should never be used; that in places where one could not say "Arkansas people" the classical "Arkansawyers" would be employed (and indeed it would be Monica who would organize on the Internet a select bloc known as "Arkansawyers for Ingledew").

Further, Vernon had no intention of raising taxes and wished to overhaul the entire taxation system. Further, Vernon fully supported the state's cultural and natural heritage. At Monica's suggestion, they agreed that Vernon was strongly opposed to drugs, although no mention was made of his inclusion of tobacco and guns in the drug category. Monica was also responsible for a plank in the platform favoring health care and mental health care with or without insurance for every person, and since this made no mention of Vernon's opposition to hospitals it was acceptable.

Monica had a live-wire assistant at headquarters named Hazel Maguire, and she not only trusted Hazel with the keys to headquarters while she and Cast took off for the state tour of campuses, but she also got Hazel to visit her apartment daily to feed her dogs, Buster the bulldog and Whiskey the part-rottweiler, and her several cats. Another way Monica emulated Lydia was in surrounding herself with pets; Lydia too had taken an apartment in Fayetteville and installed in it her dog Beanbag and several cats from Little Rock. Monica hated to leave her animals, and she knew that Lydia hated to leave hers. Whenever Lydia went out of town for overnight or longer, she hired somebody to feed her animals, and it had been Monica's ambition to be able to emulate Lydia in that regard.

The morning that she and Cast were going to depart Fayetteville, the newspapers published the first polls for the Democratic primary. Monica was amazed to see that Vernon Ingledew had got .85 percent! But she couldn't understand the arithmetic; the percentages of the other five added up to more than the remaining 15 percent, and Barnas alone had 47 percent. Then she realized to her horror that it wasn't 85 percent but only 85 percent of 1 percent: Vernon Ingledew had less than 1 percent of those polled! Arch Schaffer came to headquarters to deliver a pep talk (there were now several volunteers from the university in the headquarters) and to remind everybody that his uncle, Dale Bumpers, had pulled only 1 percent in the first poll taken after he'd announced for the primary, but that Dale Bumpers's ranking had steadily risen in the polls. "Let's get rid of those long faces!" he told them.

But Cast and Monica still had long faces when they headed south on Interstate 540. For many miles they didn't even speak to each other, although they both felt an obligation to make talk. Finally, to cheer him up and herself into the bargain, she offered, "I'll bet a week's salary against your week's salary that the *next* poll will show him with at least ten percent."

"If we have anything to do with it," Cast declared firmly. She was going to be treated to the spectacle of Cast busting his ass, an act that she thought only herself capable of. So far he hadn't seemed particularly industrious. He did his assignments, whatever they were, but he didn't hustle. Now on this trip she was going to see him transformed into an activist take-charge guy. He had overscheduled the trip: fifteen colleges and universities in seven days, but Monica had calculated the distances between schools carefully so that, if they spent as much travel time as possible on the interstates, they could get from one school in the morning to another in the afternoon.

There was nothing whatever romantic between them. Cast had never asked her how old she was, and she'd never offered to tell him that she was eleven years older. Of course there were lots of relationships between older women and younger men—look at Vernon Ingledew himself—but even though Monica thought Cast was "very cute," she couldn't see herself having an intimacy with him. Campaign workers are always on duty when in public, and any sign of flirtation or affection between them would be ill-conceived. She had been younger than Cast when she'd divorced, and she hadn't had a real relationship for seven years. If Lydia could thrive without romance, so could she.

But there was nothing wrong with becoming the best of friends with Cast, and in the course of their travels they told each other quite a lot about themselves. Cast discussed what he knew of his unusual parentage: his mother a porn actress and his father one of her costars, neither of whom he'd ever seen much of as he grew up. Monica told about her family house burning down with her mother in it. They both talked about their names, how Monica meant *advisor*, and she not only was full of political advice but was pretty good also at psychological advice and general health advice as well. He told her of the Greek legend of the beautiful Leda whom the mighty immortal Zeus had desired but had had to disguise himself in order to keep his seduction of Leda a secret from his jealous wife, Hera. So he had turned himself into a swan. Naturally Leda had laid a pair of eggs. Monica thought that was hilarious. Out of one egg had hatched Helen, who would become Helen of Troy, and her twin brother Pollux. Contrary to popular belief, Pollux had not shared an egg with Castor. Castor had been in the same egg with Clytemnestra, destined to become Agamemnon's queen, but he spent all his time growing up with his half brother Pollux. Castor was mortal, Pollux immortal, but when they died and Pollux went to heaven (Olympus) while Castor had to go to hell (Hades), Zeus took pity on them because they missed each other so much and arranged to let Pollux give his brother half of his immortality, so they could stay together, half the time on Olympus, half the time in Hades.

"Did you have a twin?" Monica asked him. "In real life, I mean?"

"If I did, nobody ever told me," Cast said, "but there might just be a Clytemnestra somewhere out there."

Monica and Cast both confided the embarrassment their names had caused them. Cast had been the victim of many puns based upon the fact that a cast may be something put on a broken limb, the group of actors in a play or movie, a throwing of a fishing line, the outward appearance of anything, even the circling of hounds to pick up a scent in hunting or a pair of hawks released by a falconer at one time, to name only a few of the forty-odd meanings. When he was a child other kids called him Castor Oil. Because at Harvard he'd read Robert Bly's *Iron John* (as recreation and did not particularly enjoy it), he picked up the nickname Cast Iron. Monica told him of a woman she'd met, who, upon learning her name, had stared at her and said, "My dear, you have something on the corner of your mouth," causing Monica to wipe at it, to the laughter of the others, until she realized the woman's joke. Then there was the woman in Louisiana at a Wal-Mart who had said loudly to Monica, "Oh, tell me, is it true that Bill Clinton has distinguishing marks on his penis?" To which she'd been constrained to reply, "Examining Bill Clinton's penis was not in my job description."

"He never even flirted with you?" Cast asked.

"He flirted with everyone, but that was all: just talk. Down home in Louisiana, they all assume I must have slept with him, but I never did."

Cast and Monica took turns driving. The Nissan practically drove itself, as if on autopilot. One time when she was driving, Cast reached into the back and uncovered his guitar case from the stack of campaign materials, opened it, took out an expensive guitar, tuned it, and then asked, "Any requests? Classical? Popular? Rock?"

"Do you know any country and western?" she asked.

"Sure." He began to play Willie Nelson's "On the Road Again" and sang it in a remarkable imitation of Willie's voice. She wanted to scream. It was one of her favorite songs and it melted her heart and she decided she might be falling in love with Castor Sherrill. At her request he also sang "Georgia on My Mind," "I've Seen Better Days," and a lot of others. From then on, she would have preferred doing all the driving herself, just so he could play.

They did Arkansas Tech, Hendrix College, University of Central Arkansas, and her own UALR in the first two days, at each campus setting up a booth, finding volunteers from student organizations to maintain it, passing out the beautiful yellow-and-purple INGLE WHO? T-shirts along with the FAQ manual to the more enthusiastic students, passing out the paper sacks of goodies to anybody who wanted one, and, everywhere they went, getting and keeping lists of names, addresses, phone numbers, e-mail addresses, and dates and times available for such work as database entry, giving talks to their classes, phoning their friends, organizing rallies. The goal was to have each student contacted provided with a sheet to recruit a minimum of ten more fellow students.

She never saw Cast sitting or standing still. He was a whirling dervish, which his campaign T-shirt accentuated, and he almost put her to shame, but she did more than her job; she gave those college kids a crash course in just who Vernon Ingledew was and why they would have better futures if they got out and campaigned for him. On some campuses it was tough sledding, and they lost valuable time just trying to find enough students to put together the simplest organization. On some campuses, their request to speak to political science classes was refused, or else the college didn't even have courses in poli sci. There was one college where they couldn't find anybody to be a volunteer coordinator to manage the assignments and contact lists for the other volunteers, so they had to hire one. Everywhere they went they offered summer jobs to the more enthusiastic and personable of the campus leaders: they looked for kids who were as kind, considerate, and hardworking as themselves.

They had no spare time. They stayed in the best motels (the idea of saving money by sharing a room never actually crossed their minds, or it certainly didn't cross Monica's), but every night before putting out the lights they were on the telephone or their computers making calls and e-mails to local students. If Monica had a free minute on any campus, she tried to visit the art department—the painty smell of these rooms was in her blood and she could sniff them out without needing directions (she suffered homesickness not so much for Louisiana as for her own studio she'd had to abandon to take this job)—where she would get into conversations with teachers and students about the connections of artists to politicians, whether kings, queens, Egyptian rulers, state or local governments, whatever. Winston S. Churchill was a painter, right? So was Eisenhower. Vernon Ingledew was an expert in art history; they could go over to their library and look up his article in *Art Bulletin.* At every art department she visited, she left behind the message that Vernon Ingledew was the first person in Arkansas politics to be passionate about art.

They had their share of unpleasant experiences: the wise-ass punks who challenged their right to be alive, the hecklers, the rude creeps who eagerly gathered up the campaign literature and made a big show of dumping it in the trash can. On every campus there are always certain students who can only establish their identities by being arrogant, contentious, contemptuous, and generally vile. Monica had to restrain Cast from throttling one of the worst; she had the notion that the kid, a twenty-year-old jock, might actually have been badly injured if she hadn't held Cast back.

He brooded for a couple of days afterwards, and she couldn't get him to play his guitar. She wasn't sure how much he was troubled by that particular incident and how much by the plain fact that most college students simply didn't care who Vernon Ingledew was and weren't at all interested in finding out. She tried to reassure Cast by pointing out that all they were really doing was establishing a base on each campus, and that once Vernon became better and better known throughout the state, those bases would be in place and could unfold.

As if to compensate for the bad encounters (and Monica strongly believed that Destiny likes to keep things in balance), they had a wonderful experience at the last school on their schedule, little Lyon College in Batesville. They were met by a delegation of seven students who had already learned about Ingledew from reading the column in the *Arkansas Democrat-Gazette* and who were united in their opposition to their school's political science teacher, an arch-conservative who, they said, would oppose anything that Vernon Ingledew might stand for just on principle. More to flaunt him than in genuine support of Ingledew, this group of students set up at once an Ingledew-for-Governor headquarters in the student union. Each of the seven began wearing the Ingledew T-shirt right away; they called themselves the Little Samurai and were bright, eager, polite, and happy: the best kids Monica had found yet. They plastered Vernon's picture all over the campus, and Monica and Cast were able to leave town early enough to start the long drive back to Fayetteville.

Partly out of relief that their tour was over, the Nissan emptied of its campaign contents, and they both could look forward to a day or two of R and R, they really relaxed and became convivial on that return drive. Monica told some of her favorite jokes, and Cast played some tunes on his guitar with hilarious showing off. They even stopped to treat themselves to a fancy supper at Otis Zark, a quirky restaurant way out in the sticks of Durham, along the Pig Trail home. Most of their meals throughout the tour had been quick, usually just fast food. Here they relaxed and did some fancy eating. Afterwards, on what little remained of the drive to Fayetteville, they were old friends, co-conspirators, and even a little bit sweethearts: Monica told Cast things she wouldn't have told anyone else. In reciprocation he confessed to her that while he had a few dates at Harvard and a few more in Cincinnati, he had never gone to bed with any of them.

Monica was both touched and incredulous. "Do you mean you're a virgin?" she asked.

"I guess that's what you'd have to call me," he said.

Oh, she could have stopped the car right there and done something about that. But they still had some miles to go before they slept.

Whiskey and Buster were so glad to see her you'd think she'd been gone a month. Bo Pharis debriefed Monica and Cast the next morning on their tour and was very pleased with their report and with the databases of student names they brought back with them. "I've been observing the local campus," he said, "and if what you established there is any indication of your work, you've had a most fruitful trip." Indeed, the flagship campus of the university system had a full-blown Ingledew organization in place and was actively recruiting. The T-shirts had become prized and were proliferating all over the place. The *Arkansas Traveler*, a student newspaper, had run a feature story on Vernon, and there was a request that he personally visit a political science class.

Monica was appointed to take Vernon to the class. It met at eight-thirty in the morning, and when she phoned his hotel to inform him of the hour he suggested that they first have breakfast together at the student union. She was thrilled, although she couldn't imagine how he would be able to overcome his woman-shyness to the point of sitting across the table from her. Instead of wearing her customary black, she wore a campaign T-shirt. When Vernon appeared at the food court of the union, she was tickled to see that he was wearing the T-shirt too! It was really funny: There was this picture of his face on his chest, with his real face right above it. If the real face couldn't look at her, she'd just make eye contact with the printed one! And of course they got lots of attention, and even a few people came up while they were eating breakfast and asked for Vernon's autograph or, trying to be funny, said, "Ingle who?" to which the candidate always laughed and said, "A couple more weeks and you won't have to ask that."

While he looked not at her but at his plate, she told him of the tour she and Cast had made, and which colleges she thought would be strongest, the colleges where he ought to give speeches. Speaking of speeches, he managed to impart to her, without a glance in her direction, that he had just returned from a few days in Washington, where he had gone to spend some time with a speech coach that Carlton Drew had recommended. He had taken with him a videotape of the disliked announcement speech; he had also been videotaped making a set speech, which was played back to him repeatedly with analysis of his weak phrasing, mannerisms, poor posture, lack of gesticulation, and so on. It had been an embarrassing experience but he had learned quite a lot, and it was well worth the expense. Jelena had gone with him, to see the sights of the capital.

"And I've been working on my timidity toward the opposite sex," he declared, but he still wasn't looking at her when he said it.

Now, this morning in the political science class, he was going to be delivering his first speech *since* having been taught a few things about his flaws as a speaker, and, he told Monica, he wanted her to monitor him closely and keep notes in her notebook. She told him she'd already arranged to have the session videotaped for possible use by the television stations, and she of course had her cassette tape recorder with her and would sit in the front row.

"Splendid," Vernon said, to his cup of coffee. "You're being a great help to me, Monica, and I really appreciate it. I don't know how I could get along without you. Besides that, you're simply a very good person, and I like you very much, and if there was any woman I could feel unnervous toward it would probably be you."

Monica had to brush away a tear on her cheek and hoped it hadn't messed up her mascara. "Thank you," she said quietly. "And I just want you to know this: I have worked for many politicians. Every last one of them was arrogant. But you're not."

Vernon smiled broadly and straightened his shoulders and said to the tabletop, "Let's go bulldoze those students."

They walked across the campus to Old Main, Vernon waving and smiling to students and stopping to shake hands or say hello. In between these greetings he told Monica he wanted her to do a little favor for him. He wanted her to record in her notebook any word he used that she'd never heard before. Also any expression. He laughed and said, "I'll pay you a hundred dollars for every word you write down that you haven't heard before, and I'll pay you two hundred dollars for any expression I use you haven't heard before." She said she'd be glad to do it, but he didn't have to pay her. It was just part of her job.

As it turned out, she wouldn't have made any money on that deal anyway. After the introduction by the professor, who simply read most of the details of the official bio Lydia had written about him, Vernon strode to the lectern so briskly he overshot it and had to back up. Then he looked out over the room—there were only about thirty students—and said, "My fellow Americans." He said it movingly, clearly, with feeling. Then he said, "Unaccustomed as I am to public speaking, in this day and age when all is said and done, but good things come to those who wait for the best-laid plans of mice and men to rush in where angels fear to tread, it is indeed a glorious and undeserved privilege for me to address such a sea of bright and shining faces. It is my considered opinion that the state of the nation and the state of the state leave much to be desired, that this tide in the affairs of men, this heat in the kitchen that men cannot take and stay out of, this position between a rock and a hard place, this can of worms that has upset the applecart—"

The professor himself, Monica noticed, had begun cackling, and his students were staring at their teacher as if wondering if he was being rude to the guest, but then they started chuckling, cackling, snickering, snorting, and guffawing too. Monica was uneasy. Vernon was speaking beautifully, such a fantastic improvement on his announcement speech, but his words seemed to be provoking an inappropriate amount of amusement.

"For want of a nail the shoe was lost, and we are waiting for the other shoe to drop. It's on the other foot now. If it fits, wear it. My friends, I am here to tell you that there is simply no use flogging a dead horse of a different color that you led to water but couldn't make drink and tried to put the cart before him. Where was I?"

Monica suddenly realized, as the roar of laughter swelled, that Vernon was trying to be silly. He had offered her two hundred dollars for any expression she hadn't heard before, but she had heard all of these expressions so often they were stupid.

"The issues of this campaign are substantive and cannot be avoided. One of life's little ironies, which I have on unimpeachable authority, is that the rich get richer and poor get poorer, and it is time to pay the piper! My opponents claim that what goes around comes around, but I beg to differ. That dog won't hunt. He who hesitates is lost. The finger of destiny has pointed itself at me and said, 'Take the bull by the horns!' Life is what you make it. Am I right or am I right? Far be it from me to put all my eggs in one basket, because, my friends, you have to break a few eggs to make an omelet! Thank you. I can't even begin to tell you what a pleasure it's been. It has been a pleasure."

They gave him a standing ovation, so Monica stood up and clapped and laughed too. She was a little worried, though. When the laughter died down, Vernon stopped being oratorical and said in a matter-of-fact voice, "I am establishing in this political science department a special award of merit for mental alertness, and the first winner of that award will be the student in this class who can tell me anything I said worth hearing. Anyone?"

After another uproar of laughter, a student raised his hand and said, "Well, that part about paying the piper wasn't so bad! But where do we find the piper?"

That brought another swell of laughter. The professor stepped to the lectern. "I think Mr. Ingledew has made an admirable demonstration of the vacuity of most political rhetoric. But perhaps he would now be willing to answer our questions about his life and work and beliefs. Let's hear those."

A girl said, "Mr. Ingledew, you never went to college yourself. Do you belief that college is useless, or did you just not get a chance to go?"

"No," Vernon said, avoiding her gaze. "College is a kind of Arcadian paradise where everyone—faculty and students alike—can retreat from the mundane realities of life long enough to explore the vast body of wisdom governing the smooth functioning of those realities. I was simply too far away from a college campus and too busy earning a living."

"You're not opposed to colleges?" a boy challenged him.

"I don't honestly believe you can *learn* anything in college that you couldn't learn better by yourself."

"So you consider yourself smart?" another boy asked.

"*Smart* sounds like a handicap if you say it like that," Vernon said. "And don't confuse intelligence with knowledge. There are unfortunately a lot of smart politicians who don't know anything. And a lot of really good politicians who aren't particularly smart."

"But you're both, right?" the boy said, and Monica made a note to get his name after class and try to recruit him. "You're smart *and* you know it all."

"Thank you," Vernon said, as if the kid had complimented him, not insulted him. "But as you've discovered every day you're in college, the more you know, the more you know you do not know. Knowledge is a lifelong process, and I've still got forty years to go, I hope."

"You claim to know so much," the same boy said. "But how do we know you know *anything*?"

Vernon smiled. "Why don't you test me? Ask me something."

The guy looked around at some of his fellow students as if for their help in furnishing questions. He apparently couldn't think of a good one offhand himself. But then he opened the textbook on his desk, letting it fall open at random, and said, "What's the difference between Hobbes and Locke?"

Vernon summarized the contrasts between the philosophies of the two thinkers, making the explanation so clear that the professor complimented him.

The student flipped to another page. "What is the purpose of the behaviorist conception of political science?"

Vernon not only outlined the goals of behaviorism but contrasted them to Greek and nineteenth-century conceptions.

"Shit," the student said. "You just got ahold of our textbook and memorized it."

"What is your textbook?" Vernon asked.

The professor showed Vernon a copy. "Looks like a good book," Vernon said, "but it's not in my library. Why don't you ask me something else?"

"Any subject?" a student asked.

"Any subject from A through P," Vernon said. "That's as far as I've got in my autodidacticism." He meant it as a witty observation and it drew much laughter. And then a student asked him to explain Laplace transform. Another student asked, "Who was the better painter, Rubens or Caravaggio?" And a third student asked him to define and give examples of "gunboat diplomacy." For the rest of the class period they asked Vernon Ingledew questions and he answered them all.

"A most impressive performance," commented the professor when it was all over. And added, "I think you've got my vote."

So Monica decided—her best idea yet—to start a radio call-in program. It would be called *Ask Me Anything*, Vernon would do it for an hour twice a week, and it would be on several different radio stations all over the state.

She didn't know whether it was that or the tour she and Cast had made to campuses or what, but the next poll gave Vernon 8 percent, almost ten times his ranking in the first poll! But Cast reminded her that she had bet him a week's salary that Vernon would reach 10 percent in the next poll, and he hadn't quite made it. Monica cheerfully paid up, even though she couldn't afford it.

Chapter Nine

At this point in the campaign he still felt pretty good about his new job. He got up every morning eager to get to work, and he no longer had to don his khaki work shirt, which all Tyson executives wore out of some kind of solidarity with the blue-collar (or, rather, khaki-collar) workers. What he was doing on behalf of the state of Arkansas in general and Vernon Ingledew in particular filled Arch with a greater sense of accomplishment than what he'd been doing at Tyson. One of the reasons he decided to take leave from Tyson was the frustration he had been putting up with for ten years, trying to convince the public and elected officials across the country that Tyson was a good corporate citizen, paid its people a fair and competitive wage, provided a safe workplace, was environmentally responsible, and concerned about food safety. This was not easy; the prevailing attitude about Tyson in the media was that like all big corporations they were interested in nothing but the bottom line. And he still bore understandable resentment over Donald Smaltz's federal case against him that got him a prison sentence for an innocent act—although President Clinton in his last days had pardoned him, and he'd never had to spend a day in jail.

Of course Bo had had some of the same frustration, which may have been part of his reason for taking leave, but his company after all was one of the top American corporations while Arch's was just a local chicken company, so to speak—even if it was the world's largest poultry processor. But apart from that difference in the relative size of the companies they left behind them, Bo Pharis and Arch were remarkably alike, even in their appearance, and more than once they got mistaken for each other. Hank Endicott in his column took to referring to them as the Smith Brothers, because of their beards. But Bo still kept his linebacker's body in trim. Arch had been a tackle at Charleston High, and if you know anything about the difference between linebackers and tackles you can imagine how his lower body weight had gotten a bit out of hand. He may as well confess something Bo himself never knew, or if he did he kept his knowledge of it a secret from Arch: In the Class AA football playoffs of 1965, Arch's Charleston High Tigers played Bo's Harrison High Goblins, where Bo was the star of the defense. Arch's job was to take him out, to knock him flat on his back. Arch did. Bo didn't know who Arch was then. But in the heat of the campaign Arch could always remind himself that if Bo needed to be taken out, Arch was the man for the job.

If Bo was correct in his search for a *Don Quixote* allusion, Arch was his Sancho Panza. But Arch liked to subscribe to the *Seven Samurai* allusion, as everybody else did, in which case, if Bo was Kambei, the leader, Arch was not necessarily Shichiroji, his adjutant, but rather Kyuzo, the all-purpose deadly swordsman. Kyuzo was quiet and kept to himself and never ran out of energy. He never lost a duel. At every turn he could be counted on to do his job. He worked best under pressure. He was always ready. That was Arch.

Without boasting, Arch recognized in himself certain qualities that set him apart from Bo Pharis. Sure, they had their similarities, which were endless, apart from their appearance. For example, they discussed art together, although Bo knew much more about nineteenth-century art than Arch did; they played golf together, although Bo's handicap at Stonebridge Meadows, the new public (Democratic) course in Fayetteville, was seven, whereas Arch's was eighteen at best; they fly-fished together on Kings River and Crooked Creek, but Bo always caught twice as many as Arch did (Arch didn't wish to give the impression that they sneaked off from the campaign constantly to go fishing or golfing or chatting up modern art, but they did allow themselves an occasional break from the stress of their jobs, and they deferred until after the election even the thought of fishing for king salmon on the Kenai River in Alaska or deep-sea fishing off the Baja Peninsula at Cabo San Lucas).

But Bo, like managers of any sort—boxers' managers, writers' managers, actors' managers—could be tough, abrasive, even mean. Arch had always tried to be nice to people. He was easy to get along with. Bo could make enemies right and left without compunction; Arch couldn't tell you the name of any enemy he'd ever made . . . except possibly his first wife, and even she, he believed, had good feelings about him overall. He had a talent for making friends, and the state of Arkansas was densely populated with his lasting go-way-backers. There was even a time, in the seventies, when Witt Stephens, the super-rich kingmaker of Arkansas politics, tried repeatedly to persuade Arch to run for governor himself. His father, Archie II, always told Witt, "Spike would have to have an ego transplant even to consider such a thing." (The nickname *Spike* was bestowed upon him in infancy by a relative and he never could outgrow it; by the way, *Arch* was his real familiar name, *Archie* his actual birth-certificate name, the same as his father and his great-uncle. The distinction confused a lot of people who thought they were being chummy when they called him Archie.) Like Monica, Arch never met a politician who didn't have a huge ego . . . until he met Vernon Ingledew, and while Vernon might have had *ambition*, a quality Arch was lacking in as well as ego, Vernon did not think he was God's gift to mankind nor—since like all the Ingledews he didn't believe in God—did he think he was put on this earth for the purpose of attracting universal love for his personality and accomplishments. If Arch had had a smidgen of Vernon's looks he would probably have had to have an ego to go with it, but he was convinced Vernon didn't even have an idea of how good-looking he was. Arch never once saw Vernon glance in a mirror.

One reason Vernon could pull off that little speech he gave to the political science class at the university was that he was not only poking fun at politicians but poking fun at himself. You had to realize that to know how funny it was; otherwise it just seemed silly. The professor of that class requested a copy of the videotape, from which he had several copies made and sent to colleagues who taught political science at other Arkansas campuses, with the result that Vernon was invited to speak at a number of campuses just before the semester was over, and to speak not only to political science classes of thirty or sixty students but to the entire campus. This helped energize the good work that Monica and Cast had already started and was one reason that so many hundreds of college students devoted themselves to the campaign in the crucial last weeks before the primary election.

It was also the beginning of what would become an essential component of Vernon's campaign: a return to stump speaking. Arch's uncle Dale Bumpers, the last of the great old-time stump speakers and recently cited by a poll of historians as Arkansas's best governor of the twentieth century, was not just a great orator but a firm believer in contact with the people, and as his chauffeur Arch had taken him to hundreds of rallies in little Arkansas towns. Arch knew that George Dinsmore intended to be Vernon's chauffeur, but when Arch learned that George, a sensible and engaging old hillbilly, had been a helicopter pilot in Vietnam and still possessed a pilot's license he hadn't had any reason to use for twenty-five years, Arch suggested, and Bo agreed, that they ought to lease a helicopter—even if it meant going to Tulsa to get a good deal—in order to get Vernon to all those campuses and, subsequently, all those little Arkansas towns. In time, the only difference between old-time stump speaking and what Vernon did was that the candidate did not arrive on a dusty winding road but out of the sky.

Vernon's candidacy became noticeable and targetable to the other candidates. Endicott's original column had scared three of them into quitting, but the others didn't really start worrying about Vernon until he jumped from 1 percent to 8 percent in the polls. Bo and Arch hired their own pollster, whose numbers were actually higher (and more accurate) than that. The other primary candidates began looking for ways to keep Vernon from getting anymore attention, and their oppo men started sniffing around Stay More in such numbers that George Dinsmore had to run them off.

The good thing about Vernon, despite those thirteen deadly albatrosses, any one of which would have killed his candidacy if it became widely publicized, was that he left no paper trail whatever: there were no documents or public or private records or anything at all on the Internet that could be used against him. Nevertheless, the other five candidates became thoroughly aware that Vernon had lived out of wedlock for thirty years with his first cousin, had no children, was an atheist, and had no experience in elective office. So it became Arch's pleasant chore to call their campaign managers, each of them old friends of Arch's, and politely inform them that the Ingledew campaign's Director of Opposition Research, Mr. Harry Wolfe, had obtained sufficient information on each and every one of them (with one exception, to be discussed below) to thoroughly discredit, defame, and destroy each of them "if the need arose." That need would not arise, Arch politely warned them, if they did their utmost to refrain from making any personal attacks on Vernon Ingledew.

These guys, who knew Arch and knew he played fair, cursed him aloud, making some really offensive insults, and if they did not do that, he could hear them over the phone gnashing their teeth and snarling in frustration. He even felt sorry for them.

This tactic didn't faze Secretary of State Leon McCutcheon, who either didn't believe Arch or else wasn't afraid of anything. In his television spots he began to refer to Vernon as "Mr. Know-It-All" because of Vernon's new radio call-in show, *Ask Me Anything*. The spot showed a not-very-bright farmer calling in to the radio show, who says, "I got a question for you, Ingledew. What makes you think that a egghead smarty pants is qualified to be governor?" And the spot ended with a smooth announcer declaring, "Leon McCutcheon may not know everything, but he knows how to govern!" Arch thought the spot was innocuous enough but Bo felt otherwise, and it was soon leaked to the press that Leon McCutcheon's wife was in the process of filing for divorce, the grounds for which would be announced at a later date. McCutcheon shut up. He killed those spots and had nothing else to say about Vernon.

Indeed, all the other candidates concentrated so fiendishly on attacking one another from top to bottom, without any further mention of Vernon, that the electorate (surely the *intelligent* electorate) must have begun to get a little suspicious. Here were these five guys slinging mud all over the place, and not a fleck of it hit Vernon. Was he a saint? Or, since he was so fabulously rich, had he bought the silence of his opponents? The Reverend John Colby Dixon, a popular television evangelist who had used his pulpit on statewide TV for the past year to drum up votes for himself, and whose campaign manager was the only one Arch hadn't fully intimidated—because all Harry Wolfe had been able to find on him was the allegation, never taken to court, that he had seduced a sixteen-year-old member of his choir (Cast had found a newspaper item about that very early on, but the news hadn't diminished the size of the evangelist's audience or voters)—made bold to denounce Vernon from the pulpit, not for his atheism, strangely enough, but for the fact that he was "nothing but a pig farmer, an ex-hippie Ozark hillbilly living in the weirdest mansion you ever saw."

George Dinsmore had his hands full trying to keep photographers and television crews off the mountain trail to the Ingledew double-bubble. Erecting a locked gate on it wasn't enough; photographers can climb fences. George had to delegate a posse of Ingledew factory workers to keep around-the-clock guard. Fortunately, the majority of snoops hunting for Stay More couldn't even find the town, let alone the trail to the Ingledew homestead. At any rate, no image of that double-bubble ever appeared in the media; the only public image of it remains the smudged and obscure final illustration in *The Architecture of the Arkansas Ozarks*.

Bo told Harry Wolfe, since he had nothing better to do, to devote his full energies to the Reverend John Colby Dixon and to find, at all costs, that alleged sixteen-year-old seductee and offer her whatever price necessary for her full confession. Harry did succeed in locating the girl's mother, who lived alone in Beebe. She informed him that the girl, now twenty and twice divorced, was living in "Boston or Seattle or one of those places" but had no mailing address, phone number, or other means of contact. "Did she have an affair with Reverend Dixon?" Harry asked the mother. "Oh, no question about that," the woman said.

But without details or proof or a confession or anything, and nothing else in Harry's meager file on Dixon (Garth Rucker had devoted a fruitless week to the task), there was no leverage to dissuade the evangelist from his weekly attacks on Vernon—or, rather, his disparagement of Vernon as a "mere" hippie pig farmer.

Bo and Lydia and Arch wondered why the evangelist never brought up the matter of Vernon's atheism. "Maybe he's saving it," Lydia suggested. After McCutcheon began to fade, Reverend Dixon rose until he was right behind Barnas in the polls.

Fourth place was the highest Vernon could hope for. The Samurai did their damnedest, each of them, but they just couldn't claw their way up those stingy polls. Vernon couldn't lift himself by his bootstraps. In his own eagerness to improve his rating he was inclined to forget some of the lessons they'd tried to teach him about keeping a lid on his radical ideas for what he was going to "extirpate." They didn't mind too much when he proposed broad and revolutionary solutions to the "highway problem," meaning not simply improving the condition of the highways, which all the other candidates were loud about, but totally eliminating litter by stepped-up patrols that would catch litterers and force them into on-the-spot cleanups: One large bag of collected litter would be the fine for having tossed an item.

What the Ingledew campaign really needed was not anymore radical ideas but a media event. Arch knew very well that politics itself rarely makes news; the newspapers don't give space to politicians' attacks on each other, or the manipulations of the campaign, or even the fluctuations of the polls. For a candidate to get noticed in the media, he or she has to be involved in something newsworthy. Every candidate knew this. When, for example, in late April a horrible tornado hit the town of Barling in western Arkansas with so much destruction and death, all six of the primary candidates, plus Governor Shoat Bradfield himself, were on the scene before the wind died down. Shoat Bradfield got himself on television with a speech that promised relief and personally absolved God from any responsibility for the disaster. Five of the Democratic candidates rolled up their sleeves and tried to get themselves photographed clearing away the debris or serving food to the victims, but they were lost in the crowd. Vernon encountered a television cameraman who was curious to know if he and George had had any turbulence bringing that helicopter into Barling, and Vernon took the occasion to give a speech in which he actually promised, if elected governor of Arkansas, to eliminate tornadoes!

Bo was fit to be tied. "Don Quixote has found his windmills!" he raged. As soon as they got Vernon and George back in Fayetteville, Bo called a meeting and, since Bo was out of control, Arch took over and politely said to Vernon that he thought it would be a really fantastic achievement if Vernon eliminated tornadoes. It would hugely benefit not just the state of Arkansas but also Oklahoma, Kansas, and Texas, all the tornado-alley states. But just how, for God's sake, did he plan to do it? Without batting an eye, Vernon launched into this complicated meteorological explanation of just how tornadoes could be—he didn't use this word, but Arch couldn't help thinking it—*extirpated*, that is, each tornado can be thought of as having a root at the base of its funnel, and that root, while the most powerfully destructive part of the tornado, is the most vulnerable and can be "tripped" and broken. But just what means would be used to trip and break the root was something that Vernon would discuss only after he was elected.

They had their media event, all right. The television commentators and all the newspapers, while they devoted the top of the news to accounts of the actual destruction and mounting death toll and the relief efforts, with just brief mention of Governor Bradfield's appearance and no mention at all of the other five candidates, made side-of-the-news references, implicitly derisive, to, as the *Southwest Times Record* of Fort Smith put it, "the campaign promise to end all campaign promises: elect Vernon Ingledew and he'll stop tornadoes!" The next day, the

Arkansas Democrat-Gazette's editorial cartoonist John Deering had a lulu depicting Vernon in the stance of Charlton Heston as Moses parting the sea, lifting his arms to split a tornado. It wasn't even a good caricature of Vernon, and because he still lacked wide recognition, he had to be identified by a banner that said INGELDEW [sic].

Although the other five candidates were loath to paint Vernon's promise as sheer folly, out of fear of retribution from the files of Harry Wolfe, the media itself had a high old time with the matter, and Hank Endicott wrote a witty, satirical, slightly vicious column in which he suggested that the real opponents in this matter were Vernon Ingledew and God, and that God ought to be put on notice that if He tried to throw a tornado after Vernon became governor, He had better expect to have to file a Tornado Permit at least forty-eight hours before attempting to unleash His twister. "Tornado control is above politics," Endicott concluded. "But Ingledew appears to have lost the Almighty's vote, even if he hadn't already lost it because of his refusal to believe in Him." That was the first clear public allusion to Vernon's atheism, and while a number of preachers lacking subjects for their Sunday sermons picked up on the matter and began to question the candidacy of a man who not only defied God by planning to stop His tornadoes but also didn't believe in Him in the first place, the other candidates did not broach the subject . . . except, as we shall see, the Reverend John Colby Dixon.

The tornado fiasco wasn't the straw that broke Bo's back, but it didn't help. Arch turned on his computer one morning to find this e-mail:

> Arch—the university has just informed me that they have decided to "postpone indefinitely" the awarding of an honorary degree to me at commencement. Only reason? "Certain members of the Board of Trustees feel that

partisan politics should not intrude upon academia." Well, fuck 'em! I thought the goddamn thing was for my past achievements, not what I'm doing lately. I'm sick about this, and I'm taking off. Catch you later.—Bo.

The first thing Arch did was try to find Cast, to see if he knew anything about his mentor's whereabouts. Monica didn't know where Cast was. Arch thought of protesting the board's decision to John White, the chancellor of the university, but he and Arch weren't the best of friends, not since Tyson, Arch's company, had countermanded White's decision to close the University of Arkansas Press by offering a gift of a million to keep it in business. So Arch went over him and called Frank Oldham, chairman of the Board of Trustees, who owed Arch, and Arch gave him an earful—politely, of course. Oldham consented to give Arch the names of the three members of the board who had been responsible for the decision to rescind Bo's honorary degree. Not all three of them owed Arch, just a couple, but Arch gave them all an earful, even dropping the politeness during several minutes, and Arch wound up getting their agreement to "strongly reconsider" their asshole stupidity.

But Arch couldn't find Bo to give him the good news that he'd probably get his degree after all, even if Arch had to hood him himself. In the wee hours of one morning Lydia called Arch, waking him, and said, "You're boss now, you know." Arch answered that he wasn't so sure but he was "acting campaign manager" for the nonce. Well, she said, she'd just got a feed from a radio station manager with a possible media event looming behind it. In Morrilton a small grocery store called Sam and LaTonya's, operated by blacks in a mixed neighborhood, was bombed earlier in the middle of the night. This very same night, meaning earlier this morning, and fifty miles west across the river in Danville, La Comida, a *tienda de comestibles* or Hispanic grocery store, was similarly bombed. Lydia thought they ought to get Vernon to both places as fast as George's helicopter could take him. So Arch phoned Vernon in Stay More about 5 A.M., told him Arch was subbing for Bo, gave him the details, and jokingly asked him to refrain from proposing the extirpation of bombs.

George and Vernon got in that helicopter and George whisked his boss down to Morrilton, arriving simultaneously with the first television trucks out of Little Rock. After making a forceful and dramatic speech to the several dozen blacks assembled there, expressing his outrage at whoever planted the bomb, Vernon was televised standing between Sam and his wife LaTonya with his arms around them. "We'll find who did it," he told them, "and this will never happen again in the state of Arkansas. Not after I'm elected governor."

Then, after they'd milked the situation for all it was worth, Vernon and George disappeared, reboarded the helicopter, which George had parked out of sight, and flew quickly to Danville, where the entire Latino population of the town, about three hundred people, was congregating in front of La Comida and the television cameras from Fort Smith. Vernon addressed them in Spanish, deploring this senseless violence and inviting their solidarity with their black brethren across the river, who had suffered an identical bombing. He told them in Spanish that when he became governor of Arkansas he would *extirpar* whatever root causes of such racism or bigotry had caused this. He told them that he hoped this incident would not diminish their pride in being Arkansawyers. He knew why they had come to Arkansas in the first place from Mexico and El Salvador: *Trabajo, tranquilidad, familia.* Work, small-town tranquillity, family. He would guarantee they could enjoy those things forevermore.

They cheered Vernon wildly and yelled, "*Gobernador! Gobernador* Ingledew!" The television stations broadcast the performance to the entire Hispanic population of Arkansas, particularly in the northwest counties, where it was strongest, thanks in no small measure to the fact that Arch's Tyson Foods had been hiring these workers in droves. The other five contenders for the gubernatorial primary could only mouth the customary pap of indignation; they had been caught flatfooted and were ignored by the media.

Vernon's appearances at Morrilton and Danville were all over the next day's papers as well as on television and radio. The three or four Spanish-language newspapers published in the state really made a big deal out of it, making it look as if Vernon Ingledew were the only friend Latinos had among the Anglo population. The Ingledew campaign couldn't possibly have bought such good publicity. Vernon practically sealed the Hispanic vote, as well as a large part of the black vote, with that single morning's work.

Never mind that sharp FBI agents sent in to examine the bombings discovered that there had been no forced entry or other way of getting the bombs inside the stores, and this led them to the eventual discovery and analysis, weeks later, that the "bombs" had actually been defective or malformed cans of food that had exploded on the shelves in the stores. It was too late to reverse the image of Vernon as a leader of the oppressed. And a lot of non-Hispanic white people began to notice and admire him because of his championing of the downtrodden and his forceful opposition to prejudice and injustice. Arch's pollster told him he had nothing to worry about. The next public poll gave Vernon an astounding 20 percent, again more than doubling the previous figure. More incredibly, some of the media began to editorialize that Vernon just might be capable of abolishing tornadoes.

One more candidate dropped out of the race, leaving only five, and Vernon was clearly in third place, even if a distant third behind Barnas and the Reverend Dixon. Surely, wherever he was, Bolin Pharis was apprised of this. Arch kept up his efforts to locate him, even calling his Cincinnati house several times. Finally, Monica reported to Arch that Cast had returned to work—or, rather, he had never left work but had been busy helping Carleton Drew plan an advertising campaign that would get around Vernon's proscription of television by extensive use not only of newspaper ads and radio but also the Internet. Since Vernon would not allow yard signs, Cast had coaxed Carleton into the idea of using a blimp: they were going to hire a large dirigible, paint its sides with INGLEDEW FOR GOVERNOR in huge letters, and pilot it constantly all over the state. "Great idea, Cast!" Arch complimented him. And then Arch asked politely, "I don't suppose you have any idea where Bo might be?"

"Yes, but I'm not supposed to tell," Cast replied.

"In his absence, I'm your boss," Arch reminded him.

"Yeah, I guess you are."

"Then I'm ordering you to tell me where he is."

After further persuasion of that nature, Cast finally relented. Some time ago Bo had gone "back to the sticks": he was spending a lot of time sitting on the whittler's bench at the Harrison courthouse square; he was walking, not driving, along the back roads of the Ozarks; he was even, supposedly, hanging out a lot around Stay More. Arch decided to see if he could find him.

But first there was one other big boost Arch needed to give Vernon in the polls, possibly even to propel him into second place. And it happened mostly by accident.

Arch's uncle, Dale Bumpers, was in Fayetteville leading a seminar at the university (the entire College of Agriculture had been named after him). Dale asked Arch to meet him for lunch, and they met at Herman's, a real institution so popular it doesn't even have any signs identifying it in its run-down stucco roadhouse along busy 71. Herman's serves the best steaks in northwest Arkansas, and that was what they ordered. It had been a long time since Arch had eaten with Uncle Dale, and it brought back memories of the hundreds of meals they'd taken together when Arch was his campaign manager in the seventies.

Arch's mother and Bumpers's wife were sisters, and Bumpers had just been talking to Arch's mother in Charleston. "Spike, what in the hell are you doing back in politics?" he wanted to know.

"I guess the political junkie in me needed a fix," Arch said.

"The last time we talked about this, you were a total cynic about politics. You were even asking me to help you talk some friends out of running for office. Do you remember you practically insulted me, calling politicians 'nasty, partisan, self-serving killjoys'?"

"There was a time, Uncle Dale, when I lost all respect for politicians. But never for *you.*"

"So tell me about this nasty, partisan, self-serving killjoy who has lured you away from a respectable job at Tyson's."

Arch told him as much as he could about Vernon. Arch even attempted to describe Vernon's appearance. He told him some of Vernon's more radical ideas, as well as his really commonsense ideas for leading Arkansas into the twenty-first century. Arch spelled out a few, but not all thirteen, of Vernon's albatrosses. And when he was all finished depicting Vernon, he asked Arkansas's greatest modern governor, "Does he remind you of anybody?"

At first Dale Bumpers looked puzzled, as if Arch were making up a riddle. Then he grinned, mildly. "So you're just trying to recapture your lost youth by reliving or re-creating those good old days."

"I hadn't thought of that," Arch said. "But Beverly's been telling me I look a lot younger. Do you think?"

"Come to think of it, you do. But I just figured you'd dyed your hair." He dabbed at his mouth with his napkin. "Well, I certainly wish you and your Ingledew the best of luck."

"You can do more than that, Uncle Dale. You can give him your endorsement."

"God's sake, Spike! You know I never endorse candidates in the primary. If he survives the primary I'll certainly endorse him in the general election. Anybody to beat that shithead Shoat."

"He needs your endorsement *now*," Arch told him. Arch sketched out the current situation: Senator James Barnas firmly entrenched in first place, the Reverend John Colby Dixon nipping at his heels, Vernon Ingledew bringing up a distant third but crowding out the remaining candidates. "All those guys, even the preacher, are career politicians, or has-beens, or never-will-bes. Vernon's the only answer."

"Sorry, Spike. If I endorsed your man, I'd hurt the feelings of all the candidates I've declined for years to endorse simply because I wouldn't get involved in primary elections."

Arch sighed. He had the greatest admiration for his uncle, who was his family. When Arch's father had died several years before, Dale Bumpers had delivered the eulogy, as fine a speech as Arch had ever heard him make. Like Dale, like Vernon, Arch's father had been an independent thinker, an idiosyncratic visionary, almost a pariah at times. "Throughout history the great men and women who left a great and enduring legacy," Dale Bumpers said at the memorial service, "never hesitated to stand alone, to swim against the tide."

From memory Arch now quoted these words back to his uncle and beseeched him to swim against the tide once more. Then, while his uncle was still debating with himself whether to take the plunge, Arch added, "I promise you that Vernon Ingledew, when elected, will appoint you Adjutant General of the Arkansas National Guard!" That was a post Arch knew that Uncle Dale, an old World War II marine, had always coveted.

They discussed the best place for the announcement: in front of Old Main? at the campaign headquarters off the square? why not the steps of the capitol building in Little Rock? or even the steps of the Old Statehouse, which Clinton had used for such dramatic effect?

"I don't want anything special," Uncle Dale said. "Why not simply the front porch of your lovely home?"

Arch may have blushed with pride, but he did have a nice big old two-story Shingle Neoclassical Craftsman in the heights west of the university. It had once been a fraternity house. Beverly and Arch had put a lot of work into its restoration.

Anyhow, that was where Vernon Ingledew came to meet Dale Bumpers for the first time, to shake his hand in front of the cameras, to thank him warmly for his endorsement in the primary, and then to make a little speech in which he said that Dale Bumpers's original campaign for governor could never be duplicated but it could certainly serve as a constant source of inspiration.

Attending that ceremony were Arch's wife, Beverly, and their daughter, Eliot, who was going to turn fifteen the week before the upcoming primary and who discovered that Vernon Ingledew was "the coolest guy" she'd ever met, even if he talked not to her but to the top of her head. Arch was surprised to notice that Vernon's woman-shyness extended to young ladies too, but Eliot would later remark that Vernon's bashfulness was what she liked best about him. Eliot was going to have some great ideas for enfranchising, as it were, the hundreds of thousands of Arkansawyers too young to vote but not too young to proselytize their parents. Eliot's finest idea was to have a great campaign poster downloadable from the Internet, and this poster would, very shortly, be seen in the rooms of all of the state's teenagers. It did not say INGLE WHO?, a question that no longer needed asking, but rather VERY VERNON. That poster became so ubiquitous that Vernon sent Eliot an e-mail in which he declared his intention to appoint her Secretary of Teenagers, and Arch didn't think he was entirely joking. Arch was also proud of Eliot because she was the first person to notice (how had it escaped everyone else's detection?) that *Ingledew* and *Governor* contain the same number of letters, eight, a handy thing to know when making posters, painting blimps, and having rich but subliminal mental associations.

Also attending the ceremony were the Samurai, all seven of them, including Bo, who had flown in with Vernon and Jelena in George's helicopter. It turned out that what Bo had primarily been doing was a combination of wandering all over Stay More and hanging out at the double-bubble, where he begged Jelena to permit him to help her plant her tomatoes (as well as the ones he'd brought from Cincinnati) and other stuff in the vegetable garden and to help her keep the weeds out of it, and where he'd had some long talks with Vernon whenever the candidate was at home. "Trust me," Bo told Arch. "He really *does* know how to stop tornadoes."

Bo had returned to the campaign without having learned from Arch that he stood an excellent chance to get his honorary degree after all. In fact, he did get it, and all of them were there watching and applauding: the Samurai, Vernon and Jelena and George, Day and Diana, and Dale Bumpers, whose endorsement of Vernon had boosted him into second place in the polls. The lengthy citation for Bo's degree, read out by Chancellor John White, carried no mention of his current occupation.

Bolin Pharis III, LLD, returned to his current occupation energetically. Arch didn't mind being second in command again. Monica found and gave him an old button for Avis, the car renters: WE'RE NO. 2, WE TRY HARDER. Monica meant for it to refer to the fact that Vernon was now second in the polls, but Arch, proudly wearing the button on his shirt, thought of it as referring to himself.

Chapter Ten

It was true that he was the only boy in a family of five girls all older than he, and it was true that he slept with his mother until he was nine years old, and there was no preventing the opposition's using such facts as these in whatever skewed psychological implication they wished. At the age of fourteen he encountered his unhappy cousin Jelena standing on the edge of Leapin Rock, that's true, and he may or may not have been responsible for the fact that she did not jump. When he was sixteen, his father, John Henry ("Hank") Ingledew, had presented him with a gold chronometer wristwatch that had been given to Hank at the age of only ten years by an itinerant peddler on his last trip to Stay More moments before his death, who had told Hank that he would keep and save the watch to give to his son, assuming that ten-year-old Hank would ever have a son, or would have one only after trying and failing five times. That (and much, much else) was true and available to any of the opposition who bothered to read the peculiar chronicle called *The Architecture of the Arkansas Ozarks*.

But the gold watch did not possess any sort of magic power, nothing that enabled the wearer of it to become aware of the fact that he was "in" a novel and could communicate with readers of the novel as well as with the Author himself. Life is hard enough without the added burden of feeling that one is merely acting out some assigned role in a made-up story.

In any case, that gold watch, which was still in Vernon's possession and still kept excellent time, although he hadn't worn it since he was twenty, did not, Vernon can assure you, endow him with any ability to communicate with you, or you, or *you*, or any other readers or viewers or witnesses or eavesdroppers or audience or whatever you would prefer to be called, you who are holding in your hands a book called *Thirteen Albatrosses*. Of course you aren't saying anything. (Or are you?) The point is, even if Vernon put on that magic chronometer, he couldn't hear you.

It was his estimable best buddy, Day Whittacker, who revealed to him the book's title and advised him that he might as well "go along for the ride" and enjoy it, as he was doing. Over the years, Day and Vernon have had some really heavy arguments, but they rarely if ever got angry with each other. Vernon was a bit irritated, however, with Day's own kind of "magic realism," nearly as bad as that gold chronometer business, which claimed that Day had already "read" each of the previous chapters of this book and knew what each of the persons—George, Bo, Jelena, Lydia, Harry, Monica, Arch—had been thinking.

"If we're only in a book," Vernon said to Day, "why don't you flip ahead a few pages and tell me whether or not I'm going to win this goddamn primary?"

Day laughed uproariously. "We're not 'only' in this book, Vernon," he said. "If we were 'only' here, the reader would know every little thought that passed through our minds. It would be awfully boring. I have a rich, full, exciting life outside this book."

"So you're telling me you can't skim ahead a few pages and reveal the outcome of the primary?"

"I can't understand," Day challenged Vernon, "why some people have to skip to the end of a book. That's gross impatience and violates the fairness of time."

So Vernon gave up. There was the Second Conversion of Bo Pharis to accomplish, the First Conversion of course being the trip to Cincinnati. Now Vernon arrived home for a short rest from a grueling trip downstate to shake several thousand hands and smile several thousand times and reiterate from memory his standard campaign speech. He arrived home, George settling their helicopter upon its pad near Jelena's garden, and there was Jelena down on her knees putting tomato plants into the rich soil, which was being spaded up by some fellow in overalls and a straw hat, whose skin was already tanned from the sun but wasn't quite as red as what one might expect to see on a Newton County farmer. After giving Jelena a big kiss, Vernon turned to look at the man, and it took him longer than it should have to recognize him. Vernon supposed it was the man's build and his dark beard that gave him away.

"So," Vernon said to him, jokingly, "I'm paying you two hundred dollars an hour to dig holes?"

But Bo Pharis did not think it was funny. "You're not paying me zip. I'm no longer working for you. And Jelena's not paying me for this either. I'm doing it for nothing. I'm doing everything for nothing."

His voice sounded a bit frantic, even unhinged. Vernon suggested that when Jelena and Bo were finished with *their* garden, they might have some gin and tonic and talk. Later Vernon asked Jelena, "How long has he been around?" and she said just a few days. "*Just* a few?" Vernon said. "You mean he's been spending the night?" Vernon's beloved explained that she'd found Bo wandering around down in the valley like a lost dog, and she'd put him in her car, fed him, given him drink, and told him to make himself at home and take over the guest room if he wanted it. They'd gotten along just fine, talking about gardening and what was to be planted and when, and she really enjoyed Bo's company and his help in the garden, although, as Vernon must have noticed, Bo was not exactly playing with a full deck. One night he had asked Jelena, straight out, "Do you think Vernon is right?" About what? she'd replied. "Everything. Anything," Bo had said. She had laughed and said, Well, no, frankly, Vernon was wrong about a lot of things, and he was certainly wrong to think that he'd be happy as governor of Arkansas. "Me too," Bo had said.

Vernon, whose primary quality, it must have been noticed by now, was not his intelligence so much as his compassion—his ability to empathize with anybody—took hold of Bo, literally and figuratively, and straightened him out. Vernon took Bo for long walks all over Stay More. He commiserated with Bo over the stupid about-face of the university board of trustees and predicted, quite correctly as it turned out, that Arch would handle the matter and Bo would get his honorary degree after all. But that wasn't the main thing troubling Bo. Bo had become increasingly pessimistic about the campaign. He had hoped there would be a way to accommodate Vernon's radical ideas to the electorate. He had intended to gloss over the fact that Vernon was extremely conservative in some respects—like Stay Morons for generations he was opposed to *prog* ress, as they had always disparagingly pronounced it—while in other ways he was dangerously liberal in his intention to abolish traditional institutions. Bo felt he could paint a picture of Vernon as a populist that would hide his extremism. But Vernon was not making it easy, with his occasional outburst of crackpot ideas like stopping tornadoes.

As chance would have it, one of their hikes along the back roads of Stay More took them into the presence of one of those common little whirlwinds called *dust devils*. Whether or not a dust devil is a miniature tornado, it behaves in basically the same fashion and funnels dust, debris, and sand to great heights. And thus Vernon was able to demonstrate, to Bo's astonishment, how he could simply extirpate the dust devil, depriving it of its root. Since

Bo couldn't believe his eyes, another dust devil conveniently came along and Vernon repeated the trick, which involved some fancy footwork and the swinging of an old board.

"Wow," Bo was moved to remark. "The next thing you'll be doing is claiming that you can extirpate cancer."

Vernon smiled. "I'm saving that for the general election."

As they were strolling down what had been the main street of Stay More, now populated by Vernon's free-ranging hogs, who had converted into hog wallows the old foxholes dug by children playing war games during World War II, they noticed that the occupant of the old Jacob Ingledew house was sitting on her porch, enjoying the early May sunshine. Vernon waved to her and, as she did not get up and rush into the house or show any shyness in the presence of the strange bearded man, Vernon decided to introduce them. But Vernon did not use either her actual name, which was Svanetian, or her well-known American pen name. Vernon assumed that Bo, like any well-read person, would have heard of her, or even read one of her many books, and would, like the world at large, have assumed that the woman had been murdered years before, as recounted in the pages both of *The Paris Review* and in the novel *Ekaterina*, by the same Author as *The Architecture of the Arkansas Ozarks.*

Vernon knew that Bo had read at least one of those, and he took the familiarity to serve as a basis for reminding him that Jacob Ingledew's mysterious inamorata, who had shared the ex-governor's last years here in this house with him and his wife, Sarah, had been referred to simply as Whom We Cannot Name and thus, for present purposes, for the nonce, it would be just as well to refer to the present occupant of the house by that same cognomen. Vernon was not ready—and might never be ready—to reveal to Bo the complicated story whereby he had conspired with the woman, and with the woman's presumed murderer, to fabricate her death in order to allow her to retreat into permanent seclusion and anonymity here in Stay More, free forevermore from harassment by her fans.

The Woman graciously invited Bo and Vernon inside the house so Bo could see what she had done to it. Bo expressed his astonishment constantly. The interior was both an attempt to restore the building to the actual rustic Victorian appearance it had had when the ex-governor lived here and an adaptation of that appearance to the Woman's needs and interests, particularly her extensive library and her music collection.

Vernon wanted Bo to see especially the way an upstairs room had been transformed. For years it had been called the "unfinished room": just a big storeroom, like an attic space filled with the accumulated castoffs of generations of occupants from Jacob onward, but now it was the nicest room in the house, a guest room never used, containing a gorgeous four-poster bed and other bedroom furniture, antique paneling, and stenciled floors; it was like stepping directly into the 1860s, not as they were known by typical Ozarkers but by that anonymous Little Rock woman who had become the governor's mistress. It had been in this room, in its former cluttered, unfinished state, that Vernon as a young man had found the nearly complete holograph manuscript of *The Memoirs of Former Arkansas Governor Jacob Ingledew.* Vernon told Bo he was welcome to read a photocopy of it, for whatever it was worth. There were only three copies in existence: the original in a bank vault, a copy the Woman possessed, and a copy Vernon would lend to Bo.

"I'd be delighted," Bo said, and then he asked the Woman, "What about ghosts? Is this house haunted?"

"Oh, yes!" she said. "But not as much as the last place I lived."

"Where was that?"

"The Crescent Hotel in Eureka Springs," she said. "Do you know it?"

Bo said he'd been there a time or two. "Do the ghosts here bother you?" he wanted to know.

"Bother?" The Woman laughed. "I'd rather think it's the other way around. I bother them."

As they were leaving and thanking her for the tour of the house, Bo asked, not entirely in jest, "What does the ghost of Governor Ingledew think about his descendant running for governor?"

"I quote," the Woman said. "He's 'proud as the devil.' "

That night Vernon gave Bo a photocopy of his ancestor's handwritten memoirs, and Bo began reading it. The next day they would be summoned to Fayetteville for a special ceremony involving an announcement by former governor Dale Bumpers. For now, Bo Pharis, who seemed to be searching so desperately for something in the rural past of the Ozarks, could be permitted to stay up late reading Jacob Ingledew's fabulous recollection of how he and his brother Noah had trekked with two mules some six hundred miles from their home in Tennessee to establish a new home in the lush paradise of this Ozark valley that was to become known as Stay More, given that name by the last Indian resident of the paradise, an Osage who had been nicknamed "Fanshaw" by his long-gone tribesmen because of his friendship with the early British explorer George W. Featherstonhaugh, and who had learned from his friend a passable, albeit British, English and had befriended Jacob.

The two men enjoyed many hours together, smoking the Indian's tobacco and drinking the white man's corn liquor and—it struck Bo Pharis as so much like his own endless talks with Vernon—discussing everything under the sun, including their philosophical differences and the inevitable question of which of them would have to yield Stay More to the other. Always at the termination of one of these long sessions of smoking, drinking, and debate, whenever the Indian tried to excuse himself and return to his own lodging, where his squaw was waiting for him,

Jacob always said, "Stay more. Hell, you jist got here." And the town's named derived from that formality or custom, which Fanshaw's wife found amusing because among their own people the exact reverse was the case: When a guest has stayed as long as he wants to, his host senses it and sends him packing with an Osage expression that, if translated into modern idiom, would most literally be "Haul ass" or perhaps even "Fuck off." Whenever Fanshaw left his wife to go visit Jacob Ingledew, he would tell his wife that he was on his way to Stay More. And that was how the place got its name.

What Bo could not quite understand, as he expressed it to Vernon, was just how Fanshaw could so easily have made his wife available to Jacob. The Osage were not like certain Eskimo tribes who consider it polite to provide guests with abundant gratification of all their needs: food, drink, sex. Jacob was still a virgin at the time of his encounter with Fanshaw's squaw, whose name, if it was ever known to Jacob, was not given in his memoirs, although the memoirs speculated endlessly not only about her background and feelings and appearance (which Jacob had seen clearly only once, as she and Fanshaw were about to depart) but also about Fanshaw's motive (and his wife's accession) for the generous gesture. Had Fanshaw just been drunk? Was he simply extremely hospitable and friendly? Or was he trying to teach Jacob the meaning of an emotion that Jacob had been very slow to grasp: joy.

There was no question what the deed itself—described in detail in *The Architecture of the Arkansas Ozarks* and in even greater detail in the governor's memoirs—actually accomplished for Jacob, not only removing his virginity but providing him with a single manifestation of female passion and joy that would forever after be a standard no white woman could match. One reason that Vernon had never considered publication of the memoirs was the amount of space devoted to Jacob's comparison of the squaw's sexual performance with that of the three other women he would eventually know: his wife, Sarah; a Confederate "recruiter" (with sexual favors) named Virdie Boatright; and the nameless Little Rock woman. It was so erotic that Bo stayed up reading long past his usual bedtime and promised himself that when he got back to Fayetteville he would ask Arch if he didn't know any nice single women.

Jacob's fabulously joyful encounter with the wife of Fanshaw was not a first-and-last experience. He was invited to repeat it, and he did, with variations, several times. The squaw became pregnant, and, as Jacob learned from Fanshaw himself, although the two men had been sharing the woman repeatedly, to their mutual complete satiation and even exhaustion, only Jacob could have been the impregnator, for Fanshaw was sterile. The Indian couple did not remain on their ancestral campground, in their basketry domicile, until the baby was born. One day they packed up and left, presumably going westward to try to find their Osage tribesmen in Indian Territory. Jacob never saw them again.

Was the impregnation of his squaw therefore Fanshaw's motive for the sharing? Vernon told Bo that if he was really interested in such things, he should feel free, eventually, to discuss it with Day Whittacker and with the Woman now living in Jacob's house, who was an authority on the Osage Indians.

But there was a campaign to run, and the current Stay More idyll was at an end. Vernon was gratified to watch as the endorsement of Dale Bumpers raised his rating in the polls until he slipped ahead of the Reverend Dixon and was right behind Barnas, with less than a month to go until the primary. The Seven Samurai had mapped out a couple of scenarios, both of which made it increasingly likely that there would have to be a runoff. In order to win the primary you had to have 50 percent of the vote plus one. There was simply no way that any one of the three front-runners—Barnas, Ingledew, or Dixon—could achieve that. The question was, since a runoff would be necessary, which of the other two would be the "better" opponent? Did they want to run up against Barnas's well-organized and well-heeled grassroots juggernaut, even if Barnas was already proscribed from attacking Vernon? Or would they rather take on the evangelist, who, because his own record was unblemished (except for the choir girl that Harry Wolfe and Garth Rucker had been unable to locate), would be free to attack Vernon on every front? Bo and Arch explained to Vernon that it would be possible for them to manipulate the primary, to determine which of those two would be the opponent in the runoff.

The last three weeks until the voting were unimaginably hectic, and any other man who, unlike Vernon, could not go without sleep would simply have dropped from exhaustion. The Samurai had to work in relays to keep up with him and with his busy schedule. Lydia arranged to have Vernon take to a leisurely lunch, one by one, each of the state's major newspaper editors. Since Carleton Drew was going to be spending most of the budget customarily allotted to television on newspaper ads, particularly an advertisement that depicted graphically why Vernon was opposed to yard signs (a photograph of a Fayetteville street with all the yards hideously cluttered with all the other candidates' names), the newspaper editors were grateful for the revenue coming in from the Ingledew campaign and were more than willing to meet with Vernon, listen to him, or rather, as he preferred, talk to him about what they considered the pressing issues of the day while he listened and took notes.

From then until the voting, the newspapers treated Vernon as if everything he did or said was newsworthy, and it wasn't uncommon to see large headlines like INGLEDEW IMPRESSES RICE FARMERS and INGLEDEW SHOWS STATE'S EDUCATORS WHY HE IS THEIR MAN, and even HELICOPTER BREAKDOWN FAILS TO SLOW INGLEDEW'S RELENTLESS MARCH TO THE STATEHOUSE. The television stations, which were peevish because the Ingledew campaign wasn't wasting a cent on TV ads, tried their best to ignore him, but he was so often and spectacularly before the television cameras that they simply couldn't edit him out. Wherever he went, he was accompanied by a large marching band, Ingledew's Instrumentalists, made up of talented college band members on summer vacation, usually accompanied by a choir, Vernon's Vocalists, who sang among other things a spirited sort of country and western campaign song, "Why I Gotta Have Vernon," that was so catchy it was soon on everyone's lips. As if the marching band and the choir weren't enough, Vernon's rallies and speeches were usually highlighted by performances by the Cheerleaders, members of the University of Arkansas Razorbacks' acrobatic cheerleading squad, male and female, who were employed for the summer by the Ingledew campaign and wore not their red-and-white uniforms but the purple and yellow associated with Vernon. When the band, the choir, and the cheerleaders came into town ahead of Vernon, you could be sure there would be such a crowd there that the television stations couldn't ignore it *or* him. "All this," Hank Endicott commented in awe, "and he hasn't even begun what he intends to call 'the rebirth of stump speaking.' "

The highest form of publicity was accidental. The incumbent governor, Shoat Bradfield, who didn't need to run in the Republican primary because the nomination was already assured him, was shown on the evening news in early June in an unguarded candid rage, waving his arms and declaiming, with much profanity that the network bleeped out, that he had never heard of Vernon Ingledew and didn't expect him to survive the Democratic primary but that if he did he'd get murdered by Bradfield in the election. If there was any person left in Arkansas who didn't know who Vernon Ingledew was, that appearance by Shoat Bradfield soon straightened them out.

The last week of the campaign, television commercial time

was almost constantly devoted to the vicious battle between the Reverend Dixon and Barnas. Since Barnas could only attack the innuendo about Dixon, he made the most of that, with TV spots showing an old photo of the minister with his arms around several female members of his choir, and a voice-over asking, "Which of these young ladies was it?" Bo and Arch eventually decided that they'd rather, in the runoff, challenge the preacher instead of the state senator, so they leaked to the preacher's men several tidbits about Barnas's connections and his past, enough to provide the preacher with all the ammunition he needed in his attack ads. Whether this violated Harry Wolfe's deal with Garth Rucker was immaterial. The preacher was able to capitalize on it sufficiently to defame Barnas in television spots. By election-day morning, most of the newspaper editorials said that Vernon Ingledew was the "clear" choice.

There was a big party planned at Ingledew headquarters for election night. Monica made sure there was plenty of food and drink, plenty of room for the crowd to spill out onto the sidewalks, plenty of room for the television cameras, and places of honor for the main participants: Vernon and Jelena and the Seven Samurai. As the returns began to come in and were chalked up on a board, Bo draped his arm expansively across Vernon's shoulders and said, "This is the best part of politics. This is the *game*, watching the score. This is the most fun." Vernon had butterflies and couldn't eat, but he tried to keep smiling and shaking hands with people (at least the men) who came to watch the board. Day and Diana were there, and Vernon preferred huddling with them.

When the final chalk marks were made on the board, voters in the primary had given Barnas 28.5 percent of the vote, just behind the Reverend Dixon, who got 29 percent. Vernon got 31 percent, and the other candidates split small pieces of the remaining 11.5 percent. Since all the Samurai had been rooting for Dixon to edge out Barnas, there was more cheering over that than over Vernon's coming in first.

Vernon got two letters in the next day's mail; Bo intercepted both of them but shared their contents with his boss. One was from Barnas, congratulating him sarcastically, cursing him to high heaven for having leaked damaging information to Dixon, and vowing that not one of his 28.5 percent of voters would vote for Vernon in the runoff. "Does he want them all voting for Dixon?" Bo asked rhetorically.

The other letter was from the Reverend Dixon, and said:

> *I knew it would be you all along. The gauntlet is laid down. I'm sure you've noticed I've refrained from maligning you thus far, apart from raising the mild question over the fitness of an ex-hippie pig farmer to move from an outlandish yurt into the governor's mansion, but now that you and I are alone together in the ring, you may be assured that I'll hammer you with everything I've got, particularly your rejection of Our Lord and Savior. Run scared, Mr. Ingledew.*

The evangelist's second-place finish, ahead of Barnas, attracted large cash contributions from some of the other former candidates' supporters, from the viewers of Dixon's regular Sunday-morning television show, and from several Democratic loyalist sugar daddies who were not above letting Hank Endicott know that they despised Vernon's fanatical ideas. The huge influx of contributions filling the Reverend Dixon's coffers enabled him to fire several of his own campaign consultants and replace them with professionals who came as close as was humanly possible to matching the Seven Samurai. They attempted to hire Barnas's oppo man, one Garth Rucker, but Rucker declared he'd already accepted an offer to be Harry Wolfe's assistant. "I might learn something," Hank Endicott quoted Rucker as saying. Bo reported to Vernon that Harry had revealed he'd been offered a substantial amount of money to "switch" to the Dixon team. Harry had declined, out of his sense of decency. Bo had made no attempt to raise Harry's salary to match the exorbitant offer made by Dixon, but he had given him a token raise and also authorized a trip Harry and Garth were making to Portland, Oregon, where, Harry was convinced, the long-lost choir girl was living.

Vernon perceived that John Colby Dixon bore two burning resentments: he fancied himself a learned man, certainly not a "highbrow" but a cultivated, educated, quick-witted sophisticate who was able to charm his vast television audiences in polished, perfect English with his wisdom about the Bible and the road to salvation, and therefore he bitterly envied Vernon's supposed knowledge of any subject; and of course he coveted and resented Vernon's Seven Samurai, any one of whom, even Cast Sherrill, was superior to his opposite number on Dixon's team. In his first Sunday-morning sermon following the primary returns, Dixon made disparaging references to Bolin Pharis as "the Pharisee" and to Arch Schaffer as "the Archfiend," to Lydia Caple as "the Incapable" and to Harry Wolfe as "Old Harry," a common Arkansas nickname for the Devil. He called Monica Breedlove "the Intern" and Castor Sherrill "the Castoff," and he probably had to tax his enlarged brain to come up with a designation for Carleton Drew as "the Cigarette," a triple allusion to the fact that there was a brand of cigarettes called Carltons and to the fact that Drew smoked cigarettes and to Drew's previous employers, the Washington tobacco lobby.

Cigarettes were just about the only issue on which Vernon agreed with the evangelist, but while Vernon intended to make Arkansas the first tobacco-free state in the Union, Dixon only wanted to make sure that the state collected as much damages as it could from the tobacco companies. Dixon's platform, as it was perceived by the public, was not notably challenging or even unusual. He was against crime. He supported the environment, welfare, term limits, health care, and most particularly the family and children. He opposed taxes and illegal drugs, as well as poverty and homelessness, and particularly moral and ethical decline. His opposition to abortion was as equivocal as he could make it.

But as far as the campaign was concerned, Dixon was indifferent to the issues and appeared to want only to attack Vernon on every possible front. Toward the end of that sermon mocking the Seven Samurai and giving them nicknames, he suddenly declared, "I hereby challenge the infidel Vernon Ingledew to a debate!"

Bo was opposed, and so was Arch. They knew that Dixon, with his enormous experience as a preacher, his smooth eloquence, evangelistic fervor, and dramatic delivery, would make Vernon at his best look dull and awkward, even if Vernon was considerably better-looking than Dixon, a gaunt, sharp-chiseled person with wire-rimmed spectacles and the look of an old-time country preacher. Lydia, however, believed that Vernon could "acquit himself handily" and, if they avoided getting into personalities, could probably outduel the preacher on the issues. The Seven Samurai (six, rather; Harry was in Oregon) spent quite a lot of time with and without Vernon, trying to come up with a way that Vernon could refuse the debate without losing face. Every day that went by, the evangelist capitalized upon Vernon's hesitation in accepting the challenge. "Have you left the state, Mr. Ingledew?" demanded his television spots and his newspaper ads. Vernon said to his team, "Come on, guys, let's do it. I can handle him!" and he sounded so confident that Bo began to have lengthy talks with Dixon's campaign manager, trying to agree on conditions, a format, and a location. Carleton Drew made sure there would be major television coverage of the event. Finally it was agreed that the studios of KARK, the NBC affiliate in Little Rock, would be suitably furnished for the debate; and that Hank Endicott would serve as moderator. The Dixon campaign wanted Meredith Oakley, less liberal than Endicott, but the Ingledew campaign pointed out that she had already declared in favor of Dixon, and would thus be biased.

"Gentlemen," Endicott declared at the outset of the debate, like a referee instructing the boxers, "this is going to be a clean fight. No hitting below the belt. You will not, either of you, get into personalities, but confine yourselves to answering my questions about your intentions for bettering the state of Arkansas. All right, my first question: Do you support the death penalty? Reverend Dixon?"

"Certainly. Where would Christianity be if Jesus had got eight to fifteen years with time off for good behavior?" The studio audience had a good laugh over this, and Vernon joined in.

When his turn came to answer the question, Vernon said, "Does it make sense to hire murderers to kill defenseless victims on death row, in order to prove that hiring murderers to kill defenseless victims is morally wrong?"

"But you are a godless man, Mr. Ingledew, totally ignorant of Christianity's support of the death penalty."

"All early Christian writers who discussed capital punishment were absolutely opposed to it," Vernon pointed out.

"Early Christian writers?" said the evangelist. "Name one."

"Lactantius Firmianus of the late third and early fourth centuries. Better known as the Christian Cicero. He wrote a fine book called *Divinarum Institutionum Libri Septem*, in which he said, 'When God forbids us to kill, he not only prohibits the violence that is condemned by public laws, but he also forbids the violence that is deemed lawful by men. It is always unlawful to put to death a man, whom God willed to be a sacred creature.' "

"Mr. Ingledew, you have no right to mention God, since you don't believe in Him!"

"I don't believe in fairies. Am I forbidden to tell fairy tales?"

"Gentlemen. . . ." Hank Endicott tried to intercede.

"You're out of your depth quoting some obscure 'early Christian writer' to me," Reverend Dixon said. "You're simply showing off your false wisdom. And you forget that the God whom you discredit has discredited your wisdom. 'Hath not God made foolish the wisdom of this world?' First Corinthians, one and eighteen."

"That's First Corinthians, one and twenty," Vernon corrected him.

"*What?*" The minister got very red in the face and demanded of those present a copy of the Bible to prove himself right but, discovering that the atheist Ingledew was correct, waved the Bible about and declaimed, "This is a sacred book and that blasphemous smart-alecky heathen has no right even to mention it!"

Hank Endicott's next column said:

> It was my dubious honor to attempt to moderate a debate between a popular clergyman who kept losing control of his temper and a savvy layman who repeatedly demonstrated that he knew far more about Christianity than the pastor did.

Other commentators were not as restrained; one columnist continued the boxing metaphor by saying, "Ingledew laid him out with an uppercut in the first round."

Just how many thousands of votes that debate cost the Reverend Dixon couldn't be calculated. But the minister's behavior cost him considerable support, even among those minions of Senator Barnas who had been instructed to vote for him. In an effort to counteract the effects of the debate, the minister made a number of television spots with his former enemy, James Barnas, in which they stressed the need for solidarity against the godless hippie hillbilly radical who was living out of wedlock with his own cousin. As the date of the runoff neared, these television spots grew increasingly virulent. Dixon seized upon a few of Vernon's thirteen albatrosses, those that were already known, and paraded them in the public view, and this was why the polls, just a week before the runoff, showed the minister several points ahead of Vernon.

Then Harry Wolfe and Garth Rucker returned from Oregon, bringing with them a young lady, a rather attractive and neatly dressed girl of twenty, who announced to the reporters and cameramen covering her arrival at the airport, "I am tired of being forced out of my dear sweet home state by that man. He can't keep me away. No amount of money will keep me away. I'm back. I have some things to tell you."

Vernon Ingledew collected 53 percent of the vote in the runoff.

Second Part

Election

Chapter Eleven

About the same time that Vernon and Bo were encountering those two dust devils on their hike around Stay More, I received an e-mail message from a stranger, a cybernetic dust devil I couldn't extirpate. On the average, I get about three e-mails from strangers each year, and on the average one of them will be a request from a teenager in Sweden who wants my autograph, another from a teenager in Arizona who has been assigned to do a theme on an American Author and wants me to supply her with my complete biography, and the third a fan letter from Wisconsin. The e-mail that whirled into my computer may have been from Wisconsin or from Sri Lanka. In keeping with e-mail etiquette, there was no salutation.

From: Heartstays@aol.com
To: dharingt@uark.edu
Subject: your book

Read your book. Wish I could say I enjoyed it but I found too much of it too painful, although I realize you wrote it trying to be funny. I notice it was published when I was only eight. I wish I had known about it before now, but our public library doesn't have it. I found a copy of the paperback for fifty cents at a yard sale, almost as if

I were fated to stumble upon it. The people having the yard sale I have known all my life and now they're leaving town and I hate to see them go. After I read the book, all of one night, I asked the woman if she had read it before consigning it to her yard sale. Some years previously, she said. Did you realize that it is about us? I asked her. Well, she replied, maybe just a little. And it didn't bother you? I wanted her to tell me. Well, maybe just a little, she said.

One question I have for you, sir, is this: Where did you get all your information? How much of it did you just "make up"? You have obviously mixed up real people and imaginary people all the way along, but my question is, If you're still alive yourself after all these years, are those people you pretend to be real still alive?

Juliana Nancy Waspe

So much for my morning. I ought to have put off checking my e-mail in-box until the afternoon, when the day's work was over, but the job of writing fiction, as I am careful to warn the students in Advanced Placement English at Fayetteville High School who each spring invite me to answer their questions about what it takes to be a writer, is the loneliest job on earth, and the Author is, unlike the Creator, fallible and subject to temptation. The urge for human contact is not always resistible.

For all its disturbing flaws, the message from this Juliana person was compelling. I am always grieved by people who announce that they have read "your book," as if I have written only one of them, as if that in itself, the writing of a book, is such a noteworthy thing that it is inconceivable there might be more than one (in my case eleven). And which of the eleven did she mean? The only clue was that she was eight when the book was published, and thus, assuming she was not merely ten or even twelve now, we could discount *When Angels Rest* and *Butterfly Weed*. If she meant *Ekaterina* she would be only fifteen now, but somehow she seemed older than that. So she could have been referring to any of the seven novels from *The Cherry Pit*, making her forty-three, to *The Choiring of the Trees*, making her seventeen. The last was the least funny of my novels, so I scratched it. My principal clue in this little detective game was her claim, or her question to the seller of the paperback, that that book was about "us." Was she perhaps a native of Stay More? Or of one of the lost cities of Arkansas described in my *Let Us Build Us a City*? That book was marketed as "nonfiction," although I'd thought of it as a kind of nonfiction novel, but nowhere did Juliana use the word *novel*, so quite possibly this was the book she meant. She was therefore twenty-four years old.

With nothing better to do, since my morning was shot anyhow, I replied at length to Ms. Waspe (a name I'd never encountered in any of the places covered in that book, but of course it could have been a married name). I explained that all eleven of the lost "cities" of Arkansas are actual places, and that the names of the inhabitants therein that my wife, Kim, and I met and interviewed were actual names of real people, and that for the most part I stuck to the facts as revealed in the considerable research I'd done, but that I had indeed, as she surmised, invented several imaginary people and "mixed them up" with real ones, which I have always considered a sure-fire legitimate means of giving verisimilitude to a story.

For example, I was currently engaged in a fascinating project called *Thirteen Albatrosses*, a political novel, wherein I was combining real-life actual people such as Archie Schaffer, Monica Breedlove, and Vernon Ingledew with imaginary people such as Bolin Pharis, Lydia Caple, Harry Wolfe, Carleton Drew, and

Castor Sherrill. Whenever I respond to the occasional fan letter, I like to mention the forthcoming book in detail, in order to drum up a little advance business for it. I said I hoped that Juliana would watch for it at bookstores in another year or so, and that meanwhile she might like to read another of my previous novels (I listed them), particularly the one most relevant to the current project, called *The Architecture of the Arkansas Ozarks*, which, despite its unusual title, was very much a novel, albeit a novel wherein I continued my lifelong practice of combining real and imaginary people.

Her reply to my e-mail was so fast that I began to imagine her sitting at her computer.

From: Heartstays@aol.com
To: dharingt@uark.edu
Subject: Re: your book

That's the book I meant! I didn't know you'd written so many. The architecture book. I don't know the lost cities book. I mean the Ingledew book is the one I read. Are you sure you spelled Ingledew correctly? It's very easy to misspell Osage, happens all the time, but the correct transliteration for panther is "Ingthonga," which could very easily have got mispronounced as Ingledew, just as "Osage" itself is a hideous French misrendering of *Wah-Shah-She*. But maybe you know this, since you appear to know so much about the Osages, at least the one you presumed to call "Fanshaw," driven away by Jacob the Panther.

My really big question to you now is: Do you mean to tell me that Vernon the Panther is alive and real??!! If so, where? And what's he doing in a "political" novel? Please answer right now. I am here.

Juliana

I replied at once that I had not realized there was an Osage word so closely resembling the Anglo-Saxon family name Ingledew. Although several panthers figured prominently in "the architecture book," I had not known that the Osage word for panther was so similar to Ingledew, and I thanked her for telling me that. I said I wished I'd known it at the time I'd written the book. My only sources for telling the story of Fanshaw, the Osage brave displaced by Jacob Ingledew, were the latter's unpublished memoirs, plus a book called *Indians of the Ozark Plateau* by Elmo Ingenthron (whose name, come to think of it, was even closer to "Ingthonga"), plus of course the classic *Wah'kon-tah* by John Joseph Mathews.

How did Juliana come by such familiarity with the Osage? It was wholly a pleasure to make contact with somebody who knew anything about them. And yes, Vernon "the Panther," if she wanted to call him that, was at this very moment running for governor of Arkansas. Where did Juliana live? Maybe her local newspaper would carry a story about the upcoming Arkansas Democratic primary, in which Vernon the Panther was facing several other candidates but had a good chance to win. He was still living in Stay More, still in the house described at the end of "the architecture book," still living with his first cousin, the beautiful and brilliant Jelena.

For the rest of the day, we exchanged several messages. Kim commented, "Sounds like you were real busy in there," referring to the fierce pecking of the keyboard in my study. Yes, I said, I was getting a lot done. Before Juliana and I discontinued our e-mail chat for the day, I had learned some basic facts about her. She was, as arithmetic had already shown, thirty-four years old, eight at the time of the publication of *The Architecture of the Arkansas Ozarks*. She lived near Pawhuska, Oklahoma, not in it but nearby. Pawhuska I already knew to be the capital of the Osage nation, and in fact I'd recently read Dennis McAuliffe's gripping *The Deaths of Sybil Bolton*, wherein he tells the story of his search for the truth about the murder of his grandmother in 1925 during a period when several Osage women were killed in order to get the money they'd made from owning oil-producing acreage. Not only had Juliana read this book, six years before reading mine, she had, a few years before that, met and talked with Dennis McAuliffe when he was living deliberately in Pawhuska for three months to track down the story and, in the process, come to terms with his own alcoholism. Juliana had attempted unsuccessfully to befriend him, but he was, as she put it, "out of it."

Was she perchance therefore an Indian—excuse me, a Native American—herself? Mixed-blood, she said. As I knew from McAuliffe's book, the population of Pawhuska contained only a very few pure-blood Osages, a number of mixed-bloods of various mixtures, and quite a large number of whites of various mixtures. Pardon me for putting it so bluntly, but did she "look" Indian? Her hair was black, she said. But her skin was not particularly "red." She could pass, and had passed, for Spanish, Greek, Italian, and so on.

In my insomnia the night after our e-mail meeting, the sound of her name kept repeating itself in my head. *Juliana Nancy Waspe.* I assumed that the sound was pronounced correctly with the last name as two syllables: *Was-pee.* The relationship among the three parts of her name was more melodious and congenial than that of any other person I'd encountered since Daniel Lyam Montross, his name "three sounds bonded at two junctions of end and beginning." The first thing I did, in my first e-mail of the next morning, about the same moment that Vernon Ingledew was shaking hands with Dale Bumpers on the broad porch of Arch Schaffer's house, was to ask Juliana about her name. Juliana was of course her given name, but the rest of it . . . ? Her parents had allowed her to pick, from several appropriate sources, her last name, and "Nancy Waspe" was a rough phoneticization of the Osage that she used to disguise her actual last name, which was Heartstays, as in her aol.com address.

Was I familiar with any of the ancient legends of the Osage? Very few, I said, although I had read V. Kelian's *Dawn of the Osage* (and had to resist the urge to reveal to Juliana that "V. Kelian" was actually alive and well and living in Jacob the Panther's old house in Stay More, Arkansas).

Well, Juliana explained, in the story of the Great Flood, when the flood struck, some of the Osages climbed up into the tops of trees and were called Top-of-the-Tree Sitters. Others climbed a forested hillside and were called Upland Forest People. A third group saved themselves among the thorny growths on the sides of a ravine and were called Thorny Thicket People. A fourth group couldn't reach high ground but took refuge on the talus at the base of a cliff and were called the Down Under People. But the fifth group, the last group, Juliana's ancestors, stayed where they were; they refused to flee but stood their ground on the hummocks of dry land amid the swirling floodwaters. They were attached to their land and could remain contented only by staying there. Staying more, as it were. Their hearts thus were quieted, and they became known as Heart Stays People. The name is rendered in Osage as Non Tze Wath Pe, sometimes spelled Nontsa Wah Spah, which the Jesuits spelled as Nantze Waspe, and which Juliana spelled Nancy Waspe.

How clever, I wrote. Would you rather I call you Juliana Nancy Waspe or Juliana Heartstays? Suit yourself, she replied. And then she wrote:

> So you see, you were entirely wrong about the origin of the name Stay More.

Her words were like a slap. In my various books I had laid out all the several possible beliefs about the origin of the name, and in "the architecture book" I had conceded that while the name was indeed based upon the common Ozark polite injunction not to rush off but to stay more, the actual name of the place had been bestowed by Fanshaw the Osage in recognition of his host Jacob Ingledew's common employment of the expression. I have the book open before me, page 8, Juliana wrote.

> You say, "Yet Fanshaw could not help but remark upon this custom to his wife because among his own people the exact reverse is the case: When a guest has stayed as long as he wants to, his host senses it and sends him packing with an Osage expression that, if translated into modern idiom, would most literally be 'Haul ass' or perhaps even 'Fuck off.' " Well, excuse me, but you didn't get that out of Jacob's memoirs and you didn't get that out of Ingenthron and you certainly didn't get it out of Mathews's *Wah'kon-tah*. So where did you get it? How did you know what Fanshaw and his wife said to each other?

I allowed as how that was one of many places in the novel where I'd given my imagination and my comic sense free rein. She responded:

> You also claim that Fanshaw's basketry dwelling was portable, that—here's another of my many X marks in the margins of your book—page 6, "A gentleman and his squaw," Fanshaw explained over the firewater, "can lift and transport their domicile over great distances where the woods are not, or, where the woods are, disassemble and reassemble." Think about that. It's wrong. Even if those basketry huts could be picked up or disassembled or whatever, the Heart Stays people never took anything

with them when they left, usually because they never left!

Sorry, I replied. You're right. That was a stupid passage. But are you saying that Fanshaw was of the Heart Stays band?

Of course he was! Juliana answered. And then she wrote:

Catch you later. Bending Bear wants to take me into town.

Was this Bending Bear her boyfriend? Whoever, he had stolen her away from me at a crucial juncture in our exchange, when I needed to confirm whatever theory she might have that Stay More had got its name because the last Indian resident of the place had been of the Heart Stays People.

Come to think of it, the site of the Osage camp in Stay More, in the rocky meadow hard by swirling Swains Creek, waiting for Bo Pharis to explore, fit the description of the traditional locale of Heart Stays people as being right on the water's edge.

I rushed to locate my copy of the Ingenthron book and to look again at the Harold Hatzfeld illustration (pp. 64–65), on which I'd based my own drawing of Fanshaw's double "bigeminal" dwelling. The depiction of an Osage seasonal hunting camp at the mouth of Swan Creek in Missouri shows several of these basketry beehive-shaped huts, with a larger lodge in the background, all of them spread out right alongside the waters of the creek, so that any hard rain might swamp them if they weren't determined to heartstay. Jacob Ingledew and the Osage Fanshaw had had many conversations during the several months that they shared Stay More before the Indians' departure, and Jacob had recorded most of these conversations in his memoirs, from an excellent power of memory that would be inherited by Vernon, but there was no mention, or none that I could recall, of any

"Heart Stays People." I must say it crossed my mind that, just as I freely admitted enlivening prosaic truth with my novelist's imagination, perhaps Juliana herself was making a few things up in order to "explain" her name.

Waiting for her whenever Bending Bear brought her home was my lengthy e-mail, in which I confessed something I'd scarcely told a soul and had nearly forgotten myself: My book she'd read had been intended originally as just the first volume in a trilogy. Volume Two was to have been called *Interiors* and would have gone more deeply into such things as whether or not the two halves of that basketry paraboloid were connected by any sort of interior door joining Fanshaw's half to his wife's half and, consequently, whether or not Fanshaw and his wife discussed at any length their (his? her?) decision that she might divest Jacob Ingledew of his virginity. Volume Three was to have been called *Outbuildings and Others*, the double O's of its title symbolizing the two holes of the privy and having in its first chapter the meaning and significance of the lodge building in Fanshaw's camp. Did Fanshaw and his squaw use it for anything? Or was it just a constant reminder that their tribesmen had abandoned the camp forever, that their hearts had not stayed?

No doubt, I told Juliana, if I'd gotten around to writing those other two volumes, I could have "corrected" some of the mistakes she'd found in her reading. But the first volume had not fared well commercially or critically; it had been either ignored completely or dismissed as a spoof, and there had been scant chance the publisher would have wanted to risk the other volumes in the trilogy, which remained unwritten.

Several days went by (what "town" had Bending Bear taken her to, Dallas?) before her answer came, in the form of a list of all the mistakes she'd caught in Chapter One, involving Osage habits, beliefs, practices, and pronunciations. (Example: When Jacob and Fanshaw went hunting together, Fanshaw would not have used his bow and arrow if Jacob was using his rifle. Fanshaw, like most Osages of the time, probably possessed a rifle too.)

> Would you have corrected all of these in *Interiors* or *Outbuildings and Others* [she asked]? More importantly, would you have revealed the name of Fanshaw's squaw, which was Kushi? More importantly yet, would you have admitted your major misrepresentation of the truth: namely, that Kushi did not freely offer herself to Jacob but was raped by him?

My service provider suffered one of its recurrent failures (probably from an overload of students doing end-of-semester work), and thus my immediate and vehement response to this question did not reach her until the following day. Hold on, Juliana! I wrote. Where do you get that? On what authority are you basing such a contentious and extravagant claim?

> How do I know her name, and you do not? Because she was of the Heart Stays People, who in their staying told their children all the old stories, the Little Old Men, the storytellers who made a profession of it, told everything about Fanshaw and Kushi and their idyllic life together in Stay More until the white men came and drove them out, told it to their children, who told their children, and all the old stories came down generation to generation as neatly and truthfully as if they had been written in stone.

How does *Kushi* translate? I wanted to know.

> The *k* is medial between *k* and *g*, and there is a slight but distinct suppression between the initial consonant and the initial vowel. Without that suppression, the name might be heard as "Kuzhi," which means far away, at a

great distance. "K'ushi" is hard to translate without knowing the whole folk joke behind it, but literally it means "gulped into the earth."

Speaking of folk jokes, stop me if you've heard this one, I wrote. It's from Vance Randolph's book of folk jests, *Hot Springs and Hell*, which I freely expropriated in my novel *Lightning Bug*, the beginning of—and the key to—the Stay More saga. There was a girl had a fellow arrested for rape, and the prosecuting attorney was asking her some questions about it. She says the fellow just throwed her down and raped her, and it happened on Easter Sunday. "It's August now," says the lawyer. "You say he hasn't bothered you since Easter?" The girl said a dirty word. "Bothered me! I'll say he has! Why, it's just been rape, rape, rape all summer, and something has got to be done about it!"

Funny. Relevance?

The relevance, Juliana, is this. According to Jacob Ingledew's memoirs, and as I indicated in "the architecture book," not only was Jacob's sexual intercourse with Kushi, if that was her name, at the express invitation of Fanshaw himself and with the express consent of Kushi herself, but also it was repeated on several occasions. Is that "rape"?

That is only Jacob the Panther's perspective, and what may have seemed consensual to him was not to her.

What I needed to do, I decided, was to quote at length to Juliana several passages of *The Memoirs of Former Arkansas Governor Jacob Ingledew*. But, as we've learned, there were only three copies in existence, the original in Vernon's bank vault, one in the possession of the Woman Whom We Cannot Name the Second, and one on loan to Bo Pharis. I had seen the original when it was still undiscovered in the "unfinished room" of the Jacob Ingledew house when I was a very young man. I hadn't fully appreciated at the time its value and significance and I didn't consider stealing it, which I could have done. Worse, I hadn't considered copying it; photocopy machines in those days were slow, awkward, and barely legible. Now I thought of asking my good friend Arch Schaffer if he could temporarily borrow Bo Pharis's copy and have a copy made of it. I certainly wasn't going to ask Vernon Ingledew to copy the original in his bank vault.

Then, when Kim and I dropped in on the Ingledew campaign headquarters to watch the returns come in the night of the primary, we ran into Day and Diana. During the course of the long evening, as Vernon's lead gradually mounted but not enough to avoid a runoff, I had a chance to speak privately with Day. I told him of my discovery of Juliana Heartstays and of our lengthy e-mail correspondence. He thought it was fascinating. As we've already seen, Day was thoroughly familiar with *Thirteen Albatrosses*. This certainly was not because I had allowed him to see any of it but because of his firm conviction that he had every right to be just as aware as you, the reader, are. Now, having heard what I had to tell him about Juliana, it was Day Whittacker who first thought of something that, I'm abashed to say, had escaped my own awareness. Because I'm so hard of hearing, he even took the trouble to write it down on a note card: *You don't suppose there's a possibility that Juliana is a descendant of Jacob Ingledew and Fanshaw's wife, Kushi?*

"Good Lord!" I exclaimed, and we both glanced at Vernon, who was standing by the tote board watching the numbers being chalked up. I knew we were both thinking, *Maybe Vernon's got another cousin he doesn't know about.*

I made my request of Day: since he was on such good terms with the Woman Whom We Cannot Name the Second (he was one of the privileged few who knew she was also the writer V. Kelian, who had written *Dawn of the Osage*), could he possibly ask her to make, on her high-speed Canon copy machine, a copy of Jacob's memoirs? And get it to me pronto?

Which he did, although it wasn't quite as pronto as I'd have liked. During the three weeks that Vernon was battling the Reverend John Colby Dixon, either Day or the Woman was taking a lot of time getting around to making that copy. My e-mail chats with Juliana continued, but I didn't tell her that I was arranging to obtain a crucial document to help convince her that Jacob had not raped Kushi. I did tell her about the campaign: how this extremely popular and smooth evangelist John Colby Dixon, the runner-up in the primary, was challenging Vernon to a debate. Could Juliana's television pick up the Fort Smith stations? Maybe she could watch. But Juliana informed me she didn't have television. Neither does Vernon, I said, but I did not posit that as evidence of their kinship. I wasn't ready yet to put forth that Juliana was the offspring of Jacob and Kushi.

> `Are you a good friend of Vernon the Panther?` asked one of her e-mails.

Hardly, I answered. I've met him only once, seen him only twice. As you may have gathered from reading "the architecture book," and as you'd know conclusively if you'd read my other books, I have never been overly fond of the Ingledews. Growing up in Stay More, I was taught to think of the Ingledews as—well, I suppose as the Osages might think of their clan chiefs. You venerate your chief and obey him and all that, but you don't necessarily love him. Stay More never had any class distinctions, but the Ingledews always had a sense of being leaders.

She repeated it back to me.

A sense of being leaders. So now Vernon the Panther wants to be the leader of the whole state of Arkansas.

He might be a good one, I allowed. He's enormously intelligent and has some visionary ideas, and he has a sense of what people want and a sense of what they don't need even if they want it . . . like cigarettes. You don't smoke?

I quit.

Good for you. So did I.

Did you quit drinking?

I gave up the hard stuff. But I have a beer now and then.

You're a writer. Can you put into words what Vernon looks like?

The best I could do was tell her to imagine her favorite movie star or, better, *all* her favorite movie stars rolled into one, and be sure that he was suave, impish, about six feet five inches tall, 215 pounds, with brown hair that looked sun-bleached, and blue eyes.

I hate him, Juliana declared. I don't care what he looks like or how smart he is. I hate all the Panthers and would kill them if I could.

It took me awhile to digest this. Trying to pace my flourishing acquaintance with Juliana, I had not yet told her an important fact about Vernon: that in his sixteen-year program of autodidacticism, he had devoted six intense months, right after spending six months on the occult, to the Osage, their whole history and culture, even their language. Eventually I intended to ask Juliana if she knew her neighbor James Big Eagle, the Pawhuska mixed-blood who had come to Stay More for two months to teach Vernon the Osage language. I questioned my own motives in wanting to dispel Juliana's hatred of the Ingledews, but I was determined to do it.

At the Ingledew campaign headquarters the night of the runoff, as Vernon's lead over the Reverend Dixon became indisputable early on, I saw Day Whittacker again, and he delivered into my hands at least a ream of copy paper, bound with a yellow bandanna, containing my request. He apologized for not having got it to me sooner; he hadn't wanted to trust it to the U.S. Mail and had hoped to see me again at this function: the celebration of Vernon's victory in the runoff. "And now," Day said, "you can deliver it personally, if your trust of the U.S. Mail is as weak as mine, into the hands of Juliana Heartstays."

I laughed and then realized he wasn't joking. Driving home late from the victory party, I told Kim that I had to go to Pawhuska, Oklahoma, a distance of about three hours or so, in order to do some research on Jacob Ingledew.

"One," she said, "what has Jacob Ingledew got to do with *Thirteen Albatrosses*? And, two, what has Jacob Ingledew got to do with Pawhuska, Oklahoma?"

I tried to explain that Fanshaw and his squaw, pregnant with Jacob's child, had eventually rejoined the rest of his clan on the Osage reservation in Pawhuska, and that the early career of the man who was Vernon's ancestor as well as a governor of Arkansas was an important subtext in the novel. But Kim and I have rarely been separated for an entire day, going separate places. I offered to take her with me, but I knew she had errands of her own to handle that day and would decline the offer. I promised to try to get home before nightfall.

* * *

In my red Jeep Cherokee I got away from Fayetteville before 7 A.M. and taking the Cherokee Turnpike reached Tulsa by 9 and turned northward on State 11 to Osage County, the largest of Oklahoma's counties, larger than the state of Delaware. I was mindful of all these Indian names, and of the names of every town large and small I passed through, concluding with my destination, which was named after Paw-Hiu-Skah, or "White Hair," a chief of the Little Osages, the tribe which included the Heart Stays People.

It was a hot day; my Jeep's external thermometer would register between 92 and 97 for most of the day, but of course I had air-conditioning. And Diet Cokes on ice. And a sense of excitement that even permitted me to fantasize, as thousands of e-mail correspondents have done, about the charm of the unseen "other" and what might transpire when two correspondents actually meet for the first time. I knew that she'd find nothing particularly charming in me, thirty years her senior and a Paw-Hiu-Skah myself. But the manuscript, still in the yellow bandanna in which Day (or V. Kelian) had wrapped it, would be delivered into her surprised hands, and I might be invited to lunch, and that would be that: enough.

The drive was not interesting; Oklahoma falls far short of Arkansas in attractiveness. I made mental note of an occasional interesting road sign, such as Little Dog Threasher Creek, which might furnish topics for conversation. Although I was prepared by Dennis McAuliffe to find Pawhuska itself unglamorous—he had used words such as "rundown," "godawful," "hellhole," "deserted," and "dump"—I was still unprepared to see what an ugly place it was, and I couldn't imagine my Juliana being imprisoned there. As in small towns all over America, most of the downtown buildings were either abandoned or had been converted into uses far removed from their original intention. One of the few busy buildings with any trace of modernity was the supermarket, called Homeland. The name struck me because I had originally intended to call *Thirteen Albatrosses* by that name.

I stopped at Homeland to look at a telephone book. I can't use the telephone, but if Juliana was listed it might give her street address. It was a yellow Southwestern Bell book for BARTLESVILLE AREA, including Pawhuska, but there was neither Heartstays nor Waspe nor Nancy Waspe in it. I drove up the town's one hill, called Agency Hill, and parked at the Osage Tribal Museum and Library, which really was not much more than a souvenir shop. I asked the lady running it, herself obviously an Indian, if she knew Juliana Heartstays, or Juliana Nancy Waspe, and got only a blank look.

Did she know anything about the band of Indians called Heart Stays People? Where had they lived? My poor hearing failed to catch several of her words, but I heard enough to understand that she really didn't know anything. She suggested I might try the Osage County Museum, which was in the abandoned railroad station and was not much more than a junk shop and used-book store, and where the couple who ran it, both of them at least mixed-blood Indians, could not tell me anything about any Heart Stays people or anybody named Heartstays or Nancy Waspe.

I was beginning to suspect that my e-mail correspondent had just invented herself and her location. It was lunchtime, and I missed the chance to be invited to have lunch with Juliana. I ate at the town's lone remaining family restaurant, where I got a decent cheeseburger. The waitress, a thoroughly non-Indian blonde, had of course never heard of anybody named Juliana. While eating, it occurred to me to try the public library, which I did. The white librarian, a very polite and helpful lady, said she couldn't reveal any information about library patrons and thus couldn't tell me if they had a patron of that name. "But couldn't you tell me if there's anyone by that name living in this town?" I begged. I think there could be, she said. But she had no idea where the person might live. "Have you ever heard of any band of Indians called the Heart Stays People?" I asked. No, but let me check, she said and disappeared into a room marked OSAGE MATERIALS.

While waiting, and waiting, I had nothing better to do than check the card catalog to see if they had any of my books. Nothing, of course. The librarian returned with a popular picture book called *The Osage*, by Terry P. Wilson, and there on page 51 was a map, OSAGE RESERVATION AROUND 1900, which showed Pawhuska on Bird Creek with five little dots upstream representing Heart Stays People. How far is that from here? I asked her.

"There's nothing up that way anymore," she said, and got a U.S. topographic survey map to show me how an "unimproved" (dirt) road led northward through a valley between Bird Creek and Mud Creek to the area where the hummocks or "lenticular bottoms" (as John Joseph Mathews had called them) had led the Heart Stays People to pick a "permanent" campground reminding them of those sites they'd had to leave behind in Kansas, Missouri, and Arkansas. There were no habitations indicated anywhere in the area, just abandoned oil wells and an old railroad grade.

"Is this road still passable?" I asked. The nice lady said she hadn't ever been up that way.

The road started near the Pawhuska cemetery, a sprawling necropolis suggesting that most of the Osages, like their oil reservation, were underground. The road cut through a ravine, stopped being blacktop, and continued on as a decent gravel road that meandered through thickets and straightened out onto the suggestion of a prairie, took a couple of sharp right angles, then roughened and weedened, climbed a hill, and meandered through woods for quite a ways. At least there were tire tracks to suggest that the road was still in use, and I stayed on it for a couple of miles until finally it dropped down into a bosky dell alongside Bird

Creek, where I caught a glimpse of what might be those hummocks or lenticular bottoms and where, finally, having seen no signs of human habitation, I came to a mailbox.

It was an RFD mailbox beside a trail, and on the side of the mailbox was a red heart, but the heart was sideways; that is, it was resting on its side; it was sleeping or it was staying; it was a Staying Heart. I turned into the trail, which wandered through the woods and then emerged onto the lenticular bottoms, where stood the most fabulous house I've ever seen. It gave a first impression of being thrown together by a horde of hippies on peyote, but on closer inspection it was obviously the work of a trained postmodern architect who knew pretty much exactly what he was doing and had at least a million dollars to spend: It was a kind of vast enlargement of the same structure that I had illustrated in Chapter One of "the architecture book" as Fanshaw's dwelling: a basketry paraboloid beehive or, rather, a giant pair of them closely conjoined with several buttresses or protuberances or annexes. It hadn't been built yesterday; it looked as if it had been there for several years at least, and thus Juliana could not have used the illustration of my book as her inspiration, not if she'd only discovered the book recently. It was a huge place, actually larger than Vernon's double-bubble (which of course I had never seen but had had a good description of from Day and from Arch Schaffer), to which it bore a kind of kinship in its bigeminality and its singularity, the principal difference being that Vernon's house was on a mountaintop and this was right beside the banks of Bird Creek. Juliana was going to have a lot of explaining to do about her extravagant house.

I sat in the Jeep, transfixed by the palace, for a long time, long enough for Juliana to become aware of my presence in her driveway. Then I got out, toting the manuscript of Jacob Ingledew's memoirs, boldly approached the house's huge oak door, and rang the doorbell. She answered at once.

She was a great disappointment: round. Many Indian women seemingly settle into a general rotundity as they mature, their faces apple-shaped and almost swollen, their waistlines disappeared. Not fat, necessarily, but just *circular*. And her dark-skinned face beneath the thick braided black hair was nothing at all like I'd fantasized. She was homeliness personified.

"Juliana Nancy Waspe," I said, trying to keep my chagrin out of my voice, "I am Donald Harington." Whatever she replied was not clear enough for my deafness. "I'm sorry," I said. "I guess I should have told you that the only way we can communicate is by e-mail . . . unless you want to use my note cards." I offered her my ballpoint and my pack of note cards, but she would not take them.

"Gone," she said, raising her voice, so I could hear it. "Not here. *Gone*."

I perked up. "You aren't Juliana?"

The woman shook her head, and tried to shape her lips carefully. "Housekeeper."

"Oh, that's good," I said, beside myself. "So where's she gone? When will she be back?"

"Homeland," she said. "Gone Homeland."

"The supermarket?" I asked.

The woman laughed. I was glad to see that Indians have a sense of humor. The previous Indians I'd met that day had never even smiled. "Not *that* Homeland," she said. "Not grocery store." And then she pointed generally eastward, the way I had come, the way Fanshaw and Kushi had also come, and said carefully, "Gone to find her ancestors' homeland. She and Threasher and Bending Bear. Left this morning."

"Who's Threasher?"

"Her dog."

"Who's Bending Bear?"

"Her chauffeur."

Chapter Twelve

Hoo, lordy, it was hot as blue blazes, and George was cussing hisself for not doing what Boss told him to do, take a few days off, which was what all the others was doing, Bo just a-cooterin around up yonder in Jelena's garden patch and Arch a-floatin the Mulberry River and Lydia gone down to Pine Bluff for something or another and Monica gone home to Louisiana, and God knows what had become of Harry and Carleton, although if George looked hard enough he could probably find Cast, who was somewheres hereabouts; George had seen him earlier this morning down at the swimming hole on Swains Creek. Bo said they all needed a little spell of rest to catch their breath before gearing up for the big campaign that would run all the rest of the summer and into November.

George doubted that Boss hisself was taking a break, but at least he'd gone back to his big easy chair in his office up under the dome of that puffball house of his, and although he was probably a-settin there reading books on how Roosevelt and Truman and Kennedy got theirselfs elected, he was just a-lollygagging around compared with what he'd been doing for the past three months.

But George didn't rightly know how to take it easy, so here he was in his Explorer running all over God's creation taking care of these razorbacks. He'd spent the morning rounding up and castrating the shoats—he allowed himself a smile, knowing what symbolism was and knowing there was a kind of symbol involved here—the rest of 'em all taking a lull to get ready and castrate that Shoat Bradfield, and George with his trusty knife (there were others at the plant who could do it but not as quickly and painlessly as George), snipping off the balls of these just-weaned piglets.

He'd also had to track down a boar named Schoonover, an old pal of his who'd somehow missed out getting castrated when he should've and had taken to roaming the high hills of Juberaw or wherever, and George had spent most of the afternoon wearing out the Explorer and a-calling and a-calling old Schoonover (couldn't nobody call a hog as good as George) and then finding him and sweet-talking him and sticking him with a anesthetic and slicing off his nuts, apologizing while he did it, and Schoonover hadn't liked it one bit. A young pig didn't seem to mind, didn't even seem to know what was happening to him, but an older hog sure did hate to get deballed. It didn't happen often, but it was one of the few drawbacks of Boss's idea of giving the hogs their freedom, which years ago Boss had explained to George, or tried to. You can't pen up a hog without getting inferior meat. You've got to keep the animals from ever feeling they belong to you. You've got to turn 'em loose. He knowed in reason that a free pig is a happy pig, and he'd understood that being happy truly makes the meat more tasty (Boss had tried to explain to George stuff about glycogen depletion and lactic acid buildup in stressed-out pigs, but George had taken his word for it).

Now he was tired and dirty from wrassling with Schoonover and he was itching to get on home and take a shower and have a drink. As he passed the old Governor Ingledew house, however, he stomped on the brakes, for there in front of the house, parked, was a sleek black vintage automobile of some kind, and a real big fellow polishing it with a chamois rag. George hadn't seen a car that old in Stay More since Doc Swain passed on, and for a moment he felt himself transported back in time. He knew the strange woman who lived here—he'd met her many a time and to himself called her "Cat"—was a rich writer lady who was hiding out from the world, and Boss had made it clear that George and everbody else in Stay More would do whatever they could to protect the woman and her privacy. So who was this giant dude with the fancy antique auto and what was he parked here for?

George got out of his Explorer to take a better look. The man had a dog, a mongrel setter or something, and the dog commenced barking at George, which he didn't like, because he had more right to be here than the dog did. The man gave George just a glance and says to the dog, "Shush," and then resumed polishing the fender with the chamois rag, but George gave the man a thorough scrutiny. He was plumb nearly seven foot tall and broad as a corncrib door and was a-wearing one of them Hawaiian sport shirts, but on his head he had a black uniform cap, like a hired driver would wear. As George got closer, he saw that the man had dark reddish skin and dark hair, and by God if he sure didn't look like he was some kind of injun! George had known only a few injuns in his life, mostly boys in Vietnam, good soldiers but hard to know. They'd all been of a average size, though, not overlarge like this feller.

"Howdy," George says, politely but warily.

"How," says the injun, proving he must be a injun, sure enough, not a Mex or a African. But then he says, "Excuse me, but you're staring at me, and it's rude."

"Well, hell, feller," says George, "excuse *me*, but it aint ever day I run acrost a car like this'un a-settin smack dab in the middle of Stay More."

"So this *is* Stay More, then," the big feller says.

"What's left of it," George admits. And then he asks, "What-all make of car is this, anyhow?"

"It's a Pierce-Arrow," the man says.

"How much did a relic like this set you back?" George wants to know.

"It isn't mine. I only drive it."

George took a glance at the house. It hit him that whoever this injun was driving the car for might be inside the house, a-visiting with the nice lady who lived there. George wasn't fixing to think that lady's name out loud right here, where any fool could see it. He was only going to notice what she herself had already observed in relation to Latha Bourne's yard full of cats: that you could call it—and her—a "cat arena." Maybe just Cat for short.

"It aint none of my business, I reckon," says George to the injun, "but how long do you figure on standing here?"

"Not that it isn't any of your business," says the injun, "but I couldn't tell you, one way or the other. I've already been here more than an hour, and my lady had just stopped to inquire if this is Stay More, which you've already told me in far less time. You aren't by any chance an Ingledew?"

"Naw, but I work for one," says George.

"Really?" says the injun cordially. "Then you're just a hired gun, like me."

"I reckon," George admits. "Though I don't tote no gun."

Both men chuckled over this, and then the injun says, "Are you married?"

"Now what in tarnation has that got to do with anything?" George wants to know.

"I'm just curious about your disposition," says the injun. "Family man? Bachelor? Male-oriented? Switch-hitter?"

George didn't rightly know what-all this feller was a-talkin about, but he sure was nosy. "B, I reckon," he says.

"B?" says the injun. "Bi? Boondagger? Bindle boy?"

"You gave me a multiple choice, A through D," George tells him. "So I picked B."

"Ah, yes. *Bachelor*!" says the injun, smiling really big. "That's *very* interesting."

Trying to change the subject, George asks, "What-all kind of dog is that you got there?"

"Threasher? He's what I suppose you would call a turtle dog."

"*Turtle* dog?" says George, and even though it might be rude he had to stare at the pooch. "I know what a turtle*dove* is, but I aint never heared tell of no turtle *dog*. You don't mean to tell me he trees turtles?"

"He doesn't tree them. He just points them."

"Huh? That's the dumbest thing ever I heared. Why would a dog point turtles?"

"So we can catch them and eat them."

Rude or not, George had to stare at the huge injun for a long moment. "They eat turtles where you come from?" he wanted to know. George had never eaten no kind of reptile in his entire life and he wasn't about to start, nor even to start thinking about it.

Probably this injun was a-fixing to tell George a few box tortoise recipes, but just then the door of the house opened and out come two women: one was Cat, who George had known for years, the other was not just a stranger but the strangest woman George had ever seen, strange like she was somebody he'd just dreamed up, somebody whose feet didn't touch the floor but floated above it, a sight, a knockout, looking like a million, which she must've been worth at least. She was wearing some kind of long silk summer dress, blue-green, and a broad-brimmed straw hat atop her long dark hair. It hit George that just maybe she was some kind of injun too, though she sure didn't look like one, not her skin, not her shape, she sure wasn't no kin to this hefty feller standing here that worked for her.

She was smiling from ear to ear, the prettiest smile George had ever seen on a woman's mouth. "*Waxkadazhi*, Ben!" she calls to her hired gun. "This woman speaks better Osage than I do! And this is Stay More! We're in the right place." And then she turned to the woman and says, "This is Thomas Bending Bear, my man."

"Hello," says Cat. *"Ha-way Washazhe. Thots-he pee-chay. Way-wenah."* And the big brave answers her in the same lingo, and they just commenced a-chitchattin. George couldn't rightly tell what they was talking about, but it seemed it was all politeness and compliments, and it lasted too long before Cat took a notion to wave at George and say, "Good evening, George."

"Howdy, ma'am," says George.

The gorgeous injun girl's smile vanished. "Not an Ingledew?" she says to Cat.

And Cat says, "No, this is George Dinsmore. He's the general manager of operations for Ingledew Ham, and you might say he's Vernon's right-hand man."

The lovely gal gave George a stern look, as if his connection with Boss didn't sit too awful well with her. Then she says to him, "How do you do?"

"I was better, but I got over it," George says to her, but winks to let her know he's just trying to be clever.

"Where is your employer?" she asks him.

"Boss? Aw, I reckon he's up to home," George allows.

"Where is home?" she asks. And then she says, "Pardon my manners. I'm Juliana Heartstays."

"Right pleased to meetcha," George says, and he meant it, he sure was tickled to pieces to make the acquaintance of such a sightly gal. He gestured toward the west, toward Daniels Mountain. "Boss lives up yonder a good little ways."

"Ben," the gal says to her hired gun, "this wonderful

woman, who lives in this wonderful house that was built long ago by Jacob Ingledew himself, just happens to know everything about the history of the Ingledews. And as you can see, she just happens to speak perfect Osage and has even written a book about us!"

"Marvelous!" says Ben.

Cat says, "And I've invited you to spend the night, because there's nowhere else. This used to be Stay More's only hotel, years after Jacob Ingledew died."

Ben says, "I am prepared to pitch a tent on the creek bank at the location of the ancient Osage camp. In fact, I'm prepared to erect an authentic wigwam."

"George, would you like to join us for supper?" Cat says.

"Why, thank ye kindly, ma'am," George says. He knew he smelled too bad to sit down at the table with anybody. "But I reckon I'd best be gittin on over home. Sure am mighty proud to make you'uns' acquaintance." He offered his hand to Ben to shake. Ben's handshake was soft for such a big powerful-built feller. George couldn't offer his hand to the gal. Her touch might melt him.

"Could I have a minute?" Cat asks George, and walked him back to his Explorer, out of earshot of the injuns but not of the turtle dog Threasher. "Tell Vernon that I'll try to phone him later tonight. But for right now I'd better tell you this much: These people, that exquisite girl and that formidable Osage warrior, are here for the purpose of extirpating all Ingledews from their ancestral homeland, meaning Stay More."

George's mouth dropped open. "You don't mean to tell me," says he. "How come?"

"It's a long story. Ask Vernon to explain it to you. But tell him there is a ravishingly beautiful Osage girl who would be pure-blood except for one thing: Jacob Ingledew was her progenitor."

Maybe it's rude to stare, but George couldn't take his eyes off Juliana Heartstays, standing over there on the porch of the old house, and it wasn't just on account of she was such a sight for sore eyes. "Lord have mercy," says he, "I reckon you're fixing to talk 'em out of it."

"If I can," says she, and pats him on the arm and goes back to join the others.

George didn't know whether to go on home and call the county sheriff, his good buddy Mark Rupp, or just to call up the posse of Ingledew workers, the same fellers who had worked so hard to keep them nosy newsmen and cameramen from finding or getting to Vernon's place. He could call up that posse and they could run these injuns out of town so fast they wouldn't know what hit 'em.

But George decided he'd first better go tell the bad news to Boss. So he turned his Explorer around and headed across the Swains Creek low-water bridge and on up the road that led to the mountain trail that climbed up to Vernon and Jelena's. He was hungry, but he could count on Jelena to offer him a bite, if he didn't have to sit at the table with them, stinking of hog balls as he did, if maybe they was just some way she could feed him out back with Vernon the cat.

The three of 'em—Vernon, Jelena, and Bo—was just a-setting out in the yard, drinking gin and tonic. George didn't much care for gin and tonic, and Boss knew it, even though he'd tried to explain to George that hot weather demanded gin and tonic with a wedge of lime in it.

Boss jumped up to fetch George some bourbon, the drink of his choice, hot weather or cold as a well-digger's balls, and George pulled him up another chair, not too close to the others, and they sat and drank and talked. "Aint this the by-goddest weather ye ever seen?" George remarks, although in fact he'd seen much worse. But Bo allowed as how it was probably a lot hotter down-state, so it was a good thing they weren't down there stump speaking already in places like Pine Bluff and El Dorado. Boss says he likes hot weather hisself. Jelena says she wonders why we're all a-settin out here in the yard instead of inside the house where it's nice and air-conditioned. George says he'd been cutting shoats all day and ought to stay out in the open air. Bo says settin in the yard is good for the constitution, and besides it puts us in touch with our Ozark ancestors.

George jumped on that remark for a excuse. "Speakin of Ozark ancestors," he says, "they's a coupla injuns just turned up down to Stay More town, in this here fancy old auto called a Pierce-Arrer, and that Woman Whom You Cannot Name is a-fixin to put 'em up for the night and feed 'em and all."

"Really?" says Boss.

"What tribe?" says Bo.

"Osage," says George.

Nobody says nothing for a little while; then Boss says, "That ought to make her very happy. Do they *speak* Osage?"

"It appears so, I reckon," George says. "There's a feller and a gal, and the feller is just her car driver, but he's this big old redskin brave looks like he ort to be on a horse with his bow 'n' arrer and his war paint and all. Nobody never told me they made injuns that big. The gal is something else. I mean, let me tell you'uns, she's *something* else. Nobody never told me they made injun women that pretty."

"Well, well," Bo says. "Maybe we ought to go meet her."

"Not me," says Boss.

"Ha!" says Bo. "I keep forgetting your legendary Ingledew woman-shyness." He turned to Jelena like he was just a-making talk and says, "Tell me, Jelena, if it's true that all Ingledews from time immemorial have been paralyzed in the presence of the opposite sex, how could Vernon be so chummy with *you*?"

Jelena smiled and says, "Because I'm an Ingledew myself."

George figured that was as good a answer as any. But it

also set him to figuring, if them injuns was out to exterminate all Ingledews, just how many Ingledews hereabouts was there? Boss and Jelena made two, Boss's sister Sharon made three, and Boss's dad, Hank Ingledew, made four. The injuns wouldn't have no trouble finding Sharon, who lived just up the road a little piece from Cat's house, but they'd probably have to search around a good bit to find Hank, who lived away off up high on the yon side of Ingledew Mountain.

And what was they fixing to do the exterminating *with*? George recalled Ben's remark about "hired gun" and wondered if the redskin brave was packing a pistol or two. "Boss," he says, "is there some reason why them injuns might be out to get you? The Ingledews didn't drive them injuns' ancestors out of town, did they?"

"I can answer that one," Bo says, "based on my reading of Jacob Ingledew's memoirs. There were only two Native Americans remaining in Stay More, an Osage brave named Wah Ti An Kah, called Fanshaw, and his wife. Jacob and his brother Noah, who was shy not just toward women but toward anyone, especially Native Americans, lived in peaceful coexistence with the Native Americans through a whole winter and into the spring, when Fanshaw decided to leave and go westward in search of his kinsmen.

"Fanshaw had freely shared the sexual favors of his wife with Jacob on many occasions. Like all Ingledews, Jacob couldn't tolerate the thought of seeing or being seen by a female, but apparently it was always pitch dark when he'd succumbed to her allure and her passion. Fanshaw knew that he himself was sterile because his constant efforts to impregnate his wife had failed. So the baby his wife was bearing when they departed Stay More was Jacob's, but that was not by any means their reason for leaving. They left because . . . well, I suppose because they were lonely for their tribesmen and, like people everywhere at all times who have to choose between love of place and love of family, decided they would sacrifice their ancestral homeland in favor of their kinfolks . . . if they could find them."

Bo finished his little lesson, and then he nudged Boss with his elbow and says, "Is that the way it was, Vernon?"

"In a nutshell," Boss says, "although I suspect it's a bit more complicated than that. I think Fanshaw didn't harbor any jealousy toward Jacob's being the father of the baby, but on the other hand he didn't want to raise the child with two fathers, as it were. So he had to leave."

"Whatever reason they left," George says, "they've come back. What I mean is, this scrumptious injun gal I'm telling you about, right down in the town yonder, is a offshoot of Jacob Ingledew."

They all three stared at George so fixedly he was of a mind to repeat back the immortal words of Thomas Bending Bear, "Excuse me, but you're staring at me, and it's rude." But he didn't say this.

"How do you know?" Bo says.

"The Woman Whom We Cannot Name tole me to tell ye," George says. "And something else too. She said she'd try to phone ye, Boss, sometime tonight. But she says to warn ye, them injuns is here to wipe ye out. She said they was here for the purpose of extirpating all Ingledews from their ancestral homeland, meaning Stay More."

"*Why*, for heaven's sake?" says Jelena.

"We had better find out," Bo says. "Surely they don't think that the Ingledews drove the Native Americans out of Stay More."

"Bo," says Boss, "do me a favor. You don't have to say 'injuns' like George, but I think it's hypocritical to say 'Native Americans' after they've been identified as Indians forever."

"Political correctness is the first aim of politics," says Bo.

"Let's eat supper and talk some more about it," says Jelena.

And, to George: "You stay to supper with us, hear?" George says he'd be mighty glad to, excepting he's so smelly from wrassling them pigs he couldn't sit at the table with them. Jelena says, "Dear heavens, Uncle George, Bo and I have been working in the garden all day, and we smell just as bad as you do."

So they sat at the dining table and ate. George didn't much care for the cold gazpacho soup, but the tuna-fish casserole was edible, and Jelena's homemade bread was always real good eatin. Right in the middle of supper the phone rang and it was for Vernon, and he took it out of earshot and it went on for quite a time. His food got cold and Jelena decided not to wait for him to serve dessert, which was blackberry cobbler, and George had to have seconds on that. Nothing like hot cobbler with cold ice cream on top to make the whole meal just right.

They were still waiting for Boss to get back when Bo says to Jelena, but with a glance now and again at George to let him know he's not left out, "One thing I don't understand. If these two Native—if these two *Indians* are here for the purpose of extirpating Ingledews, how would the Woman Whom We Cannot Name have found out about it? Did they just come right out and tell her? Assassins have to work in secrecy. Why would they have declared their intention to her?"

George says, "You got me on that one, but I reckon she let it be knowed right off she wasn't no Ingledew herself."

Boss finally returned, smiling, and the first thing he says is maybe he won't have to go meet that Indian lady after all, which suits him fine. George knows Boss would probably have fainted from shyness if he'd ever had to meet up face-to-face with that peach of a female.

"Well, *I* would certainly like to meet her," Bo says.

"Nothing's stopping you," Boss says to him. "But you better wait until tomorrow. The Indian woman is going to be busy for the remainder of the night reading the memoirs of Jacob Ingledew, which the Woman suggested she read, to disabuse her of the notion that her ancestor, Fanshaw's wife, was raped by Jacob."

"Raped?" says Bo. "That's preposterous."

"Tell her that, when you see her," Boss says.

Before leaving, George told Boss just to say the word and he'd round up the boys and give them injuns a escort out of the whole country. But Boss said that probably wouldn't be necessary, even if it weren't so inhospitable. "The least we can do," Boss says, "is let them reclaim their ancestral campsite."

So George just went on home and put it out of his mind for the rest of the night. But the very next morning, bright and early, while George was eating his Lucky Charms cereal, there come a knock at his door, and George snuck a peek out the window to see that there shiny Pierce-Arrow getting chummy with his Explorer. He opened the front door, and there was the heap big injun. He was wearing a different Hawaiian shirt than he'd had on yesterday, but he still had that hired driver's cap on his head.

"Good morning, George!" says Thomas Bending Bear, singing it more than saying it. "I hope I didn't wake you."

"Naw, I was just eating my breakfast," George says, and knew it was rude not to invite a guest, even a strange injun, to join you. "Come in and have you a cup of coffee." George poured him a mug, and even says, "Lucky Charms?"

"No, thank you very much," says Ben. "Our hostess has already filled us with *khinkali*, an exquisite breakfast dumpling common to her native Georgia."

"Georgia?" says George. "I thought she was from some'ers in Europe."

The injun laughs. "There's a Georgia in Europe too, you know."

"Where's your boss-lady?" George asks.

"She's very busy reading. Very busy reading."

He says it twice, as if George might be feebleminded, which he aint.

When their coffee was finished, Ben says, "Would you care to go for a drive?"

Actually George wouldn't, but he needed a good excuse not to go to work for Ingledew Ham this morning. He'd overdone it yesterday; and besides, he had to get used to letting others take over his job, because when this here campaign really got clicking, he wasn't going to be around very much anyhow. "In that thing?" George says, and pointed at the Pierce-Arrow.

"If you want to sit in back, you could pretend I'm your chauffeur," says Ben.

"I'd as lief sit up front with you," says George.

"How sweet!" says Ben, and pats him on the arm. "You wouldn't happen to have a chain saw I could borrow?"

George fetched his chain saw and after thinking it over decided not to ask the injun what he wanted it for. If he was a-fixing to use it on human beings, leastways I aint a Ingledew, George reminded himself.

That there Pierce-Arrow was some automobile. As they rode around, hither and yon, not going nowheres in particular, Ben told him all about the car, its whole history, how many cylinders it had, etsettery. Seems that when the Osages commenced getting rich from all that oil, back in the twenties, the Pierce-Arrow was their vehicle of choice and became as common as clothes, though you hardly ever saw one anymore, leastways not in Osage country. It sure was a fine-riding car, and George felt rich just a-setting in it.

Ben interrupted his harangue about the Pierce-Arrow to say, "What beautiful country! These glorious mountains! All my life I've lived in flat country, Oklahoma, with scarcely a hill. And my people—you know, the Heart Stays band—always had to have a flat but hummocky creek bank to settle upon . . . like *that* one."

Ben pointed, and George all of a sudden caught on that the injun hadn't been just gadding about without no purpose but had been heading all along for this particular spot, which George knew was where the Osage camp had stood when Jacob and Noah Ingledew came to settle Stay More. There wasn't ary trace of it left behind, not a piece of pottery or nothing, maybe an arrowhead somewheres but not in the camp itself. There was just this hummocky stretch of meadow right beside Swains Creek. Hadn't no white man ever built on it; it had been the Duckworths' pasture at one time, and during World War II it had been a bivouac for army tanks on maneuvers, and then the Duckworths reclaimed it and it had stayed a pasture for some years until Boss had cut down all the barbed wire so the hogs could run free.

Ben stopped the car. He just sat there and looked out at that meadow for a while, kindly wistful-like. George had him a idea what the injun might be thinking and, recalling what Boss had said last night about letting the injuns have it back if they cared to, and what Ben had said yesterday about pitching a wigwam on it, George says, "It's yours if you want it."

Ben's eyes was full of water when he turned his head back to look at George. "Really?" he says. "On whose authority? Is it yours to give me?"

"It's Boss's," George says. "All the land hereabouts belongs to him. And he says you can have that piece where your ancestors made their home."

Ben swept his mighty arm to take in the whole world. "My ancestors had 'all the land hereabouts,' which now belongs to your boss. Of course my ancestors did not have it, because they did not know the meaning of property ownership, but it was theirs."

"You wouldn't settle for that there meadow?" George asks.

"It appears your swine have already taken full possession of it," Ben says. And sure enough there was a whole bunch of hogs a-rooting and a-wallowing all over the place.

George laughed. "I reckon them swine sorta feels the same way about it your ancestors did. They don't own it, because creatures, like men, can't own the earth. And if you was to set up your wigwam or whatever, even right atop their favorite wallow, they'd just move on across the creek or somewheres else."

Big Ben real sudden gave George a mighty hug. It was embarrassing. While Ben was a-hugging him, with arms that could've crushed him if George wasn't pretty darn sturdy hisself, George could only pat him on the back and say, "There there. There there."

"Can I cut down a few of those trees?" Ben asks, and points at a thicket of bodark saplings.

"It's your land," George says.

George had nothing better to do this morning, so he helped Ben make his wigwam, or rather a pair of them, a sort of double hut bound tight together. Ben explained that the sapling George called bodark was the bois d'arc, *Maclura pomifera*, also called Osage orange, not just because of its orange-colored wood and its fruit, which looks like an oversized orange ("We call 'em horse-apples," says George) but also because the Osage Indians had used the tree to make their bows and arrows and build their houses. What Ben and George would do was, they'd use the chain saw to cut down a long slender trunk of the bodark, sharpen both ends with an ax (which Ben already had, maybe to do some ax murders with), and then the two of them would bend that pole into an arc and stick both ends deep into the ground.

"I could never have done this by myself," Ben says. "Thank you so much. Thank you so very much."

Then, when they had about ten of them poles interwoven and arched into a big circle, they covered the sides with reeds and cattails, which grew all along the creek bank.

It took just two days to finish the job, hooking the second beehive wigwam to the first one on the second day. There wasn't no door connecting one beehive with the other'n in between. "What's the point of joining 'em?" George wants to know.

"Now that is a mystery," Ben said. "My lady's mansion in Oklahoma is constructed in pretty much the same design, only infinitely larger, of course, and there are several connecting doors between one 'beehive' and the other. But here . . ." Ben fetched from the Pierce-Arrow a book, called *The Architecture of the Arkansas Ozarks*, and showed George one of the pitchers. The pitcher was exactly what they'd just been doing. "I'm just following orders," Ben says, and his voice was kind of wistful. "I'm just doing what my lady asks me. All my life it has been that way."

When they had the double wigwam all done, Ben's lady come down to take a look at it, and she had the Woman, Cat, with her, and also Bo, who was driving 'em in his Nissan 4-by-4, and even the dog Threasher. But no Boss. "Wonderful," the lovely gal says, and gives Ben a big hug despite he's all wet from the sweat of his work.

"Half the work was his," says Ben, and the smiling eyeful goes to give George a hug too, but he backs off, not on account of he's soaked with sweat but because he knows if she touches him he'll turn into a pillar of mush.

"You've been more than kind," she says to George.

"Aw, it wasn't much of nothing," George says. "I just did what he told me to."

"Is it ready for me to try it out?" she asks Ben.

"I haven't put the bedding in it yet," he says, "but the structure is finished."

"You're going to sleep here?" Bo asks her. "May I have the other side?"

The gal laughs. "Bo, you'd have incredible dreams if you did. No, I have to spend at least one night here all alone."

George has been thinking that if these injuns really intended to use this beehive combo for living purposes, that the reason there are two of them without no door in between is that one is hers, the other'n is his, but it appeared that's not what she had in mind. Bending Bear wouldn't sleep here at all, or not unless he built another beehive combo for hisself.

Ben had been sleeping in one of the spare rooms at Cat's house, although just last night when he drove George home he stayed a awful long time, drinking George's bourbon and making hints so plain any fool could've figured out that Ben was trying to get hisself invited to spend the night. George had a terrible time getting rid of him.

"Look, Threasher's pointing!" Ben says, and sure enough that dumb dog was just a-standing there with his tail straight as a rod. Ben ran and searched and came back a-holding this here big soft-shelled turtle, who was trying his best to bend his neck and bite Ben's hand.

"My supper!" says Juliana Heartstays, as if she'd been in that Maisonette restaurant in Cincinnati. George would have puked but he had a empty stomach. "Good boy, Threasher! Point a few more, and I'll invite all these people to a feast."

And sure enough, that turtle dog rounded up a whole bunch of terrapins and box turtles and softshells, and even a snapping turtle out in the creek. That crazy dog just went wild, pointing them critters as fast as Ben could catch 'em and chop off their heads with his ax, the same ax he'd used to build the wigwam with.

And Juliana Heartstays declared they'd have a real feast that evening for supper, right here on the creek bank, to "housewarm" the new habitation. An old-style injun celebration. Cat said she'd be glad to take a couple of the turtles and use a old Svanetian recipe on 'em and contribute 'em to the feast.

Near about everbody was invited: Day and Diana, Sharon and Larry, Boss and Jelena, etsettery. Cast showed up with a local girl, Sheila Kimber, who was the bookkeeper at the plant and was a real looker herself. But Boss never showed up. Jelena said he claimed he was rehearsing a speech he was a-fixing to give in Pine Bluff next week—and George realized his services as helicopter pilot would remove him from the presence of these injuns in just a few more days. But when Jelena was making excuses for Boss, George noticed she winked at Bo, as if she and Bo knew the real reason Boss wouldn't come, but so did everbody else, practically, except Juliana herself—not that he was scared of the threat that these injuns was out to assassinate him, but pure and simple that he couldn't face womenfolks on account of his congenital Ingledew disorder: pathological woman-shyness. The way it worked was, the prettier the woman was, the worse the Ingledews' disorder. And Juliana Heartstays was just about as pretty as they make 'em. Even if Boss hadn't laid eyes on her yet, but just had to go by George and Bo's descriptions.

She threw a real spread. Right out there on the creek bank. George was happy to tote in a bunch of sawhorses and planks to set up some tables, and Cat and Jelena covered 'em with nice tablecloths, and all the womenfolks contributed their very best desserts: you never in your life saw such a passel of tasty pies and cobblers and a fancy Georgian lemon tea cake made by Cat that George couldn't wait to set his teeth into, but first he had to at least pretend like he was a-sampling some of that turtle meat. Why couldn't one of the women have brought a platter of fried chicken? There wasn't nothing but turtle: The main course was little meat pies made with turtle, but there was side dishes of turtle stew, fried turtle, and turtle soup, with plenty of good wines and George's own contribution of a case of Molson's ale. When Thomas Bending Bear saw that George wasn't even tasting any of them turtle dishes, he practically held him down and forced him to bite into a piece of fried snapping turtle, and George was amazed to discover it wasn't uneatable; in fact it was pretty tasty, sort of like a cross between chicken and ham. George was just half kidding when he told Ben the two of them ought to put Threasher into business and start a turtle-packing company to compete with Ingledew Ham. "I'd love to be your partner," Ben says.

All and all, it was one of the best eatin parties George had ever attended. He just wished Boss could've been there. Juliana and Ben both made little speeches, saying they was so happy to be here and so happy to get to know all these good people, and although they had come originally with ill feeling in their hearts toward the descendants of the Ingledews who had forced their ancestors away from this homeland, they realized that such removal and change had been inevitable, almost a part of Nature's plan, and now we were privileged to witness this handsome edifice as testament to the cooperation of an Osage Indian, Thomas Bending Bear, and a near-Ingledew, Mr. George Dinsmore.

At home later that night, after getting rid of Ben, who wouldn't hardly take no for a answer, George was just a-setting around digesting that big supper and the three pieces of lemon tea cake he'd eaten, and he got to pondering about Juliana spending the night all by herself out there in that wigwam. George knew she didn't have nothing to fear from the hogs, even if the hogs was resentful that Juliana had forced them out the same way that Boss's ancestors had supposedly forced out Juliana's ancestors. No, the hogs wouldn't bother her. And there wasn't no coyotes or wolves or bears or nothing hereabouts. But George wondered if that fine woman might get any trouble from human beings. Who knows? That Bolin Pharis sure had the hots for her. George had noticed how Bo had kind of cozied up to her during the party, always talking to her and laughing with her and what-all. Obviously the fool had his heart a-sliding down his wrist. No telling but what he might take a notion to see if she didn't need some company in the wee hours of the night.

George couldn't put it out of his mind. Nigh on to midnight, he got into his Explorer and drove over pretty near the Osage camp, switched off his headlights, drove on closer, stopped, and walked the last quarter mile or so. It was a dark night, dark as pitch, no moon, and George stumbled a couple of times. He wasn't young anymore. He was thinking, when this here campaign was all finished and done with, and Boss was either elected governor or defeated enough to drive some sense into his head, George might just take a early retirement.

He crept as soundlessly as he could to the vicinity of the Osage camp. There was no light of any kind inside the wigwam; she'd be fast asleep this time of night. But George could hear voices. One of the voices was some man's, but George couldn't tell if it was Bo or not. George tried to creep closer, but then Threasher caught wind of him and commenced barking, and George hightailed it out of there, falling down more than once.

Just as he was making it back to his Explorer, he happened to detect the looming bulk of some other vehicle parked off the road amongst the brush. He went up to it until he could tell, practically by feel, that it wasn't Bo's Nissan. It was a Land-Rover. George was abashed that it took him awhile to figure out who it was, hereabouts, that owned a Land-Rover. It ought to have hit him all at once, all of a heap: fellow name of Ingledew, better known as Boss.

Chapter Thirteen

They were made to wait in the reception lounge of Republican headquarters, which was not in customary downtown Little Rock but in an elegant new building on Chenal Parkway in the upscale western suburbs. They were offered their choice of beverages, even alcoholic ones, but still they had to wait. Bo explained to Cast that this was just a transparent ploy that Billy Joe Slade was using to put them in their place. "He knows we're here," Bo told Cast, "and he's not particularly busy. But he wants us to cool our heels as an additional reminder that we're on his turf, this is his show, and he's going to call all the shots." But if any of this explanation was getting through to Cast, there was no way of telling.

Bo had invited Cast along for three reasons: one, the kid needed the experience, especially of how to sit at the bargaining table with the enemy; two, on the long drive in the Jaguar from Fayetteville, Bo preferred for a change not his haunting solitude but a sounding board for his ideas, not just about the campaign; and three, Bo wanted somebody on his side of the table in this showdown. But it may have been a mistake: during the recent interlude, Cast too had fallen under Stay More's magic spell, had apparently become deeply involved with some local girl he'd found picking flowers in the forest, and couldn't get her off his mind.

Bo had thrown enough loaded questions at Cast to be able to determine that, sure enough, Cast had managed to rid himself of his long-standing virginity. *Maybe he's the only one who got any*, Bo reflected. He certainly hadn't gotten any himself. Bending Bear's lust for George Dinsmore had apparently gone unrequited. And Vernon . . . despite Bo's best efforts as a pimp, after all the trouble Bo had gone to, setting up an assignation for Vernon and Juliana that would've circumvented Vernon's appalling shyness toward women, in much the same fashion that his ancestor Jacob had been able to get around his shyness toward Juliana's ancestor (using full darkness but without benefit of whiskey), you would think that Vernon might at least have reported back to Bo on the success or failure of the venture. But Bo still did not know if anything sexual had ever transpired between them.

"Did you catch a word of what I said?" Bo asked Cast, who was staring dreamily off into space, his gaze narrowly missing a huge poster of Shoat Bradfield smiling and offering his hand to the world.

"Sir?" Cast said. "Oh, yes, sir, we have to sweat it out to take the starch out of us, so we'll be meek and nervous when he tries to put one over on us."

Bo chuckled. "Good enough. We didn't have to do this, you know. We could have insisted he come to Fayetteville, on *our* turf. Or we could have met him for lunch at a neutral place." The first polls following Vernon's victory in the runoff had shown Vernon trailing Bradfield by 24 points, 57 to 33, with 10 percent undecided. Of course, part of that lead was from Democratic supporters of the Reverend John Colby Dixon (and of James Barnas), who were still bitter over Vernon's win. But as of right now, Billy Joe Slade could afford to gloat over his man's commanding lead. Still, Bo felt very condescending toward Billy Joe, whom he hadn't seen for years and was then just a deputy assistant campaign manager, who had supposedly risen from the ranks of *salesmen*: Slade had made his reputation as a live-wire peddler of pharmaceuticals, winning national awards for his prowess as a pitchman.

"So why did we come *here*?" Cast wanted to know.

"Just to let him know we're not afraid of him," Bo said. "But listen, we've got to stay focused. This campaign is going to be all uphill, and we can't let our recent adventures distract us from the matter at hand."

Speak for yourself, Bo, he thought. He was having the devil's own time keeping his mind clear of the two enthralling women whose company had given him so much recent pleasure. If he were not already madly in love with Jelena, he could so easily have fallen in love with Juliana (Bo took credit for being the first to notice, even before Vernon did, the great similarity of their given names). And because he had lost his head and his heart over Jelena, it was easy for him to want, even without thinking about it, to push Vernon toward Juliana. Had there ever been a situation in politics comparable to this one? Had a campaign manager ever become a pimp to get a woman for his candidate so he could steal his candidate's woman? That was a blunt way of putting it, but that was the way it was going to look in Bo's memoirs whenever he got around to writing them, and the more complicated this situation became the more determined Bo was to put the whole story on paper eventually. *But that's the distant future, Bolin Pharis! Get ahold of yourself!*

"Sir? What's the distant future?" Cast asked.

"What? Was I talking aloud?" Bo muttered.

Finally Billy Joe Slade came out of his inner sanctum and greeted them. "Sorry to keep you guys waiting," he said.

"Like hell you are," Bo said.

"Doin all right, Bo?" Billy Joe said. "Aint seen you in ages. Welcome to Li'l Rawk again." He gestured expansively with his hand and ushered them into a room where there were four chairs facing a blackboard, one of those portable flip-over two-sided blackboards on casters. There was no table and nothing else in the room. "Just have you a seat, and he ought to be here any minute."

"Who ought to be here?" Bo asked.

"The guv'nor."

"Hell, Slade, you didn't tell me that Bradfield was going to be in on this," Bo objected.

"You wouldn't want to leave His Excellency out, would ya? That would be downright rude and disrespectful."

"But it would only have been fair, then, if Ingledew could have joined in also."

"I heard tell he was real busy starting a wham-bang stump-speakin rally down to Pine Bluff."

That was true. Vernon himself had chosen to inaugurate his new tour of Arkansas towns—almost a hundred of them scheduled—by throwing a gala party-cum-speech at one of Arkansas's less prepossessing locales: the populous but downtrodden city of Pine Bluff, where equal numbers of blacks and whites would turn out (they hoped) to feast on Ingledew Ham and to watch and hear Ingledew's Instrumentalists, Vernon's Vocalists, and the Cheerleaders in a three-ring extravaganza opening for an old-fashioned demonstration of oratory by the Democratic candidate. Lydia and Carleton had used good chunks of their recent vacation planning it all.

It had been hard for Bo to decide whether or not to give the staff the brief vacation in the first place. Arch had argued against it, and had only grudgingly agreed to take a few days off, go to Turner's Bend (where, Bo knew, Arch would love to reside permanently if Beverly would allow it), and kick the campaign out of his canoe for a while. As for himself, Bo had needed and thoroughly enjoyed every minute of the vacation . . . although he'd not exactly consummated his passion for Jelena.

While the Samurai had been on brief vacation, Shoat Bradfield himself had lost no time in beginning the contest . . . although, characteristically, he had stuck his foot in his mouth. As soon as

Vernon's victory in the runoff was announced, the governor had gone on television to declare, "If he thinks beating a two-bit preacher-man earned him a shot at the title, let him come on. The lowdown scumbag deserves to be kicked to death by a jackass, and I'm just the one to do it!" Moments passed before Billy Joe Slade whispered something into Bradfield's ear, and Bradfield blushed and said, "Let me rephrase that."

And now here was the jackass himself. Bo and Cast rose from their seats respectfully as he entered the room. Even if the man was a crook, a lowlife, and an asshole, he was still the governor of Arkansas, the state's highest elected official, and you couldn't help feeling some sense of awe in his presence.

"We meet at last," Shoat Bradfield said to Bo, pumping his hand. "I've heard so much about you. You're a legend in Arkansas politics, even if you turned your back on us and went east." Bradfield was physically imposing, in much the same way that Bo himself was, but his face, up close, was pocked and sallow, and whatever handsomeness he had once possessed had been corroded by alcohol.

"I never turned my back on you, Governor," Bo said. "I just had more important things to do."

"But now we've got the *most* important thing to do, and I've got another meeting at the statehouse in an hour, so we'd better get cracking. Billy Joe, light into 'em!"

"Yessir," Billy Joe said. "If y'all will just make yourselfs comfortable. Anybody want a drink or anything?" Billy Joe moved to the blackboard and gave it a flip so that the empty front turned away to show the backside, which had writing all over it. "Now let's see what we got here," Billy Joe said.

There were thirteen items written on the blackboard. In the margin at the beginning of each was a crude drawing, like restroom graffiti, representing some kind of bird, a cross between a chicken and a seagull, except that its wingspan was extremely long and thin. After Bo had read Item One on the blackboard, he suddenly realized what the crude drawing was supposed to represent: an albatross.

1. Refuses to believe that Jesus Christ is the Son of the Living God.
2. Never elected to any office anywhere at any time.
3. Has slept for thirty years out of wedlock with his very own first cousin. No children, no experience with child-raising.
4. Never worked. Owns a large unregulated pig farm managed by others and earns income from ham-processing operation in which he takes no part.
5. Said pig farm is in remote Ozark Mountain boondocks, out of touch with the rest of Arkansas.
6. Resides there with said first cousin in outlandish homemade "house" consisting of two huge bubbles, unlike anything ever seen elsewhere.
7. Never been to college. High school diploma only.
8. Uses big words to make himself seem smart, although this makes everybody else feel dumb.
9. No military experience whatsoever. Could have served in Vietnam but never signed up.
10. Walks and moves around like he's got all day; laziness is infectious.
11. Really just a pretty boy. Like all very good-looking men, he's vain and obsessed with appearance.
12. He's opposed to things that give enjoyment, like television, cigarettes, and guns. He thinks schools and prisons and hospitals ought to be abolished.
13. Despite being handsome, he's scared to death of women or anything female. Can't even look at them, let alone talk to them.

"Isn't that just beautiful?" Governor Shoat Bradfield declared admiringly. "Good job, Billy Joe!"

"Where did you get this?" Bo demanded.

"Well, I'll tell ya," Billy Joe said. "You've been known to mention the Albert Ross bird to other people, haven't you?"

"Who? Oh, yes, I'm the originator of the metaphor of the albatross, but I didn't spell out all these items."

"But there they are!" said Shoat Bradfield. "And boy, are we gonna have us some fun with 'em! Billy Joe, do you want to give him the big news or do you want me to do it?"

"I can do it, Chief," Billy Joe said, and he and the governor exchanged huge smirks. "Hate to tell you this, Bo, 'cause I know it will just break your heart, but Mr. Carleton Drew aint working for you folks anymore. As of day before yesterday, he is in the employ of His Excellency Shoat Bradfield."

Bo was infuriated, but he kept himself in check. It was understandable that Carleton, given his fondness for television advertising and his frustration over Vernon's refusal to sanction it, would have wanted to work for a man who would appreciate his talents. But to betray his former employer by giving the opposition all thirteen albatrosses was incomprehensible.

"I thought he was a good man," Cast remarked mournfully, "but he's just a greedy shit heel."

The governor snuffled. That was the only word for the man's inability to laugh or chuckle or chortle. Billy Joe Slade began to describe in detail just what they intended to do with their information about Vernon, but Bo found he couldn't pay attention; his mind was deliberately wandering, not just to escape the dishonor of Carleton's defection but to seek out more attractive objects of contemplation: a pair of fabulous women. Even if the holiday in Stay More hadn't afforded any sexual consummations (other than Cast's), it had certainly *started* something. At least Vernon was willing to report to Bo that he and Juliana had talked into the wee hours not just one but three nights, or perhaps four. After Bo had had to leave Stay More, Vernon had remained until it was time for George to helicopt him down to Pine Bluff. And Vernon was willing to admit to Bo that he had quickly discovered the essential difference between Jelena and Juliana: Jelena was lovely and warm and almost unbearably intelligent, but Juliana was unimaginably beautiful and earthy and vigorous.

During his own lengthy conversations with Juliana, in the gradual process of "introducing" her to Vernon, Bo had learned much about her background and her original motive for coming to Stay More. Bo and Juliana had in common that they were recent readers of the memoirs of Jacob Ingledew, and Juliana was willing to admit that it was difficult for her to cling to the notion that Jacob had raped Kushi, as Fanshaw's wife was called, after having read the memoirs—or even to blame Jacob in any way for the out-migration of those last two remaining Osages. Juliana had showed Bo her .38 Smith & Wesson, had told him of the arsenal of weapons that Thomas Bending Bear kept in the trunk of the Pierce-Arrow, and had declared that she had fully intended to employ the weapons on all of the Ingledews, but after reading Jacob's candid and apparently truthful memoirs she had told Ben they wouldn't be killing anybody.

"Excuse me, Mr. Pharis, are you paying attention?" The governor's unpleasant voice brought Bo back from idyllic Stay More to the harsh reality of Little Rock.

Bo looked at the governor, taking in his sneer, his clouded eyes, his haughty jaw, and for a moment—just a moment—he felt sorry for him.

"You may call me Bo," he said. Then he rose from his chair, moved to the blackboard, and gave it a flip that turned away the thirteen albatrosses and revealed a clean slate. He took up the chalk, silently thanking Harry Wolfe and his sidekick, Garth Rucker. He drew a bird, a cross between a pelican and a bald eagle, and said,

"This, gentlemen, is not an albatross but a foo bird. Have you ever heard the legend of the foo bird? Stop me if you've heard it. The bird is native only to areas of Africa where elephants live, although the connection between the bird and elephants is not certain.

"Anyway, a group of explorers quickly discovered the foo bird's habit of dive-bombing them from the air with excrement, as we've all experienced from pigeons and other birds. Several of the explorers thus besmirched quickly washed it off and just as quickly died a painful death. A native explained to the last remaining explorer that the only way to survive the droppings of the bird is *not* to wash it off. The moral of this story, gentlemen, is: If the foo shits, wear it."

The governor's snuffle was feeble. Billy Joe's laugh was perfunctory and impatient. Cast cackled.

"All right," Bo said. "Foo Bird Number One." And he began to sketch thirteen numbered foo birds on the blackboard, and with each number he spoke these words:

1. Sent to principal in fourth grade for calling Abraham Lincoln "a Jew niggerlover."
2. Suspended from school in fifth grade for calling principal "a cunt."
3. Expelled from school in the sixth grade for drilling peepholes through the wall into the stalls of the girls' rest room. And for charging admission.
4. Insufficient credits for high school graduation. Purchased for $100 an equivalency certificate from a school official later jailed.
5. Did not actually receive diploma from Southern Arkansas University; registrar's records show sixteen hours of incompletes and thirty hours of Fs.
6. Defeated in three high school elections and four college elections.

7. Never elected to any office before running for governor.
8. Spent most of military service in the brig for insubordination and goldbricking.
9. Made fortune in real estate, mostly from selling poor properties at twice their value.
10. Of all promises made in his first campaign for governor, not one has been kept.
11. Three different physicians have urged him to join AA, but he refuses. Gave January's state of the state address while plastered and incoherent.
12. Has not been able to keep a chief of staff longer than three months and has had six of them so far.
13. His Republican predecessor, Mike Huckabee, has privately called him "inept, foolish, and disappointing."

Bo's thirteen foo birds nearly covered the blackboard, but he could squeeze in one more. "I see you, and I'll raise you one," he said to Billy Joe Slade, who was sitting open-mouthed and dumbstruck. And he put one more foo bird on the board:

14. His teenage daughter is residing at a private mental hospital, Charter Vista.

"I assume that when you stole Carleton Drew from us you also attempted to steal Harry Wolfe," Bo said. "But you didn't. So he's busy, even as we speak, tracking down those five former chiefs of staff of yours to learn their reasons for quitting. And he has dispatched his lieutenant, Garth Rucker, to Charter Vista to learn by hook or by crook the reasons your daughter is incarcerated there. Their next project is to find out why your wife wears such heavy makeup. To cover her bruises, perhaps?"

Shoat Bradfield was standing, his hands on his hips, his face as red as a baboon's buttocks. "You filthy scum," he said. "Have you no decency at all?"

"Have you?" Bo asked.

The governor glowered, or tried to glower, but his lip was trembling, and suddenly he burst into tears. He lost control completely and shook with sobs. Billy Joe Slade had to embrace him and hold him for a long time and then lead him out of the room into another chamber.

"Gosh, sir," Cast said, when they were alone, "I've never seen such a display of swordsmanship in my life. You shredded him!"

"He has shredded himself," Bo observed.

They waited for a while but remained alone. "Maybe we should just go?" Cast suggested.

Bo held up a finger. "One minute."

In less than a minute, Billy Joe Slade returned. "Shame," he said. "Shame on y'all. That was uncalled for, and it was disrespectful to the chief executive of Arkansas, and you've hurt a good man in such a way that it just makes my blood boil!"

"It was tit for tat, plain and simple," Bo said. "If you don't know that, you haven't learned the first thing about politics."

"But y'all have got such an unfair advantage over us!" Billy Joe observed.

"Thank you," Bo said. "I intend to keep it that way."

"What are your plans, could I ask? Do you plan to start leaking that stuff right away? Or are you gonna save it for later in the campaign?"

"We would prefer never having to use any of it," Bo told him. "It depends on what *you* do with what you've got on Ingledew. If you don't reveal anything, we won't. That's tit for tat too, you know."

"But that's not the way people campaign anymore. You know that. Even the public expects us to tear into each other; if we don't, they'll wonder if we've made some kind of deal."

"Let 'em wonder," Bo suggested. Then he asked, "*Have* we made a deal?" He offered his hand.

Billy Joe didn't take it. "I'll have to clear it with the governor first. I'll get back to you soon as I can."

So that was that, for the time being. Mission accomplished. Bo and Cast got into the Jaguar and headed back to Fayetteville. Bo had considered going on down to Pine Bluff to watch Vernon's big rally, but he had seen it before and he hated crowds and there really wasn't much that he or Cast could do to lend a hand down there. But he intended to promote Cast to Carleton Drew's position and told him so on the return trip to Fayetteville. Cast protested that he wasn't a media expert like Drew. "But didn't you learn anything from him?" Bo wondered. Oh, yes, lots, Cast said, but he just wouldn't know how to do all the things that Drew could do. "Like turn traitor?" Bo said. Cast said he couldn't understand why Carleton would have done that. "Then you're not as smart as I've been giving you credit for," Bo said.

Once again, he permitted his thoughts to drift away from the machinations of politics, away from the self-serving dishonesty of such as Carleton Drew and toward the halcyon contemplation of those two goddesses in Stay More. Or *three*, if we count the Woman Whom We Cannot Name, who had told Bo that the coming of the two Osages must have been ordained by Anangka, the name she gave to her personal Fate-Thing, a sort of fairy godmother. Bo knew the Woman had spent years researching a book she'd published on the Osage, and he also knew the Woman was rumored to have been a novelist before she went into seclusion. Maybe, Bo reflected, she would beat him to the pleasure of telling the story that was unfolding before them.

At Russellville, Bo abruptly left the interstate and headed north on State Highway 7. He told Cast they'd done enough work for the day, maybe enough for two days, so why didn't they just take a little detour and drop by Stay More to see if it was still there? Cast of course was thrilled beyond words, but he did have to call Bo's attention to the fact that they were driving the Jaguar, not the Nissan 4-by-4, and the roads of Stay More were rough. Bo suggested they could just leave the Jag at the Stay More Hotel and get people to come pick them up. Didn't Cast's girlfriend have a car? Sure, Cast said, and then he asked, Hotel? And Bo explained the history of the Jacob Ingledew house, how after the death of the original Whom We Cannot Name, one of the Ingledew women had converted the house into a hotel, which had never done much business during the decline of the village. Bo told Cast that if he ever found the leisure to do so, he ought to read *The Architecture of the Arkansas Ozarks*.

Stay More in the heat and drought of July was still a luxuriant garden, nearly swallowed up in dense and unrestrained plant life; the contrast with the city they'd just left a few hours before was fantastic. The only vehicle in town was the Pierce-Arrow, parked in the shade of a giant maple tree beside the former hotel, and that made it seem as if they were escaping not just from the city but from time, back into the thirties. On the long porch of the house, whose frilly roof sheltered them from the late afternoon sun, sat three people, the Woman and Juliana in rocking chairs and Bending Bear in the porch swing.

Was it just Bo's imagination, or were the women dressed as they would have seventy years before? At least Bending Bear wasn't wearing one of his loud Hawaiian shirts but a collarless broadcloth dress shirt, and his chauffeur's cap had been replaced with a straw sombrero. The women were wearing calico cotton dresses such as Bo had seen in old pictures of countryfolk. With the pointer Threasher sprawled out on the porch floor, the scene was a tableau of yesteryear.

Cast used the car phone to ask his girlfriend to come and

pick him up, and Bo reflected that the technology of the car phone was out of keeping with this setting. It was hard, though, to step out of the Jaguar's air-conditioning into the heat.

There were other chairs, including another rocker, lined along the porch, and they could sit in these, after exchanging greetings. "Too hot for the wigwam?" Bo asked Juliana.

That radiant smile. "I don't think the original Stay Morons spent much time in their wigwams on days like this," she said.

The Woman observed that they ought to be inside enjoying the air-conditioning, but nobody anywhere sits on their porches anymore. If you have a porch, why not use it? Bending Bear remarked that when Threasher wasn't able to move because of the heat, he couldn't move either. He was fanning himself with an old-fashioned funeral-parlor fan. Where had he got *that*?

They all sat on the porch and watched the world fail to go by. Eventually Cast's girlfriend arrived, and Cast introduced her to Bo, although he'd already met her, briefly, at the turtle feast. Sheila Kimber was a very pretty young lady whose people went way back in the history in Stay More. You could tell by the way that she and Cast looked at each other that they were fast becoming a number. Before leaving with her, Cast asked Bo when and where they should meet the following day, for the return to Fayetteville, and Bo said they ought to meet right here around two o'clock, or whenever lunch was finished.

When Cast and Sheila were gone, Juliana said, "So you're spending the night?"

"If I can find a place to crash," Bo said.

"Oh, I'm sure Jelena would love to have you!" she said.

Did he blush? Bo abruptly had a disquieting thought: Juliana and Jelena had become friends and were comparing notes on both Vernon and Bo. Well, actually, he told her, he was thinking of doing something he hadn't done since he was a kid: worm fishing by lantern light for catfish.

"Down at my creek?" Juliana asked, smiling, always smiling.

"*Your* creek?" Bo said. "I didn't realize you owned it."

"Osages own nothing, I've told you that," she said. "But Guckah Wazhingah—Swan Creek—is a major source of our food supply, including those turtles."

He said that unless he was mistaken it wasn't Swan Creek but Swains Creek, named after the family of Swains who were early settlers.

The Woman spoke up. "*Wazhingah* means any kind of bird, and Juliana's home in Oklahoma is on Bird Creek."

They made chitchat about Oklahoma and birds and creeks and turtles and worm fishing by lantern light for catfish. The subject of birds tempted him to relate the morning's battle between the albatross and the foo bird, but he decided to put politics out of his mind. Eventually Bo stole a glance at his watch and announced that he supposed he ought to at least give Jelena a ring and get himself invited to her place.

"She's not at home," Juliana said. "She's having supper with Diana and Day."

How could Juliana know that unless they were becoming friends? Bo was only mildly disappointed to learn Jelena wasn't at home. He could catch her later. He was really more interested in talking with Juliana for now. But he needed to get her away from the Woman and from Bending Bear. Half of that problem was solved when the Woman excused herself to go inside and start supper, first inviting Bo to dine with them if he wanted (and where else would he get a bite?). The other half was solved shortly thereafter when Ben announced that it was just too damned hot for him and he was going up to his room to cool off before supper.

So they were alone. Bo discovered he could tell her privately what he couldn't tell the others, the battle of the albatross and the foo bird, which greatly amused her as well as made her admire his swordsmanship, as Cast had called it. His summary finished, he remarked that somehow it all seemed as if it had happened in another decade in another continent to another person.

"I'm glad you're *here*, Bo," she said.

"So," he said. "Where were we? I was about to ask you, What do you think of your cousin Vernon?"

The radiant smile became more effulgent. "He's the most charming man I've ever met."

"In utter darkness how could you tell?"

She laughed. "Just his voice. But I saw him in daylight too. I have laid eyes on him. After you left. Before he left. He had George land the helicopter near the wigwam the other morning. George kept the rotor running and Vernon kept his head down so it wouldn't get chopped off or that's the way it looked, but actually he was keeping his head down so he wouldn't have to look at me because he still couldn't stand to see me. They were on their way to Pine Bluff, and he wanted to say goodbye and tell me he was so glad I hadn't murdered him, and he hoped I would stay here forever. And then he kissed me and took off."

"Forever?" Bo said. "Kissed you? Wow."

"He had kissed me before, in the dark, in the wigwam."

"And that's all he did? He didn't suggest that you and he reenact the first meeting of Jacob Ingledew and Kushi?"

"He didn't bathe beforehand in three waters, in rainwater, in creekwater, in springwater." Juliana laughed.

Bo laughed with her. In Jacob's memoirs, as well as in *The Architecture of the Arkansas Ozarks*, the Indian Fanshaw, after finally persuading the reluctant Jacob to accept his offer of his wife, explains to Jacob that Indians can't tolerate the smell of white people and therefore Jacob should first wash in three waters, rainwater, creekwater, and springwater, and then, instead of putting his buckskins back on, arrive naked at the wigwam. "If I bathed in three waters, could I come to the wigwam tonight?" Bo boldly asked her.

She stopped laughing and stared at him, as if she were trying to decide. She asked, "You wouldn't rather stay with Jelena?"

Bo lied. "You are much more desirable."

They reparteed. Juliana wondered aloud why Bo wanted her if he had been so intent on getting her and Vernon together. Bo countered that since Vernon wasn't here, and alluring Juliana was all alone, Bo would be a fool not to avail himself of the opportunity. Juliana said that sounded like an excellent excuse for availing himself of Jelena. They bantered with each other over this topic until the Woman returned to the porch to announce that supper was ready. After an excellent dinner of *kuchmachi*—a Georgian dish combining chicken giblets and walnuts—served with a surprising bottle of Pouilly Fuissé, Bo and Juliana returned to the porch while Ben remained with the Woman, who wanted to continue a conversation they'd started about Maria Tallchief, the Osage ballerina, another cousin of theirs.

Bo remarked that Ben and the Woman seemed to enjoy each other's company, and Juliana said they spent all their time together, now that George was gone. "You know, of course, that Ben's crush on George is nearly as strong as my crush on Vernon," Juliana said. "But quite possibly neither of us will ever accomplish our desires."

Bo scoffed. "Oh, if you want Vernon, I'm sure you'll get him sooner or later. But Ben—for heaven's sake, George Dinsmore is old enough to be his father!" Bo remembered his own first impression of George in Cincinnati as a somewhat uncouth and tough but kindly hillbilly, and he could not imagine why a refined person like Bending Bear would have fallen for him.

Juliana explained to Bo that Ben was what was called a *berdache*—that is, a person of two spirits—a woman actually, but a woman who appears to be a man. A *berdache* is not exactly a homosexual, not in the conventional sense. Bo observed that they must be as rare as turtle dogs. Turtle dogs are not rare at all,

Juliana said. And she explained that Bending Bear was more of a cousin than Vernon was; they were both descended from Saucy Chief, the last of the Heart Stays chiefs. Bo could not come right out and ask her how much she was worth, but he gathered, from what they discussed that evening on that porch, that her Osage great-grandfather, a son of Saucy Chief, had wisely invested his share of the oil rights, had taken it out of the stock market before the crash, and had built it into a tidy fortune, which she'd inherited when her father and mother were killed in an automobile accident at the time she was fourteen. Bo learned another thing Vernon and Juliana had in common besides their descent from Jacob Ingledew and their great wealth: Neither had been to college. Or, rather, Juliana had spent only a semester at Stanford before being overcome with homesickness. Bo wanted to hear about her love life, but the best he could do was to ask, "Had you ever been in love before Vernon?"

Her laughter must have made Ben and the Woman, inside the house, think that Bo was telling his favorite jokes. "Do you think I'm in love with Vernon?" she asked him.

"It's written all over you," he declared.

As the evening settled in and the air darkened and cooled a bit, Juliana told Bo the short history of her love life, beginning not with the loss of her virginity at fifteen (she hadn't loved the guy, an Indian classmate) but with her first true love, a white guy she'd known in her last semester of high school. She had dropped out of Stanford to go home to him, only to find he'd already married somebody else. She hadn't dated anyone else for years after that, and then had an affair with a married man.

This was in Pawhuska? Bo wanted to know. Juliana said, Oh, no, she'd grown up in Tulsa, gone to school there, thought of it as home, returned to it. Spent most of her life there until, visiting the Thomas Gilcrease Museum one day and seeing all the Indian art there, she had suddenly become interested in her heritage. She had never been to Pawhuska before then. But she became obsessed with the Heart Stays People and wanted to track down whatever she could find about them; finding nothing except the approximate location of their final encampment up Bird Creek a few miles from Pawhuska, she had bought the land and commissioned a Tulsa architect, a disciple of Frank Gehry, to erect a great manor house done in the fashion of the conjoined reed-thatch wigwams of the Osage.

She had devoted her life for the past six years to learning the Osage language and culture. She had no social life in Pawhuska, although for a time she had been a habitué of a Main Street dive called the Phoenix Lounge and had met a very few men who appealed to her and whom she'd taken home with her, purely for sexual purposes. "You could say I was a bad girl, for a while," she declared.

"What did those guys think when they saw your fabulous mansion?" Bo was curious to know.

"Either that I was some kind of screwball, because of its architectural design, or that I was, as one of them put it, 'rolling in it.' I didn't care what they thought. I fucked them and forgot them."

It was the first time Bo had heard her use a dirty word. He found it both shocking and endearing. More to the point, he began to hope that her experience with casual sex might make her willing to accept him into the wigwam that night.

The lightning bugs had come out. He knew of course why the male lightning bug flies around flashing his illuminated advertisement, and why he searches constantly for a flash coming in response from a female waiting in the bushes. It was too dark now for him to see Juliana's face. But he could see Jelena's. Jelena had a charming habit of winking at Bo. He supposed she winked at Vernon too and, for that matter, at Uncle George and everybody else. But he had only seen her winking at him, and he had even winked at her in response. There wasn't anything necessarily sexual about the wink, it was sort of conspiratorial, or not even that, just friendly, just her way of saying, "You and I are in this together, this situation, this moment, this life." Now in his mind's eye he saw Jelena winking at him, and it was disconcerting.

"How did you know Jelena was having supper with Day and Diana?" he asked. "Are you becoming friends with her?"

"Oh, no!" Juliana said. "But they invited me too, and told me she was coming. I simply told them I had other plans. I'm not ready to sit at the table with Jelena. I'm not ready to pretend to be her friend."

"I suppose I should call her," Bo reflected out loud. But he made no move to fetch his car phone. Moments, and lightning bugs, drifted by. Then he said, "I keep thinking perhaps instead I should take those three baths. . . . But where would I find springwater?"

"If you wanted springwater," Juliana said, "the same spring in which Jacob washed is still there. You would have more trouble finding rainwater. Nobody has a rain barrel anymore. And even if they did, I'm told it hasn't rained since early June. But really you wouldn't need all that washing. Maybe a quick dip in the creek would do."

"And you could join me for that?" he suggested.

"Bo," she said, "you should know a couple of things. First, Fanshaw was putting one over on Jacob when he made him wash in three waters. It has been a joke among the Osage ever since. We don't think you stink. Jacob didn't need those three baths. And second, I really do think you ought to phone and see if Jelena is home yet. If she isn't, then . . . well, I have no choice but to invite you to the wigwam."

Chapter Fourteen

Really, she was glad Vernon was gone for several reasons. He was removed from the temptation of that Indian woman. He was off somewhere in some godforsaken south Arkansas town throwing one of his campaign parties and giving one of his eloquent speeches and shaking hands with everybody (at least with all the men) and maybe enjoying himself for a change. When he was just sitting in his study totally immersed in his books she never could tell if he was having fun or not. It is difficult to live for thirty years with a companion who doesn't reveal whatever delight he receives from life.

While he was gone, she didn't have to *do* anything to delight him: She didn't have to prepare his meals, she didn't have to listen to his philosophical rants, and she didn't have to adjust her sexual responses to match his. She didn't have to adjust *anything*. She could do whatever she liked. Or, if she chose, she could do nothing at all.

When Vernon had first left her to hit the campaign trail, she had gone to Harrison and purchased a television set, a small one, the smallest she could find, but a good one, which she kept hidden in the food pantry covered with a dish towel whenever Vernon was home. As soon as George's helicopter lifted Vernon off the premises, she got out the TV, plugged it in, and watched talk shows. She even watched a few soap operas, ashamed of herself but helplessly trapped in their stories.

She openly smoked cigarettes while watching television. Maybe she smoked too much; when Vernon was around, she could get by with sneaking maybe one or at most two cigarettes a day; when he was gone, she'd smoke almost a pack. She might have smoked more than that, but the cat Vernon didn't like smoke and avoided her when she was smoking, and she really enjoyed having him (the cat) around. When Vernon was here, Vernon the cat was strictly a yard cat; when Vernon was gone, he became a house cat and sat in her lap whenever she wasn't smoking. When Vernon the man was here, she hid her Bible and her journal and got them out only when she knew he was taking his six-mile hike or was at the ham plant. Now she could indulge her desire to write in her journal long letters to her grandchildren, whom she had never seen and whose names she had to invent: Jacob and Sarah and Isaac and Salina and John and Sirena, all names of her Ingledew ancestors. Beautiful kids.

Vernon had wanted her to get a dog, as protection during his absences. Just as a sentry, Vernon called it. You know, a *watchdog* to bark if anybody tried to approach the house. But she didn't want a dog. There was no telling how Vernon the cat might take to the idea of a canine on the premises. He might run away from home. She had never had a dog, and while there were some things she wasn't too old to try for the first time, dog ownership wasn't one of them.

Her diet went to hell. Since she didn't have to prepare meals, she could eat Skippy peanut butter for lunch and a bowl of popcorn for supper and plenty of Lady Godiva chocolate for dessert, and that was that. It was a shame not to be eating all those wonderful vegetables her garden was producing, which Bo had helped her nurture—beans and squash and peppers and eggplant—and they'd have gone to rot if she hadn't found someone to give them to. For a while she'd given them to the Woman Whom We Cannot Name—hell, Jelena could damn well name her and did: Ekaterina—but then those Indians moved in with Ekaterina and Vernon started taking a too-deep interest in the Indian girl, and Jelena could not stop there anymore to unload her uneaten vegetables on them.

She couldn't really bear to look at the Indian girl, whose name was so like her own but prettier: they were both long-haired brunettes but "Jelena" suggests a country girl, an aging courtesan, housemate to a genius running for governor, whereas "Juliana" suggests an exotic enchantress of indescribable beauty whose very walk, Jelena observed during the turtle feast, was lithesome and graceful beyond compare. Never mind even the fact that Juliana must have been at least twenty years younger than Jelena, Jelena was smart enough (boy, was she smart enough!) to realize she was no competition for that trophy doll.

For a while, Jelena had had only her secure knowledge of Vernon's ludicrous woman-shyness to ward off the thought that he might be drawn to her. So long as Vernon couldn't even speak to the Indian woman, Jelena was safe. But she hadn't reckoned with the idea of darkness. She hadn't realized that if somehow Vernon could speak to Juliana without seeing her he wouldn't necessarily be shy, any more than his ancestor Jacob had been shy with her ancestor Kushi—or, rather, both their ancestors, because in a way Juliana was an Ingledew, which, as Jelena had tried to tell Bo, was the only reason that Vernon wasn't shy with Jelena.

Jelena knew that Vernon had spent at least three nights with Juliana. Whether or not he had actually slept with her Jelena didn't know, and couldn't know, without asking him. The first night she had awakened around 1 A.M. and ordinarily would have made nothing of Vernon's absence from the bed; he habitually stayed up reading in his study until and beyond the wee hours. But something—intuition, perhaps—made her look into his study and discover he was not there, and then to throw on her kimono and hike up to the parking space atop the mountain and discover that his Land-Rover was not there. She went back to bed but couldn't sleep. Around dawn she looked into his study again, and he was asleep in his Barcalounger. She didn't wake him, and she didn't later confront him with the fact of his absence. That night the situation was repeated, and the third night. It was not like Vernon to get into the Land-Rover and drive around at night; she could only surmise that he had been going down to the wigwam that Uncle George had helped that queer Indian gorilla build, a wigwam in which Juliana had expressed her intention to sleep each night. Was Juliana openly attempting to re-create the setting in which Jacob and Kushi had screwed? Whenever she had got the chance, Jelena had given Vernon a hug and a kiss on the morning after and attempted to pick up any scent of the Indian woman, or any of the musky scents of sexual activity, but there had been none.

Earlier tonight she had told Day and Diana of her suspicions. Or, rather, she had told Day first, in the living room, while Diana was busy preparing supper. Jelena wanted so much to say to Day, Well, if Vernon is fooling around, now you and I can fool around at long last. But she knew beyond question she could never say that. Diana was her best friend. The only way she would ever be able to actualize her sexual fantasies for Day would be to ask Diana for permission, which quite possibly Diana would be happy to grant but which Jelena could never request.

"Even if it's just a fling"—Day had tried to reassure her—"he's going to be too busy between now and the election in November to give her any more of his attention."

And later, when she'd told Diana too (did she detect a jealousy in Diana, as if Diana wished it were *she* with whom Vernon was fooling around?), Diana simply reminded her that skeptics are imperturbable, and that Jelena was the most imperturbable skeptic on earth, and there was nothing Vernon could *ever* do that would stir Jelena up. Then Diana, trying to be light or even funny, had said a disquieting thing: "Since you don't want to live in the governor's mansion anyhow, let him take the redskin chick to Little Rock with him!"

They had laughed, but Jelena had only been able to remark, "Her skin is lighter than mine."

Which was true. Jelena had spent so much time in her garden this summer that she was sunburned. In fact, the vegetable garden hadn't satiated her; as one more secret from Vernon, from everyone (she hadn't even told Day and Diana about it), she had created a secret garden: about the time Vernon had announced his candidacy, back in March, she'd begun the digging and the planting and the transplanting, on a quarter acre of forest-enclosed clearing not too far from the house but not at all visible from it. She had a secret path to it that she could use from a corner of the vegetable garden, so that Vernon would never see her going to the other one. Not that he'd ask her anyway. He never once asked, "Where have you been?" She could take a five-mile hike through the woods and he'd never ask, "Where have you been?" She could spend the whole day driving around to the nurseries of Harrison and other towns in northern Arkansas, hunting for the most exotic plants for her secret garden, and when she got home long after suppertime, he would never ask, "Where have you been?"

Because she was so proud of that other garden, which now in July was thriving luxuriantly and blooming spectacularly despite the drought (she ran an underground hose from her vegetable garden hose to keep the secret garden watered), she had been tempted to show it to Bo, who would've appreciated it, but if she'd done that, it wouldn't be secret anymore, it wouldn't be her very own. It was so hidden, so secluded, so private that she could do things there she couldn't even do in her house when she was all alone in it, because even in the house with Vernon gone she still had the thought that it was Vernon's house too and he was still somehow *involved* if, for example, she masturbated. Which she did, more often than she wanted to reflect, so she didn't reflect, she just did it. The shower had been her favorite place until she had created the secret garden, and then she much preferred doing it out-of-doors, surrounded by flowers and weird shrubs and the idea that plants themselves couldn't ever stop thinking about sex and did it constantly, all the time, their lives devoted to it entirely.

Jelena wanted to be a plant in her reincarnation, which she didn't believe in despite Day and Diana's involvement with it. But thinking of Day, she realized that although nobody had seen her secret garden, not even Bo, she always took Day with her when she went to visit it for the purpose of autoeroticism, a word she wouldn't ever have thought except it was such a good match for Vernon's autodidacticism. It was Day, the outdoorsman, the forester, the plant specialist, who crept into that secret garden with her, at least in her mind, and held her, and touched her, and kissed her, and licked her, and entered her, and made her gasp and sigh and come. Their lovemaking was like that of the flowers, burgeoning and bursting and bright, in all colors.

She didn't do this because Vernon was undersexed or inept or undesirable in any way. They had a rich and full life—she almost thought *in bed* but realized they didn't spend very much time together in bed, except maybe in the middle of the afternoon or late Sunday morning—they had a rich and full sexual life, which was probably, she thought, better than most couples'. But after thirty years it was something you just *did*, not because you particularly wanted to but because you'd been trained through thirty years of repetition to keep on doing it. Jelena had no standards for comparison except her ex-husband Mark, who had been even worse than Vernon in one respect: When he ejaculated, not too long after he started getting busy, that was it, that was all. She was left high and dry.

When she'd first started her affair with Vernon, while she was still married to Mark, they often did it in the woods, mainly because it was safer than doing it in her house, where she might be discovered, and she still treasured her memories of those wild abandoned frolics, with all their clothes off, on pine needles and fallen leaves or even the hard earth. They hadn't had sex outdoors since then, even though Jelena had broadly hinted that she'd like to re-create the passion and abandon and naturalness of doing it in the open air.

Thinking of this now, she decided to take a kerosene lantern to light her way and pay a visit to her secret garden. She hadn't been there at night before. She wanted to go out there and lie down among the flowers that did their fucking by moonlight or starlight and try to keep count of their orgasms and her own.

But as she was preparing to leave the house, the phone rang. "Hi. Guess where I am. Guess who I've been talking to. Guess where I'd rather be."

"First I have to guess who you are," she said, laughing. "Uncle George?"

"Oh, come on," he said. "Do I sound like George?"

"Where are you?"

"The Stay More Hotel. I have the Jag or else I'd have driven straight up to your house. Could you come and get me?"

If she went and got him, she'd have to give up her immediate intention, going to the secret garden in the night to count the orgasms of the flowers and herself. Or would she? She could take him with her. "Is Juliana around?" she asked.

"As a matter of fact, she's sitting on the porch, and I've been talking to her for hours. Why?"

"I would be embarrassed if we saw each other."

"Oh? Well, I suppose I could ask her to go inside when you arrive."

She knew of course that if she went and got him he would spend the night. He had spent the night a few times when Vernon was gone. Nothing wrong with that, although there ought to have been. He ought to have at least flirted with her, or have made an outright proposition, but although they'd talked and talked and drank and drank, finishing a bottle of Glenfiddich between them, to the point where she herself had almost blurted, "Want to sleep with me?" he had never *done* anything, never even hinted at doing anything. They had talked about Harrison, Arkansas, and Harrison High School until they had exhausted the subject. They had talked about gardening until there was nothing left to be said. Naturally, he was Vernon's campaign manager and therefore his employee, and you don't fuck the boss's wife, even if she wasn't a wife and Vernon wasn't really a boss and it wouldn't have been fucking, but something, she hoped, far grander than that.

She sighed. "Why don't you just start walking in this direction, and I'll pick you up at whatever point you've reached when I get there."

"Fine. Starting now?"

"Start walking."

And that was the way it happened. She set aside the kerosene lantern that she'd been preparing to use to light her way to the secret garden, and, first checking to see that the guest room was tidy, the bed neat, everything in its place, she walked instead up to the place where her Isuzu 4-by-4 was parked, got into it, and drove down the mountainside. Her headlights picked him out as she rounded a hairpin; he had covered maybe a mile from the village. He was carrying only his briefcase, in which, she supposed, he had his toothbrush, comb, and a change of underwear. She was always glad to see Bo; he was a physically imposing man, quite muscular, and his neatly trimmed beard gave him character and kept him from looking like a businessman, which he was.

When he climbed into her car, he gave her a kiss. It was quick but it was on the mouth. Then he said, "Sorry to put you out. I didn't know I was coming, or I'd have brought the Nissan. Cast and I spent the day in Little Rock, sparring with the governor himself; I'll tell you about it. And on our way back to Fayetteville I decided I deserved to see you again and inspect our garden and pick a few hornworms off the tomatoes."

"But you spent hours talking to Juliana."

"Only because I was invited to dinner, and because I learned you were having dinner with Day and Diana."

"How did you know that?"

"Didn't they tell you that they had invited her too? But that she declined?"

"No," Jelena said. "Maybe they were going to surprise me. And what a surprise that would have been! I'm glad she turned them down. Did she say why?"

"For the same reason that you don't want to see her."

It was after ten o'clock when they got back to the house, too late to visit the secret garden. Maybe she could show it to him in the morning. She offered him a nightcap. He said he'd do the honors and poured a Glenfiddich for each of them. They sat side by side on the sofa. She came right out and asked, "How much do you know about her and Vernon?"

"If it will make you feel any better, I'm almost certain they haven't made love."

"How do you know? Did he tell you?"

"She did."

"What else did she tell you? I'm not stupid, you know. I have an idea that Vernon has spent quite a lot of time in her company, late at night."

"Oh, they've spent hours talking. In Osage as well as in

English. There's no denying that they're fascinated with each other . . . the same way I'm fascinated with you."

She laughed self-consciously. "Bo Pharis, that's the first flattering thing you've ever said to me."

"No, it isn't, but if you'd like to be flattered, I could do it all night."

"Do *what* all night?"

He blushed. "Accidental. Oh, hell, maybe it was deliberate." They both laughed, and she couldn't help winking at him. "I love your wink," he said. "Did you know that you wink at me?"

"It's just a nervous tic," she said.

"No, it makes me feel as if you and I exist together in a world of our own, that we have our own secret way of communicating."

"What a nice thing to say. Flatter me some more!"

"Gladly." He finished his drink quickly and poured himself another. "Remember Miss Nettleship? Eleventh-grade English? She certainly remembered you. Whenever she returned one of my papers, it would have an A plus on it but it would say something like 'This reminds me of the good work that Jelena Ingledew always did. It is almost worthy of her.' All my life since high school, Jelena, I've wanted to be that worthy." She was so touched by that she didn't know what to say, and she was thinking, *If ever there was a moment for a real kiss, this is it,* but he didn't move to kiss her, and she didn't know what to say, and it was something a wink couldn't answer. After a while, he went on. "My ex-wife—I don't suppose you ever knew Patricia Harmon or heard of her?—when she divorced me she said one of the problems was that whenever she said or did something wrong I would always remark, 'Jelena wouldn't have done that!' even though I'd never known you. I guess it wasn't fair to her, but she wasn't the only victim. I've always, whenever a woman did or said *anything*, asked myself,

'Would Jelena have done that?' You have made life difficult for dozens of women."

She gathered enough aplomb to remark, "After years of setting me on a pedestal like that, it must have been a terrible letdown to see what I'm really like."

"On the contrary. From the very first I discovered that I hadn't raised the imagined standards high enough. I discovered that you are far more beautiful and charming and wise and intelligent than I had ever dreamed."

"Oh, Bo!" she said. "That's enough. That's enough flattery to last me for the rest of my life."

"One more thing," he said, and put his big powerful hand on top of hers, and her breath caught in the expectation that he might really be getting ready to give her a passionate kiss. "When I was with Juliana earlier, our chat reached the point where she practically invited me to join her in the wigwam tonight, but I turned her down because I'd rather be with you."

"Now *that* was a dumb choice," Jelena said. "If you had that opportunity, you should have taken it. Unless you're already beginning to think of her as Vernon's woman."

"You're much more Vernon's woman than she could ever be," Bo said, "but that doesn't stop me."

"Doesn't stop you from *what*?" she wondered aloud.

"Doesn't stop me from telling you I love you."

When he said that, there really was nothing for her to do, no choice for her, nothing to say. Since he still didn't make the first move, she made it. She scooted closer to him on the sofa and inclined her head to his and waited for their lips to meet. Which they quickly did. Quickly and ardently, and for a long time. She knew she wouldn't have to take him to the secret garden. He had already created his own secret garden and surrounded her with it. It was a garden that had the power to enchant her to the point where she couldn't even think of Vernon, let alone of Juliana. She did have one brief thought about Miss Nettleship, a very nice teacher and one of her favorites. But then she thought of no one except Bo and herself, and she said to him, when at last they broke their long kiss, "Now you've made it supremely difficult for me to allow you to sleep alone in the guest room."

He was just a little slow in getting that, and she realized it sounded a bit as if she were going to refuse him sleeping privileges. But he said, "Then why don't you join me?"

She preferred it that way, to use his bed instead of theirs. In fact, for the convenience of their rare guests that bed was king-sized, a larger field for sport, whereas hers and Vernon's bed was only queen-sized, for sleeping closer together if the chance ever occurred.

He declared, "I'd like to shower first. And you could join me for that." He was grinning as if he knew a joke, as if perhaps he'd already said that to someone else and was enjoying his repetition of it to her. Or maybe he was grinning because he meant not the guest-room shower but the shower in the master suite, which could accommodate all the Samurai at once if need be. It had been a very long time since she and Vernon had used the shower together. And they had never used it *before* making love, always *after*. What about *during*? which was what she did by herself.

But Jelena was mildly reluctant to reveal her body naked for the first time in thirty years to anyone other than Vernon. "I'm sorry," she apologized. "I'm just much too modest for that."

"My goodness, honey, I've worked hours in the garden with you when you were dressed just in shorts and a T-shirt without a bra, and I had no trouble pretending you were totally nude. You have a sensational body."

"Flattery again," she said, but she was pleased beyond words. "You might not think so if you saw me without a stitch."

"Would another drink help?" he offered. "Or another kiss?" He enfolded her in his arms and gave her another vigorous kiss, and she twisted and squirmed with desire for him, and thought *To hell with modesty*. When the kiss was over she ran into the kitchen and came back with two large plump tomatoes, which she'd picked that afternoon, intending to take them to Day and Diana but forgetting, what with all the other thoughts on her mind. They were the first ripe fruits of the Brandywine variety that Bo had started in his Cincinnati windowsill and brought with him to Arkansas. Brandywine, thought to have been started by the Amish, is an heirloom tomato whose taste is far more assertive and luscious than conventional tomatoes.

"Recognize them?" she asked him.

It took him just a moment. "My Brandywines?"

"Yes, but old-time Ozark folks called them 'love apples,' because they were rumored to be aphrodisiac."

They didn't need aphrodisiacs. But they took the love apples into the master bath, where they removed each other's clothes quickly and got into the huge shower with their love apples, which they both began munching as if they were peaches, a very sexy, messy thing to do. He traced his juice-dripping fingertips along her backbone. "You have the most lithesome long back," he said. Nobody had ever complimented her back before, and she was overwhelmed.

"You look good all over," she said. He was broad-shouldered, very muscular, and for a man his age his belly didn't bulge very much. Below the slight paunch she couldn't help seeing that his penis was already well risen, and not because of the love apple. It was huge, almost too big. She'd seen only two others for comparison—Mark's and Vernon's—and theirs had been plentifully expanded when aroused, but nothing like this. She couldn't resist wrapping her fingers around it and her thumb came nowhere near meeting her fingertips.

Bo shuddered and wriggled. "What a marvelous hand you have," he said. They gobbled down the rest of their love apples and then turned on the shower to wash away all the tomato juice trickling down their fronts. There was a big fresh bar of bath soap, an aromatic loaf bar scented with gardenia, and Jelena was the first to grab it. She rubbed it all over him, and it sudsed and foamed and lathered, and the fragrance turned him into a flower. She gave so much attention to his cock and balls that he had to say, "Easy." And then he took the bar of soap from her and applied it to her body, gently and soothingly, to every convexity and every concavity of her flesh, coming finally to the bump that rose from the lips of her sex, and stroked and twiddled it in almost the very same fashion that she did to herself. In this very same spot, this shower, this very same spot, this place here, this, this, this. She was so close to coming.

"Have you ever made love standing up?" he asked.

"Not that I can recall," she breathed, trying to remember if, long ago, she and Vernon might have done it.

"Here we go," he said, and pressed against her, bending his knees, spreading hers, raising her on tiptoe, touching, meeting, and then the one sliding up into the other. She gasped; it was painful, he was so big, it was worse than childbirth for a little while.

He was attuned to all this. "If it hurts, we can wait until we're more comfy, in bed."

She loved him for his thoughtfulness. "But I'm so close to the edge," she said. "Could we just hold still a bit? To let me get used to it?"

And he understood that perfectly too. He did not attempt to thrust. He was deep inside her and just stayed there, for a long time, the water coursing over them, washing off all the lovely suds. Eventually, he flexed his penis. She could feel it give a throb of expansion inside her. She squeezed her vaginal muscles around it in return. And then she decided she could stand it. She could stand standing and stand his stand. She could understand. She began rising on tiptoe and coming down, lifting and settling, impaling herself and levitating, slowly at first but then faster, until he too began moving, with great gentleness, gentleman that he was, until he realized he was no longer hurting her and could let go, exert himself, drive into her. He held her buttocks in his hands and steered his driving with them. He talked the whole time. He kept her informed of his progress, his destination, and the pleasures of the trip, the feelings that he was having.

Vernon never talked during sex. Mark had never talked, period. Bo was almost too much, like a tour guide. Rising on our left, ladies and gentlemen, is a monumental edifice called a multiple orgasm; we shall soon not only see it but feel it, and we will never have felt anything like it before. She knew she was going to come uniquely, and multiply, and she did her share to make it happen, and he, considerate sweetheart that he was, took note of her every inch in progress toward that goal and kept always just an inch behind her, always with her, but letting her get there first, as if, racing toward the finish line as all-time scholar of Harrison High, she beat him by just a fraction of an inch, and gasped and shook and cried aloud in victory and collapsed against him, who held her as his own crossing of the finish line shook him and shook him, and she could feel that thick flesh of his emptying itself inside her. Then they both slid to the tile floor of the shower and just lay there panting and sighing, and Bo had to shut up, at last. The water continued to pour down on them, washing away every trace of tomato juice and love juice, until the water began to turn cold, and she rose up to turn it off.

They spent the night together in the king-sized bed of the guest room, but it was a long time before they slept. That big bed was a challenge to try it out this way and that way, south, north, east, and west, south over north and east over west, the great variety of things they were doing and feeling only briefly giving her the jealous thought that he must have had a lot of experience with all these things. Vernon, alas, did not. As far as she knew, Vernon had never made love to anyone else (except possibly that one time when he had a chance, with Diana). Jelena had been his original teacher, and while surely his vast reading had exposed him to an entire kama sutra of possibilities and variations, he had never seemed to realize that she had more than one opening, or even that there were more than two or three positions available to them. Now to add to her list of all the things that were secret from Vernon she wanted to have Bo take her anal virginity. "I am not too old to start," she declared. But it wouldn't work. He was simply too large. He gave her plenty of lubrication and stretching with his gentle fingers but it wasn't enough, although he blamed himself, not for his being too large but for being too soft: after his second coming of the night he simply couldn't become stiff enough again.

"But we can try again tomorrow," he said. "Or any time." And she reflected that this night was not, as she'd been thinking, a onetime spur-of-passion fling but just the beginning of something that could conceivably continue a long time.

She gave him his third coming with her mouth, and then they fell asleep. It must have been long past midnight. But she woke before dawn, her intuition on fire, and slipped out of Bo's bed and returned to her own. She lay there for quite a long while trying to get back to sleep, kept from it not by any guilt over her infidelity or even any further jealous thoughts of Juliana, but by the conviction, not suspicion but conviction, that Vernon was in Stay More, that he would be home any minute now but that he was still in the process of taking leave of the wigwam, where he had discovered that the Osage bedding was not nearly as commodious as the king-sized bed where she and Bo had been cavorting, but that, in contrast to the square shape of the king-sized bed, the Osage field of sport was *round*, like the wigwam itself, and that there is something about fucking in a round space that gives a whole new dimension to the frolic. So what Jelena found herself being jealous of was not that Vernon and Juliana had been screwing (you can't be jealous of something you've just been doing yourself) but that the round space of their act(s) was a creative cosmos unlike any she'd ever imagined or would ever experience . . . unless she and Bo borrowed the wigwam some night. This last thought caused her to laugh aloud, wondering when was the last time she'd laughed aloud alone.

"You're awake," Vernon observed. She turned, and there he was, under the sheets beside her. He must have sneaked into bed so stealthily she hadn't even felt the bed move. "What's so funny?" he asked.

"When did you come in?" she asked.

"Oh, a while ago," he said, which could have meant anything: thirty seconds or an hour. For a moment she had the panicky thought that he might have already been here while she was in the guest room with Bo, but she convinced herself that that wouldn't have been possible if the sexual activities of the two couples were truly simultaneous, as she knew them to have been. "George and I decided to leave right after the rally was over. Pine Bluff is no place to spend the night."

"How did the rally go?" she asked politely, wondering if by any chance she might possess any aromas of sexual activity or of Bo. But there was only the gardenia, a pervasive fragrance.

"There wasn't much of a turnout," he said. "In this hot weather, nobody wants to attend an outdoor rally. I don't think I gave a very inspired speech."

Perhaps your mind was elsewhere, she nearly said. Instead she asked, "How did you get here? I didn't hear the helicopter land."

"Bending Bear brought me."

"In the Pierce-Arrow?"

"Those things can go anywhere."

"How did you happen to run into Bending Bear?"

"It's complicated. Basically, George landed down in the village, because he suspected engine trouble. He decided to wait until daylight to work on it, and so there we were, and Bending Bear offered to bring me on home."

"Did you see Juliana?"

He was spared answering that question by the ringing of the bedside phone. He reached for it, and she tried to hear enough to determine who was calling. She could only determine it was a woman's voice. Did Juliana have a cell phone in the wigwam? He talked awhile, keeping his voice low. Or rather he listened, mostly. Then he said, "Hang on, I'll ask Jelena. She's already awake." And he put one hand over the mouthpiece and said to her, "It's Lydia. She's trying to locate Bo. All hell has broken loose down to Little Rock, and she can't find Bo. You wouldn't happen to know anything about him?"

"He's sleeping in our guest room," she declared.

"Ha! No wonder he couldn't be found." Vernon got out of bed. He said into the phone, "Lydia, it just so happens he's right here in my house. I'll get him." Vernon headed for the guest room. Jelena tried to think if there might have been anything incriminatory about the guest room. No doubt it smelled like gardenia in there. She got up and put on her kimono and stepped into the master bath just to look around and be sure there wasn't anything left behind. Sure enough, Bo's and her clothes were still on the floor! She snatched up Bo's things and hugged them into a bundle and sneaked into the other bubble, into the guest bath, where she dumped them on the floor there. As she was returning to her own bedroom, she bumped into Vernon. "He's talking to Lydia," Vernon said. "Why don't you make some coffee? I had better shower and get dressed. We'll be going to Fayetteville, whether or not George fixes the helicopter."

"What's this all about?" she wanted to know.

"Governor Bradfield apparently has decided not to back down in the face of all the goods we've got on him. We hoped—or Bo did—that if we had enough evidence against him, he wouldn't use his evidence against me; it seems Carleton Drew went over to his side and divulged all my albatrosses. We hoped we could run a clean campaign without mudslinging and concentrate on the issues. But it seems that my crafty opponent—my powerful opponent—went on television last night to announce that he has elected to confess each and every one of the black marks that we've got on him. And then to make capital of those he's got on me."

"Can he defeat you with that?" she asked, politely but hoping, as she had been all along, that *something* could stop Vernon from moving into the governor's mansion.

"Quite possibly," Vernon said glumly, and then, changing the subject, lowering his voice, he said, "Did you know that Bo sleeps in the nude?"

Chapter Fifteen

For a long time after becoming aware of the contents of the previous chapter, Day was thrown, to put it mildly, and he began to wish that he did not enjoy his privilege of being privy to this novel's events as they unfolded. Now, when it was his turn to take charge of a chapter, following the same sequence as in the first half of the book, he felt as if some unruly strangers had left behind a hideous mess for him to clean up. Not knowing how to do this, he seriously considered begging out of the responsibility of his second chapter. Why couldn't Cast Sherrill do it? Or Larry Brace? Or Sharon? Or, perhaps best of all, since she had so much experience at writing, Ekaterina?

He wanted desperately to confide in Diana and complain to her about this impossible onus: not only of knowing about Jelena's secret garden literally and figuratively but of having to comment upon it in chapter 15. Of course he couldn't say anything to Diana. How could he possibly explain to her *how* he knew the contents of chapter 14? He wasn't completely sure, himself, just how he possessed that privilege. He hadn't seen the words written on a page, even in typescript or computer printout. Unlike you, the reader, he hadn't even seen the words at all. He just *knew* that Jelena Ingledew, the woman in all the world he loved most next to Diana, had wanted so much to say to him, "Well, if Vernon is fooling around, now you and I can fool around at long last"—but she had not said that; she had instead fooled around with someone else. He just *knew* that Jelena had created a secret garden in which she imagined making love to Day, "their lovemaking like that of the flowers, burgeoning and bursting and bright, in all colors." Worst of all, he just *knew*, as if he'd been in that shower and in that bed with them, that Jelena and Bolin Pharis had started a passionate affair. Rightfully, Day was feeling more jealous than Vernon himself might have, under the circumstances. *Why couldn't it have been me?* he kept asking of the woods, aloud.

Diana and Jelena had been such intimate friends for so many years that quite possibly Jelena would confess the affair to Diana anyway, and then perhaps Day could talk to Diana about it. But not now. Day doubted that Jelena would ever confess to anybody, not Diana, certainly not Vernon, that she made herself come with fantasies of Day. He was most uncomfortable with that, yet at the same time he had to face up to the simple fact that when he "saw" her in her secret garden with her eyes closed pretending he was with her, holding her, touching her, kissing her, licking her, and entering her, making her gasp and sigh and come, he had become so aroused that he himself had been required to masturbate, then and there. No way could he tell Diana about *that*. Even thinking of it swept him back some thirty-odd years to the time when, as kids in the forest of Five Corners, Vermont, he had been so embarrassed to learn that Diana had seen him masturbating that he had tried to hang himself.

Years ago he had told Vernon that story, needing to talk about it at last to somebody, not just the embarrassment of being caught jerking off but the humiliation of failing in his attempt at suicide (he'd tripped and got tangled in his rope, and Diana had to climb the tree and get him down), and he had been surprised and relieved to hear Vernon explain how commonplace and incessant the act of masturbation is. "Do *you* have to do it?" Day had asked him. "With Jelena available?" And Vernon had delivered a little lecture on how self-sex is more "ready" and "personal" and "expert" than sex with another.

"Jelena does it too," Vernon had said.

"How do you know? Have you watched?"

"I found her vibrator," he had said. "If she used it simply for other parts of her body, why would she hide it from me?"

Day wondered if possibly the other things that Jelena was hiding from Vernon—her cigarettes, her journal, her Bible, her TV set, her *other* garden, and, now, her affair with Bo—were not as secret as she thought. Vernon was no dummy. And what about his casual remark to her: "Did you know that Bo sleeps in the nude?" That sounded to Day as if Vernon had a suspicion, even if he hadn't noticed the clothes on the floor in the master bathroom and the scent of gardenia in the guest room. Day was convinced that if Vernon did not already suspect the affair between Jelena and Bo, he would soon find out. And then what? Would he simply shrug it off, or use it as an excuse for his own affair with Juliana Heartstays? Day was mildly amused that Vernon had started his affair with Juliana before knowing that Jelena was starting one with Bo. Or had he? Diana had told Day that on several occasions when she'd gone up to visit Jelena, she'd found Jelena and Bo working together in the garden (not the secret one), and on at least two of those occasions Vernon was out of town, and Jelena had told Diana that she thought Bo "exuded virility." Day still wasn't able to understand how Bo could permit himself with impunity to become involved with his employer's woman, and right in the middle of a hectic political campaign.

Now, in this chapter under Day's aegis, the campaign was going to become more hectic. Governor Bradfield, surrounded by his family, including a daughter recently removed from a private psychiatric hospital and even the family's cocker spaniel, had appeared on television to say, "Yes, I have sinned. I am no better than the next man in this regard. I have misused alcohol. I was a problem child in school and a goof-off in college. My military service to my country was hampered by misfortune due to my own stupidity. The Democrat-controlled legislature has kept me from carrying out my vision for the great state of Arkansas, and I have made enemies right and left. But *you* are still my friend. And when *you* compare my character and my record with Vernon Ingledew's, you will reach the firm conviction that I am the lesser of two evils." The governor and his campaign had launched a thirteen-part program of spending an entire week of newspaper ads and television spots (under the fiendish direction of Carleton Drew) on each one of Vernon's so-called albatrosses, starting with his atheism, in which Vernon was being presented not just as a disbeliever in the divinity of Jesus Christ but as an Antichrist, who, if elected, would guilefully abolish the state's houses of worship. Week One of this campaign was already pretty ugly, with the Arkansas Ministerial Alliance up in arms and unanimous in their opposition to Vernon, and making a large number of widespread Sunday sermons denouncing him, several of which were reprinted in the state's newspapers. Monica Breedlove was appearing regularly at church youth groups and socials and fellowship meetings to deliver a spirited talk in Vernon's defense, in which she, a good Christian, claimed that Vernon had the highest respect for Jesus Christ even if he did not believe that He was the son of God (for the simple reason that there was no God).

Vernon himself was valiantly trying to combat the attack by temporarily abandoning his stump-speaking rallies, with their ham feasts and bands and singers and cheerleaders, and going instead to any church that would accept him (he hit seven the first Sunday morning, but three of those were Unitarian) and professing his profound knowledge of the Bible and his abiding faith in the existence, if not the divinity, of a Savior.

It would be three weeks before Vernon would get a chance

to return to Stay More. When Day saw him again, he was stunned to see how haggard Vernon was. Day had always admired and envied Vernon's indefatigability, but now Vernon looked as if he couldn't get out of his chair if he wanted to, which was good, because he didn't want to. So he just sat and told Day of some of the rough encounters he'd had with ministers and church elders and one woman churchgoer who had spat in his face and called him Satan. And then, Diana not being present, Vernon confided in his best friend, telling Day that he was hopelessly in love with Juliana. He began with a question, "Day, old friend, do you think it's possible for a man to be equally in love with two women?" Day, who was in love with Jelena himself but not as much as he was with Diana, perhaps for the simple reason he'd never gone to bed (or the shower) with her, had protested that he couldn't really answer the question since he'd never had any experience along that line. He said he supposed it would take great powers of concentration and greater powers of feeling and, above all, supreme powers of diplomacy in the event that one woman found out about the other.

"Does Jelena know?" Day asked.

"Not yet," Vernon admitted. "I mean, she doesn't yet know that I'm crazy about Juliana, although she probably suspects that we're fooling around."

"No wonder you're all worn out," Day observed.

Vernon laughed. "Not from *that*. Although I've got to tell you—" and he described, in intimate detail, not one but two sexual encounters he'd had with Juliana, the first three weeks ago, the second just last night. Day was just a bit uncomfortable listening. Vernon had never once told Day anything about his sex life with Jelena. Now he was being erotically frank in describing just what he and Juliana had done. Not boastfully, not lasciviously, but just matter-of-factly as if he were recounting not his own adventure but that of Jacob Ingledew and Kushi a hundred and sixty years before. As a matter of fact, whether by design or by disposition—whether she was trying to imitate her ancestor Kushi or whether that was simply the way she was—Juliana had at the moment of climax unclasped her legs, which were around his back, and straightened them out, and then her whole body had arched itself into a long quivering arc: a bow, a soft but taut arch that held him suspended up from the ground for a long moment until he had his own stupefying climax. That was a nearly exact duplication of the orgasms of Jacob and Kushi as described in Jacob's memoirs.

Vernon also spared Day no amplification of the various sexual supplements that enhanced Juliana's sensuality, things she'd done that Jelena had never known. "I've suspected that Indian women simply have a greater repertoire of sexual turns and tricks than white women. At least my reading into American Indian customs has led me to believe that. But Juliana claims it isn't true. She says Indian women have stronger libidos, and that's all there is to it. Where there's the appetite, there's the inventiveness."

"Apart from her prowess in the sack," Day said offhandedly, "what do you see in her?"

"Oh, come on, Day!" Vernon chided him. "She's *exotic!* She's *gorgeous!* And she's *dynamic!*"

"But how on earth can you keep your mind on the business of running for governor?"

"Now *that* is a problem," Vernon admitted.

Day congratulated himself, later, that he had not even hinted at the possibility that Jelena herself might be enjoying a sexual adventure. But Vernon's brief stopover in Stay More was accompanied by the Samurai, who were holding a planning session to get ready for Bradfield's weeklong assault on the matter of Vernon's thirty-year relationship with his first cousin. Once again, Day and Diana had overnight guests in Lydia and Arch; Monica and Harry were staying with Sharon and Larry; Cast was staying with his girlfriend Sheila; and Bo was ensconced in his familiar guest room at Vernon's house, where, presumably, when Vernon sneaked away to visit Juliana, he would sneak out into the secret garden with Jelena or use the shower again, or the king-sized bed.

Diana and Day were happy to have house guests, and they genuinely liked Lydia Caple and Arch Schaffer. But Day was not at all amused by the irony that Stay More, long a ghost town, was beginning to fill up with characters and their intrigues. Even apart from the Samurai, who appeared to love the town so much they might as well have set up their campaign headquarters here (which Monica had actually suggested at one time, a not altogether frivolous or wistful idea), and even apart from the newsmen and television people who prowled around in search of local color—or scandal—there seemed to be a steady rise in Stay More's population, which abnegated its charm as a ghost town.

When Day and Diana had first arrived here at the beginning of the seventies, they had the whole place practically to themselves. Then Larry Brace had come to town, and Sharon had joined him, and then Ekaterina, and as the ham works had expanded, its employees had bought up the outlying abandoned houses. Nobody was keeping count, but it seemed Stay More had as much occupancy of dwellings as it ever had, even in its heyday. And now here were the two Indians, apparently considering themselves permanent residents or reclaimants of their ancestral lands. The house of Day and Diana was still at the end of its road and still enjoyed abundant privacy, yet Day sometimes found his sleep troubled by the thought that there were in the neighborhood dozens of other humans, sleeping or having exceptional sex.

But the population was going to be reduced by one. The planning session of the Samurai, apparently, did not come up with any better counter to Bradfield's intended attack than to suggest that Jelena ought to start accompanying Vernon on his campaign tour. Was that Bo's idea? Did Bo think it would permit him to see more of her? No, it was Vernon's idea, who argued thus: If Bradfield was going to call public attention to the "illegitimacy" of Vernon's relationship with Jelena, the public was naturally going to be very curious about her. Keeping her hidden back in Stay More would just make it look as if he were trying to keep his relationship secret. So why not put her on display? Let the world see what a lovely lady she was. Somehow Vernon (perhaps with an assist from Bo) persuaded the reluctant Jelena not only to do this but also to buy herself a new wardrobe of smart summer separates and suits, and to visit a hairdresser, and to appear at a number of rallies looking like what Vernon proudly introduced her as, "the next First Lady of Arkansas."

For the whole week that the Bradfield campaign was attacking her—or attacking the *idea* of her as an unmarried consort and cousin of the candidate—Jelena diffidently but boldly appeared with Vernon at rallies all over Arkansas. Monday night, anyone who watched reruns on television would repeatedly see a commercial consisting of footage of Jelena (not in her First Lady garb but taken by some paparazzo who'd caught her in unbecoming dishabille) superimposed with the letters P.O.S.S.L.Q. and a voice-over that asked mockingly, "People of Offensive Sexual Situations Living Quietly? Partner Opposing Safe Sex Laughs Queasily? Perhaps Occupants Shouldn't Save Leftover Q-Tips? Please Omit Such Sinful Lifestyles Quickly?" And then on Tuesday, at a rally in Jonesboro, thousands of people would turn out to see her waving and smiling at the crowd and then affectionately holding Vernon's arm. All of their head-shakings and *tsk-tsks* and their disapproving sneers and scrapings of one forefinger with the other would dwindle and disappear as a barbershop quartet from Vernon's Vocalists would serenade her with a rousing takeoff on "The Sweetheart of Sigma Chi."

She was a drawing card, there was no question of that, and the idea of flaunting her instead of hiding her began to plant an idea in Day's mind. Nobody had asked him for any advice on the campaign, and he certainly had little interest in and less knowledge of politics, but this whole contest between albatrosses and foo birds was beginning to seem absurd to him, although he understood that it was what people expected in any sort of political campaign. He had given a lot of thought lately to how to put a stop to it, and Jelena's public humiliation—if that was what it was, and he *knew* she hated every minute of it—made him determined to come up with a solution.

Before he got any opportunity to offer his unsolicited advice to Vernon's people (he chided himself for that excluding expression, as if he himself were not the utmost of Vernon's people), he was solicited to give advice in his field of expertise. One day in August he arrived home for lunch (he'd been thinning some stands of cedar in the nearby Ozark National Forest) to find on his message machine (Diana had gone shopping in Harrison for the day) this throaty message: "Hi, Day, this is Juliana Heartstays. I didn't have much chance to speak with you during the turtle banquet last month. When you get a chance, could you drop by the wigwam? Or, if you prefer, or if I'm not there, could you drop by Ekaterina's?"

Day smiled. For a brief moment he allowed himself the fantasy that since Vernon had been gone for a while, Juliana's notorious Indian libido was acting up and she needed a substitute. After lunch and a shower, Day drove his Jeep Cherokee to the wigwam; one good thing about being your own employer is that you don't have to return to work after lunch if you don't feel like it. She came out of the wigwam (wasn't it awfully hot in there?) and sat in the Jeep beside him. He left the air-conditioning running.

"Vernon tells me you're a forester," she said to him. My God, up close she was breathtaking. And her simple words in that deep vibrant voice were as if she were professing her love for him.

"I don't live in the forest," he said. "Not at night, anyway. Maybe dendrologist would be a better word."

"What's that?"

"A student of trees."

"Exactly why I want to see you," she said, and there was the pinprick in the bubble of his fantasy. "Can a dendrologist look at a piece of land and tell what kind of trees used to grow there? I mean, for example, this pasture was cleared by white settlers at one time. Would you be able to tell me what was growing here originally?"

"That's easy," he said.

She got out of the Jeep and came around to the driver's side and opened the door and took his hand. "Come," she said, and his fantasy leapt into his vision again, full-blown. But she didn't lead him to the wigwam. She led him to a spot between two hummocks of earth and pointed at the turf. "Here, for example," she said. "What was growing here two hundred years ago?"

"Right where you're pointing," he declared, "nothing grew, because one of your ancestors had cut down an elm tree to make room for another wigwam. But *here*"—he pointed to a spot just to the west of where she'd pointed—"there was a giant maple."

"You're good," she said. "Now my question is, Would it be possible to put that giant maple back? Or one just like it."

"Do you mean transplant a mature maple to this spot?" She nodded and he hedged. "It would be awfully complicated. It would require some heavy machinery—backhoes and a truck-mounted tree spade and a huge flatbed hauling truck—but it could be done."

"When can you start?"

He laughed. "I don't normally contract heavy equipment, and in any case you'd have to wait until the cooler weather of autumn to do it."

"Day," she said earnestly, in her throaty voice, sweeping her hands to encompass the whole area, "whenever you can do it.

And not just the maple but *everything*. I want to make all of this look as it used to look before the white men came. I want to restore this piece of earth to its original appearance."

"It would be terribly expensive," he pointed out.

"That doesn't give me a moment's thought," she said. "Can you do it? I know it may take you a good bit of time just to do the planning, and deciding what goes where, and finding the trees and all, but I'll pay you whatever you want."

"Have you asked Vernon what he thinks of the idea?" Day had a suspicion that Vernon might not like the idea of a drastic reshaping of this part of Stay More's landscape.

"I don't need his permission," she said. "He has given the Heart Stays site back to us. My lawyers have drawn up the papers. The only permission I need is *yours*."

Day knew he could do it if he had to. It would be a challenging assignment, to determine what large trees had originally grown all over the pasture when it was forest, and to replace them, and to turn the entire site into a kind of laboratory where he could watch a climax forest coming into contact with humanity.

She raised her eyebrows. "Do you think it's preposterous?"

"I think the idea is radical, but it's feasible and even exciting. As the old song goes, 'If you got the money, honey, I got the time.' "

"I would have just one requirement," she said. "I would want you to hire Bending Bear as part of your crew. Well, I mean, you wouldn't have to give him a salary; he's already got one. But I want him to participate, and he needs some busywork, because he doesn't have to do much driving for me anymore."

"Be glad to have him," Day said. He liked Bending Bear. He knew the big fellow was a deviate; Day and Vernon had joked about Ben's crush on George, who didn't know what to do about it. But Day couldn't imagine that Ben's sexual orientation would create any problems for the job of moving trees.

"So back to my question: When can you start?" she asked.

"Might as well start now," he said. "Let me get my notebook from the Jeep." He got his notebook and his pencil and began making a sketch of the site. "You'll have to let me know where your property lines are," he told her.

She laughed. "Osages don't believe in property. But if you can simply tell by looking at the land where the trees were, can't you tell where the encampment was?"

"I'd say it included both sides of the creek." He squinted toward the west. "Possibly from yonder bluff"—he pointed to the rocky banks beyond a meadow on the other side of Swains Creek—"to just about the edge of the road up there. And from where the old Duckworth place stood, to the south, on up to just this side of where the canning factory used to be. Maybe about thirty acres, all told."

"You're good," she said again. "You really are very, *very* good. Especially by including the other side of the creek. Because that's where I'm going to build my house."

"Oh?" he said. "The wigwam's not big enough for you?"

She laughed. "The wigwam's a playhouse. For now, it's just a playhouse."

"So I've heard," he said.

She gave him a look and then remarked, "You're Vernon's bosom buddy, aren't you?"

"We go way back," Day admitted.

"Has he told you about *us*?"

"Jacob Ingledew had already done that," Day said.

She poked him in the ribs. "Day! So you've read the memoirs too? I hope you don't think I've just been trying to relive the past. Osages believe the past is over and gone, change is inevitable, and the course of history can't be reversed."

"Then why do you want the trees back?" he asked.

"If anybody asks, tell them that I value my privacy."

And that was that. Day spent another hour by himself,

tramping around the former location of the Indian encampment, making notes in his notebook. A great oak stood here. A cluster of elms here. There was a green ash, and a stand of white ash, there were several swamp chestnut oaks, along with cherry-bark oaks, hickories, black gums, and winged elms. Day took pride in his ability to *be* a tree, to think like one, to know where, for example, if he were a sassafras, he would want to stand. When the time came to give each of these trees a personal name, he'd have to ask his "client" for actual Osage names.

Juliana had briefly returned to her playhouse, stayed there awhile, and then, as Day was concluding his inventory of the former arboreal citizens of the campsite, came to him briefly to say she was going back to Ekaterina's house. "I neglected to ask," she said, "and it's not even important and you don't have to tell me, but what should I be paying you? Could I give you some sort of retainer now, or should I start a salary, or what?"

Day decided that if she didn't yet know that he and Diana had no need for remuneration, she would probably find out soon enough. Day hadn't worked for wages since he'd bagged at a supermarket at the age of seventeen. The U.S. Forest Service had sent him periodic checks for the services he was rendering on government lands and he had simply forwarded them to Diana's team of accountants, who spared him from ever having to think that he was gainfully employed. Diana herself had no interest in money. Neither of them had ever bothered to estimate her incredible net worth, and neither of them ever discussed the subject or gave any thought to it. Day knew that Juliana too was fabulously rich, but probably not as rich as Diana. The mention of the subject gave him a headache. "Let's not discuss it," he told Juliana. "I'll just let you know what my expenses are, when they occur."

"If I start building my house now," she asked, "would the construction crews be in your way? Would you rather I waited until you've finished the job in the autumn?"

"No, it would be better if the house was finished first."

"Good," she said. She offered him her hand for a shake, and she held his hand too long.

The next time he saw Vernon, he told him that he'd been thinking about it and had reached the conclusion that it was indeed possible to love two women at the same time. In fact, he said, it was even possible to love *three* women at the same time, but he didn't tell Vernon which three. He might have, but Vernon was in a hurry. The Samurai were assembling in emergency session at Vernon's house. Again, Lydia and Arch would be Day and Diana's house guests for a couple of nights; each of them brought gifts, house plants from Lydia and very fine wines from Arch. Governor Bradfield's campaign had reached the seventh week of its attack on Vernon's albatrosses and planned a concentrated effort calling attention to Vernon's having never gone to college. Going back to Jeff Davis, nearly all the governors of Arkansas had gone to college, even if, like Orval Faubus and Win Rockefeller, they hadn't graduated. Bradfield's TV spots (craftily authored by Carleton Drew) were going to be careful not to offend the great mass of Arkansawyers who had never been to college themselves, but they were going to leave the indelible impression that a man without *any* college education is simply not qualified to lead the state government. It wouldn't be sufficient for the Ingledew campaign to counterattack with the information that Bradfield had flunked thirty hours at Southern Arkansas University and had never actually received a degree himself. Bradfield, like Faubus and Rockefeller, had at least thought enough of college to matriculate (although Carleton Drew insisted on never using that word in the Bradfield campaign because it sounded naughty).

Now the emergency session of the Samurai was considering Cast's suggestion that they call in a team of professors who were experts in each of the fields that Vernon had mastered in his self-education program (thirty-one so far, from art history through philosophy, but not yet including politics, which he was still in the process of mastering), and having these professors testify that Vernon was worthy of having a PhD in each of their fields; therefore, he was far better than a college graduate; he had, in fact, the equivalent of thirty-one doctorates.

Day did not get a chance to tell Vernon of his own idea for putting a stop to the negative campaign of mudslinging. Nor did he tell Vernon that Juliana was building a house in Stay More and had arranged for Day to restore the arboreal landscape; he assumed Vernon would find that out soon enough from Juliana herself. He decided to try out his idea of the campaign on Arch and Lydia, perhaps at supper. But although they were sleeping at his house, they were having their supper at Vernon's. So he tried it out on Diana and she bought it, wholeheartedly.

This inspired him. He knew that what would really give him the confidence to present the idea to the Samurai would be not so much the approval of Lydia and Arch but the approval of the one man in whose realm of expertise it most resided. So later that night, after the meeting of the Samurai had broken up, he told Diana to make Lydia and Arch right at home and tell them he'd be back in a jiffy. Then he drove to Sharon and Larry's house, the former Stay More post office (where, his first months in town, thirty years before, he'd "mailed" letters to Diana and received hers in return, every day when they were experimentally living apart from each other for a while). They were all sitting on the porch, Sharon, Larry, Monica, and Harry, enjoying the cooling darkness of early September.

"Howdy," Day said to them, and they exchanged howdies with him, although Harry said, "Mohammed of the Mountains."

Day smiled at Harry. "I'm taking it to the mountain, and you're the mountain. Could I have a few minutes of your time in private?"

Harry looked at the others and then back at Day. Then he hefted himself out of his chair and walked down the steps of the old store and post office. He brought his drink with him. "Lead on," he said to Day.

They strolled up the road, not the main road but the Right Prong Road that Day had come in on.

"I know nothing about politics," Day began, "and I don't understand the refinements of negative campaigning, your bailiwick. But it has occurred to me that while the public has learned to expect two candidates to assault each other with innuendo and accusation and slander, the public possibly has a point of saturation. Do you agree?"

Harry snorted. "If the public's got a saturation point, I've never seen 'em reach it."

"But don't you think it's possible, hypothetically, that if two candidates attack each other incessantly and viciously, the public will simply eventually tune them out?"

"Yeah, it's possible," Harry admitted. "But calumny is like gossip for most people: You can't get enough of it."

"We won't listen to gossip if it's outrageous. If the calumny were inflated and overdone beyond a certain point, wouldn't the public get sick of it?"

"So?"

"So I've been thinking. Here are Bradfield and Vernon having at each other with everything they've got, and you have certainly provided Vernon with an arsenal of serious accusations against the governor, but it hasn't particularly helped. The latest polls show Vernon falling farther and farther behind. My idea is this. Instead of trying further to counteract Bradfield's calumny, why not help it along, until it is so bloated it self-destructs? Pad it, in other words. If necessary, fabricate all kinds of sins and errors and crimes that Vernon has committed and have him confess to them on a daily basis, until the public begins to take a 'So what?' attitude. The populace will be *inoculated* against any further scandal. If a saturation point can't be reached, supersaturate the public!"

Day waited, but for a long time Harry Wolfe did not respond. They continued strolling, and once or twice Wolfe raised his glass to his mouth and took an audible gulp. At length he said, "You're Vernon's asshole buddy and you want to stick all those knives in his back?"

"Maybe," Day said, "people would start feeling sympathetic toward a guy with a back full of knives."

Harry continued to ponder for a while longer before saying, "It's risky. You're suggesting that I take my cannons, turn them around, and shoot in the wrong direction."

"Good metaphor," Day said. "Possibly in all the noise and smoke of the cannons firing there might grow up a general wish for quiet and clarity and peace. Who knows? The candidates might even be compelled to concentrate on the *issues*."

"Heaven forbid!" Harry said mockingly. "I don't know nothing about no *issues*." He began laughing. He finished his drink and stopped and turned to face Day. "Mr. Whittacker, you know, I think you've really got something here. I'll take it up with the others and we might even give it a try. Will you take all the blame if it backfires?"

"I'd prefer to remain anonymous," Day said. "Is there some way you could introduce the idea as if it's your own?"

"And if it works, I'll be a hero?" Harry said. Day tried to catch a note of sarcasm in Harry's words, but Harry really meant it. "I could even parlay this ploy into fat oppo jobs for the rest of my life. Only I wouldn't be researching the opposition, I'd be researching my own man!" Harry continued laughing. He finished his drink and stared into his empty glass. "What's this local moonshine called? Chism's Dew? It's pretty good stuff, you know. I could develop a real liking for it. Let's go back to the house and get another one." Harry turned around and began strolling homeward. "Say, you know, amongst all the other turpitudes, we could leak the news that Vernon Ingledew is the head of the operation manufacturing Chism's Dew!"

"Why not?" said Day. He permitted himself a chuckle, as he envisioned all the vilification that could be heaped on Vernon.

"I've got a better one," Harry suggested. "A real one! Did you know that those two Indians use peyote? It's part of their religion or whatever, but I believe it's a controlled substance and illegal. We could claim that Vernon and Juliana get high together!"

"I should have guessed you already knew about Vernon and Juliana," Day said.

"Yeah, and we'll throw that in too, right on top of the heap, piling the dirt so high that the people of the great state of Arkansas won't give a flying fuck what Vernon does or does not do in his private life!" Harry began cackling. "Of course, Vernon will have to deny everything. When we hit him with the peyote, he can say, 'Yes, I used peyote, but I didn't inhale!' " And Harry laughed so loudly Day wondered if the others could hear.

"Just out of curiosity," Day inquired, "how did you know that Juliana uses peyote?"

"I asked her," Harry said.

"Does anything escape your all-seeing eye?"

"Thank you, no. Not even the possibility that, even as we speak, Juliana may be pregnant."

"You're kidding me!"

"For the moment, I'm just speculating. Mr. Whittacker, I take it you're just as familiar as I am with *The Architecture of the Arkansas Ozarks.* You know, therefore, that Jacob Ingledew impregnated the Indian squaw who was, supposedly, the ancestor of Juliana Heartstays, and therefore if Juliana is trying to recapture the lost times of her people she is bent upon getting herself impregnated. No?"

"No," Day said firmly, "because that book also makes clear that Vernon is the very last of all the Ingledews because the woman he loves, Jelena, cannot have children. Of course, it doesn't say anything about Juliana coming along many years later, but it does make quite clear that there will never be any more Ingledews after Vernon."

"Yes, it draws a fabulous parallel between the lives of the Ingledews of Stay More and the lives of an ancient family of Arcadian Greeks, as expressed in a book in Latin that Vernon found in a bookstore in Rome on his first trip around the world. The book is called *De Architectura Antiqua Arcadiae*, or *The Archaic Architecture of Arcadia*."

"The book we're talking about—the Arkansas architecture book—makes clear that the Roman book tells the whole story of Vernealos Anqualdou, the last of the line of Anqualdous. The *last*, who could have no children because the woman he loved could not bear a child."

"And it also tells everything that will happen to Vernealos for the rest of his life—including whether or not he becomes elected as provincial eparch, or governor, of Arcadia, like his ancestor Iakobus Anqualdou."

"Which is the reason that Vernon deposited his copy of the book in the Library of Congress with instructions that they never let him see it, because he doesn't want to know what is going to happen to him for the rest of his life."

"But which doesn't stop a good pal of mine in DC from going to the Library of Congress and getting a copy made, which he sent to me, and which I have commissioned a fellow at the University of Arkansas, Professor Daniel Levine of the Classics Department, to translate for me. Any day now I'll know not only whether or not Vernon will have a child with Juliana but also whether or not he'll be elected governor of Arkansas in November."

"If you believe in fairy tales," Day said. "I find it hard to accept that a man of your cynicism and objectivity would believe that an ancient book can accurately predict what's happening *now*. Shades of Zoroaster!"

"I think it's Nostradamus whose shades you want to invoke," Harry Wolfe said, then thanked Day for the "brilliant" idea of extirpating the negative campaign by supersaturation and returned to the house of Larry and Sharon to get himself another Chism's Dew.

Day was to discover that there were no trucks with tree spades for hire in Harrison. He made several calls and discovered the closest place he could find a big tree spade was Fayetteville. He decided to go have a look at it and, while he was at it, have a little chat with the Author and ask him if he knew this Professor Levine, who was translating this *Architectura Antiqua Arcadiae* and finding out everything that happened to Vernealos Anqualdou.

Day decided not to tell Vernon that the ancient book was being translated from the Latin at Harry's request. And of course he couldn't tell Vernon that he himself had "planted" the idea of dumping so much scandal on Vernon that the populace would grow jaded and indifferent. But there was one thing he wanted to ask Vernon, and it was this: "Do you use contraceptives when you're with Juliana?"

Vernon looked baffled. "Now what would I be doing with a contraceptive in my possession? I've never used one in my life. I've never had to."

"Don't forget that personal motto of yours: 'I'll try anything once.' "

Chapter Sixteen

Lydia had never particularly liked Harry Wolfe, but now she had to wonder if the man wasn't some kind of genius. She thought he was physically repulsive: obese, disheveled, constantly reeking of booze, and usually wearing a facial expression dominated by what seemed to be a sneer contemptuous of the whole world. Once when he was thoroughly sloshed he had slapped her on the butt and she had been required to slap him on his flabby jowl, and that was the only time they had ever touched. She admired him for his sleuthing powers at the same time she disdained the entire aspect of politics that his powers fed: the intrusion of personal lives into campaigns. "Gotcha" politics. Whatever disappointment she'd had with her old boss Bill Clinton, she had always felt Clinton's personal life should never have been an issue, as long as he performed his duties as governor and as president to the best of his considerable abilities. What we do in our bedrooms, she believed, should have no more bearing on our performance in our jobs than what we do at our dining tables.

Harry Wolfe was therefore some kind of serpent, and she had as little to do with him as possible. But now he appeared to be proposing a bit of strategy that would seem to contravene his own principles, rendering the whole apparatus of smear campaigns ineffective. Her first reaction to his idea, which she sensed was shared by her fellow Samurai, was doubt and caution. The plan could so easily go haywire. What if the public was *not* surfeited by all the scandal that Harry proposed to heap upon their own candidate? What if the plenitude of muckraking simply increased the public's appetite for it? In the Samurais' discussion, Lydia had offered this idea: "What if they, the populace, think this whole big blob of mud is actually chocolate cake? And they want seconds? And thirds?"

But the more she thought about it, the more tempting the plan seemed. It might be a huge gamble, but a gamble worth taking in view of Bradfield's determination to concentrate his entire campaign on Vernon's albatrosses. If Bradfield could devote a whole week of spots to each of the thirteen albatrosses, at God knows what expense, what could he do if there were two hundred? Might not the very size of the intrusion sheet discourage him from continuing his smears? There were still two months left until the November election. Quite possibly the people of Arkansas in their goodness and wisdom might prefer that those two months be spent in an honest contemplation of the ideological differences between the two candidates instead of their peccadilloes. Might that be too much to expect?

The Samurai decided to take an extra day and night at Stay More, in order to complete their consideration and discussion of Harry's proposal before presenting the idea to Vernon himself. Bo certainly approved of this extension of time; Lydia suspected it would give him more time to be with Jelena, and Lydia was the first of the Samurai, other than Bo himself, to imagine it true that Bo and Jelena were having an affair; when Lydia had called early one morning to tell Vernon that they needed to find Bo because of Bradfield's bombshell, Vernon hadn't seemed to know, at first, that Bo was right there in his own house! And of course the Samurai had already speculated among themselves that there was something going on between their candidate and that ravishing

Indian maiden who had taken up residence in a quaint little wigwam. When Lydia had first heard this gossip, it had hurt her as if someone had slashed her with a knife, because she herself was very much in love with Vernon. One thing that made Lydia receptive to Harry's radical scheme was that whatever hanky-panky was going on between Vernon and Juliana and Bo and Jelena would be smudged over and obscured in the onslaught of slanders.

When Lydia had made that early morning phone call to Vernon, she hadn't expected to find him home; she had a hunch that possibly Jelena might know of Bo's whereabouts. Lydia was irritated that her bosses—her candidate, Vernon, and his campaign manager, Bo—had both taken to mysterious disappearances without any word to her. Pine Bluff had been a fiasco, and Vernon had simply got into his helicopter right after the rally petered out. After all the work she and Carleton had done—planning and setting up the rally and getting as much publicity for it as they could squeeze out of the media, and with a considerable expenditure for TV and radio spots, posters, and what Lydia had been led to believe was a good Democratic organization in the town—a little more than one hundred people had turned out, scarcely more than the numbers of Vernon's hired troops, the band and cheerleaders and singers and all.

Either owing to the meager crowd or because his heart was elsewhere, Vernon had not given an inspired speech, and the whole thing was desultory and discouraging. Lydia feared, against the sincerest wishes of her heart, that old-time stump speaking was dead, dead, dead, and nothing would revive it. She had been left to do the postmortems and cleaning up, without any help from Carleton, who at least had the courtesy to come to her and inform her that after much soul-searching he had decided to take a lucrative offer from the Bradfield camp to switch sides. Lydia did not tell him or anyone else, then or now, that she herself had also received a very good offer, delivered in person by Billy Joe Slade,

Bradfield's manager, and the offer was so high it should have caused her some soul-searching too, but she hadn't needed to search her soul because she knew her soul would never give her a minute's peace if she had accepted it.

Slade had told her that if she wouldn't accept the exorbitant figure, they were going to offer it to Harry Wolfe. Apparently Harry had also turned them down. Could it be that Harry, for all his other shortcomings, at least possessed a conscience? A sense of loyalty? Once before, during the primary, the Reverend Dixon had put in a very high bid for Harry's services, but Harry had turned him down too. And Lydia knew, because her friend Monica was in charge of the payroll, that Harry hadn't received a raise for turning down Dixon or Bradfield. Lydia wondered if she could have held out for a higher salary herself. She needed it on her résumé for whatever future campaign might employ her. But she was not going to sell out for any amount of money.

Still, she was not a happy camper. She wanted more than anything in this world to see Vernon Ingledew installed in the governor's mansion, which was at least a reasonable desire, compared with her unreasonable desire to have him return her love. There was a good chance that if he were elected he would make her his press secretary and they might have some moments of intimacy behind his office door. And whether he was elected or not, she knew she'd always want to be a part of Stay More. She genuinely loved this place. If only she could relax here and have nothing political to preoccupy her, it would be heaven. She had fantasies of dressing as sometimes she'd seen the Woman Whom We Cannot Name and her new friend the Indian maiden dressing—in country calico cotton—and sitting on the porch of the old Governor Ingledew house watching the world go by . . . or failing to go by.

During her previous stay in Stay More, Lydia had taken a hike up to the dogtrot log cabin where Vernon's grandmother,

Latha Bourne Dill, persisted alone and fiercely independent beyond the age of a hundred, and Lydia had a delightful visit with the old woman, who knew everything about the history of Stay More. As press secretary, Lydia had an ulterior motive: perhaps a human-interest story could be written about the colorful old lady, who kept a yard full of cats (many more than Lydia's half dozen), and whose pastoral kindness and keen-wittedness had been inherited by her grandson. But when Lydia had mentioned the idea of an interview and of photographers, the woman had said, "Miss Caple, whatever that boy Vernon does has always been okay with me, but when it comes to his wits and his ways and his twists, he takes after his momma, my daughter Sonora, and I'd just as soon not have anybody looking at me as if I had anything to do with it." Sonora Dill Ingledew had of course been dead (of breast cancer) since Vernon was only ten years old.

"What about his daddy?" Lydia had asked. "Did Vernon inherit any of his character or features?"

"You haven't met Hank Ingledew?" Latha had asked.

"I wasn't aware he existed," Lydia had said. Vernon had never talked about him, nor had any of the other Samurai mentioned him, and Lydia had written nothing about him in Vernon's press bio.

"I'm sorry to say my son-in-law and I don't visit, but I reckon that's as much my fault as his," the old woman had said.

Lydia had made a mental note to make the acquaintance of John Henry "Hank" Ingledew on her next visit to Stay More, and now it was time, although now she had the weighty matter of Harry's radical scheme to think about. She didn't ask Vernon or Bo for their permission to visit Hank Ingledew or for directions to the house. She asked George, who had been her favorite of these local people until she'd met Latha. George was only too glad to get away from the attentions of Thomas Bending Bear and give

Lydia a ride "up high to the yon side of Ingledew Mountain," where Hank Ingledew lived alone in a "modern" house he had constructed for his large family back in the fifties, just before Vernon was born. Lydia was more curious to see the house Vernon had grown up in than to meet his father. The house was indeed remote from the rest of Stay More, which somehow made Vernon's father seem like a hermit.

Hank Ingledew was a well-preserved man past eighty, and Lydia saw at once that Vernon had fallen heir to his handsomeness, his height, and, alas, his congenital woman-shyness. Hank managed to shake Lydia's hand while studying the rug as if searching for an invisible insect. And for the whole length of her visit he was never once able to look her in the eye. "I've heared about ye," he allowed, and, gesturing toward his television set, a surprisingly large and recent model, he said, "I keep up with the news and politics and all, and I've known ye to work for other fellers before you went to work for my boy. Democrats one and all. I've got to tell ye, I've voted Republican all my life."

"Really?" Lydia said. "Well, I assume that's going to change in the next election."

"Last I heared tell, my boy was a-fixin to run as a Democrat, and if that's so he won't get no vote of mine."

"Oh, what a thing to say!" Lydia lamented. But she had a sudden inspiration. If Harry's proposal was accepted by the Samurai, and they did in fact embark upon an operation to heap defamation upon their own candidate, wouldn't it look great if the public knew that Vernon's own father wouldn't vote for him? "Don't tell me you have any admiration for Shoat Bradfield," she said to him.

"He's a upstanding member of the Republican Party, and that's good enough for me," Hank said.

Lydia wondered if she should try to explain Harry's scheme

to the old man, and decided against it. "Would you actually do something to help Bradfield against your own son?" she asked boldly.

"If it would keep Bradfield in office," Hank Ingledew said. "Besides, Vernon would be a right smart happier if he'd just stick to raisin hogs. Right, George?"

"Sure thing," George put in. "I'd vote for Bradfield myself if it would help keep Vernon here in Stay More. But I got to admit, I'm just as much a lifelong Democrat as you are a lifelong Republican."

"Never held it again ye, George," Hank said. "There's lots of idjits in this world. We don't blame 'em for their mental deficiency, we just try and humor 'em along."

"Wal, don't ye go tryin to humor me, Hank. I can cuss the Republicans more thundery than you can cuss the Democrats," George replied.

Lydia would have liked nothing more than to listen to George and Hank argue politics. But there was business to tend to. She asked Hank, "What if a reporter came up here and asked you to reveal all the bad things Vernon did when he was just a boy? What would you tell him?"

Hank needed more than a moment to think. "Hmm," he said. "Well," he said. He scratched his stubbly chin a bit and said, "Well, now." He stared out the window and finally cleared his throat and said, "I do seem to recollect there was a time, when he wasn't but about six or seven, when he didn't have the sense to latch the pasture gate behind him, and the cow—we didn't have but one cow in them days—she got out and wandered off and we had to go for purt near a whole week without ary milk." Hank looked at George for confirmation of the severity of this deed.

"That was a real dumb thing to do," George admitted.

Lydia kept silent and did not reveal her disappointment that no capital could be made of such a minor misdeed. At length,

Hank said, "Then there was the time, he must've been maybe eleven or so, when he was shootin at tin cans with his BB gun, just a-tossin 'em up in the air and tryin to hit 'em, and he shot an eagle! Hit that eagle right in the eye. Didn't kill him but put his eye out. Grady Bullen, the game warden, found the eagle and took him home and nursed him back to health and that darn eagle never would leave the Bullen place but hung around for years afterward, and Vernon used to go and watch it, but he never told Grady it was his BB gun which done the deed."

"That might explain why Vernon is so opposed to guns," Lydia observed.

"He is, is he?" Hank asked. "Well, heck fire, aint nobody gonna vote for the fool if he is. Ever man has got the right to keep and use all the shootin arns he needs, to pertect his fambly and kill him some game and what-all."

"Darn tootin," George said. "Many a time I've told Boss that I don't see how he can make any friends among the voters if he wants to do away with guns."

Lydia herself greatly admired Vernon's stance on gun control (or *extirpation*, not to split hairs), but she didn't say this to the men. "Still, the two misdeeds you've mentioned were both accidents, more or less, wouldn't you say? Didn't Vernon ever deliberately do something that was wrong, or illegal, or very bad?"

"Nothing that he was ever arrested for, or even taken to account for," Hank said. "But because I wouldn't give him money to waste on the pitcher shows—I wanted him to have to earn his own spendin money—he used to sneak into the pitcher show, the Buffalo Theater over to Jasper. I don't rightly know just how he got in, but he did it, more than once, until he was caught. But Tim Barker, the Buffalo's manager, just gave me a phone call about it, and I told Vernon that I was going to cut off his—"

Hank faltered and grew red in the face. Lydia asked, "Yes? Cut off his what?"

"His nose?" Hank offered. "I just told him that what I'd been threatening to cut off ever since he was just a pup if he ever did anything real bad that I was now a-fixin to do it." Hank chuckled. "That boy just run away from home. He was gone for three days, God knows where. But I couldn't hold that again him, because I run away from home myself, to join the circus, when I wasn't but the same age. We both came back, of course."

Lydia wondered if Harry Wolfe might have better luck worming some information out of Hank Ingledew. She suspected that because she was a woman Hank was not only very shy about speaking to her but also reticent about revealing any of Vernon's childhood or adolescent conduct that might have involved sins of the flesh.

Before the Samurai reconvened to discuss Harry's proposal, Lydia learned from her host, Day Whittacker, of the Indian maiden's plan to build a house (or mansion) in Stay More and of her intention to conceal it with transplanted trees. Day brought the subject up because he needed Lydia's advice: Would the busy activity of the building and transplanting attract attention from the occasional journalists and photographers who snooped around town, and, if so, might it harm Vernon's campaign?

Now Lydia realized that if the busy activity were to occur under "normal" times, that is, when Stay More was as sleepy and undisturbed as usual, it would draw a lot of attention, but if it happened in the midst of the initial furor over all the "scandals" revealed about Vernon, it would go unnoticed or unremarked. In fact, as she thought about it, the building of the mansion might even be used as one more potential scandal: If it was true that Vernon was involved with the Indian maiden, that in itself was going to be a major scandal, and her construction of a mansion on land that Vernon had simply given her would further embellish the scandal in the eyes of the public, already disaffected by the reports of Vernon's extravagant double-bubble house, which Bradfield had given considerable time and space to exposing in the sixth week of his attack on Vernon's albatrosses. Although they had not been able to photograph the house, even from the air, they had hired an artist to render an imaginary conception of it, inaccurate and misleading but at least emphasizing that it consisted of two huge round globes bonded together. "Would anybody who chose to live in a place like this be happy in the governor's mansion?" asked the advertisements and TV spots. It was a noisily rhetorical question, and perhaps more than Bradfield's use of the other albatrosses it left the populace convinced that Vernon was simply not One of Us.

So Lydia's last expedition, before the Samurai reconvened, was to interview Juliana Heartstays. Several days were needed to talk herself into it, because her jealousy of the Indian maiden was bitter and galling. Lydia had expected to find her at the wigwam, but she was instead at the home of the Woman Whom We Cannot Name. Going there to talk to her, Lydia realized that when all the "scandals" broke and the village began to fill up with snooping newspeople, it might cause problems for the Woman Whom, who guarded her privacy, who was almost desperate not to be discovered as the famous novelist who had supposedly been murdered several years before. Lydia decided that if the Samurai did indeed decide to embark upon the supersaturation campaign, she should have a talk with the Woman and suggest that she might want to take a vacation (go home to visit Svanetia?) for the duration of the breaking scandals.

Swallowing her animosity, Lydia gave a little white lie to Juliana Heartstays: as Vernon's press secretary, she was intrigued by the reports that Vernon had "donated" a parcel of thirty acres, more or less, to Juliana, a descendant of the Indians who had once lived on that land, and she wondered if a human-interest story might be made of it.

"I'd much prefer to keep it as quiet as possible, if it's all the same to you," Juliana said, cordially but firmly.

"But if the story gets out, we should be prepared to offer our 'official' version," Lydia said. "Couldn't we simply say that some Osages had regained possession of their tribal lands through Vernon's generosity?"

The Indian maiden smiled, with perfect teeth. She truly was an unutterably fine-looking woman, and Lydia knew that if Juliana became a centerpiece of "Vernon's Vices," as Lydia was beginning to think of the scandals, her picture would not only be in every newspaper in the state but would probably appear in a few national magazines. "Vernon doesn't like to think that he gave the land back to us," Juliana said, "because indeed he didn't. We simply reclaimed it."

"Whatever," Lydia said. "You plan to stay, right? You're going to build a house on it?" The Indian nodded. "You're going to become a permanent resident of Stay More and sell your Oklahoma house?"

"I didn't realize anyone knew anything about my Oklahoma house," Juliana said.

"I'm just assuming you had a home there somewhere," Lydia said.

"Yes, I did. I do. I haven't put it on the market yet. I might have trouble selling it. It's a peculiar house."

"As peculiar as Vernon's?"

"I haven't seen Vernon's house yet," Juliana said.

"Oh," Lydia said. "You don't visit him. He visits you. Because of Jelena."

The Indian maiden stopped smiling. Her look was fiercely challenging. "What do you mean by visit?"

"You and Vernon are having a relationship," Lydia declared flatly.

Juliana Heartstays looked so stunned that for a moment

Lydia wondered if possibly she'd been mistaken to believe that. "Where on earth did you get such an idea?" she demanded. Lydia simply smiled knowingly. "Who *told* you that?" Juliana persisted. "Was it Bo?"

"Bo hasn't told me anything. Nor has Vernon."

"Then who did? You're staying with Diana and Day. Did one of them tell you they thought I was having an affair with Vernon?"

Lydia decided not to reveal to Juliana that it was practically common knowledge, or at least common rumor, among all the Samurai and everyone else in Stay More, including Day and Diana. Instead she said, "I just have a pretty good hunch. For years I worked for a newspaper, and reporters often have nothing to go on but their hunches."

"But you're putting two and two together and coming up with the wrong sum," Juliana protested. "Why *me*?"

"You're beautiful," Lydia said, honestly but painfully. "And I know Vernon."

"Have you told Vernon—or anybody—of your suspicion?" Juliana asked.

"Just you," Lydia said.

"Well, you're dead wrong, and I hope you'll keep your suspicion to yourself," Juliana requested. "You had *better* keep it to yourself. If it gets out, I'll hold you to blame for any trouble it causes."

But when the Samurai got together—in the store part of Sharon and Larry's house, the one available meeting place other than Vernon's living room that would hold the six of them—the first subject that came up, even before anyone proposed a vote on Harry's suggestion, was the matter of Vernon's "recreational activity during his too-frequent visits to Stay More," as Harry Wolfe put it. Monica Breedlove boldly delivered herself of the opinion that it was just terrible. Arch Schaffer said that as long as they were going to refer to it as "recreational activity" they ought not begrudge the man his dalliance. Cast Sherrill said that under ordinary circumstances the story would be romantic and exciting and even thoroughly American, but that the timing couldn't be worse for a gubernatorial candidate. Bo Pharis said he was personally appalled by the situation but didn't see that it would damage the campaign unless it "got out."

" 'Getting it out' is what this meeting is all about," Lydia reminded them. "We're here to consider Harry's radical proposal that we disclose all the possible damaging goods on Vernon in order to give the public a stomachache. So if we decide to do that, the crown jewel of the damaging goods is going to be Miss Juliana Heartstays."

"You beat me to it, Lydia," Harry said. "But I was going to make a case for bringing in the redskin lady as a kind of pièce de résistance of a full seven-course feast that will not only give the public a bellyache but cause such dyspepsia and vomiting they won't have any appetite for months afterward . . . or at least until after the election."

"But do we want to bring her in at all?" Bo wondered. "Couldn't we accomplish our motive without her?"

"What have we got so far?" Arch wanted to know.

The Samurai got down to work, and each reported on whatever he or she had found, or knew about, that could be used against Vernon. Lydia related in detail her visit to Hank Ingledew and all that she'd managed to learn from him. "We can't do anything with the business of letting the cow out of the pasture," she observed, "but maybe we can make something out of shooting the eagle and sneaking into the movies. Best of all, maybe we could divulge the information that Vernon's own father plans to vote against him."

"No!" Arch said. "He didn't say that."

"He most certainly did," Lydia maintained. "And imagine what the Bradfield campaign could do with it."

Bo said, "Good work, Lydia. But we have to decide at what point to leak that news to the best advantage. Indeed, we have to establish some sort of order for these revelations, perhaps in ascending rank of vilification. Maybe we could start with something simple like sneaking into the movies and build up from that."

"Look, guys," Arch said, "if this fantastic scheme is going to work at all, it's got to hit all at once, like a ton of bricks. If we just leak out one little scandal at a time, it will, to use Harry's metaphor, be like hors d'oeuvres to whet their appetite, not quench it."

"I stand corrected," Bo allowed.

"Could I get some clarification on one essential point?" Cast interjected. "Are we going to confine ourselves to *actual* bad things that Vernon Ingledew has done? I mean, if we're limited to only the *truth* about his past, we might not have enough food in the pot to quench anyone's appetite. As long as we're going to heap scandal upon him, why limit ourselves to verifiable misbehavior? Let's fabricate aspersion and innuendo!"

There was a long silence as the Samurai considered Cast's suggestion. Harry broke it by saying, "That's what I assumed we'd do when I first made the suggestion."

Bo remarked, "Yes, Harry, but it was Cast who made it clear. Brilliant idea, Cast, my boy. Now let's brainstorm!"

The rest of the meeting was a lot of fun. Each person taxed his or her imagination to come up with a whole disgraceful history for Vernon, and before the afternoon was over they had enough, as Bo put it, "to utterly crucify him, which it might do if it backfires." Harry offered up all the most flagrant misdeeds he had anthologized throughout his sordid career. Lydia herself contributed no small portion of the outrageous sins and transgressions of Vernon Ingledew. Their detraction of him was so ingenious and thorough that they all became rather disrespectful, even antagonistic, toward their candidate. "Why are we working for this jerk?" Harry wanted to know, and his remark drew the intended laughter, as well as a feeling of guilt and unease.

Vernon Ingledew slept with his mother until he was nine, at which point they were discovered in a posture that was not sleeping by Hank Ingledew, who forthwith expelled Vernon from his mother's bed. Thereafter he systematically seduced each of his five older sisters ("Make it only four," Monica suggested. "It might look more credible if one of them held out.") He also relieved his carnal appetite with the family cow. He was expelled from school in the seventh grade for persuading a girl to accompany him to the cloakroom for immoral purposes during recess, but his expulsion was rescinded when he began an affair with the school's young principal. He was only fourteen when she had to leave her job—and the state—because she had become pregnant. Two of his sisters had to have abortions. The cow ran off and was never found.

His adult misbehavior included such things (actual) as feeding his hogs the leftover corn mash from the Chism's still, which kept the swine constantly inebriated, the real secret of the superiority of Ingledew Ham, and (fabricated) he kept them shot full of steroids and other chemicals to enhance their growth and succulence. His immoderate income from the ham processing business was supplemented by his secret ownership of Chism's still, and the trademark Chism's Dew was registered in his name. Further, he devoted the most secluded parts of his vast acreage to the growing of marijuana, of which he and everybody else in Stay More were constant users. Although he'd been living with his first cousin Jelena since he was nineteen, when he paid her husband a large sum of money to move to California, he had confessed an ambition to get it on with every female in Newton County and was keeping a list; at last count, he still had a few hundred to go.

The reason there are no churches in Stay More—the closest being the Buffalo church four miles to the north—is that Vernon owns all the land (almost true) and has made a pact with the Devil to keep churches out. And the reason the Stay More school has been shut down for forty years is that Vernon has such unhappy memories of being in trouble during his school years (the young principal, etc.) that he hates education: the main reason he never went to college. He was now actively engaged in an orgiastic intrigue, abetted by peyote, not only with a Native American beauty but also with her homosexual manservant.

When they were all finished brainstorming, the portrait of Vernon Ingledew they possessed was so nefarious that they cringed in revulsion. "Do you think anyone will buy it?" Bo wondered.

"The point is," Arch reminded them, "that no one will *want* to buy it."

"It's beyond my wildest dreams," Harry Wolfe observed. "It's the dirtiest dirt I've ever seen. Such a pity that almost none of it is true."

"How are we going to leak all this stuff?" Cast wanted to know.

"I can take care of that," Lydia assured them. She did not want, not yet anyway, to tell them that she had received a handsome offer from the Bradfield campaign to become a renegade. But she had begun to entertain a devilish stratagem: She could pretend to switch sides and, in the process, leak all these tidbits craftily so that the Bradfield campaign would use them. In effect, she would be a double agent. The prospect was almost like something you'd read in a spy thriller, and it excited her. She noticed now that everyone was looking at her, waiting for her to continue. "Just leave it to me," she told them. "I can think of all kinds of ways to get this dirt disseminated."

"Well, then," Bo said, "are we agreed that we want to do this, or should we put it to a vote?"

"Your call, Boss," Arch said. "But hadn't we better find out what Vernon thinks of the whole thing?"

The meeting concluded after a lengthy discussion of whether or not they should summon Vernon forthwith to present him with the scheme they'd devised, and the ugly picture of himself they'd fabricated, or have a special meeting for that purpose the following day, perhaps up at Vernon's house. If the latter (and it was too late in the day now to think of extending this meeting), should they make an effort to hold the meeting so Jelena would be excluded? Should she be made privy to their falsehoods and, worse, their truths, such as the "orgiastic intrigues abetted by peyote"?

Cast Sherrill, who continued to be a house guest of Vernon and Jelena during these subsequent visits of the Samurai to Stay More (although he was spending more and more of his nights with Sheila Kimber at her house), and who consequently knew Jelena better than the rest of them (except Bo, of course), offered the opinion that Jelena be given full rights as participant in the "plot"; she might thus even reveal some things, true or false, about Vernon that nobody else knew or could invent.

Harry Wolfe said, "Hell, for that matter, why don't we ask Vernon himself to confess to any misdeeds that nobody else knows about?"

Lydia was unable to determine who fiendishly cackled at this idea; maybe all of them did. *What bad people we are!* she reflected. It was decided to reconvene the Samurai the following day at Vernon's house. Arch gave Lydia a ride in his Chevy pickup to Day and Diana's, where they would spend one more night.

Lydia was beginning to miss her cats and her apartment in Fayetteville. But there was one more thing she wanted to do here in Stay More. Because she had heard so much about Daniel Lyam Montross, whose bedroom study she used, and had taken the trouble to read a copy of *Some Other Place. The Right Place.* that Diana had loaned her, she had developed a suspicion that his spirit—not exactly his ghost—still inhabited the place. Just last night, sometime after midnight, she had had insomnia, and had taken the silver flask out of her purse, and had several swallows of vodka, and—of course it was quite possible she'd just dreamed all this—a man had sat on the side of her bed and asked her for a swig, and she'd given it to him, more than once (certainly the silver flask was empty the next morning), and they had talked, and he had told her that he was going to be her protector. "What do I need protection for?" she'd asked him. *You'll see*, he'd said. And the next thing she knew it was daylight and she was left with the conviction that she was waking up from what had not entirely been a dream.

After supper, Lydia asked Diana if she could tell her how to find the grave of Montross, which was supposedly nearby. Diana said she'd be very glad to take Lydia there, but Lydia insisted that she'd prefer to visit it by herself. It wasn't far, Diana said; you just go up that old logging trail, straight up the mountainside a little ways, and you'll come to a thick grove of cedar trees (which Day maintained), in a glade on a bench of the mountainside. And the tombstone is in that glade. You can't miss it.

So in the gathering dusk, Lydia took a little hike to the cemetery-of-one, the gravestone in the clearing, and stood there reverently for several minutes to gaze upon the inscription:

DANIEL LYAM MONTROSS
June 17, 1880–May 26, 1953
The last Montross of Dudleytown

The only Montross of Stay More
"We dream our lives, and live our sleep's extremes."

She recognized the last line as a quotation from his own poem, "The Dreaming," and thought it was very appropriate and perhaps even meaningful, in view of her dream (or vision) the night before. It was growing dark, and she wanted to be back at the house before she'd need a flashlight to get there. But she felt a special kinship for Montross. The man who'd sat on her bed last night—assuming that was him, or his ghost—was extremely appealing: kind and rugged and good-natured and witty.

She closed her eyes to see his face again. And that was her last sight of anything. Suddenly something shrouded her—a blanket or a large bag—and she felt herself covered and clutched by massive arms. She tried to lash out her fists, but her arms were held tightly within the cloth container. She screamed. Somebody had slipped a sack over her and was now lifting her and carrying her off! She tried to scream again but a hand clamped over her mouth within the sack and she could only mutter. Nothing like this had ever happened to her before; it was undignified and unheard of and terrifying. Whoever was carrying her—or was there more than one?—must be very strong because she wasn't exactly a lightweight. The feet of the person were pounding down the trail; she had enough sense of gravity to know they were going down, and she overcame her panic enough to reach the decision to wait until they were nearer to Day and Diana's house before she tried to scream or struggle again.

But when they were approximately where—she could only guess—the logging trail emerged onto the Whittacker property, a man's voice said to her, "Hush, and you will not be harmed." She tried to identify the voice, but it was no one's she had heard before, not even the singular voice of Daniel Lyam Montross, so she could dismiss her fleeting thought that she was being abducted by the ghost of a man who didn't want her visiting his tombstone. She believed the voice's warning and did not try to scream, although instinctively she kept trying to struggle within the confines of the sack.

They went on and on, until she knew they were no longer anywhere near Day and Diana's. Finally the voice said, "Now I am going to set you down upon a seat, and you must not try to move until I tell you or I will have to hurt you."

She came down off the man's shoulder and found herself sitting on something cushioning, her back and bottom supported almost in comfort after being carried aloft down the trail. Then she heard a motor start and realized that she was inside an automobile. Just what kind of automobile she couldn't begin to guess. It didn't sound like any car she'd heard before, just as his voice didn't sound like any voice she'd heard before. The car began to move.

"Who are you?" she asked. But he did not answer. "Don't you realize you could be getting yourself into real big trouble, doing this?" she demanded. He did not answer. "I assume you know who *I* am and that you've got a motive for kidnapping *me*, but I wonder if you realize the consequences." When he made no response to that, she told him about the consequences. "The Samurai will track you down and bring you to justice, and you'll spend the rest of your life in jail!" That provoked no response from her abductor either, so she continued. "Are you employed by Governor Bradfield, or his manager, Billy Joe Slade? Are they pissed off because I wouldn't accept their offer to defect from the Ingledew campaign? Well, then, the joke's on you, because even before you snatched me I'd made up my mind to switch over to the Bradfield team. Not only that, but I'll tell you all you could ever possibly want to know about Vernon Ingledew's shady history. Now why don't you take this bag off me and we can discuss this like civilized people?" When that had no results, she demanded, "Do we have to drive all the way to Little Rock like this?"

But they were not, apparently, going to Little Rock. After a long while on what felt like a bumpy dirt back road, and then a longer while on a jolting logging road or forest path, the car came to a stop, the motor was turned off, and her kidnapper said, "Now you must walk, because I can't carry you. It's steep and uphill from here on."

Chapter Seventeen

The bejeweled fucking fairyland that is Little Rock from the air at night on landing was beginning to pall for Harry; he scarcely gave it a glance. He'd made this trip so often he felt like a commuter, a feeling that was confirmed when the particular cabdriver at the airport said, "The Capital, right?" The more trips he made to Little Rock, the more he began to appreciate the occasional idyll in Stay More. A city man all his life, he never dreamed he'd develop such affection for the sticks. He'd even discovered something wondrous: Saturday nights in Stay More he didn't seem to need as much booze to make him happy as he required elsewhere.

But now he appreciated the parallel: that this, his second and last chapter, was beginning in exactly the same way that his first, chapter 7, had begun: arriving in Little Rock by air, checking into the Capital Hotel, plugging in his modem, and getting ready to go out and conquer the goddamn world. It was not just closure, it was *enclosure*, a fucking parenthesis seeming to suggest that life was not utter chaos after all.

There was a big difference, though. That first trip, he'd made contact with his old pal the political paragrapher Hank Endicott, made the useful acquaintances of librarian Bob Razer and of oppo man Garth Rucker, lured the last-named away from his employer, and compiled some handy dossiers on the opposition. Not much, but a good week's work that had played no small part in getting Vernon Ingledew past the primary.

Now his mission was far more serious and far more demanding of his talents, not as a muckraker but as a sleuth. He was going to infiltrate the goddamn Bradfield organization. He was going personally to find out what they had done with poor Lydia, and he was going to rescue her. And into the bargain, giving a grand climax to the whole operation and to this, his final chapter, he was going to effectuate the crafty plan to bring down Bradfield not by impugning him but by making the public sick and tired of his impugnings of Vernon Ingledew. To amuse himself before going to sleep in his nice room at the Capital, he mentally projected onto the ceiling a whole Hollywood movie of the story. His part was played by Drew Carey or John Goodman, and Lydia was played by Michelle Pfeiffer. Maybe they'd have to get Diane Keaton or Kathleen Turner. But central casting would really have to scrape the bottom of the barrel of slimy villains in order to cast Billy Joe Slade and Carleton Drew and oppo man Rafferty Oates and especially Governor Bradfield himself. Harry grinned with considerable satisfaction over the scene where John Goodman whips out his gun, informs those rascals that he's been a counterspy all along, and demands to be taken to wherever they're keeping Lydia.

But Bo hadn't permitted Harry to purchase a gun. "If they've got her," Bo had said, "and if you can somehow find out where they're keeping her, you'll have to go in and get her out without the use of any force. That's too dangerous." And Bo had impressed upon him the need for haste: the Newton County sheriff's department had agreed to wait not more than forty-eight hours before reporting the kidnapping to the Arkansas state police and the FBI and thus presumably to the newspapers and television. But Harry knew enough about the mechanics of kidnapping to realize that the longer they waited, the longer she was kept alive, the better her chances for coming out of the ordeal unscathed. So while he was mindful of the forty-eight-hour deadline, he was in no great hurry.

One problem, as he told Hank Endicott the next day, not over drinks in the Capital Bar but over coffee at a nice place called Community Bakery, was that it was only a supposition that the Bradfield people had kidnapped Lydia. In fact, as soon as the news was permitted to break, all the attention would be focused on the Bradfield people anyhow.

"Who else would have taken her?" Hank asked.

"Well, the sheriff has been questioning everybody in Stay More," Harry said. "Even me."

"Is it assumed she's been harmed?" Hank asked. "Was there any evidence of blood or anything?"

"That long-overdue thunderstorm we had yesterday morning washed away all the tracks, car tracks and people tracks, near the spot where Lydia was last seen, or rather where she had gone to inspect this little cemetery off in the woods. So it's not even known if she actually left that cemetery. She simply failed to return to the house where she was staying."

"Whoever took her," Endicott said, "should have realized she is such a well-known figure in Arkansas politics and journalism that this is going to be big news. I'm eager to do a column on it, as soon as I can. I'm getting antsy, Harry."

Harry had already debated with himself whether or not to reveal to Hank his plan to infiltrate the Bradfield organization and had decided against it. He and Hank were good buddies, but you don't tell even your best friend something so secret. You shouldn't even tell it to yourself, for God's sake. "I'm meeting Slade and Drew and Oates this afternoon," Harry said.

"And you're saying what, 'Please give Lydia back to us'?"

"I'm making them an offer they can't refuse," Harry said with a smile.

"Damn you, Harry, don't keep me in the dark. If I haven't heard from you again by sundown, I'm calling the police."

Harry assured Hank Endicott that he would report back to him, he hoped before sundown. Then he spent the rest of the morning at the Little Rock Public Library, not that there was anything he needed to research but just to touch base with librarian Bob Razer, who had become his good friend since their first meeting months earlier. Razer had helped him research the dossiers on the five former chiefs of staff who had worked for Governor Bradfield, not one of them for longer than six months, and had permitted him access to some arcane databases not open to the public. Razer made no secret of his own contempt for Shoat Bradfield and was only too happy to help Harry "dethrone" him (Razer's word). Now Harry just wanted to chat. He said nothing about Lydia's kidnapping or his own plan to infiltrate the Bradfield organization. The only reference to the campaign was indirect: He told Bob Razer that he had stopped en route to the Northwest Arkansas Airport yesterday to visit with Professor Daniel Levine at the University of Arkansas in Fayetteville and had picked up a copy of his translation of *De Architectura Antiqua Arcadiae*, which Harry had mentioned to Razer before, and the existence of which Razer knew about because of his familiarity with *The Architecture of the Arkansas Ozarks* (though he was suspicious about the book because he had stopped believing in fairy tales in the fourth grade).

Harry patted his Compaq laptop. "I've scanned it right into my hard drive. I read most of it last night. And it does indeed reveal everything that would happen to Vernealos Anqualdou for the rest of his life. Wouldn't you like to know?"

"Maybe you'd better not tell me," Razer said. "It would take all the fun out of watching Ingledew rising up against Bradfield."

Harry laughed. "I know. I sort of wish I hadn't already learned the outcome of the election myself."

Harry did not tell him, because he couldn't divulge Lydia's kidnapping, that there was no mention in the ancient Roman text of any female on Anqualdou's staff who was abducted by the opposition. This had slightly disappointed Harry, just as he'd been disappointed that there was no mention that Anqualdou had a crafty henchman whose job was to uncover all the secrets of the opposition and rescue that female assistant. The trouble with prophetic stories is they can't always bother themselves with every little detail of the future.

Before he could go off for his showdown with the Bradfield thugs, Harry had one more visit to make. For lunch at Cuzins, a sports café, his companion was Garth Rucker. Garth was flabbergasted that Harry didn't order a drink, and Harry had to fabricate an excuse.

"My stomach's been bothering me," Harry said, which wasn't entirely a fib. Out of consideration, perhaps, Garth ordered simply a beer instead of his usual scotch and soda. In their close association, Harry had gradually developed a tolerance if not a liking for the fiendish rat-faced little fellow in tweeds and spectacles, who was now officially his Deputy Director of Opposition Research and who indeed had been earning his salary. Harry had decided he didn't want Garth involved in the plot to rescue Lydia, so he wasn't even going to tell Garth that Lydia was missing, but he did explain the motive of his own trip to Little Rock: He told Garth about the scheme of killing off the negative campaign by making it too intrusive and unpalatable. Garth was incredulous at first, but the more Harry told him about the idea, and the more examples Harry offered of Vernon's Vices, the more Garth began to understand and appreciate the maneuver. Garth wasn't simple-minded, his tongue to the contrary. It had been Garth's clever observations and hunches that had led to the discovery in Portland, Oregon, of the Reverend Dixon's former child mistress, the hymn singer, and it had also been Garth's powers of persuasion, slicker than Harry could have mustered, that persuaded the young lady to return to Arkansas.

"So very shortly you'll be the *Chief* Director of Opposition Research for the Ingledew campaign," Harry informed him.

"I will? Where are you going?" Garth wondered.

"I'm joining the Bradfield campaign," Harry said with a smile.

"What?" Garth cried. "You couldn't!"

"But I am. Tell me, do you think they'll let me replace Rafferty Oates, or just become his assistant, or what? Do you personally know Rafferty?"

"Hell, yes, Raff and I go way back. And he's not going to give up his job to you, even if you *are* Harry Wolfe. They'll probably have to fire him! Which they could easily do. After all, what has he done for them? Except for enhancing some of those albatrosses, which he never discovered in the first place. No, I think they'll give him the bum's rush as soon as you show up. But I can't believe you'd do it."

"Thanks, Garth. That's all I need to know, that Rafferty Oates is dispensable." And when lunch was over, he got Garth to give him a ride over to Republican headquarters in its swank location on Chenal Parkway.

As they were shaking hands, Harry said, "Be sure to watch the ten o'clock news tonight. You might see me. You might see me and Lydia too."

"Oh? Is she in town?"

"I believe she is," Harry said, and then got out of the car and entered the site of his showdown. He was impressed with

Republican headquarters; the place looked ultrafestive and ultra-patriotic and ultra upper-class. If Lydia was being held hostage in Republican headquarters, she was living in style. It lacked the homey touches that Monica had imparted to Democratic headquarters in Fayetteville. The contrast between the two pointed up a central difference in the candidates' support: Anybody who was well off and comfortable and satisfied with life and the status quo was going to vote for Bradfield; Ingledew would pick up only the less wealthy and the discontented and people who thought too much for their own good.

His appointment was for two o'clock and he was fifteen minutes early, but they were waiting for him. "Welcome to Li'l Rawk," Billy Joe Slade said, pumping his hand. "I 'spect it aint your first visit, though, is it? Ah moan make ya comfy."

"Good to see you again, Harry," Carleton Drew said. "Make me happy when I guess why you're here."

Did Carleton know that he'd come to get Lydia? "Guess away, Carleton," Harry said.

Rafferty Oates's handshake was only halfhearted, and he wasn't smiling. "I don't believe I've had the chance to make your acquaintance, Mr. Wolfe. I wish I could call it a pleasure, but I can't."

"I doubt if anything pleases you," Harry observed.

Billy Joe Slade asked, "Y'et yet?"

Harry had a bit of difficulty understanding him. "Excuse me?" he said.

"Y'et yet?" Slade said again, and when Harry still failed to grasp his meaning, Slade pantomimed the forking of food into his mouth and Harry realized he was asking him if he had yet eaten.

"Oh, yes, I had lunch with Garth Rucker at a place called Cuzins," Harry declared.

They ushered him into an inner sanctum with comfortable

chairs. Billy Joe closed the door and said, "Ah moan fix ya a drink. Whatja like?"

It was the second time Slade had uttered *Ah moan* and Harry was beginning to realize it was short for *I am going to.* He shook his head. "Thanks, but I haven't had a drop for a week. Doctor's orders. My stomach."

"Well, then, I reckon none us boys gonna drink nothing neither," Billy Joe said. "But they's sody pop ov'are if ya git thirsty." He gestured and Harry understood that *ov'are* meant *over there.* Billy Joe sat down and clapped his hands together as if summoning a servant. "So. Well, now, yessiree bob. Let's us hear what-all goodies you've brung us."

"You made me an offer," Harry said. "Remember?"

"What kind of a offer?" Slade said. "Oh. Yeah. Back when we tried to give you a job?"

"Yes. In fact, you said that if I'd tell you how much Ingledew was paying me, you'd double it." He turned to Carleton Drew. "Did they double your salary?"

Carleton grinned. "Pretty much," he said.

"We figured you must have had an offer you couldn't refuse," Harry said to him. "But we also figured you must have had other reasons for leaving us."

"Like the leopard, I couldn't change my spots," Drew said. And when nobody laughed at his wit, he took the trouble to explain. "My TV spots. I'm proud of my spots, and Ingledew wouldn't let me make them."

"So you had an ulterior motive besides the money," Harry said. "Likewise, I'm not just looking for money. But let's start with that. I'm making seven a month. Will you pay fourteen?"

Billy Joe Slade coughed and said, "Well, heck now, that's a whole lot and I'd have to clear it with the Big Boss. But a man of your talents, shit, you'd be worth every bit of that. Why don't you just hang on a second, and I'll put in a quick call to the top."

Slade reached for the phone, punched one button, and said, "Martha. Billy Joe. Is he in? Let me talk to 'im." A few moments later, he said, "Boss. Yeah, just like you figured, he's ready to talk turkey. But this is one humongous turkey. He wants fourteen a month. . . . Yeah, that's right. . . . What? . . . Well, hang on and I'll ask him." Slade redirected his attention to Harry. "He wants to know what you've got on Ingledew that we don't already know."

"I don't know where to begin," Harry said, picturing all of Vernon's Vices in his mind. "For starters, how about this? He's been ingesting peyote with a redskin chick who would knock your eyes out."

"Huh? What's pay oatie?"

"It's a cactus. Produces tubercles that have narcotic properties. It's also called mescal."

"Aw, yeah," Billy Joe said. "Hang on." And he relayed this information into the phone. Then he reported back, "He wants to know how come Raff never found out nothing about that. Huh, Raff?"

"I think Wolfe is making this up," Rafferty Oates said. "Ingledew doesn't know any redskin chicks."

"Have you seen his little black book?" Harry asked Oates.

"What book?" Oates wanted to know.

"He keeps this black book," Harry said. "Only it isn't so little. I've not only seen it, I've scanned it into my computer." He patted his Compaq laptop. "It's pretty damned extensive. Did you know he has in it the names and phone numbers of hundreds of women in Newton County and all over northwest Arkansas?"

"You're making that up!" Raff Oates protested petulantly, but Billy Joe was back on the phone excitedly relaying this information to the governor. The conversation continued awhile and then Billy Joe said, "Will do, Boss! Let the good times roll!" and he hung up and said to Raff Oates, "Boss said for you to take a walk."

"Take a walk where?" Oates wanted to know.

"Go to N'Orleans and have a good time. Whatever. We don't need you no more."

"Well, screw that!" Raff recommended, snapping shut his briefcase and preparing to leave.

"Don't let the door hit you in the ass, Raff," Billy Joe said.

Actually, Harry was pleased to notice, the door did strike Rafferty Oates on his hip as he slammed it behind him. Harry conjectured that a man like Oates, seeking revenge for his dismissal, would promptly offer his services to the Ingledew campaign and would tell them all he knew about Bradfield's sins. Here was a situation Harry hadn't bargained for but was potentially very useful, because in order for the antidefamation scheme to succeed through oversaturation, the Ingledew campaign had to be able to match the Bradfield campaign's imputations, slander for slander. That would not only give the public indigestion that much sooner but also, just in case anybody believed any of the shit about Ingledew, it would give them plenty of fresh shit about Bradfield.

But one thing was beginning to bother Harry. Didn't Rafferty Oates know about the kidnapping of Lydia? Why hadn't he threatened to expose them, if he did? Or maybe only Slade and the governor himself knew about it. Maybe they'd kept it secret even from Carleton Drew.

"*Fourteen* a month," Billy Joe said to Harry. "Jesus, I don't make that much myself! But welcome aboard. You need a office or anything? A car maybe?"

"There's one little catch," Harry said.

"Aw-aw!" Billy Joe exclaimed. "I was afraid of this. What is it?"

"I suppose I should have mentioned it before you told Oates to take a hike. You might want him back if you're not willing to make this deal with me. I will make the switch and accept fourteen a month, but like Carleton I've got an ulterior motive besides the money. *I want you to let Lydia go.*"

Billy Joe looked genuinely puzzled, a great job of acting. "Lydia *who*?" he said. "Go *where*?"

"Lydia Caple!" Harry snapped. "What other Lydia is there?"

Billy Joe exchanged looks with Carleton Drew, and Carleton looked as puzzled, if not more so. "Let her go?" Carleton said.

"Okay," Harry said. "Maybe she voluntarily joined up with you people, just like I'm doing. If so, I want to know that. If you've forcibly taken her, I want to know *that.* My services for Bradfield do not begin until she appears, one way or the other, is that clear? *Where is she?*"

"Well, holy shit, Harry," Billy Joe said, spreading his hands. "Fuck a duck and crying out loud. This is total news to me. Let me check with the Boss." And he punched his phone again and said, "Martha, git him quick." And then, "Hey, Boss, Harry Wolfe thinks we've got Lydia Caple. Look under your desk and see if she's hiding anywheres. No kidding. . . . Okay, here." He handed the phone to Harry. "Boss wants a word with ya."

Harry Wolfe spoke for the first time with his former arch nemesis, the object of all his snooping, Governor Patrick Thomas "Shoat" Bradfield, who said, "Hey, Mr. Wolfe, let me say how thrilled I am to have you as part of my team, and I sure do hope we'll make beautiful music together. But what's this about Lydia Caple missing? I haven't heard a word. How come it's not on the news?"

Harry tried to determine the degree of sincerity in the man's words and had to admit to himself that there was no tinge of dissembling. "She's apparently been kidnapped," he said. "She just disappeared. Naturally, suspicion has fallen upon you."

"Well, goddamn it, why would we kidnap her? Do they think we'd do something like that without giving a thought to being the number-one suspect? Of course we wouldn't! I'm not that dumb.

Here, I'm on another line to the head of the state police, and we'll have every available man out looking for her. Hell, we'll call in every available man from his sleep or his fucking or his fishing spot!"

Harry was obliged to explain to the governor the agreement with the Newton County sheriff's department to keep Lydia's disappearance a secret for forty-eight hours, but he realized he was talking to a vacant line. The governor was on another line, talking to someone else, and when he came back and Harry had to repeat himself, the governor said, "Too late, I've already mobilized the entire state police. Naturally the FBI will come in too, and if they want to grill me, or grill any of my men, they're welcome to do it. But believe me, Harry, I didn't have anything to do with it. Now let me talk to Billy Joe again."

And Harry passed the phone back to Billy Joe and listened intently to catch any note of complicity or duplicity in Billy Joe's voice, but Billy Joe sounded genuinely alarmed by the news. Harry's lovely dream of the Hollywood movie disintegrated, and he realized it wouldn't have done him any good if he'd had a pistol. Now all he could do was turn his attention to the big question: If the Bradfield people hadn't abducted Lydia, who had?

"My God, this is just awful," Billy Joe said to Harry when he hung up. "You might just have to hold back a little on all that juicy stuff you've got on Ingledew, until this is over. Boss says he's going to call a moratorium on the whole fucking campaign until Lydia has been found." Billy Joe turned to Carleton Drew. "He wants to go on the evening news to make an announcement to that effect. Tonight."

When Governor Bradfield appeared on the ten o'clock news, Harry was already drunk in his room at the Capital Hotel and had just enough sentience to make out what the governor was saying. From the moment that Lydia had first been discovered missing,

Harry had denied himself the sustenance of his liquor, because he needed to remain absolutely clear-headed throughout his plot to rescue her, but now that he was convinced Bradfield hadn't perpetrated the deed, there was nothing holding him back, and he killed off a quart between supper and ten o'clock. He tried to call Garth Rucker, but got no answer and could only leave a drunken message on his message machine. He succeeded in calling Hank Endicott, and Hank offered to come and help him get drunk, but he had passed the point of social drinking. He managed to slur to Hank the basic facts: It did not appear that Bradfield had anything to do with Lydia's disappearance, goddamn it. Watch what the fucking governor has to say on the news and then finish your fucking column and stick it in tomorrow's paper.

The next morning's issue of the *Arkansas Democrat-Gazette*, when Harry retrieved it from beside his door sometime in the late afternoon, did indeed have a whole column of Hank Endicott's devoted to the disappearance of Lydia Caple, but it was overshadowed by a front-page article on the subject, with lesser articles on the reactions of Shoat Bradfield and Vernon Ingledew, and even an editorial decrying the disappearance of a woman who had once been a dear colleague of the paper's editorialists. Harry phoned room service for a turkey sandwich and another quart of bourbon and stayed in bed.

The next several days were a total blank in the history of Harry Wolfe. He had the vaguest memory of having showered and dressed and gone downstairs to the Capital Bar and spent some time there staring at the TV, and of a barmaid who was nice to him for a while but then became rude and summoned some goons to return him to his room. Or maybe that whole scene was just one of the several weird dreams he had, off and on, in the course of those several days. His first clear awareness of anything, eventually, was of the red light on his bedside phone. It kept flashing.

Somebody was trying to give him a message. He picked up the phone and identified himself and was told that a Garth Rucker had been trying to reach him. He punched in Garth's number.

"For fuck sake, Harry," Garth said. "Where have you been? I've been trying for *days* to get you."

"I've been indisposed," Harry said.

"Drunk, you mean?" Garth said. "Did Bradfield turn you down or something? Or, more likely, you know something about all of this and you're keeping it to yourself by hiding away with a bottle."

"That sounds sort of like it," Harry admitted.

"Did you see this morning's paper?"

"What day is this?" Harry asked. When Garth told him the day of the week and the date of the month, Harry had to admit that he hadn't seen a newspaper in recent memory.

"Or watched TV, even?" Garth wanted to know.

"I was watching some TV down in the bar the other night," Harry allowed.

"Well, you're in the dark. Sorry I woke you up. But I *am* the present holder of your previous job, and my services have been requested in the search for Lydia. Especially because, as today's paper said, Vernon Ingledew is offering for her safe return a reward of one hundred thousand dollars."

Harry whistled and then could say only "*Wow.*"

"Go out and get yourself a newspaper," Garth said. "No, you can just read mine; I'll be there in half an hour. If you need a ride anywhere, be ready to go."

Harry asked room service for a pot of coffee, and then he retrieved the day's *Arkansas Democrat-Gazette* from outside his door, scanned the headlines, and found the story not on the front page but inside. Vernon Ingledew was indeed offering $100,000 for information leading to the safe return of Lydia Caple, whose abduction he decried as "an act which, if it is political, casts all politics in an ugly light."

While Harry was in the shower, the phone rang, and he stepped out dripping to get it, in case it might be Garth again. But it was his new boss, Governor Bradfield, and he was not in a good mood. He said he'd been trying for three days to reach Harry. "I know you're a mystery man and you hide yourself and lurk in the dark and all that crap, but you sure are hard to reach."

"Sorry," Harry said. "That's just the way I am. What's up?"

"Have you fully convinced yourself that I am not in any way responsible for Lydia Caple's kidnapping?'

"I'd already done that last time I talked to you," Harry said.

"I am strongly tempted to match Vernon's offer and make it two hundred thousand dollars. But our campaign coffers are running low."

"That's white of you," Harry said. "Even the thought."

"But as you know, we're not going to do anything more in the way of campaigning, negative or otherwise, until Lydia is found, which could happen any moment now that the reward is in place. So I thought I'd keep you busy with a little assignment, if you have nothing better to do, and I assume you have nothing better to do, right?"

"I always have something better to do," Harry said.

"Maybe not better than this. You know, you mentioned some Native American woman that Ingledew was involved with, smoking dope and whatever. That intrigues me. Where'd she come from?"

"Oklahoma," Harry said.

"But Ingledew is keeping her in Stay More?"

"Maybe keeping isn't the word. She's richer than he is, I'd guess," Harry said. "So what do you want me to do about it?"

"I want you to check her out," Bradfield said. "I want you

to find out *everything* about her. I want to know her whole history, everything she's ever done, all the men she's been involved with, everything. I want a *complete* dossier on the girl."

"That's a tall order," Harry muttered.

"I'm paying you fourteen thousand dollars a month," Bradfield reminded him. "Plus expenses. Get your ass in gear and, if you have to, go over to Oklahoma and talk to everybody who ever knew this girl. Prove to me that you're as good as they say you are." Without waiting for Harry to say "Yes, sir" or "Righto" or anything, the governor disconnected.

Harry told Garth Rucker about his new assignment. "Want to drive me to Pawhuska, Oklahoma?" Harry asked.

"I'm not beholden to you that much," Garth protested.

"Okay, forget it," Harry said. "We could just start in Stay More. Maybe the Indian would tell us most of what we need to know."

"*We?*" Garth said. "I'm not your assistant anymore."

"But don't you want to sniff around and see if you can win a hundred thou?"

They drove to Stay More, or as close to it as they could get. There was a roadblock a mile from the village set up by state troopers, who wanted to know their business. Harry told the troopers that he and Garth both worked for Vernon Ingledew and were friends of Lydia Caple. The trooper radioed somebody else and gave Garth permission to drive on, but warned him that they might have trouble getting past the FBI roadblock farther down the road. And sure enough, the FBI agents wouldn't let them proceed. The agent in charge explained that many people, eager to get the reward, were trying to enter Stay More and were turned back by the troopers, so the FBI was interested in *anybody* who got past the troopers as possible suspects.

"Can I make a phone call?" Harry asked the agent, and he borrowed Garth's cell phone and called the number of Larry and

Sharon in the village, his usual host and hostess during his visits to Stay More. Monica answered.

"Harry," she said. "Where are you?"

"Right outside of Stay More, at the FBI roadblock. Garth's driving."

"You might not get any closer," she said. "It's a madhouse around here, with all the cops and FBI. I don't think Stay More has ever had as many people in it, and everybody seems to think that *this* is the command center or information office. Sharon and Larry have gone to Harrison to stay in a motel until it's all over. So has Ekaterina."

"Sorry to hear that," Harry said. "I was hoping to have my room for a night or two."

"Well, I'm sure Larry and Sharon wouldn't mind if I let you in. But what are you doing here? I thought you had defected to the Bradfield camp."

"To all intents and purposes," Harry said. "But Garth and I are still pals, and he's driving me. Can you tell me how to reach Bo?"

"He and Arch and Cast are up at Vernon's," she said.

"Do you know if Bo is packing his Nokia? I need a number to reach him."

"It's a very private number," Monica declared. "I don't know if he'd want me to give it to you."

"Monica, honey, if you must know, I'm just pretending to be working for Bradfield. I'm as loyal as you are." *There*, Harry said to himself, I've said it.

The FBI agent asked them to step out of their car and took them to a large van, like a house trailer, where they were fingerprinted, separated from each other, and interrogated at length. Garth was finally permitted to leave and left word for Harry that he'd contact him later, but meanwhile they were keeping Harry, because, he learned, his name was on the "short list" of suspects.

They asked Harry all kinds of questions, and they wanted his driver's license for identification, but he had to explain he'd had to surrender it in DC after a DWI conviction. The only identification he had was his old Social Security card, and they wanted him to duplicate the signature on it, but he'd got the card when he was only fourteen and his signature had changed considerably since then. He tried his best to sign his name as it had once been signed, and fortunately among the several FBI agents was a signature expert who could determine that his present signature still bore certain characteristics similar to his fourteen-year-old signature.

They grilled him for the better part of an hour, wanting to know when he'd last seen Lydia and what was the nature of their "working" relationship as well as their "personal" relationship. Wasn't it true that they were rivals within the Ingledew organization? Wasn't it true that because Lydia was nominally Harry's boss—since oppo men answer to press secretaries—that he resented her?

Finally they said to him, "You can make one phone call," and he wanted to know if he needed a lawyer. "You haven't been arrested," they told him. "Yet." So he called the special Nokia number of Bo's that Monica had given him.

"Busy?" he asked Bo.

No, Bo told him, they were just loafing around and waiting for suppertime, and Harry was welcome to join them for supper. "If you can get away," Bo said. "Garth arrived a little while ago and told me they've got you in custody."

"Bo," Harry said, "could you talk to them? Can you tell them I have no reason on God's earth to have kidnapped Lydia?"

"Why would they believe me?" Bo said. "They've got my name on their list of suspects too. I take it, by the way, that your Little Rock operation was a failure. Are you completely convinced that Bradfield had nothing to do with Lydia's disappearance?"

"Yeah, he's innocent," Harry declared, believing it.

"But you went ahead and made the switch . . . or pretended to."

"I did a good job of pretending," Harry said, and hoped the Nokia cell line was secure.

"So if you're now part of the opposition, what are you doing in Stay More? Spying on us already?"

Harry told him about his assignment from Bradfield: to compile a dossier on Juliana. He supposed he'd have to go to Oklahoma to do most of it, but he might as well start here.

"If you wanted to interview Juliana," Bo said, "you might have to go to Oklahoma anyway, because she and Ben have gone back to her house there. But I could tell you all you need to know about Juliana."

"Her whole history? Bradfield wants to know *everything* about her, the works: every detail of her life. I suppose it's academic if she's gone for good and out of Vernon's life."

"Oh, she'll be back," Bo declared. "Eventually. It was just getting too crowded around here with all these state troopers and FBI agents."

"Bradfield is paying me fourteen a month."

"You're not worth it."

Monica came and got him. The FBI agent told him not to leave town until they'd had further opportunities to talk with him. Monica drove him to Larry and Sharon's house. She herself was dressing up to go to dinner at Vernon's, and although Harry was invited, he didn't much feel like it, especially because he had already been replaced by Garth Rucker and would be considered a turncoat. So Monica showed him what was available in the fridge and freezer, plenty for supper, and she produced a stoneware demijohn of Chism's Dew, and Harry got comfortable with his hosts' copy of *The Choiring of the Trees*, his favorite of all the Harington novels, and he spent his evening drinking and refreshing his memory of those parts of the novel that told about the fabled "glen of the waterfall," which had figured importantly as a setting in several of the Stay More novels and was especially crucial to *Choiring*. He was asleep—or passed out—when Monica returned, and she must have lifted the book from his lap.

The next morning the FBI wanted to talk with him some more, and he obliged. He had nothing to hide, and he didn't need a lawyer. No, he told them, he had no idea, since he'd never been there, where the cemetery of Daniel Lyam Montross was located. They tested him, trying to trick him, but he really had nothing whatever to hide.

They let him go, and he took a stroll out across the fields to the double wigwam that Thomas Bending Bear, with the help of George Dinsmore, had constructed for Juliana Heartstays. It was still very much there, its arched doorway open and a few of the younger free-ranging pigs wandering inside. He shooed them away and stepped into it and looked around. There were just a few items: woven mats, a bed of sorts, some cooking utensils. He probed and pried but found nothing of interest. Nothing in writing; he might as well have been transported back to the dawn of the Osages in preliterate times. The only thing of interest that attracted his professional eye was outside the wigwam, in the dirt: the imprint of the tire track of a Pierce-Arrow.

He returned to Larry and Sharon's house and made a couple of sandwiches, which he packed into a paper sack with some fruit and chips. He poured himself a last drink of the Chism's Dew and took one final glance at the copy of *The Choiring of the Trees* and studied a particular passage of it again.

"Where are you going?" Monica asked him, but he simply said he was restless and needed some exercise and had decided to take a hike. He'd see her at suppertime.

Then he climbed to the first benches on Ledbetter Mountain behind Larry and Sharon's house. He passed through what he realized, from his reading of *Lightning Bug*, was the old orchard that had once been Latha Bourne's. When he reached the first bench of the mountain, he had to pause a long time for breath, realizing how out of shape he was and realizing also his mistake: he should have brought along a jar of water to serve as a canteen. He grew impossibly thirsty. But he climbed on, and in time found a spring trickling out of the earth, and knelt to drink.

It was almost noon before he finally located what had been the sheep pastures of Nail Chism, the hero of *Choiring*, and from there he followed the instructions as given by Latha Bourne in describing it in a letter to Nail:

> There's this one place, way up against the corner of your upper forty, where the two tree lines sort of converge at the edge of the pasture on what looks like a dead corner up against the mountainside, and is a real dark shade of green, like the mouth of a cave, and you feel sucked into it, or drawn up thataway, and when you get into it you see there's an old road there, just a trail, if you know the spot I mean, and if you follow that trail up through the woods for quite a ways, a mile or more, with the woods growing deeper and darker, you come to this glade where a waterfall comes down off the very top of the mountain, as if it was gushing up out of some powerful spring up there. The glade is sunny, with the sun shining right on the waterfall, but it's dark all around, and dark in these several sort of half-caves where it looks like Indians must have lived. It was kind of scary, and I didn't stay up there very long, but while I was there I thought of you, a lot, and I had a strange vision as if I could see you just living and dwelling in that hidden glade.

Harry found the trail. He not only found the trail but he detected quite clearly, coming from a different direction, the tracks of the tires of an antique automobile once popular and widely owned by the oil-rich Indians of Oklahoma, and at that moment he knew the hundred thousand dollars was his, and he even began to think about ways to spend it. The tracks were fairly fresh, and in celebration of finding them Harry stopped and sat on a rock and ate his lunch and had no trouble finding a spring where he could lap up enough to wash the sandwiches down. Fastidiously, he spread his handkerchief for a tablecloth and ate slowly and leisurely, in no hurry at all now. When he was finished, he dusted the crumbs off his clothing, enjoyed a cigarette, and then he went on, the trail growing steep and the tire tracks finally stopping but being replaced by clear footprints: many footprints, the prints of a big man and the smaller prints of two—no, *three*—different women, as well as of a dog. He happily joined his footprints to theirs.

Harry Wolfe had never in his life been out in such a wilderness, and the very wildness of the forest, the fragrances of it, the bird sounds, filled him with awe, he who was so blasé about everything. He had not yet quite reached the glen of the waterfall when the dog got wind of him and began barking and then appeared.

The dog approached him and snarled ferociously, but Harry held out his hand for the dog to sniff in recognition of him. And Harry said, "Good dog, Threasher. Nice dog, Threasher. That's a boy."

Chapter Eighteen

From the moment back in March when she had first eagerly joined the campaign, she had constantly enjoyed a sense of being on top of things. She was not only an in-charge manager but also a *take-charge person*, quick to see what needed to be done and doing it herself if she couldn't teach her underlings to do it. She required virtually no supervision from those among the Samurai who outranked her (as all of them did); in fact, the most common expression among them, whenever anybody needed to find out something or get something done, was "Ask Monica." She had her fingers on all the strings, and she knew many things that nobody else knew.

For instance, she knew that unless the campaign started an active fund-raising drive, they would be all out of money within a matter of weeks. And if anybody did claim the reward for finding Lydia, they'd not only be flat broke but in serious debt. She had been meaning for some time now to approach Vernon and ask him if he was aware of how close to insolvency the campaign was, and that was before he'd made that sensational offer of a reward. She knew that fabulously wealthy Diana or almost equally rich Juliana could help, but only to a point, since there was a $2,500 cap on contributions. Bo and Arch were going to have to get off their duffs and solicit hundreds of such amounts from the state's usual political contributors.

The money problem didn't really bother her. What troubled her most right now—what in fact actually frightened her—was the way she no longer felt in charge, of the campaign or even of her own destiny. Oh, these FBI guys and state troopers deferred to her as if she were the commanding general of the whole operation, and she could make them all jump through hoops if she wanted. She had chosen to reveal her first name to none of them, and she distinguished among them by whether they called her "Ms. Breedlove," "Miss Breedlove," or "ma'am." Although the FBI's base was on the front porch of the Woman's—Ekaterina's—temporarily abandoned house, just about everybody else, including a lot of the FBI agents themselves, considered the old store and post office, Larry and Sharon's house, to be the nerve center of the investigation, and they acted as if Monica were in charge of it all.

But from the moment poor Lydia had disappeared, Monica felt she was losing her authority, her ability to make anything happen. She herself couldn't find Lydia and had no idea what might have happened to her. She had a clear intuition that Lydia was still alive, and when one of the FBI agents had reported to her (as if she were in charge and could say something significant about it) that Lydia's pets (a dog named Beanbag and several cats) had been abducted from her apartment in Fayetteville, Monica understood that whoever Lydia's kidnappers were, they weren't compounding their crime by exterminating her pets; they were compassionate enough to kidnap the animals too because Lydia missed them so much. Wherever Lydia was being held—and it could be anywhere in the Ozarks or the whole state of Arkansas—she at least had the comfort now of having her pets with her. The FBI guys didn't believe Monica's theory when she told them this, but she assured them that the second kidnapping was good news.

Still, Monica couldn't help dwelling on the possibility that she herself might be kidnapped—and would the kidnappers bother to take her dogs and cats also? Hazel Maguire practically lived now in Monica's Fayetteville apartment, because Monica was spending so much time in Stay More—even before this hubbub surrounding Lydia's disappearance—and Hazel was in charge of feeding the dogs and cats . . . and protecting them from kidnappers.

"If you hear of my disappearance," she had told Hazel by phone just this morning, "take the animals and move into some out-of-town motel where nobody knows where you are." She told Hazel that Harry Wolfe too had been kidnapped, or was missing for several nights now, and the FBI and state troopers were keeping a round-the-clock watch on Monica for her protection. And presumably on Bo, Arch, and Cast as well, the only other remainders of the Seven Samurai. Monica tried to explain to her favorite among the FBI guys, at least the man who was most respectful and even obsequious toward her and called her *ma'am*, that Harry Wolfe was no longer in Ingledew's campaign anyhow; he had recently defected to the Bradfield team, so whoever had a political motive for kidnapping Lydia would not have kidnapped Harry for the same reason.

She was scared and she didn't sleep well at night, not even with a wide-awake sheriff's deputy sitting in the next room. This latest kidnapping, and the renewed investigation surrounding it, was a guarantee that Larry and Sharon were not going to come home, and it was lonely in this house without Harry, even if there were always deputies or troopers or agents watching over her. Bo told Monica that if she wanted to, she should feel free to go on back to Fayetteville, where her presence could be used in campaign headquarters, even if the campaign was in limbo. He also told her he'd request constant protective surveillance for her in Fayetteville. She told Bo she'd just as soon stay more in Stay More, if she could be useful here. She didn't love the town as much as she had before its population had filled up with all the agents and cops, but it was still, as she had once suggested to the Samurai, a better place for a *real* campaign headquarters than Fayetteville. And apparently Bo, Arch, and Cast, not to mention Vernon himself, liked it here too, for a variety of reasons: Cast, as she well knew, was deeply involved with a local girl, Sheila Kimber, and could scarcely bear to spend a moment away from her. And Bo . . . just as Monica knew practically everything about everyone (except who might have kidnapped Lydia), she knew that Bo was head over heels in an affair with Jelena Ingledew, and possibly even Vernon knew about it but couldn't feel too jealous because he himself was scandalously involved with the Indian Juliana.

Now that the Indian woman and her pansy bodyguard had left Stay More—for the same reason Larry and Sharon and Ekaterina had left: it was just too overpopulated and raucous—presumably Vernon would have to start paying attention to Jelena again. That was fine with Monica; she'd much rather be jealous of Jelena than of Juliana.

The truth that Monica had been facing for some time now was that she was hopelessly in love with Vernon Ingledew, not because he was so powerful and possibly could become much more powerful as governor but because he was just such a very nice man, the kindest man she'd ever known as well as the smartest. She hated the idea that he was being unfaithful to Jelena. At churches all over Arkansas, when Monica had given her standard Ingledew-is-really-a-Christian-even-if-he-doesn't-think-so speech to youth groups and ladies' socials and men's Bible classes and such, she had invariably been required to answer questions about Vernon's living out of wedlock with his first cousin, and she had mastered a lovely little set speech in which she pointed out that they were common-law husband and wife (which was true) and had simply avoided marriage because first-cousin marriages were not a good idea.

There was no way Monica was going to be able to give any speeches defending Vernon's affair with that Indian woman. Even though she was skeptical of the Samurai's plan to counterattack Bradfield's dirty politics by supersaturating the public with Vernon's real and imagined vices, she knew it was the only way they could slip the fact of Juliana Heartstays past the public's curiosity.

Just as Cast Sherrill had been required to take over Carleton Drew's responsibilities after the latter had defected, the disappearance of Lydia had thrust Monica into a position as substitute press secretary for the Ingledew campaign. She'd been required to deal with the newsmen and TV crews who had slipped into Stay More in search of developments about the kidnappings and, during moments when there were no new leads at all in the search for Lydia and Harry, taken to quizzing Monica about the progress of the campaign; and with Cast's help she'd started giving daily briefings to the media. Governor Bradfield had gone on television to announce that while he still fervently prayed that Lydia and Harry would be found, it was time to return to business as usual, and therefore he was rescinding the moratorium on politics that he had declared. Then Bradfield had the effrontery to suggest what he called a fourteenth albatross: that Lydia and Harry were missing because they had become disillusioned with Vernon Ingledew, with the implicit suggestion that Vernon himself might have done away with them.

One by one the state troopers and sheriff's deputies disappeared from Stay More. One by one the FBI agents packed up their gear and left town, most of them having the courtesy to say goodbye to Monica and to thank her for her help. Only a skeleton crew of state troopers and sheriff's men were still bivouacked in town, assigned to protecting the remaining Samurai from being kidnapped. Surely the newsmen were growing tired of hearing Monica announce the same thing at each day's briefing: Vernon Ingledew refused to continue the campaign until Lydia and Harry were found, even if Harry had defected to the Bradfield camp before he was kidnapped.

"But what if they're both dead?" a reporter had asked her.

Monica shuddered but replied, "Vernon Ingledew will make another statement if that should prove to be the case."

Larry and Sharon returned to their home and thanked Monica for having taken such good care of it during their absence. Ekaterina did not return. Had Larry and Sharon seen her in Harrison? No, they suspected she might have gone to a larger city or even gone home to Georgia or Svanetia or wherever.

Now that Larry and Sharon were home, Monica felt tempted to take Bo's advice to go on back to Fayetteville. She missed her pets; it had been a long time. Sharon suggested that Monica could go to Fayetteville and get her pets and bring them here to live. Monica appreciated this hospitality but knew she was putting a strain on it, especially when the deputy who had been assigned to protect her had moved into what had been Harry's room.

Larry and Sharon wanted to know all about Harry, whose disappearance disturbed them as much as Lydia's, if not more so (after all, Lydia had "belonged" to Day and Diana, whereas Harry was theirs). Monica told them that she'd been the last to see Harry, that morning when he'd told her he was restless and needed some exercise and had decided to take a hike. She hadn't bothered to look out the windows to see which way he was hiking, north, east, south, or west. The state troopers had brought a pack of bloodhounds, and Monica had fetched Harry's pillowcase, which bore his scent, for the dogs to sniff. But in a whole day of roving the countryside, the hounds had not apparently picked up that scent. Everybody currently in the Stay More population had been questioned, but nobody else had seen Harry. It was almost as if Monica had uttered an enchantment that made him vanish, but if that were so she had no witching words to make him reappear. It never occurred to any of the searchers—as it would eventually occur to Arch Schaffer before he personally took up the quest in the next chapter—to glance at the copy of *The Choiring of the Trees* that Harry had left open facedown at a crucial passage.

"Next chapter?" Monica said aloud to herself. She began wondering why she had thought those words and decided that life is sort of like a book and there would be another chapter after this one. She did not feel, as Harry himself and Day Whittacker felt, that she was actually a character in a novel that had a beginning, middle, and, if not an end, the promise of a future.

But she definitely felt everything that was happening—or failing to happen—was quickly turning into past tense, something over and done with and finished and final, irrevocable, that she could no longer control with her managerial skills. She really ought to go home. She told Larry and Sharon that she intended to go back to Fayetteville in another day or so.

Then Vernon came to see her. It was a warm day in early October, unusually warm, almost like summer still, so they sat on the front porch, Monica in the swing that so many people, young and old, had sat in during the heyday of this building's service as a store and post office. Vernon sat in the captain's chair.

He *still* could not look at her (would he ever be able to?) but at least he could talk freely, although for a long minute they could only sit there like a couple of country people enjoying the store porch and watching the autumn color emblazon the surrounding trees. And then he spoke.

“I’m awfully sorry about Lydia. I know what she meant to you. Don’t you worry, she’ll turn up.”

“I sure hope so,” she said.

“It looks like you’re my press secretary now,” he said to the post that held up the roof of the porch.

“If you say so,” she said, and did not tell him that she’d been acting in that capacity for many days. “I couldn’t even begin to replace Lydia, though.”

“I’ll bet you could,” he said. “You’re like her in so many ways. Whether you know it or not, you’ve tried real hard to be like her. You’ve watched her so much you even *seem* like her. You don’t look like her, or sound quite exactly like her, but in many ways you’re better than she.”

Monica’s heart skipped a few beats, and she realized that when Vernon spoke these last words he was looking directly at her for the first time. Now it was she who could not look at him. Her eyes could only study her hands in her lap. She didn’t know what to say. She thought of saying, “If you say so,” but she had already said that and didn’t want to sound repetitious. Finally she managed to say, “That’s real kind, sir. It makes me proud. But you don’t really need a press secretary if you’ve canceled the campaign until after Lydia is found. And after she’s found, of course she will be your press secretary again.”

“Certainly we hope that Lydia will turn up any minute now, safe and sound,” he said. “But if she does, that doesn’t mean you’ll lose your new job to her. You’ll still be press secretary. And after I’m elected, you’ll be my press secretary for four years in Little Rock. Would you like that?”

Oh, she would like that! Again she hung her head modestly and said, “That would be just fine. But right now I’m supposed to be running campaign headquarters in Fayetteville.”

“We’ll get somebody else to run the headquarters,” he said. “You’d rather be in Stay More anyway, wouldn’t you?”

She almost told him of Sharon and Larry's offer to let her keep her dogs and cats here, but she didn't want to sound too chummy. Instead she voiced a concern. "When Lydia comes back and finds out I've got her job, what will you do with her?"

"If Lydia comes back—*when* Lydia comes back—we'll appoint her to a different job. Maybe we'll give her Bo's job. I'm thinking of firing Bo."

Monica caught his eyes. "You *are*? How come?"

"I think you know why," he said.

She had thought it was her own secret that she knew everybody else's secrets, but somehow she hadn't been able to hide it from her boss. It put her on the spot. All she could answer was kind of flippant. "I could make a pretty good guess." But then she couldn't resist adding, and surprised herself at how much her voice sounded like Lydia's, "But how could you fire him for *that*, when you yourself have been fooling around?"

Vernon laughed. "I don't hold Bo's liaison against him. What I don't like is that he's so wrapped up in it he can't concentrate on his work." Vernon laughed again, and added, "I hope you understand all this is strictly between you and me."

"Does he know you know?"

"Not yet." Although she waited to hear him add something to that, such as *But he probably suspects I do* or *I'm going to let him know soon,* Vernon added nothing.

"As your press secretary, what spin am I to put upon these various Stay More liaisons?" she asked, surprised at herself for her matter-of-fact firmness. She added quickly, "Assuming, of course, that we resume the campaign."

"You don't have to worry about Juliana, because we probably won't see her again until after the election."

Monica was thrilled to hear that but wondered how Vernon knew. Of course, quite possibly Juliana and Vernon had one last fling before she left town, during which she had told him—or he had requested it of her—that she would become invisible until after the election.

"Doesn't that weaken the plan of the Samurai to overload the public with your sins, to the point where nobody will care anymore?"

Again that laugh of Vernon's. Monica was beginning to wonder if she possessed a sense of humor she didn't fully understand. "I like the way you put that," he said. "I haven't heard the crackpot plan described so succinctly. But no, I can assure you the Samurai have such a long list of my sins ready to glut the public that Juliana's absence will scarcely be noticed. You've seen the list, haven't you?"

She nodded. She had a copy of it, nearly a hundred real and brazenly fabricated instances of Vernon's misconduct, enough to make the most slavering citizen surfeited, jaded, and eventually indifferent. "Let me ask you," she said. "Are you keeping in touch with Juliana? Have you phoned her? Or vice versa?"

Vernon studied her for a moment, as if he were trying to determine why she would be asking that question. His reply wasn't evasive, just pensive. "No, I haven't. I don't have her number in Oklahoma, which is unlisted. She has her own reasons, I suppose, for not calling me."

"You're not even sure she's in Oklahoma?"

"No."

"How do you know she's coming back after the election?"

"Well, *look*," he said, and gestured in the direction of the wigwam, where there was much activity going on: workmen were laying the foundations for her mansion. Just this morning a fleet of rumbling cement trucks had groaned into town and out to the construction site of Juliana's house. Monica also knew that Day Whittacker was busy in the woods, marking trees to be uprooted and transplanted laboriously to Juliana's homesite.

"If she's not coming back until after the election," Monica

asked boldly, "and there's no way you can contact her, how can you ask her for a financial contribution to the campaign or to your generous reward offer?"

Again he studied her as if it were taking him awhile to answer his own question about why she would be asking that question. "I wasn't planning to ask her *that*," he said.

"Sir," she said, not comfortable to be calling him *sir* but needing to preface such a statement respectfully, "the campaign is nearly broke. You need money. Much money, and soon."

He smiled. "You really do know everything, don't you?"

"Not quite everything." She was proud of her restraint in not telling him that she had seen and studied the FBI's files on Lydia, as well as on Juliana Heartstays and Harry Wolfe. The agents who had been so deferential to her hadn't even questioned her right to read the files.

"I'll take care of the money," he said. And he rose and patted her on the shoulder and went off into the world to get it or do whatever he had to do.

As long as the campaign was still in abeyance, Monica didn't have much to do in her new position as press secretary, and the few stragglers among the newsmen and TV people who had invaded Stay More finally gave up and went on back to their cities. The town was almost back to normal. Monica wished Ekaterina would come back, because Monica had really enjoyed talking with her. That mysterious woman from Svanetia knew all kinds of things about Stay More that nobody else knew. But Ekaterina did not come back, and her big house, now that the FBI were no longer using its porch as a command center, seemed forlorn. Monica wasn't bored; she found time to read a novel called *Butterfly Weed* that Larry loaned her, which she found very interesting not only because it was about Stay More but also because it was full of people named Breedlove, her ex-husband's family.

On the day that her private sheriff's deputy politely informed her that he was being recalled back to Jasper, the county seat, and there wasn't much danger she'd be kidnapped too—although he said to her in parting, "Watch your back, sweetheart"—she had another visit, this time from Bo Pharis. Bo even sat in the same porch chair that Vernon had sat in, and Monica again sat in the swing, although the weather had turned a bit chilly and they both kept their coats on.

He started with a question. "Monica, honey, did you ever see the movie called *The Seven Samurai*?" She knew the allusion but hadn't seen the movie, so she had to shake her head. Bo gave her a plot synopsis and pointed out, "One by one, the samurai are killed defending the village, until in the end there are only three left. I too lost my sheriff's deputy this morning, but I'm not complaining, and I'm not nervous. You shouldn't be either. If we followed the script exactly, the remaining three would be Cast, Arch, and myself. But I don't believe that life follows art. Do you?"

She knew a lot about art, and she appreciated that Bo was being cultural with her and was avoiding politics, at least for the moment. "I always believed that art's job was to follow life," she said. "Was there a samurai like me in the movie? How did she get killed?"

"None of them were women," he said. "You know, I've thought about renting that film from a video store and showing it to everyone. But it might disturb us. The capture of Lydia and Harry are a bit too analogous to the movie."

"But in the end," Monica said, "the village is saved, the bandits are destroyed, and goodness triumphs, right? That's all that matters."

Bo smiled at her. "I'm glad you're philosophical about it." And then he abruptly changed the subject. "Now, if you will, tell me: What did Vernon say about me?"

The question caught her by surprise, and of course she wasn't going to reveal the contents of Vernon's conversation with her to anybody. She certainly wasn't going to tell Bo that his job was in danger. So she lied. "We didn't mention you," she said.

"No? What did you talk about?"

"Lydia, of course. He's giving me her job. If that's all right with you?"

"Think you can handle it?"

"What's to handle? I don't have anything to do until we get the campaign back in gear."

"Okay, that's the main thing I wanted to talk to you about. I *am* curious if Vernon mentioned me in any way, shape, or form, but my main motive for this conversation is to say this: Certainly we hope the two missing Samurai will be restored to us, but we simply cannot afford to keep the campaign in hiatus. The election is less than a month away, and the Republican campaign is back in full steam. If we're going to beat Bradfield, we've got to proceed with Plan B: the self-smear procedure revealing Vernon's Vices."

"Try telling Vernon that. He won't let us use it until Lydia is found."

"I'm afraid that Vernon and I are not communicating these days."

"Then how did you know he'd talked with me?"

"I was watching from a distance. I saw the two of you here on this porch. For quite a while."

"Why aren't you and Vernon communicating?" she asked with a straight face.

"There's been a misunderstanding between us," Bo replied.

"Is the misunderstanding named Jelena?" she asked.

He shot her a look that was part astonishment, part annoyance. "So Vernon *did* talk to you about me! Did he say anything about me and Jelena?"

Press secretaries, if they aren't born that way, must learn to be good liars. But what she said wasn't a lie. "Vernon was not my source of information about you and Jelena."

"Then who was?"

"Bo, this is a small town. It's a *very* small town. It's practically an unpopulated town."

"Monica, I'm still your boss, and I request that you tell me not only who told you but what was said."

"If newspeople are permitted to protect their sources," she declared, "I think press secretaries should be able to protect theirs too. I'm not telling. Sorry."

"Okay, but can you tell me what you know about me and Jelena?"

"Just that you've put yourself in a compromising position for a candidate's campaign manager. In other words, you ought to be ashamed of yourself."

He winced. And then he blurted, "But we're *in love*!" Having blurted, he blushed.

"Really? Does Jelena know this?"

"She certainly does."

"Maybe she's using you," Monica suggested.

"*Using* me? How?"

"She doesn't want to move to Little Rock if Vernon is elected governor. So maybe she hopes that you can help her avoid that. I mean, not that she hopes you can keep him from getting elected. But that if he does move to Little Rock, you can steal her away."

Bo Pharis studied her. "Monica," he said, "you're a lot more perspicacious than anyone gives you credit for."

She wasn't completely sure what the word meant, but she knew she was being complimented. "You're not planning to become Vernon's chief of staff, are you?" she asked.

"Heaven forbid!" he exclaimed. "I wouldn't want to live in Little Rock if I were made CEO of Alltel!"

"So what are your plans after the election? Are you going to take Jelena back to Cincinnati?"

"I couldn't go back to Cincinnati if I were made CEO of Procter and Gamble!"

"Then you plan to stay more in Stay More," she declared.

He smiled. "That's not outside the realm of possibility."

"Well." Monica sighed. "I suppose if we're going to go ahead and publicize Vernon's Vices, we might as well throw in all the juicy details of your affair with Jelena." One thing Lydia had told her, before her disappearance, was that once all the monotonous revelations of Vernon's Vices had been piled up, they could get away with anything; they could reveal the affairs between Vernon and Juliana and Bo and Jelena without consequence, because if the public was truly inoculated against scandal, one more wouldn't even be noticed. ("We could even reveal," Lydia had suggested to Monica, "that Vernon is using *you* more flagrantly than Bill Clinton used that other Monica.")

"I'd rather keep that quiet, if we can," Bo said. "My hope is that with all the other tidbits in that flapping flock of a hundred albatrosses, the public won't need to see the lame bird of the candidate's common-law wife losing her heart to the candidate's campaign manager."

Monica studied him for a moment before replying. "If you say so, I'll do what I can to keep a lid on it."

"Okay. Tomorrow is VV-Day. Tomorrow we leak to the Bradfield people the whole list of a hundred of Vernon's worst iniquities. How do we make the leak?"

Monica knew it was a rhetorical question asked of himself, but since she was taking charge in so many other ways, she answered it for him. "Send Bradfield a fax from Harry. Tell him that Harry is being held captive by the Ingledew campaign—no connection with Lydia's kidnapping—and that he's alive and well but they won't let him go because he had defected to Bradfield. He has escaped his captors just long enough to access this fax machine, on which he sends the enclosed: a list of one hundred trespasses of Vernon Ingledew."

"Monica, you're a genius."

"If you say so."

That night she had a third visitor, in the middle, alas, of only one of her dreams, in which Lydia appeared and congratulated her on the way she had taken over the press secretary's job. Lydia said she was alive and well and even happy, since she had her pets with her. "Where are you?" Monica called out in the dream, and called it again, louder and louder, and opened her eyes to see Sharon, who told her she must have been having a nightmare.

But although that was only a dream, dreams have a way of getting us ready for life, so it did not surprise Monica when, before breakfast, upon going out onto the porch to stretch and watch the sun come up over Dinsmore Hill, she found on the edge of the porch a heavy rock weighing down a folded sheet of paper, which she took and unfolded and discovered a message, written to herself and signed by Lydia. Her first thought, since she'd just suggested to Bo the idea of forging a fax under Harry's name, was that somebody was playing a cruel joke on her. But it was unquestionably Lydia's handwriting. And it said:

Dear dear Monica:

My captors are allowing me to write and send one note, like when you're arrested and allowed one phone call. You're my choice; you're the one I want most to know that

I'm still alive and I'm not being mistreated or abused in any way and I'm fairly well fed, and as you may know I even have my precious cats and my dog with me, and they are just fine too. For whatever it's worth, my fellow prisoner is Harry Wolfe, who hasn't been acting like a prisoner at all.

I am making a good guess that you've already replaced me as press secretary, and that doesn't bother me in the slightest. I know you can do a great job. My captors told me that you were virtually the commanding officer during the busy operations of the state troopers, sheriff, FBI, et al. You're a multitalented woman, Monica, and I'm proud of you, and proud if I was able to teach you anything during our long friendship. You will go far.

I suppose it's time to go ahead and put into effect the precarious Operation Vernon's Vices, if you haven't done so already. We should have started much earlier, but my kidnapping distracted everybody. I wish I could be there to make sure it's handled adroitly, but I have the utmost confidence in you, dear Monica.

My captors wish for me to request of you that you do not reveal this message or its contents to anybody. You must agree to this. They say they will harm me if you do not. If you have received this message, and agree to keep it to yourself, indicate your willingness by opening the shade in your room's window which you customarily keep closed, just for one day and night. Burn this sheet of paper, now.

I hope I'll see you again, when the election is over, and I know our man Vernon is going to be victorious. Don't waste any prayers on me, honey. Pray for him.

Love,
Lydia

How had this been delivered to her? She searched the dirt in front of the porch and found a set of man's footprints, but she could tell nothing about them. Possibly a plaster cast should be taken of them, but how could she request that without revealing the reason? It was terribly frustrating not to be able to tell anyone that Lydia was alive and well. But she went at once into her room and opened the shade that covered her window. It made her feel exposed, and she'd have to be careful tonight to turn off the light before undressing or anything. She did not like being ordered around, by Lydia's captors or anybody, and for this reason she did not burn Lydia's note but folded it several times and buried it in the bottom of her purse.

Later that morning she called Cast Sherrill, who was staying, as usual, at his girlfriend Sheila's house, having abandoned his room at the Ingledew double-bubble even before he'd become involved with Sheila, and Bo had become involved with Jelena. Cast had speculated to Monica that the affair between Bo and Jelena might not have developed if he, Cast, had still been resident up there.

Now she told Cast, who of course had replaced Carleton Drew as their media expert just as she had replaced Lydia and that creepy Garth Rucker had replaced Harry, that today was VV-Day and she was getting ready to use Larry's fax machine to send "Harry's" message to Bradfield, along with the list of a hundred of Vernon's Vices. Monica wanted Cast to be prepared for the media blitz.

"Have you cleared this with Vernon?" Cast wanted to know. "You know he won't allow it as long as Lydia is missing."

Monica was in a bind. If only she were able to get word somehow to Vernon that Lydia was alive and well, Vernon might consent to the full resumption of the campaign. But the shade in her room was up, a reminder that she was giving her solemn word not to reveal Lydia's existence to a soul.

A kindly soul, a fourth visitor, appeared to Monica later that morning. It was Arch, who had continued to stay at the house of Day and Diana and who was nominally second-in-command or, as far as Monica was concerned, since Bo was no longer on speaking terms with Vernon and since Arch once before had been required to take command when Bo was missing, was now in charge. Monica liked Arch more than any other Samurai next to Lydia. He was a person you could feel comfortable with, and open up with and feel close to, and trust and have confidence in, and who you could feel completely untroubled when speaking prepositions at the end of sentences to.

"How goes it?" Arch said, sitting himself down in the same captain's chair where Vernon and Bo had sat. Somehow he seemed like he belonged to such a chair more fittingly than they had.

"Well, in case you haven't heard, it's VV-Day," she said.

"That's what Bo tells me," Arch said. "Are we ready?"

"Except for having obtained approval from the candidate himself," she said.

"Which he won't give without Lydia," Arch observed.

"Arch," she said, and realized this wouldn't be directly violating the covenant of the open shade, "I know Lydia's alive. I have a powerful hunch. Call it woman's intuition, or better yet call it the result of being on the same wavelength with Lydia for many years. And also she appeared to me in a dream last night and told me she was alive and well."

"I've never stopped believing she's alive and well," Arch said. "Not only that, I think she's probably being held somewhere in the vicinity." He swept his arms to encompass the world around them. "Anywhere out there, in some abandoned house or deep holler or forest fastness, she could be a prisoner."

"But who is holding her? And why?" Monica said, and wondered, since her captors could deliver a message to Monica, why they hadn't ever bothered to deliver a ransom note. Whoever it was didn't need any ransom. Whoever it was—and Monica began to have a new suspicion—was too rich to need any ransom and must have some other motive.

"I have a hunch too," Arch said. "Day and Diana and I were talking about it last night. The three of us were searching our memories to recall anything Lydia might have said the last time we saw her, which was at suppertime just before she went up to look at the grave of Daniel Lyam Montross. The four of us had sat around the table after dessert, and we all talked awhile about Montross. Lydia had been reading about him in another of Harington's novels.

"Lydia and I had agreed beforehand that we wouldn't reveal to Day and Diana the plot of the Samurai to dump all of Vernon's Vices on the public, even though I knew it had been Day's idea in the first place.

"But these were not the things we remembered having talked about after supper that night. Diana recalled that Lydia had asked them—or us, including me—what we thought of Juliana's plan to build a house and become a permanent resident of the part of Stay More that had belonged to her ancestors.

"Then Day recalled the exact words that Lydia had spoken. 'Do you realize Juliana Heartstays has no idea that all of us know about her affair with Vernon?' And Lydia told us how she'd gone to interview Juliana, on the pretext that the public would be fascinated with the story of how Juliana was building a new home on ancestral lands that Vernon had given to her, and the conversation had led to Lydia's knowledge, or suspicion, of Juliana's affair with Vernon, and Juliana had become upset and alarmed that Lydia knew.

"And Lydia told us one other fragment of the conversation. It was my turn—not Diana's or Day's—to remember almost her exact words: Juliana had said to her, 'You had *better* keep it to yourself. If it gets out, I'll hold you to blame for any trouble it causes.' "

Things were meshing for Monica now. She said, "So Juliana went on believing that only Lydia knew about her affair with Vernon."

"Right," Arch said. "You're starting to catch on. And you'll recall also how Juliana had come to Stay More in the first place intending to wipe out all the Ingledews. You'll recall how her manservant had a whole arsenal of weapons in the trunk of that Pierce-Arrow."

Monica wanted desperately to tell Arch about Lydia's message to her, which showed convincingly that whoever was keeping Lydia was somewhere in the neighborhood. But she couldn't violate that part of the open-shade agreement. "So why didn't the FBI consider them prime suspects?" she asked Arch.

"What did the FBI know about them? The FBI had to let them leave town along with several other people, like your hosts, Larry and Sharon, and Ekaterina, and they had never said or done anything while they were in Stay More that would have made the FBI suspicious of them."

Monica told Arch about having read the FBI file on Juliana, which contained nothing suspicious or even interesting, except that her childhood had been marred by abuse, from both her father and an uncle. Juliana had never been in any trouble with the law.

"Did they have a file on Ben?" Arch asked. Monica shook her head, and Arch said, "Maybe they should have. I suspect he may have had some run-ins with the law."

"So you think Juliana and Ben are the kidnappers, and they're still somewhere in the neighborhood?"

"That's my hunch," Arch said, "and I'm going to follow it. Could you let me have a look at Harry's room?"

The past tense is coming to an end, Monica thought, knowing they were nearing the end of her chapter, after which time would shift. Time would take a dramatic leap into the present. She said, "I suppose we should ask Larry and Sharon permission for that." But Larry and Sharon had gone to Jasper for the day. So she took Arch into the house and let him into Harry's room. There wasn't much there: Harry's suitcase, which contained a few changes of clothes and his shaving kit. He had left nothing much behind, and the FBI had already gone through it.

Arch tapped the black Compaq laptop on the table. "This his computer?" he asked. "Or Larry's?"

"It's Harry's," she declared. "But I'm sure it's password protected."

Arch found the copy of *The Choiring of the Trees*. "The novel he was reading," Monica said. "I haven't read it myself. I've been planning to."

"You ought to. It's great," Arch declared, careful to keep it open as he had found it. "This must have been the page he was reading just before he took off. Get me a blank sheet of paper." She got him the paper, and he wrote down on it a long passage describing a sheep pasture and an old road and a trail leading through the woods to the glen of a waterfall. Monica's eye caught one phrase: "several sort of half-caves where it looks like Indians must have lived." She brightened and knew the past tense was near an end.

"Take me with you," she requested.

"Sorry, honey," he said, "it's too dangerous. And besides, aren't you supposed to be putting VV-Day into effect?"

She nods, and the past tense is past.

In the present tense, she doesn't even tell Arch that half of that hundred thousand he's about to win ought to be hers.

Chapter Nineteen

His first big problem is to find that pasture on Ledbetter Mountain where those two upper corners converge on a hidden entry to the woodland trail leading to the glen of the waterfall. He asks Day and Diana, when he goes to change into his hiking boots and warm outdoor clothes, if they know where Nail Chism's upper pasture was located, but not being natives of Stay More they do not. They want to know where he's going. He simply tells them that in the absence of anything better to do he wants to visit the old Chism home place, as described in *The Choiring of the Trees*. Diana offers to go with him (Day is very busy planning the transplanting of huge trees), but he thanks her and says he'll find it by himself.

Diana packs a picnic lunch for him, with a bottle of good Châteauneuf-du-Pape, and he takes also a spare gallon of water in plastic jugs. He wears his Big Smith bib overalls with a flannel shirt and a light jacket. He unlocks the toolbox on his Chevy Silverado 4-by-4 and gets out the German Luger and checks his supply of ammunition. His father had brought the Luger back from World War II in 1946, a magnificent weapon. The holster has a wooden back that is designed to serve as a stock so the pistol can be converted into a rifle. He has never used it as such, but he knows how to do it. He hopes fervently not to need it. He can't remember the last time he shot anything. He is a member in good standing of Handgun Control, Inc., and completely supports Vernon on the extirpation of all firearms. He decides not to wear the holster strapped to his overalls waist but just to leave it on the seat of the Chevy, ready to hand.

All the rest of the morning he drives the back roads and trails on and around Ledbetter Mountain, looking for any sign of a promising turnoff where perhaps tire tracks would indicate a Pierce-Arrow having entered repeatedly. He broods just a bit over the fact that this is VV-Day and his presence and advice and authority might be needed. He consoles himself with the thought that, if his hunch is correct, what he is doing is far, far more important than VV-Day. He also broods just a bit over being alone. He has asked himself if he ought to have had someone to help him or back him up and has realized the foolhardiness of making himself into a lone paladin. If the search is successful, does he want all the reward money for himself? No, he doesn't need or want the reward, or even the glory, or even anyone knowing that it is he who has found Lydia and Harry. He considers that after he's found them, he'll take them back to Stay More and make them promise they'll never tell anyone who found them. Two women (both natural blondes) have already offered to accompany him on his quest, and he has turned them both down. Because they are women? No, Monica could hold her own in any job requiring a man's strength or wits. He just doesn't want anybody else. If he is so certain of his hunch, and so certain now just where the kidnappers are hiding (as Harry has been certain before him), why doesn't he just notify the sheriff or the state police? Let them do it. Well, why hadn't Harry? Maybe Harry too had said to himself what Arch says now, "If this doesn't work, there's nobody to blame but me." The big difference between him and Harry, of course, is that Harry didn't have any weapons.

Odd that he should be thinking about this matter of being

alone when he happens to run across George Dinsmore. George is in his Explorer, and they roll down their windows as the vehicles meet and stop on a high back road. They exchange howdies. They exchange comments on the weather (partly cloudy, occasional sun, upper 40 degrees Fahrenheit).

"Just out for a drive, maybe?" George says.

"Yeah, I'm looking for the old Chism place that I read about in a book," Arch says.

"Which old Chism place was that?" George wonders. "The Chisms was thick as possums all over this here mountain."

"Where Nail Chism grew up and raised sheep," Arch says.

"Aw, yeah," George says. "The Seth Chism place. But I misdoubt if you could git to it, even in that four-by-four truck. And there aint nothin up there left to look at, nohow."

"No old trail that still leads to it?"

George seems to need a moment to think. "Not from this side of the mountain, I reckon. If you could find the old Bourne place, you could cut back up through one of them loggin trails behind it, and maybe you'd come out in the Chism back forty."

"Could you tell me how to find the old Bourne place?"

"I could *show* you. I couldn't rightly *tell* you."

"I don't want to put you to any trouble."

"No trouble a-tall. Just follow me." George drives on down the road and waits while Arch finds a place wide enough to turn in and back up and turn around. Then Arch follows him as they negotiate a few forks in the road and reach the east face of Ledbetter Mountain. It is close to noon when they finally come across a long-abandoned home place, of which nothing remains except the stone chimney and the stone well with its pulley hoist collapsed. They pull into the yard and stop. Arch notices that the high weeds of the yard and the wagon path to wherever the barn was, weeds that have been killed by frost but are still thick and tousled, have been mashed down in parallel indentations as if by the tires of a car. He gets out of his truck and takes a close look and discovers that there are fresh tire tracks beneath the weeds.

"Looks like somebody else beat you to it," George observes, and gets out of his Explorer to take a close look at the tracks. "Don't look like anybody's tires I've ever seen before, except on that there Pierce-Arrer them injuns has got."

George and Arch look at each other for a moment, and Arch watches George's face as it begins to take on the lineaments of comprehension. Arch has been wondering if he should reveal his actual mission to George but has decided not to. He still wants to go alone, even if it might be a great advantage in this wilderness to have George as guide and backup. But George is a sharp old hillbilly, and in the same moment that Arch observes George's face reaching awareness, George has also developed a suspicion of why Arch might be trying to find the Chism place. "Well," is all Arch can say.

"Well, *hell*," George says. "You aint lookin for the Chism place just on account of some book you read. You're maybe trying to find how Nail Chism's upper pasture is a-hidin the way you git to that there lost holler where the waterfall is at."

"You caught me," Arch admits. "I've got a real strong suspicion that's where Lydia is, and these tracks sort of confirm it, don't they?"

"Now how come a nice feller like big ole Ben would want to take her off?"

"That's what we all want to know, when we find him . . . and her. He was probably just following orders from his boss. And she had her own good reasons for wanting to silence Lydia."

"I'll be switched," George says. He thinks just a little while more, and then he asks, "Are we gonna ride in your rig or mine?"

"I was planning to go alone," Arch says.

"You want all that reward money to yourself, do ye?"

"I don't want any of the reward money," Arch says.

"Hell, Vernon wouldn't pay it to me nohow. I'm just a employee of his'n."

"So I'll just go on by myself, then," Arch declares.

"You don't think you could stop me, do ye?"

"Probably not."

"Let's go in your crate. Might scrape hell out of the bottom and knock off the tailpipe."

So they go in the Chevy, George first retrieving his shotgun from the Explorer. Getting in, George notices and admires the Luger. They follow the tracks up the back of the property and across a rusty fallen barbed-wire fence and into the woods. There the tracks become clearer, impressed into the dirt of the forest, as the weeds are left behind. It is an ancient trail, and Arch follows it, up and up the mountain, his vehicle slipping and lurching and jolting and straining. "Maybe we should have taken your Explorer," he admits. He has never driven a 4-by-4 onto a path as wild as this, and he cannot believe that a Pierce-Arrow has been able to negotiate it without drives in all four wheels. "Maybe we ought to go on foot," he suggests, but George tells him they are still a good long ways from their destination.

"Aint been up this way since I was a boy," George declares, "but I reckon I can still find it."

Eventually the trail levels off and breaks out into a pasture, an old pasture grown with brush and briars and weeds. Arch smiles to see that one corner of the pasture is up against a steep part of the mountain, and in the darkness of that corner can be detected the entry as described in the passage from *The Choiring of the Trees.*

"That's it, huh?" he asks, and drives to that corner and discovers there the trail that will take them to the glen of the waterfall. "Here we are," Arch says. "We just follow this, right?"

"If we can," George says.

"Let's stop for a bite first. You haven't had lunch, have you?"

"Naw, but there aint no McDonald's or Wendy's hereabouts."

Arch fetches the sack that Diana has prepared for him and tells George who gave it to him. There are enough sandwiches in there to feed a platoon. And he discovers a bunch of paper cups. Did Diana think he'd have company? He opens the bottle of Châteauneuf-du-Pape and pours a cup for George. Arch doesn't want to drink enough to cloud his mind, but he does want to drink enough of it to wash down the excellent sandwiches Diana has prepared.

While they are eating and drinking, he spies a cigarette butt out there on the ground and fetches it and shows it to George. "Pall Mall," he says. "That's Harry's brand."

"I sure do hope they're still alive and kicking," George says.

"We'll soon find out," Arch says, cranking the truck and driving on.

"There's one samwich left," George says. "You want it?"

"You can have it," Arch says.

"Maybe we better save it for the dog," George declares. "You know them injuns has got this pointer name of Threasher who'll come a-yappin at us when we git close. Maybe he'll hush if we throw him some lunch meat."

"There might also be Lydia's dog," Arch remarks. "Let's hope the dogs like roast beef."

The trail comes to an end when the tire tracks of the Pierce-Arrow they've been following abruptly turn off into a thick brake of cedars and disappear. There is but a footpath from there on.

"What's in there?" Arch asks, pointing to the cedar trees, as he stops the car and gets out.

"I'll cover your back," George offers with a grin.

Arch walks into the brake and discovers a makeshift but

substantial shed, one end open, constructed of scrap boards and tree branches and the same basketry interweaving as the wigwam down in the valley. It is obviously the work of Ben, intended as a garage for the Pierce-Arrow, but the car isn't there.

He returns to his Chevy. "That's where the Pierce-Arrow ought to be," he tells George. "There's a primitive sort of garage behind those cedar trees. But there's no car in it."

"I reckon we'll have to go on foot from here," George says. He carries the shotgun in one hand and the meat for the dogs in the other. Arch straps the Luger in its holster to his waist and puts his Motorola cell phone into the bib pocket of his overalls. George too has a tiny Nokia in his jacket pocket, but neither man has mentioned calling back into the village, or to George's boss, to let them know what they're doing.

They haven't gone far on the footpath when they hear a motor and turn to look back down the trail to see the Pierce-Arrow arriving behind their vehicle. Ben is alone in it, and after he stops and gets out, he walks only a slight distance toward them and waits. They retrace their steps toward him. He is holding a shotgun cradled in his arm but pointing toward them.

"Is that *you*, George?" Ben calls. "Who's that with you?"

"Just Archie Schaffer," George says, and Arch isn't sure how he feels about that "just," which sounds somehow belittling.

They walk on until they are face-to-face. George and Ben have their shotguns pointed at each other, but Ben suddenly reaches out with both arms and bear-hugs George mightily and even lifts him up above the ground. "I've missed you!" Ben exclaims.

"Nothing was stopping you from calling me to let me know you was okay," George says, and pats his Nokia. "You know my number."

Ben laughs. "Oh, yeah. Sure," he says sarcastically. "I couldn't call my own mother to wish her a happy birthday." And then, remembering his manners, he holds his hand out to Arch for a handshake. "Mr. Schaffer," he says.

"Mr. Bending Bear," Arch says, shaking his hand.

The Indian says something in his Osage language that Arch can't understand, but Arch can tell from the tone of it that Ben is not very happy that Arch is here.

George says, "First big question, of course, is have you been taking real good care of Lydia Caple and Harry Wolfe?"

"You'll soon see for yourselves," Ben says, a bit petulantly, as if the question impugned his hospitality. "But first I must ask you gentlemen to put your weapons down on the ground." And he passes the muzzle of the shotgun back and forth between them. George lays his shotgun down, and Arch removes the Luger and its holster from his waist and lays it down, and Ben picks up the two weapons and takes them to the Pierce-Arrow, where he opens the trunk and puts them in, but before locking it, he says, "I'd also appreciate having possession of your cell phones." They give him the Nokia and the Motorola and he adds them to the guns and locks them in the trunk. "Now," he says, "if you'll give me a hand with the groceries, I won't have to make two trips." Ben opens the rear door of the Pierce-Arrow and loads their arms with grocery sacks bearing the imprint of the one supermarket in Jasper. "Would you mind getting that sack of cat food?" Ben asks Arch, who takes up the twenty-pound bag of Special Kitty®. Ben, holding his shotgun casually in the same hand with a bag of groceries, motions them back onto the trail. "It's not quite a mile," Ben says. "I would have preferred to have built the garage much farther in, but neither my car nor yours could negotiate the crossings of the little creek that winds through the hollow. A little exercise never hurts anyone, does it?"

"I reckon not," George allows. They have to walk across some foot logs to get across that creek, which is tricky with arms full of grocery sacks. The little creek, Arch realizes, is probably the runoff of the fabled waterfall, whose cascade in the distance he seems to be able to hear already.

"Monica has her shade up," Ben says to Arch offhandedly, as if just commenting on the weather. Arch doesn't know what he's talking about, unless, in addition to being some kind of homosexual, Ben is also a Peeping Tom. When he gives Ben a quizzical look, the latter asks, "She didn't tell you about the shade?" Arch shakes his head. "Have you talked to Monica today?" Arch nods his head. "What did you talk about?"

"All kinds of things. The campaign. The weather. The possibility that whoever kidnapped Lydia is still somewhere not too far from Stay More."

"Monica didn't tell you about a message she had from Lydia?"

"No, she didn't," Arch says, wondering why she hadn't.

"Then what are you fellows doing here?" Ben wants to know.

"I suppose the same as Harry was doing here: trying to find Lydia."

"Well, you'll soon see both of them," Ben declares, and guides them onward into the glen of the waterfall, where suddenly two dogs come charging toward them, yapping and woofing. They sniff around Arch and George until they're satisfied that, since Ben is with them, they're not intruders. "Threasher and Lydia's dog Beanbag," Arch declares, and gives them a pat. Arch looks around at the glen and the bluffs surrounding it and the cascading waterfall, a sylvan paradise. There are ferns growing everywhere, and mosses on everything, and big old virgin trees that nearly blot out the sky even without their leaves. Arch has read about this place in several of Harington's books, which didn't do justice to it. The bluffs surrounding the glen are pocked with the dark mouths of caverns, and the largest of these mouths has been partially covered over with the same sort of basketry-and-board construction Ben used for the garage. There is a door, and Ben holds it open for them with the pride that comes from having made it. They enter the snug confines of the large shelter, one commodious cavern extending deep back under the bluff. Four people sit on improvised chairs at a table rigged from branches and boards beside a large open fire, its smoke vented through the top of the shelter's front wall: the hostages Lydia and Harry, their captor Juliana, and Ekaterina. Or is Ekaterina the captor?

"You idiots," Harry says jovially to Arch and George, rising to meet them and shaking their hands. "What makes you think you could do something I couldn't do?"

"We were armed," Arch says. "For a while." And then he asks, "Are you okay, Harry?"

"At least I'm not tied up anymore," Harry says.

"Ben, you've got to stop taking captives," Juliana says. "We'll run out of beds." She gestures at the rear of the cavern, where there are several beds made from ticking filled with leaves. Then she addresses Arch and George. "Welcome to our cozy but temporary home. I'm sure we can make room for two more. But here, let's put away those groceries." Juliana and Cat and Lydia sort and store the groceries in various niches of the cavern, and then Juliana says, "I'm sorry we can't offer anything better to drink than sassafras tea or its cousin, sarsaparilla." So everyone sits around the fire with their drinks (Arch has never had sarsaparilla before and discovers it is just carbonated sassafras tea), and Juliana asks Arch, "So how did you find us, when all the resources of the law failed to do so?"

"The law but not Harry Wolfe," Arch says. "We used the same method he did. I took the liberty of looking to see what he'd been reading lately and came across the key passage in *The Choiring of the Trees*. I knew this glen of the waterfall has traditionally been a really good hiding place, going all the way back to the Bluff Dweller Indians who used to live here."

"Ah, yes," Juliana says. "The Bluff Dwellers. We've taken over one of their shelters, just as my ancestors did when they first came to Stay More, long before the white man, and found that the Bluff Dwellers had lived here for hundreds of years." Juliana smiles somewhat apologetically. "I suppose we should never have blamed the Panthers for usurping our ancestral lands, when we usurped the lands of the Bluff Dwellers."

"But they were already long gone when your ancestors got here, weren't they?" Arch observes.

"Yes, although I can't imagine why they would've wanted to leave. Not a place like *this*."

Ekaterina speaks up. "It's assumed that disease, an epidemic perhaps, did away with the Bluff Dwellers. And it's quite possible that the Osage who inhabited the valley down below never discovered this lost hollow."

They just sit around for the rest of the afternoon, all seven of them, talking about Indians. Then Juliana says, "If you gentlemen would like to go explore the hollow and have a close look at the waterfall while we womenfolk prepare supper, we'll trust you to return in time to eat with us. But just to be sure you don't attempt to escape, I'll have to ask Ben to guard you."

Harry, who seems to have been allowed to explore the neighborhood previously, acts as their guide and conducts them, under Ben's supervision, on a little tour of the hollow and points things out: There is another cavern concealed behind the waterfall, and there are in fact not one but two waterfalls, which seem to be one because of the closeness of their juxtaposition although they come from different springs. Harry shows them a few artifacts left behind by the Bluff Dwellers and unmolested by later explorers: shards of pottery, fragments of cloth woven of grasses, and a few graves where Bluff Dwellers were buried. The late afternoon sunlight enhances the autumn color in the trees and makes the waterfalls seem like a deluge of diamonds. When this is all over, Arch tells himself, I've got to bring Beverly and Eliot up here to see this.

At supper they are treated to the fruits of Threasher's labors, an assortment of the same dishes that had been served at the great banquet Arch missed (he'd been canoeing the Mulberry River): tiny fried turtle pies made from an ancient Osage recipe and a hearty turtle stew made from an ancient Svanetian recipe, the two cultures alike in their ability to create fabulous feasts from humble reptiles. Arch isn't sure he'll like the stuff, but after watching George Dinsmore attack his first few bites of stew with gusto, Arch gingerly nibbles a turtle pie, discovers it's delicious, and even has thoughts about suggesting its inclusion in the Tyson line. But such a meal deserves imported beers and good wines, and there is only water and coffee to wash it down. Still, he thoroughly enjoys it, as well as the Svanetian dessert, a *churchkhela*, fabulous, which Ekaterina explains is a walnut roll made with walnuts and muscadines foraged right here in the lost hollow.

"That was terrific," Arch comments, when supper is over. "I could almost make up my mind that I don't want to leave."

"That's good," Juliana says, "because you're not going to leave."

"Never?" Arch says, becoming a bit alarmed.

"Not until the election is over," she says, "and maybe not until—when, January?—Vernon has been sworn in as the new governor."

Arch is beginning to understand why Lydia was kidnapped. But now he takes this opportunity to ask Juliana to answer the question that has most bothered him: Why did they take Lydia in the first place?

"Maybe I should let Lydia answer that," Juliana responds.

"Before I explain," Lydia says, "let me ask Arch and George something. Did either or both of you guys know, sometime back in the summer, that Juliana and Vernon were carrying on together?"

"I don't know about Arch," George declares, "but naturally I did, on account of I was in charge of settin down that helicopter beside that there wigwam in the middle of the night so they could get together."

"I was possibly one of the first to know," Arch admits, "because Vernon sort of asked my permission. That is, he wondered what effect it could have on the campaign. But it was common knowledge, or gossip, among all the Samurai."

"See?" Lydia says challengingly to Juliana. "I *told* you everybody knew! Harry knew, didn't you, Harry?"

Harry nods. "Nothing ever happens anywhere that I don't know about."

Juliana broods. There is a long silence, and then Lydia explains to Arch. "Juliana had me kidnapped because she thought I was the only one who knew about her and Vernon and she wanted to ensure my silence."

Arch fixes Juliana with a harsh look. "Excuse me, but that was a pretty stupid thing to do."

Juliana bristles at his remark and then protests. "I don't think you understand, Mr. Schaffer. I never intended any harm to Lydia, or to Harry, or you or George. I wanted to hold her incommunicado for the remainder of the campaign, to keep her from revealing anything about Vernon and me that could damage his candidacy. I intended to release her as soon as he got elected."

"And how," Arch wants to know, "did you intend to keep her from revealing to the authorities who had kidnapped her?"

Juliana does not answer. She hangs her head, and Arch knows she can't answer because she never considered it.

"For that matter," he goes on, "how are you going to keep *us*—Harry and George and me—from disclosing who kidnapped us?"

At once, he regrets having asked, because there is only one answer: They would have to be killed.

Arch takes a deep breath. "Maybe if you'd just release them and we could take them back, nobody would have to know what you did. We could just tell everybody that Lydia got lost in the woods and Harry got lost trying to find her, and we would all agree with a solemn oath that we'd never implicate you and Ben."

"That would be nice," Juliana says, "but I'll have to sleep on it. Does anyone want more coffee?"

For the rest of the evening they talk about other things, as if the serious topic just discussed is too serious to continue. Ekaterina tells the story of a group of Osages during the nineteenth century who were pursued by the U.S. Cavalry and fled into a lost hollow in the hills perhaps very similar to this glen of the waterfall. All attempts to find them failed. They were given up for dead or lost. But twenty years later the same Indians rode out of the hollow, and they hadn't aged a day!

"I've heard that story," Juliana says. "But of course it's just a legend."

"I believe it," Harry says. "Not only have I not aged a day since I've been here, I've subtracted all the days from my age!"

They laugh, and Lydia observes, "So has old Beanbag. So have I, for that matter."

Arch sneaks a glance at his hands, as if he might discover they are younger. He allows himself the fantasy that, if he stayed here, he'd find time stuck in the present tense forever. But he is concerned about Beverly and Eliot. He usually calls them once a day, about this time of evening, to wish them good night and to ask Eliot how she's doing in school and all. He realizes that in a day or two the newspapers will be full of these latest disappearances, and Hank Endicott will be commenting on how the Samurai are reduced from seven to only three, as in the film *The Seven Samurai*, and if Shoat Bradfield isn't the guilty party he probably knows something about it. Arch realizes Lydia is still talking, and she's asking him a question.

"Arch, what's happening with the plan to divulge Vernon's Vices to the Bradfield people?"

Arch looks nervously at Juliana and asks Lydia, "Does she know about the scheme?"

Juliana answers for herself. "Yes, Lydia told me all about it. How ironic that I went to such pains to protect Vernon when you people are hatching such a plot."

"Well," Arch says, "today was supposed to be VV-Day. Monica was going to go ahead and leak the list of Vernon's Vices to the Bradfield campaign. Vernon himself called a moratorium on campaigning until you, Lydia, return safe and sound, and the Samurai—what's left of us—are violating that moratorium with VV-Day. But Monica is convinced that you are safe and sound. She even had a dream about you last night."

"Bless her heart. And she got my letter this morning?" Lydia asks.

"I couldn't tell you that. If she did, she didn't tell me."

"She wasn't supposed to," Ben puts in. "She had to agree not to tell anyone and to leave her window shade up as a signal that she agreed to it, and when I went to Jasper this morning I noticed her shade was up."

"Tell me," Arch says to Ben. "How can you drive the Pierce-Arrow into Stay More without anybody seeing you?"

"I don't drive into Stay More," Ben says. "I leave the car on a back road above the village and sneak in on foot."

"And nobody has ever noticed the Pierce-Arrow there or on the road to Jasper?" Arch asks, and looks at George for confirmation.

"I seen it a time or two," George allows.

"Why didn't you tell us?" Arch wants to know.

"Aw, I figured ole Ben was jist being standoffish," George says. "I had no idee he was involved in this kidnap business."

It grows late, and Juliana announces that she wants to sleep in order to resolve a solution to this problem. Ben prepares two new beds for the two new guests by stuffing ticking sacks with leaves in the rear of the cavern. Juliana hears but rejects Arch's request to phone his family just to let them know that he's okay. One by one the seven people, using flashlights to see their way, use the latrine that Ben has erected in the woods nearby. When his turn comes, Arch realizes he could quite easily use the flashlight to make his way on back to his truck and to escape. But he does not. He couldn't leave the others. Harm might come to them if he did. He returns to the cave and crawls into his bed. Everyone essentially is in the same huge bedroom, but he is some fifty or sixty feet away from where the women are sleeping, although George's bed is not far from his. Arch has never slept on a mattress made of ticking stuffed with leaves, and although he can hear the leaves rustling whenever he turns he is surprised at how comfortable it is, and he has three blankets over him to keep him warm, and perhaps because of the excitement and activity of this busy day he drops quickly off into a deep and restful sleep.

Sometime in the middle of the night he is awakened by the sound of a voice loudly whispering, "No, now, you jist caint do that. I won't stand for it." And another voice whimpering. And then silence.

Arch listens for a brief moment before falling back into his heavy slumber. And when he awakens again, the sunlight is shining over the top of the cavern's front wall. He climbs out of bed and finds all the others up, everyone except Harry, but Harry's bed is empty. Ekaterina is standing at the fireplace with a frying pan in her hand, and she asks Arch how he likes his eggs.

Juliana asks him, "Did you sleep well?"

"Like a baby," Arch says. "I haven't slept so well in ages, and I didn't have a moment of trouble with my sleep apnea. I've had this condition for some time and tried various medicines without much luck, but it didn't bother me at all last night."

"Maybe you don't want to leave," she suggests.

"Yeah, I've considered staying as long as you have to keep me," Arch says. "Until Vernon is sworn in. But believe me, Juliana, Vernon's not going to get sworn in if you've got three of his best campaign strategists in captivity. Not to mention his helicopter pilot and general factotum."

"I've considered that," she says. "And I've given serious consideration to your kind offer to keep the kidnapping a secret if we let all of you go. You're an honest man, Arch Schaffer, and I'll trust you that you will keep a solemn oath never to give us away."

"Do you mean you'll do it?" Arch asks, elated.

"Let's all have breakfast and discuss the details," she says. "As soon as Harry gets back."

She has scarcely spoken these words when the door opens and Harry comes in, wrapped in a large towel, his hair wet. He hops on one foot and then the other and says, "Brrr! It's a cold morning." Then, seeing the way Arch is looking at him, he explains. "Every day before breakfast I take a shower in the waterfall. Nothing like that icewater to get the circulation going! And to keep from wanting a cigarette."

He is soon dressed and joins them for breakfast. They eat and wait for someone to bring up the serious matter again. Ekaterina is the first to speak. "Just let me say that I hope no one will ever mention my involvement in this escapade. I can't bear publicity."

Arch understands. He isn't sure just how much "involvement" she has had, but he knows it would never do if her name reached the outside world.

Juliana remarks wistfully, "I'd like to go off in the woods by myself and let go of a good loud scream."

Harry chuckles and says, "I recall a bit of advice I heard one time: 'If you are falling off the mountain, stop screaming and flap your arms. If that doesn't work, you can always go back to screaming.' "

There isn't much laughter.

Arch, whose chapter this is, stuck in the present tense, will take upon himself the privilege of switching it to the future tense, because only in the future tense will solutions happen, and that is how he will be able to think about getting back to "civilization." He will wonder, or will observe, just as Monica will have observed the shift from past tense to present, that they all will have been transported into the future tense. A practical man, he will even try testing it. He will pour himself another cup of coffee, and he will notice carefully that he did not pour himself a cup, nor does he pour himself a cup, but he *will* pour himself a cup. And he will realize that maybe it will be appropriate, because although they will have to give up this sylvan paradise of the glen of the waterfall, this storied hideaway of magical grottoes and arbors, they will in a sense be permitted to leave parts of themselves here forever. Arch will smile. But then he will recall that while this idyllic dell will have had such purposes long ago as sheltering Nail Chism after his escape from prison, and sheltering McPherson's raiders (who also called themselves samurai) during their war games, it was also the place where Sull Jerram was assassinated, and where Daniel Lyam Montross likewise was killed, and where Dawny Harington at the age of not quite six was lost in the woods. It will not be entirely a place of Arcadian memories, Arch will realize.

So when he will hear the sound of the helicopters, it will be almost as if he will have invented them himself. The four hostages and three captors will rush outside the cavern to look up at the sky and see the helicopters, several of them, hovering above. More suddenly than they will be able to think, the woods of the sylvan dell will disgorge dozens of men, all dressed in black and all armed to the teeth. With precision and incredible speed the men will surround the seven former occupants of the cave and will seemingly know the difference between the good guys and the bad guys, separating them from each other. These helmeted and black-clad men will immediately and quickly take captive Thomas Bending Bear, who will offer only minimal resistance. And then they will also place handcuffs on Juliana Heartstays.

Juliana will scream at Arch, "You tricked us!"

Arch will reply, "I didn't have anything to do with this." *Except to invent the future tense*, he will say to himself.

Dozens more of this SWAT team will arrive, until the glen of the waterfall will be practically filled with them. The swarm of helicopters overhead will drift away. One of the SWAT team, who will be dressed like all the others in black but will have curly blond hair, and will be female, will rush to Lydia and exchange powerful hugs with her.

"You always looked good in black," Lydia will say to her.

"Don't I?" Monica will say.

Chapter Twenty

He will think often of the basic belief of Taoism, that we must be passive, like nature. He will sometimes chant aloud to himself, like a mantra, *Wei wu wei*: to do without doing, to act without action. He will decide to do nothing more to get himself elected governor. He will honor those few engagements already scheduled, but he will permit his Samurai to make no new ones nor to do anything beyond what will have already been done (and having given the opposition all those secrets was plenty) to win further votes. He will realize that his crucial mistake in running for governor was not that he will have failed to prevent all these things from happening around him and to him but that he will have failed to remember that central precept of the Tao: Let well enough alone. He will deeply regret that he was not *pu shih*: independent and uninvolved and truly removed from all these things that will have happened.

"It's okay," Harry Wolfe will console him. "You aren't going to win anyhow." Harry will have returned to drinking, after his idyll in the woods. Not serious or bilious drinking but enough to liberate his tongue. After consulting with Vernon, he will be planning to make one last flight to Little Rock, where he will attempt to get Bradfield to accept this fabrication: that the Ingledew campaign, who had kidnapped him (and from whom he had escaped just long enough to fax those hundred damaging calumnies to Bradfield), will have permitted him to follow his hunch and attempt to find and rescue Lydia, only to have been captured himself. Which will explain to the Bradfield people what Harry would be doing kidnapped by Indians instead of by Ingledew.

"That's fine with me," Vernon will confide to Harry. "But out of curiosity, just what makes you so sure?"

And tipsy Harry will say, "Do you recall a little donation you made to the Library of Congress many years ago, an old Roman book called *De Architectura Antiqua Arcadiae,* which tells the story of an Arcadian Greek named Vernealos Anqualdou? Well, I took the liberty—and the trouble—of having a friend in DC make me a copy, which I commissioned a professor at the university in Fayetteville to translate from the Latin for me. I take it you haven't read it yourself, even though you read Latin."

"I don't want to read it," Vernon will tell Harry. "I gave it to the Library of Congress on condition that they never let me see it."

"But don't you want to know whether or not Vernealos won the election to become governor of Arcadia?"

Vernon will recall the conversation he had with Day Whittacker, before the primary, over this whole matter of magic realism and Day's awareness of the contents of *Thirteen Albatrosses.* Vernon had wanted Day to tell him the outcome of the primary, but Day had claimed he hadn't got that far yet. Now here will be Harry Wolfe, offering to tell him—or, indeed, having already told him by saying, "You aren't going to win anyhow"—the outcome of the election in which his metafictional ancestor, Vernealos Anqualdou, was running for governor of ancient Arcadia.

"You've already told me, haven't you?" Vernon will say.

"But it was close," Harry will elaborate. "It was *real* close."

"Did that campaign also involve the brilliant scheme to

publicize one hundred of Anqualdou's vices in order to inoculate the voters against scandal?"

Harry will chuckle. "Not exactly. But Anqualdou is figuratively stabbed in the back by his best friend, who corresponds to your Day Whittacker, author of our brilliant scheme. Oops. I wasn't supposed to tell you that."

"Tell me more," Vernon will request.

The revelation that Day was the originator of Operation Vernon's Vices will disturb Vernon, and once he will have sent Harry on his way he will go out looking for Day, to get him to confirm or deny the imputation.

Harry Wolfe will return, for a final time, to Little Rock, where he will remain with Bradfield's people, watching the Vernon's Vices scheme going beautifully, watching the electorate growing increasingly fed up with any mention of either candidate's unsavory past or present, watching Bradfield becoming apoplectically frustrated over Vernon's refusal to answer to or comment upon any of the new charges brought against him, watching the final opinion polls going awry (13 percent Bradfield, 12 percent Ingledew, 8 percent other candidates, 19 percent undecided, 48 percent totally indifferent) for the last few days of the campaign, and the election itself, in which Harry will not be able to vote, even if he were so disposed, because he is not an Arkansas citizen, a condition he will eventually remedy. Although he will have been offered, even before the election, a good job in the Bradfield administration, and will later also receive offers elsewhere in the country to be an oppo man for important candidates the following year, Harry will surprise all those who will have known him by joining a Franciscan monastery near the Ozark village of Witts Springs. In time, Vernon will receive a letter from him, a humble letter, a self-deprecating letter, an apologetic letter. "Only God should be permitted to make predictions," it will conclude. "And He already has."

"Did Harry tell you?" Day will ask of Vernon, who will have found him at the construction site of Juliana's mansion, where with a crew of men he will be excavating an enormous hole for the transplantation of a seventy-year-old red oak tree. "Well, damn him! Anyhow, I just planted the seed. He and the rest of your Samurai developed it into a workable scheme."

"It has certainly worked," Vernon will observe.

"I'll say! Apparently the voters are completely disgusted with you and Bradfield both."

"Not disgusted," Vernon will correct him. "Just overdosed and apathetic." The newspaper editorials will have agreed that Shoat Bradfield will have appeared to have committed an act of desperation by revealing all of Vernon's Vices. Hank Endicott will have commented, "Aren't we all a little sick and tired of hearing what's wrong with Vernon Ingledew?"

"Diana and I may not vote," Day will say.

Vernon will know it's just good-natured ribbing. "Bo tells me that a low turnout at the polls will probably be in my favor."

"Oh? So you're back on speaking terms with Bo? You didn't fire him?"

"I couldn't. He said that if I fired him, he'd keep on working for me voluntarily, because he's determined to see me get elected governor. He said he'd personally canvass door-to-door if need be."

"He wants you out of Stay More," Day will observe. "But if you spoke with him, did you and he finally discuss this little matter of your mutual interest in Jelena?"

"You want to report all the little details to Diana." Vernon will laugh and punch him on the shoulder. "And also to your friend the Author. Speaking of whom, and the matter of revelations and metafictions and all that, did you know that Harry possesses an English translation of the Latin *De Architectura Antiqua Arcadiae*?"

"Yes, he told me."

"Did he tell you he knows how the story ends? So you can tell your Author friend how *this* story ends?"

"Harry didn't say anything about endings. And as you ought to know, none of my Author friend's books ever have endings. He won't allow them."

"But *Thirteen Albatrosses*, as you call it, is going to have to say whether or not I win the election, and that's going to be the end."

"No, it's not. It's probably more a beginning than an ending."

"Don't you want to know what Harry said happens in that ancient election in Arcadia?"

"I'd rather not know," Day will say. "And I'm sorry that you've found out."

Vernon will be sorry too, but he will not blame the knowledge of it for the depression that will hit him and will last for the remaining days of the campaign. He will attempt to shake himself out of the depression by reawakening his former self, in its customary milieu: his secluded study, his nest in the top of the double-bubble, where he will go to read books on quantum theory, his next biannual course of study. Never mind that elsewhere on the premises his true love Jelena will be living it up with his unfired campaign manager. Usually, when weather permits, they will be out in Jelena's "secret" garden.

Vernon, turning a page of D. Z. Albert's *Quantum Mechanics and Experience*, will smile to himself, thinking that Jelena for all her intelligence will have never realized that her secret garden will not have been a secret from him, Vernon, for the simple reason that each and every time George brought the helicopter down to its landing pad Vernon had spied the secret garden from the air. He will not yet have confronted her with his knowledge of it. Just as he will not yet have confronted her with his awareness of her affair with Bolin Pharis, which, for that matter, she will not have attempted to hide from him, as she will have hidden her

Bible, her journal, her cigarettes, her chocolates, and her little TV set, the existence of all of which he has known about for quite some time.

The only mystery about Jelena remaining to him will be the question: Why has she tried to keep all those things secret but has really made no effort to keep her love of Bo a secret? Possibly because, just as he will have persuaded himself that it is indeed possible for a man to love two women equally, she has persuaded herself that her love for Bo has not diminished her love for Vernon. Because if it will have, there will have been no sign of it; she will still sleep with Vernon whenever he will be at home, or whenever he will come to bed after late hours in his study, and she will still bring him his lunch while he is reading in his study, and she will still kiss him and hug him and speak sweetly to him and, as far as their daily conduct will be concerned, Bo Pharis might very well never have existed, even if he is living permanently in the guest room.

Oh, of course Vernon will miss Juliana, and not just sexually (although Jelena's desire for Vernon will also be undiminished by the presence and the prowess of Bo). Juliana and Thomas Bending Bear will be inmates of the Washington County Jail, awaiting trial sometime in December or January. They will have obtained the very best legal counsel available, but their team of high-powered lawyers will not have been able to arrange bond for them because of the severity of their crime: not one but four kidnappings. All the newspapers will have given front-page coverage to the dramatic rescue effort that will have been engineered by Vernon's new press secretary, Monica Breedlove, which will have sent into the wilderness a SWAT team to liberate the four members of Vernon's staff being held hostage by, as the newspapers will have put it, "a pair of deranged Indians."

The expensive lawyers will have been tight-lipped about any possible motive their clients had for the kidnappings, other than a wish to depopulate their ancestral lands. There will have been no mention of, or implied connection to, Vernon Ingledew. Another team of lawyers, according to the newspapers, will have arranged quickly for the release of the woman who will be identified as Ekaterina Vladimirovna Dadeshkeliani, forty-nine, whose address will be given as Stay More but who will not be revealed to have the pseudonym V. Kelian, by which she will have once been known to many readers of American fiction. The lawyers will convince the arraigning judge that she will have had no real part in the kidnapping and was simply visiting the Native Americans, who were friends of hers. Upon her release, she will return only briefly to her home, the former Jacob Ingledew house, and will close it up, remaining only long enough to tell Vernon that she is taking an extended vacation back home to Svanetia and Georgia but will vote for him by absentee ballot. With her house vacant once again, the village will soon return to its sleepy tranquillity, in which it will drowse forevermore.

Vernon will go on loving Jelena (and sharing her with Bo) for as long as he can stand missing the very sight, sound, and scent of Juliana, and then he will ask Arch Schaffer to see if there will not be some way that Vernon could quietly, secretly visit Ben and Juliana in jail. Arch will agree to look into it and to use his connections in the Washington County legal establishment; Arch Schaffer will always have been good at pulling strings. His conduct in the closing days of the campaign will be exemplary and beyond the call of duty; he will even surpass Bo in his zeal to get Vernon elected. And when it will all be over, and his leave at Tyson's will be up, Arch will return to his old familiar desk at Tyson corporate headquarters, where he will exercise the same zeal and string-pulling, as well as his trademark bonhomie, to help his company and to further his career. In time, Arch Schaffer will be moved upstairs to become CEO of the Tyson empire, which he will vastly extend, until Tyson's, having acquired the nation's largest beef producer and then the nation's largest pork producer, will become purely and simply the largest *meat* producer in the world (including a line of turtle-meat fried pies).

Although Arch will have urged Vernon to throw his heart into the last days of the campaign, Vernon cannot. Vernon will justify his new pessimism and Taoist passivity, not to mention the prediction of that old Latin book on Arcadian architecture, on the grounds that he will have become practically broke. But Monica, who will decline the reward of a hundred thousand dollars on the grounds that Vernon can't afford it, will have been *almost* right: The campaign coffers will indeed have diminished to nothing. But those funds, which he had set aside back in February after first deciding to try his hand at politics, were only a part of his fortune; he will still possess enough money to keep him (and Jelena and Juliana and Bo and Sharon and Larry and Monica and anybody else who asks) comfortable forever. Once the hectic campaign is but an unpleasant memory, talented Cast Sherrill, who will marry Sheila Kimber of Stay More, will be appointed to the position of Director of Media, Public, and Governmental Affairs for Ingledew Ham and will help extend its markets to the four corners of the globe.

But Vernon will have solemnly promised himself (and Jelena) that once his "political allotment" is spent, he will not dip into the rest of his fortune, and therefore economy measures will have to have been taken in the last days of the campaign. One of the first of these will be the use of the helicopter. The panoply of Vernon's accompaniment—the marching band, the choir, the cheerleaders, most of whom will have had to return to their colleges for the fall semester anyhow—will disappear, and even the largesse of his feasts will no longer feature Ingledew ham but just hot dogs and hamburgers. So the last use of the helicopter, the last stump speech of the campaign, indeed the last stump speech that will ever be delivered in the state of Arkansas, will occur at the town of Mountain View, where seventeen people, five of them children, and three dogs, will listen to Vernon's halfhearted chat, promising that under his leadership things will get better in the state of Arkansas. Afterwards, after dropping Vernon off at Stay More, George will fly the helicopter back to its lessor in Tulsa, Oklahoma, and Vernon will personally drive over there to bring George home. On the way back to Arkansas, Vernon will ask him, "George, if by some miracle I were to get elected, what kind of job could I give you in Little Rock? How about Highway Commissioner? Or Director of Veterans' Affairs? I could make you Adjutant General, how about that?"

"You caint scare me, Boss," George will respond. "You aint gonna git elected and you aint gonna do no such of a thing as that. Why would you want to punish me? Aint I been good to you?" George will insist that *if* in the dog's chance Boss will git hisself elected, and will give George his druthers, he'll a whole heap druther keep on working at the pig plant until he reaches retirement, which is just around the corner anyhow.

And sure enough, that is precisely what will become of George. He will continue to manage Ingledew Ham and will work closely with Cast Sherrill in expanding its operations and making it global. He will be given a nice bonus upon his retirement at sixty-seven and will live happily in Stay More to a very ripe old age.

But for now, Vernon will tell George that he plans to stop in Fayetteville on the way back to Stay More, and Vernon will say, "George, I'm planning to say hello to Juliana and Ben. Do you want to say anything to Ben?"

George will ponder, but will say, "Naw, you can jist tell 'im we're all pullin for him, and we hope he gits out soon."

"It's not likely they're going to get out for a long time," Vernon tells him.

"Then jist say I'll miss him," George will tell Vernon. "He was my friend."

Arch Schaffer will have arranged for Vernon to enter the Washington County jail without attracting any attention and to have as much time as he wants to visit with the defendants.

Vernon will first visit with Ben, who will be brought from his cell in an outlandish bright-orange jail jumpsuit, with his hands shackled to his waist, and will sit across a table from Vernon, who will convey to him George's good wishes and the fact that George misses him and will continue to miss him.

"But you didn't come here to see me," Ben will remark.

"No, but I want to thank you for having been so kind and considerate to Lydia during her detainment. I want you to know that I understand why you were ordered to kidnap her. I am still your friend, I hope."

Ben will laugh. "That's nice. You know, I came to Arkansas in the first place intending to kill you, so maybe it's fortunate I'm just facing a kidnap rap, not a murder rap."

"Take care of yourself, Ben." Vernon will not be able to shake his hand, which is manacled to his waist.

Ben will be led away and then they will bring Juliana to him. She too will be dressed in a Day-Glo orange jail jumpsuit and will have her wrists cuffed and attached by a thin but strong chain to a chain around her waist. She will not be able to hug him. He will give her an awkward embrace but will be aware that a guard will be standing with his arms folded, directly behind her.

Vernon will speak to the guard. "Would you mind if we had some privacy for a few minutes?"

"I aint sposed to let her outa my sight," the guard will say.

"She's not going anywhere," Vernon will say.

"Still and all. . . ." The guard will hesitate.

"Do you know who I am?" Vernon will ask him.

"Yessir, you're the next governor of Arkansas. Leastways if my vote means anything. My old lady don't plan to vote for you, but I sure do."

"Thank you. So could you just step outside for a few minutes?"

"Well." The guard will continue to hesitate. "Don't tell nobody I did it." And he will leave the room and leave them alone.

And they will kiss. It will be a lovers' kiss, serious and urgent and eloquent, her solid breasts mashed against his heart. But she will burst into tears as they will be sitting down across the table from each other, and between her sobs she will say, "I made such a mess of things."

"You did indeed," he will agree, forcing himself despite his shyness to look her in the eye, "but Lydia doesn't hold it against you, and Harry doesn't, and I certainly don't."

She will stop crying and will change the subject, grinning at him. "You're such a bad boy. They let us watch TV, you know, and I've heard about all those awful things that Governor Bradfield says you did. Is any of that stuff true?"

"Believe as much of it as you want to believe," he will offer, and his shyness will make him remove his eyes from hers.

"I don't want to believe *any* of it."

"Then don't. It's all just politics."

"But I told myself, if people are going to vote for you despite all your sins, then one more sin won't make any difference, if they knew about me."

"They don't know about you yet," he will say, and will try to look at her again. "Maybe Bradfield is saving you for next week, the last week before the election. But truly it won't make any difference if he does, not after all those awful things he's already revealed about me. The public simply doesn't care anymore."

"So if I wanted to, I could live in the governor's mansion with you, and the public wouldn't care?"

He will put his hand over hers. "Juliana, I don't think I'm going to be elected. Really."

"Don't say that!" she will plead, and then she will offer, "Let me pay for a media blitz or anything. Let me *buy* you the election."

"That's generous of you, but it would be illegal. I've resigned myself to defeat. As I once explained to you, this whole campaign has just been a part of my education in politics. Now I need to learn how to lose."

"But—" She will tilt her head and toss her lovely long black hair and will say "But—" again before finding the words. "But Ben and I are counting on you to become governor so you can pardon us if we're sent to prison." When he will not comment immediately on that, she will say, "You know our lawyers think there's a chance we'll have to serve time, maybe years and years. I've heard so much about how people like Ben get treated in prison. You've *got* to become governor so you can keep that from happening!"

"Maybe it can be arranged that Ben won't be kept with the general prison population," Vernon will suggest.

Juliana will resume crying, not sobbing this time but allowing the tears to flow down her cheeks. "You know what I do with all my free time here? I have fantasies about living in the governor's mansion with you and decorating it and turning one room into a nursery and throwing parties and thumbing my nose at prying reporters. Wouldn't we have fun?"

"I'd be delighted," he will say, to console her, but he will be slightly disturbed about that reference to a nursery. "Especially since Jelena has made it clear she'd never want to live in the governor's mansion herself."

Juliana will laugh with pleasure. "I'll just take her place! She'll stay in Stay More and Bo can have her."

"That would appear to be the likely arrangement," he will observe, but then will insist, "assuming I got elected. Believe me, it seems much more probable that you and I won't be living it up together in the governor's mansion."

"Then you can just come to my Stay More mansion any time you feel like it."

"Juliana," he will say with dead seriousness, "it's not probable you'll be living there. It's more likely you'll be living for a number of years in prison."

"But I can't have my . . . I don't want to let the . . . prison's no place to have a—" She will struggle to find the words, but then the guard will return.

"Folks, let's say our goodbyes," the guard will suggest.

Juliana will say hers. "If you don't get elected, and therefore you can't pardon me, will you pardon me anyway?"

"There is nothing for me to pardon you for," he will say.

Moments of silence will pass during which they will be able to hold each other only with their eyes. He will reach across the table and touch her hands as they are held to her waist. He will smile and try to think of something cheerful to say. The guard will take one of her arms gently and raise her to her feet.

Wanting not to lose the conversation, she will ask, "Is my house still going up?"

"Last time I looked, they were nailing on the rafters," he will tell her.

"Whatever happens," she will say, "I intend to live there. Someday. For the rest of my life."

"Our lives will be long," he will predict, accurately enough. And then they can merely touch hands before the guard leads her away.

For a while afterwards, for a little while at least, he will have regained his determination to be elected governor, just so he will be able to issue pardons for Juliana and Ben.

George will suggest, since they will be only a few blocks away, that they ought to drop by campaign headquarters and say hello. So they will go there next. Vernon will be surprised to find the place a hive of activity: Everybody will be on the telephone or the fax machine or the computers' e-mail, and Monica will be using two telephones and a laptop simultaneously. Lydia Caple, although she will have gracefully surrendered her position as press secretary to Monica, will be very much in the middle of things.

"I just thought I'd better hang around and keep an eye on Monica," Lydia will say to Vernon. "But she doesn't need any advice from me. Now you be a good boy and say howdy to all these people."

Everyone will be looking adoringly at their candidate. Vernon will obligingly go from person to person, shaking hands, smiling encouragingly, and thanking the person for doing such good and hard work. Most of them will be female, and Vernon will feel a bit panicky in his shyness, but, having gained the practice with Juliana, he will force himself to look each of the women in the eye.

"Our office at that statehouse will be a picnic compared with this," Monica will say to him, when her turn will come to shake his hand.

"Indeed it will," he will say. "Especially if you're in charge there too."

He will have intended to have another chat with Monica, to tell her to take it easy for the rest of the campaign because it's all a lost cause anyhow, but somehow he will not be able to say such things to her. And she will go on.

In the new year, Lydia Caple will give herself a long vacation before she returns to politics again. She will fulfill a long dream by taking a safari into darkest Kenya, and will follow that up with a bicycle tour of Tuscany. But she will be heard to say, and in fact will be quoted in the *Democrat-Gazette* as having said, that none of her adventures will have equaled the weeks she spent in a lost hollow with a great waterfall near Stay More, Arkansas.

Her penultimate words to Vernon will be, "I know nooks and crannies of the governor's office at the statehouse that I'll be waiting to show to you." And then, at the door to campaign headquarters, her ultimate words to him will be, "Straighten your shoulders. Walk like you have somewhere to get to."

The newspapers, all of them, that last week of the campaign, will have little or nothing to say about the campaign or the candidates. "What else is there to say?" Hank Endicott will demand in print, of his journalistic colleagues, of the public, and especially of himself. And then he will attempt an answer: "It's all been said."

Vernon will drive George back home to Stay More. This time, when he will notice, as he has noticed every time he's come back to Stay More after being away, how the very sight of home sends little tinglings up his spine, he will decide, spontaneously but conclusively, that he will not want to leave again. He will want to hole up in his study and forget this damned election and become the world's foremost authority on quantum theory. But first he will simply drive around what's left of Stay More, taking it all in. It will seem that the hogs who overrun the place will be looking at him and grinning at him, as if they know, all of them, that he will be home to stay. His drive will take him by the construction site for Juliana's mansion, just to observe the progress. They will have not merely nailed on the rafters but will have completed the roofing. It is going to be a fabulous house, not just a vast enlargement of the wigwam but an elaboration upon it, as if the wigwam is the statement of a theme that the mansion will endlessly embellish. It will make his own double-bubble seem somehow very old-fashioned and outmoded.

So his first thoughts, as he approaches home, will not be

the formulation of the long-delayed serious chat with Jelena, but rather will center upon what he needs to do to his property to make the house seem not like some sixties freak but a truly post-modern dwelling belonging to the twenty-first century—or, better yet, timeless. In fact, this will still be very much on his mind when he enters for the first time Jelena's secret garden and finds her there down on her knees, planting bulbs, alone except for that overstuffed feline she named after him.

She will appear to levitate suddenly at his approach. Jumping up, she will protest, "Don't sneak up on me like that!" And then, wiping the soil off her hands so that she will not get any on him, she will give him a hug and a kiss and will ask, "How did you know where I was? How did you know about *this*?" sweeping her hand to indicate the expanse of the secret garden, where now in November nothing will be growing but everything will still have been arranged by the loving hands of a woman who will be a genius and an artist as well as a descendant of Governor Jacob Ingledew.

He will ask her if she has not realized that her secret garden is visible from the air, and that he has often landed nearby in the helicopter. Hadn't she heard the helicopter? "Why did you want to hide the garden from me?" he will ask.

She will ponder the question before answering. "I wanted just one thing in all the world that was my very own," she will say.

"But you shared it with Bo," he will point out.

"How did you know that?" she will bristle. "Did Bo tell you?"

"No, I just assumed that since he shares your interest in gardening you'd want him to see it."

"I did."

"But you didn't share with him your other secrets, which are your very own."

"What other secrets?"

He will name them: her Bible, her journal, her little TV set, her box of chocolates, her cigarettes, and her vibrator.

She will blush but will become angry. "You snoop! Do you search through everything in the house looking for my secrets?"

"Not deliberately. But over the years it's hard to keep all those things hidden. For example, sometimes there is the smell of tobacco smoke on your breath."

"Why haven't you ever told me?"

"You're entitled to your own life. If I had told you I knew you read the Bible, even if I told you I approved of it, you might quit. If I told you I knew you made yourself come with a vibrator, you'd be so embarrassed it might screw up our whole relationship."

"If you've found my journal, did you read it?"

"I did not. I swear. You're entitled to your own life."

"You keep saying that. Are you getting ready to tell me that when you've moved into the Executive Mansion in Little Rock, it's all right for me to have my own life here with Bo?"

"I'm not moving into the Executive Mansion."

"You're not?"

"No. I'm reclaiming full possession of my house, and I'm going to stay in it. Where is Bo, by the way?" Vernon will decide that his next act will be to evict his former campaign manager from the premises.

"He's over at Sheila Kimber's house, working with Cast Sherrill. They're brainstorming a strategy to reawaken the public's interest in the campaign and get you elected."

"Well, you can tell him—no, I'll tell him myself—that I have ceased running. I am no longer a candidate for governor of Arkansas. It's obvious why he's knocking himself out to get me elected. He just wants to get me into the Governor's Mansion so he can have my house and my true love all to himself."

"Bo doesn't want your study."

"I'm talking about *you.* And don't try telling me that Bo doesn't want you. Or hasn't been having you."

"I've never tried to keep Bo a secret from you. Except maybe the first night, when you asked me if I knew that he sleeps in the nude and I lied and said I didn't."

"The two of you have been conspiring behind my back, not only in bed but also in the process of plotting your life here together after I've gone away to Little Rock to live for four years. Don't deny it."

"I won't deny we've talked about it. But I've never told Bo that I would, or could, live with that arrangement. In fact, I think that if I tried to do that, after a few months of it I'd miss you so much I'd change my mind about living in Little Rock."

"You would?" Vernon will be incredulous.

Jelena will smile, and Vernon will notice, as if he will not have noticed it before, that there will always have been a certain charm about her smile, a certain cuteness and warmth, that Juliana's broader and more beaming smile does not possess. For all her glamour and sexiness, Juliana will be seen to lack the sort of down-home sweetness that Jelena possesses. "I suppose I could stand it for just four years," Jelena will say. "It would be kind of like a sentence to prison, but I can imagine that a woman sent to prison for four years could endure it with the thoughts of her eventual freedom."

Vernon will of course catch the allusion she is making to Juliana. "It's purely academic anyhow," he will point out, "since my chances of getting elected have disappeared."

"But Bo and Cast—and no doubt all the rest of the Samurai—are busting their asses to make your chances reappear."

Vernon will smile at that allusion to Monica's remark in her original letter, which got the whole thing started. Then he will ponder the fact that when he and Jelena had made one of their extended trips away from Stay More—in the sixties they'd gone all the way around the world for months, and in the course of his courses of study they had lived in Ireland and Japan and New York City for long stretches of time—they had simply closed up the double-bubble house, draining the pipes, and George had kept a periodic check on the place (break-ins were unknown in that part of the Ozarks). "If we closed the house for four years," he will now ask her, still purely hypothetically, "could you live without your secret garden? Could you live without Bo?"

"Why would we have to close it? Couldn't we visit on weekends?"

Vernon will think about that. "I suppose we could," he will say.

"As for Bo," she will say, "I suppose I could live without him. But I know I could never live without you."

When he will be an old man, and you may be sure that he will live to an age as old as all his Ingledew forebears, Vernon will look back at his long life and reflect that in the entire course of it there were only two moments that he will regret. One was when he was a boy of ten, and his cousin Jelena, eighteen, was walking down the aisle of the schoolhouse church to marry Mark Duckworth and she paused to whisper into little Vernon's ear, "I was going to wait and marry you when you grew up. Will you marry me when you grow up? If you say 'yes,' I'll call off this wedding." And Vernon looked into her eyes to understand if she were teasing him and, understanding that she was serious, shook his head and declared, "I will never marry." And even though he was right, and never would get married, he would always, *will* always, regret that he had not said "Yes." The other thing he will regret is that when, in her secret garden, Jelena will have said, "I could never live without you," he will not have immediately and passionately enfolded her in his arms and taken her straightway to bed or even to a soft patch of the cool November secret garden.

Instead, he will say, "I'm going up to my study for a while. I'll see you at supper."

And the moment will have been lost. Just as he will have expected the election to be lost. From his study he will call Sheila Kimber's house and ask to speak to Bo and without giving Bo a chance to say a word he will tell him that he has made up his mind to do nothing further to gain the statehouse, that in accordance with Taoist principles he will strive no more, that while he will be deeply appreciative of Bo's and Cast's efforts he will not be interested in hearing what scheme they are hatching up to reestablish the reputation that was tarnished by the one hundred Vices, and that Vernon will intend to remain here in his study until such time as he will have utterly mastered quantum mechanics, and if Bo will need a place to sleep tonight he ought to ask Sheila and Cast if they have an extra bed. Thanks, and goodbye.

Vernon will, at least, not only sleep with his beloved Jelena this night but also, in accordance with Taoist principles, will withhold his own orgasm until she will have had more than enough of them.

The next morning, after a good workout in his gym in the annex and a three-mile run, he will seclude himself in his study and virtually memorize three books on quantum theory. Then he will go out to his lab, also in the annex, and will conduct some experiments involving reduced temperatures, magnets, electrons, and superconductivity. At supper Jelena will offer him a thick sheaf of the day's phone and fax messages, but he will politely tell her that he will have managed to get through the entire day without one single thought of politics, and this will be no time for him to break that incredible willpower.

In fact, the only time he will think about politics will be a couple of days later when he will have decided to pay a long overdue visit to his father, John Henry "Hank" Ingledew. He will not have hated his father, or anything like that, but will simply not have had much to say to him.

"I changed my mind, boy," Hank Ingledew will say to his son. "Come Tuesday, I'm a-fixin to vote fer ye."

Vernon will be flabbergasted, because his father will have been a lifelong die-hard Republican. "You don't have to do that, Dad. I don't want you going against your beliefs just on account of I'm your son."

"Boy, you may think I live up here by myself on this mountain without knowing nothing about what's going on in this world. But I read the papers. And I watch the TV. And I have reached the solemn conclusion that Shoat Bradfield is a low-down miserable egg-sucking son of a bitch."

In not quite the same words, former governor and senator David Pryor, the best-loved former politician in Arkansas, will lambaste Bradfield on election eve. Vernon will relent and permit Jelena to bring her little television set out from under its dishcloth in the pantry (where he will have discovered it months before while searching for a jar of marmalade) because Jelena will have heard from Cast (who will have arranged it) that the popular Pryor will be planning to make an important television appearance, not as a paid political advertisement but at the invitation of the networks: all the local affiliates of NBC, CBS, ABC, and Fox will broadcast the interview. "I have refrained from speaking out on this election before now," Pryor will declare to his statewide audience, "because I didn't think Vernon Ingledew would need any help from me, considering all the other endorsements he has had. But now it would appear that there are still a few voters in this great state of ours who plan to vote for Bradfield. Friends, you must not allow this to happen. You people know I can be trusted, so please trust me when I tell you this: Shoat Bradfield is beneath contempt. In all my years in politics, I have not encountered a more despicable excuse for a man. He is an embarrassment to the whole state of Arkansas. He must be driven from office, and Vernon Ingledew is the man to drive him!"

Despite this ringing endorsement, and all the commentary that will follow it, in which dozens of the state's celebrities—solons, academics, business leaders, writers (including the Author), and a movie star or two (all recruited and arranged by Cast)—will be interviewed and will be unanimous in concurring with Pryor that Shoat Bradfield is disgraceful ("He makes my flesh crawl," the Author will comment to an interviewer at KHOG, a Fayetteville affiliate of ABC), Vernon will not change his mind about being passive in the best Taoist tradition. But he will do one thing that is active rather than passive: he will decide to vote, and, of course, he will have been persuaded by all those people on Jelena's TV set not to vote for that wretch Bradfield.

Because of Stay More's declining population over the years, Swains Creek Township will no longer have a polling place; the nearest such will be in Parthenon, itself scarcely more than a dying village, some seven miles away. On election day morning, Jelena will prepare and serve to Vernon his favorite breakfast, Swedish pancakes. While eating it, he will read the morning paper, in which the lead editorial will call him the lesser of two evils, one columnist will call Bradfield "the more experienced of two blunderers," and Hank Endicott will observe, "When all the mud is cleared away, Vernon Ingledew is still at least recognizable." After breakfast, Vernon will get into Jelena's Isuzu and allow her to drive him to Parthenon. By coincidence they will be casting their votes there at the same time as Diana and Day, Sharon and Larry, George, and Vernon's father, the sum of the eligible voters at Stay More. Eight votes right there.

But statewide, voters will stay away from the polls in droves. Or voters will go to the polls to vote for their county judge or sheriff but will leave blank the boxes marked BRADFIELD and INGLEDEW. All of those close to him will urge Vernon to accompany them to campaign headquarters in Fayetteville for the counting and announcing of the vote totals, but Vernon will elect to remain at home. Jelena will elect to remain with him, but he will not again allow her to get that little TV out of the pantry, so the only way she will be able to find out how the tabulations will be going is from phone messages from campaign headquarters, where Monica will be busy as ever but will take a moment now and again to call Jelena and tell her that Vernon is ahead in Pulaski and Washington counties but Bradfield is ahead everywhere else.

Throughout the evening, the vote totals will show Bradfield slightly ahead. "Maybe you were right," Jelena will remark to Vernon at her bedtime, which she will defer. "It looks like the bastard has got it." Just to make conversation, Vernon will tell her about *De Architectura Antiqua Arcadiae* and about what Harry Wolfe had said. Jelena will remember the book; she will remember Vernon's having found it and blown the dust off it in an obscure basement bookstore in Rome, during their travels around the world. She will remember his refusal to read it and his donation of it to the Library of Congress.

"According to Harry," Vernon will tell her, "it was a close vote. But Vernealos lost."

The phone will ring several times before midnight with requests from television stations to capture Vernon's concession speech, if he will give one. He will not. "I conceded a couple of weeks ago," he will remark, off the record, to one caller. And then he will announce to Jelena that he must get up to his study and resume his investigation of quantum mechanics. He will kiss her good night. She will turn on the phone's message machine and go to bed.

The messages on the machine the next morning she will take and collate and bring to him in bed with a cup of coffee. Bradfield will have maintained his slim lead until the absentee ballots will have been tabulated. Customarily absentee votes come from people who are travelers, and travelers are usually broader if not more intelligent than nontravelers. ("The Arkansas Traveler" is a figure of legend.) The absentees will have been nearly all for Vernon Ingledew and will have been sufficient to elect him as the next governor of Arkansas.

Briefly and quickly now but in no particular order: The Author and his wife, Kim, will be invited to the inaugural gala in Little Rock, and will attend and will dance, but will not be given an opportunity to speak to the new governor himself. Arch will introduce them to Bo and to Cast, and they will overhear the three Samurai standing proudly together as Arch will remark, "The people always win," a takeoff on the state's motto, *Regnat Populus*.

Vernon Ingledew will not succeed in extirpating the public school system, nor the hospitals, nor the prisons, although the latter will be radically overhauled. His attempt to abolish or even to reform the school system will die in the legislature, and his attempt to extirpate hospitals will languish in committee for the duration of his term.

He will succeed in extirpating the smoking of tobacco, although it will take him his entire term to eradicate the weed entirely. He will not quite succeed in extirpating firearms but will make the ownership or possession of a handgun virtually impossible.

Most notable about the Ingledew administration will be that it will be so inconspicuous and low profile. In accordance with the ideas of the Tao, the less you do about governing people the better your government will proceed.

Also, such an inconspicuous approach will allow you to accomplish things without attracting a lot of attention. Vernon will pardon Juliana and Ben from their prison sentences with scarcely any mention in the newspapers, just in time for them to return to live in Stay More in Juliana's fabulous new mansion surrounded by Day Whittacker's forest and there give birth to her baby.

But that will be another book, another episode in the story that will never end.

Acknowledgments

Thirteen Albattrosses (or, Falling off the Mountain) is not purely a work of the imagination. Like its predecessor or first half of its parentheses or bookends, *The Architecture of the Arkansas Ozarks*, the Acknowledgments to which began identically, this novel conflates real people and fictional characters. I have always been amused by authors' declarations that "any resemblance to actual persons living or dead is purely coincidental," tantamount to declaring the characters pasteboard and unconvincing. There are *real* people in this novel, and I have used their actual names and identities, to the point of my publisher's lawyers asking me to have those people who actually play a role in the book's events sign a "character release," the document title suggesting to some of them that I have requested them to relinquish their character, if they possessed any to begin with.

In the Acknowledgments to *The Architecture of the Arkansas Ozarks* I bemoaned my exile or isolation in the pastoral state of Vermont, where I lived and taught and wrote for many years, and I thanked the many people with whom I had corresponded, not one of whom I had met, and I even thanked the people who had written me appreciatively about my previous novels, only two of whom I'd met. I was consumed with homesickness for my native state, Arkansas, a situation I alleviated some twenty years ago when I came back home to live for good and marry Kim.

Several years ago two students signed up for my evening art history course, Twentieth Century European Art: one of them was Barbara Pryor, wife of the distinguished former governor and United States senator from Arkansas, David Pryor. The other was Archie Schaffer III, vice president for public relations at giant Tyson Foods. In the course of time, both Barbara and Archie became my good friends, and when I decided finally to ask Vernon Ingledew to run for governor in a new novel, I sought their advice. Archie and I discussed Vernon's candidacy over several lunches and in the course of time exchanged dozens of e-mails about it, and naturally I decided, with his permission, to appoint Archie as one of Vernon's campaign staff. I am deeply grateful for all his help and for his permission to use him as not just a character but a key player in this story. His daughter Eliot also signed a "character release."

While I have met with Arch frequently, I have yet to meet Monica Breedlove, who is just as real as he is but lives in Louisiana and has hardly ever visited Arkansas since the days she was one of Bill Clinton's aides in the statehouse. Her expertise in politics made her a logical person for that part in the Samurais' machinations, and I thank her for her willingness to jump in and help.

Other people in the book who are "real" include Bob Razer at the Little Rock Public Library, my longtime advocate among Arkansas readers, and of course both former Arkansas governors and U.S. senators, Dale Bumpers and David Pryor. My colleague at the University of Arkansas, Professor Daniel Levine of the Classics Department, while he may not actually have undertaken the translation of *De Architectura Antiqua Arcadiae*, furnished the title for it.

One of my art history majors, Rhonda Pitman, is an Indian

from Oklahoma, and she provided me with much information about her people, particularly women such as Juliana Heartstays.

The first people to hear me describe this project were my beloved wife Kim's parents, Micky and Jacque Gunn, lifelong observers of the Arkansas political scene, and they encouraged their son-in-law's idea for a novel about the subject. *The Architecture of the Arkansas Ozarks*, same number of chapters, same setting, also about Ingledews, but written when Bill Clinton was getting his law degree at Yale, was dedicated to my father and mother. This end of the parenthesis is dedicated to my father-in-law and mother-in-law.

When the novel was finished, its first readers included Barbara Pryor and also Lisa Morgan, whose responses to the story are greatly appreciated. The first truly to sense the merit and appeal of the story was my editor, Tom Bissell, who did such a bang-up edit on the book that I hereby appoint him honorary Eighth Samurai.

Eagle-eyed copy editor Janet Baker caught each and every one of an astonishing number of errors in mechanics and sense, and made the whole thing much more readable. My publisher's legal wizard, Lauren Field, bothered to read the entire manuscript and ferret out any potential problems. Authors may be omniscient and omnipotent, but they are not above the law.

Just before launching the writing of the novel, at Arch Schaffer's suggestion we held a grand picnic at Stay More (or "Drakes Creek," as its model is known), with former governor David Pryor and his wife Barbara attending, along with the wives of all the rest of us, who ate not turtles but a fabulous pot of beans and a cake furnished by the present occupant of the "Governor Ingledew" house, who is not the Woman Whom We Cannot Name, because we *can* name her, Jo Lewis. Also at the picnic, in addition to the president's cousin, Roy Clinton, was my good friend Roy

Reed, author of the recent biography of former governor Orval Faubus, which had considerable influence on this novel, and Michael Dabrishus, head of Special Collections at the University of Arkansas.

It was a splendid occasion, for which Arch furnished the beverages, and I gave a reading from the first half of the parenthesis, the story of the idiots who gathered on the Ingledew store porch, which is still standing and served as a platform for our picnic. The final words of the Acknowledgments for that first half of the parenthesis still echo in my ears: "Most of these structures no longer stand, but that fact makes them no less 'real.' They stood, and that is, like all of us, what matters."

There are still real buildings standing at Stay More. And there are real people in the pages of this novel. But nothing that happens in this novel ever actually took place, except in your mind, where it matters most.

About the Author

Although he was born in Little Rock, DONALD HARINGTON spent all the summers of his growing-up years in the dying Ozark village of Drakes Creek, which serves as the model for Stay More. On his mother's side he is descended from Ozark hillbillies and Sir Francis Drake. On his father's side he is descended from Sir John Harington, the Elizabethan humorist and inventor of the flush toilet. Harington is a tenured professor of art history at his alma mater, the University of Arkansas in Fayetteville, where he lives with his wife, Kim. For many years he lived and taught in New England before finding his way home to Arkansas. His novels include *Some Other Place. The Right Place.*, *The Architecture of the Arkansas Ozarks*, and *Ekaterina*, and his nonfiction includes *Let Us Build Us a City. Thirteen Albatrosses (or, Falling off the Mountain)* is his eleventh novel.